Ed McBAIN

LIKE LOVE

LADY, LADY I DID IT!

THE EMPTY HOURS

Ed McBain is one of the most illustrious names in crime fiction. In 1998, he was the first non-British author to be awarded the Crime Writers' Association/Cartier Diamond Dagger Award and he was also holder of the Mystery Writers of America coveted Grand Master Award. *Alice in Jeopardy* is his latest novel in Orion paperback. He passed away in 2005. Visit his website at www.edmcbain.com.

By Ed McBain

The 87th Precinct novels

Cop Hater • The Mugger • The Pusher • The Con Man
Killer's Choice • Killer's Payoff • Killer's Wedge • Lady Killer
'Til Death • King's Ransom • Give the Boys a Great Big Hand
The Heckler • See Them Die • Lady, Lady, I Did It!
The Empty Hours • Like Love • Ten Plus One • Ax
He Who Hesitates • Doll • Eighty Million Eyes • Fuzz • Shotgun
Jigsaw • Hail, Hail, the Gang's All Here • Sadie When She Died
Let's Hear It for the Deaf Man • Hail to the Chief • Bread
Blood Relatives • So Long As You Both Shall Live
Long Time, No See • Calypso • Ghosts • Heat • Ice • Lightning
Eight Black Horses • Poison • Tricks • Lullaby • Vespers • Widows
Kiss • Mischief • And All Through the House • Romance
Nocturne • The Big Bad City • The Last Dance
Money Money Money • Fat Ollie's Book
The Frumious Bandersnatch • Hark! • Fiddlers

The Matthew Hope novels

Goldilocks • Rumpelstiltskin • Beauty & the Beast
Jack & the Beanstalk • Snow White and Rose Red
Cinderella • Puss in Boots • The House That Jack Built
Three Blind Mice • Mary, Mary • There Was a Little Girl
Gladly the Cross-Eyed Bear • The Last Best Hope

Other novels

The Sentries • Where There's Smoke • Doors • Guns
Another Part of the City • Downtown • Driving Lessons
Candyland • The Moment She Was Gone • Alice in Jeopardy

Ed McBAIN

LIKE LOVE

LADY, LADY I DID IT!

THE EMPTY HOURS

Like Love
First published in Great Britain by Hamish Hamilton in 1964

Lady, Lady I Did It!
First published in Great Britain by Pan Books Ltd in 1980

The Empty Hours
First published in Great Britain by Pan Books Ltd in 1981

This omnibus edition published in 2010
by Orion Books Ltd
Orion House, 5 Upper St Martin's Lane
London WC2H 9EA

An Hachette UK company

A CIP catalogue record for this book is available
from the British Library.

ISBN 9781407230207

Printed in Great Britain by Clays Ltd, St Ives plc

www.orionbooks.co.uk

LIKE LOVE

Before 1995, it was only like love.
Then I met my wife, Dragica. This new
edition of the book is dedicated to her.

The city in these pages is imaginary. The people,
the places, are all fictitious. Only the police routine
is based on established investigatory technique.

1.

THE WOMAN ON the ledge was wearing a nightgown. It was only three-thirty in the afternoon, but she was dressed for sleep, and the brisk spring breezes flattened the sheer nylon fabric against her body so that she looked like a legendary Greek figure sculptured in stone, immobile on the ledge twelve storeys above the city street.

The police and the fire department had gone through the whole bit – they had seen this particular little drama a thousand times in the movies and on television. If there was anything that bored civil service employees, it was a real-life enactment of the entertainment cliché. So the firemen spread their nets in the street below, and got their loudspeakers going, and the policemen roped off the block and sent a couple of detectives up to the window where spring flattened the girl against the brick wall of the building.

She was a pretty girl, a young girl in her early twenties, with long blonde hair caught by the April breeeze and whipped furiously about her face and head. Andy Parker, one of the sweet-talkers sent over by the 87th Squad, was wishing the girl would come in off the ledge so he could get a closer look at the full breasts beneath the sheer nightgown. Steve Carella, the other detective, simply didn't think anyone should die on such a nice spring day.

The girl didn't seem to know either of the detectives was there. She had moved away from the window through which she had gained access to the ledge, had gingerly inched her way towards the corner of the building and stood there now with her arms behind her and her fingers spread for a grip on the rust-red wall of the building. The ledge was perhaps a foot wide, running round the twelfth floor, broken at the building's corner by one of those grotesque gargoyles which adorned many of the city's older structures. The girl was unaware of the grinning stone head, unaware of the detectives who leaned out of the window some six feet away from her. She stared straight ahead of her, the long blonde hair whipping over her shoulders in a bright gold tangle against the red brick of the wall. Occasionally she looked down to the street below. There was no emotion on her face. There was no conviction, no determination, no fear. Her face was a beautiful blank washed clean by the wind; her body a voluptuous, thinly sheathed, wind-caressed part of the building.

'Miss?' Carella said.

She did not turn towards him. Her eyes stared straight ahead of her.

'Miss?'

Again, she did not acknowledge his presence. She looked down into the street instead and then, suddenly remembering she was a good-looking woman, suddenly remembering that hundreds of eyes were fixed upon her nearly naked figure, she moved one arm across her breasts, as if to protect herself. She almost lost her balance. She tottered for an instant, and then her hand moved quickly from the front of the gown, touched the rust-red brick again in reassurance.

2

Carella, watching her, suddenly knew she did not plan to die.

'Can you hear me, miss?' Carella said.

'I can hear you,' she answered without turning towards him. 'Go away.' Her voice was toneless.

'Well, I'd like to, but I can't.' He waited for an answer, but none came. 'I'm supposed to stay here until you come off that ledge.'

The girl nodded once, briefly. Without turning, she said, 'Go home. You're wasting your time.'

'I couldn't go home in any case,' Carella said. 'I don't get relieved until five forty-five.' He paused. 'What time do you think it is now?'

'I don't have a watch,' the girl said.

'Well, what time do you think it is?'

'I don't know what time it is, and I don't care. Look, I know what you're trying to do. You're trying to get me in conversation. I don't want to talk to you. Go away.'

'Listen, I don't want to talk to you, either,' Carella said. 'But the lieutenant said, "Go over and talk to that nut on the ledge." So here I . . .'

'I'm not a nut!' the girl said vehemently, turning to Carella for the first time.

'Listen, *I* didn't say it, the lieutenant did.'

'Yeah, well you go back and tell your lieutenant to go straight to hell.'

'Why don't you come back with me and tell him yourself?'

The girl did not answer. She turned from him again and looked down into the street. It seemed she would jump in that moment. Quickly, Carella said, 'What's your name?'

'I don't have any name.'

3

'Everybody has a name.'

'My name is Catherine the Great.'

'Come on.'

'It's Marie Antoinette. It's Cleopatra. I'm a nut, isn't that what you said? All right, I'm a nut, and that's my name.'

'Which one?'

'Any one you like. Or all of them. Go away, will you?'

'I'll bet your name is Blanche,' Carella said.

'Who told you that?'

'Your landlady.'

'What else did she tell you?'

'That your name is Blanche Mattfield, that you come from Kansas City, and that you've been living here for six months. Is that right?'

'Go and ask *her*, that nosy bitch.'

'Well, *is* your name Blanche?'

'Yes, my name is Blanche. Oh, for God's sake, do we have to go through this? I can see *clear* through you, mister. You're made of glass. Will you please go away and leave me in peace?'

'To do what? To jump down into the street?'

'Yes, that's right. That's exactly right. To jump down into the street.'

'Why?'

The girl did not answer.

'Aren't you a little chilly out there?' Carella asked.

'No.'

'That's a strong wind.'

'I don't feel it.'

'Shall I get you a sweater?'

'No.'

4

'Why don't you come in off there, Blanche? Come on. You're gonna catch cold out there.'

The girl laughed suddenly and startlingly. Carella, unaware that he had said anything funny, was surprised by the outburst.

'*I'm* ready to kill myself,' the girl said, 'and *you're* worried about my catching cold.'

'I'd say the chances of your catching cold are better than the chances of your killing yourself,' Carella said softly.

'You would, huh?'

'I would,' Carella said.

'Mmm-huh,' the girl said.

'That's right.'

'Then you're going to be in for a hell of a surprise.'

'Am I?' Carella asked.

'I can guarantee it.'

'You're pretty set on killing yourself, huh, Blanche?'

'Really, *must* I listen to this?' she said. 'Won't you please, please go away?'

'No. I don't think you want to die. I'm afraid you'll fall off the ledge and hurt yourself and some of the people down below, too.'

'I want to die,' the girl said softly.

'Why?'

'You really want to know why?'

'Yes. I'd really like to know.'

'Because,' she said slowly and clearly, 'I am lonely, and unloved, and unwanted.' She nodded, and then turned her head because her eyes had suddenly flooded with tears, and she did not want Carella to see them.

'A pretty girl like you, huh? Lonely, and unloved, and unwanted. How old are you, Blanche?'

'Twenty-two.'

'And you never want to get to be twenty-three, huh?'

'I never want to get to be twenty-three,' she repeated tonelessly. 'I don't want to get another minute older, not another second older. I want to die. Won't you please leave me alone to die?'

'Stop it, stop it,' Carella said chidingly. 'I don't like to hear that kind of talk. Dying, dying, you're twenty-two years old! You've got your whole life ahead of you.'

'Nothing,' she said.

'*Every*thing!'

'Nothing. He's gone, there's nothing, he's gone.'

'Who?'

'Nobody. Everybody. Oh! Oh!' She put one hand to her face suddenly and began weeping into it. With the other hand, she clung to the building, swaying. Carella leaned farther out of the window, and she turned to him sharply and shouted, 'Don't come near me!'

'I wasn't . . .'

'Don't come out here!'

'Look, take it easy. I wouldn't come out there if you gave me a million dollars.'

'All right. Stay where you are. If you come near me, I'll jump.'

'Yeah, and who's gonna care if you do, Blanche?'

'What?'

'If you jump, if you die, you think anyone'll care?'

'No, I . . . I know that. No one'll care. I . . . I'm not worried about that.'

'You'll be a two-line blurb on page four, and then nothing. Nothing lasts a long time.'

'I don't care. Oh, please, won't you please leave me alone? Can't you understand?'

'No, I can't. I wish you'd explain it to me.'

The girl swallowed and nodded, and then turned to him and slowly and patiently said, 'He's gone, do you see?'

'Who's gone?'

'Does it matter? He. A man. And he's gone. Good-bye, Blanche, it's been fun. That's all. Fun. And I . . .' Her eyes suddenly flared. 'Damn you, I don't want to live! I don't want to live without him!'

'There are other men.'

'No.' She shook her head. 'No. I loved him. I love him. I don't want any other men. I want . . .'

'Come on in,' Carella said. 'We'll have a cup of coffee, and we'll try to . . .'

'No.'

'Come on, come on. You're not going to jump off that damn ledge. You're wasting everybody's time. Now, come on.'

'I'm going to jump.'

'Sure, but not right now, huh? Some other time. Next week maybe, next year. But we're very busy today. The kids are turning on fire hydrants all over the city. Spring is here, Blanche. Do me a favour and jump some other time, okay?'

'Go to hell,' she said, and then looked down to the street.

'Blanche?'

She did not answer.

'Blanche?' Carella sighed and turned to Parker. He whispered something in Parker's ear, and Parker nodded and left the window.

'You remind me a little of my wife,' Carella said to the girl. She did not answer. 'Really, my wife. Teddy. She's a deaf-mute. She . . .'

'A what?'

'A mute. Born deaf and dumb.' Carella smiled. 'You think you've got problems? How'd you like to be deaf and dumb and married to a cop besides?'

'Is she really . . . deaf and dumb?'

'Sure.'

'I'm sorry.'

'Don't be. She never even *thinks* of throwing herself off a building.'

'I . . . I wasn't going to do it this way,' the girl said. 'I was going to take sleeping-pills. That's why I put on the nightgown. But . . . I wasn't sure I had enough. I had only half a bottle. Would that have been enough?'

'Enough to make you sick,' Carella said. 'Come on in, Blanche. I'll tell you all about the time I almost slashed my wrists.'

'You never did.'

'I almost did, I swear to God. Look, everybody feels like hell every once in a while. What happened? Did you get your period today?'

'Wh . . . ? How . . . how did you know?'

'I figured. Come on.'

'No.'

'Come on, Blanche.'

'No! Stay away from me!'

From inside the apartment there came the sudden shrill ring of a telephone. The sound was clearly heard by the girl. She turned her head for a moment, and then closed her mind to the ringing phone. Carella pretended surprise. He had sent Parker downstairs to call

8

the girl's number, but now he pretended the ringing was unexpected. Quietly he said, 'Your phone's ringing.'

'I'm not home.'

'It might be important.'

'It isn't.'

'It might be . . . him.'

'He's in California. It's not him. I don't care who it is.' She paused. Again, she said, 'He's in California.'

'They have phones in California, you know,' Carella said.

'It's . . . it's not him.'

'Why don't you answer it and find out?'

'I *know* it isn't him! Leave me alone!'

'You want us to answer this?' someone in the apartment shouted.

'She's coming,' Carella said. He extended his hand to the girl. The telephone kept ringing behind him. 'Take my hand, Blanche,' he said.

'No, I'm going to jump.'

'You're not going to jump. You're going to come inside and answer your telephone.'

'No! I said no!'

'Come on, you're getting me sore,' Carella shouted. 'Are you just a stupid broad, is that what you are? You want to squash your brains on that sidewalk? It's made of cement, Blanche! That's not a mattress down there.'

'I don't care. I'm going to jump.'

'So jump, for Christ's sake!' Carella said angrily, using the tone of a father whose patience has finally been exhausted. 'If you're going to jump, go ahead. Then we can all go home. Go ahead.'

'I will,' she said.

'So go ahead. Either jump, or take my hand. We're wasting time here.'

Behind him, the phone kept ringing furiously. There was no sound in the apartment, no sound on the face of the building except for the ringing of the telephone and the sighing of the wind.

'I will,' the girl said softly.

'Here,' Carella said. 'Here's my hand. Take it.'

For a speechless, shocking moment, he didn't realize quite what was happening. And then his eyes opened wide, and he stood stock-still at the window, his hand extended, his hand frozen in space as the girl suddenly shoved herself away from the wall and leaped.

He heard her scream, heard it trailing all the way down the twelve storeys to the street below, drowning out the frenzied ringing of the telephone. And then he heard the sound of her body striking the pavement, and he turned blindly from the window and said to no one, 'Jesus, she did it.'

The salesman was going to be a dead man within the next five minutes.

Some twenty blocks away from where Blanche leaped to her death, he entered a street flirting with Spring, carrying a heavy sample-case in one hand, and attributing gender to the vernal equinox. To the salesman, Spring was a woman who had come dancing in over the River Harb, flitting past flotsam and jetsam, those two old-time vaudeville performers, showing her legs to the passing, hooting tugs, winking lewdly at the condoms floating on the river's edge, flashing fleshy thighs to Silvermine Road and the park, and then airily leaping over tenement rooftops to land gracefully in the

10

middle of the street. The people had come outdoors to greet her. They wore smiles and flowered house dresses, smiles and open-throat sports shirts, smiles and sneakers and T shirts and shorts. Grinning, they took Spring into their arms and held her close and kissed her throat, where you been all this time, baby?

The salesman didn't know he was going to be a dead man, of course. If he'd known, he probably wouldn't have been spending his last few minutes on earth carrying a heavy sample-case full of hairbrushes down a city street making love to Spring. If he'd known he was about to die, he might have saluted or something. Or, at the very least, he might have thrown his sample-case into the air and gone to Bora Bora. Ever since he'd read *Hawaii*, he had gone to Bora Bora often. Sometimes, when selling hairbrushes got particularly rough, he went to Bora Bora as often as ten or twelve times a day. Once he got to Bora Bora he made love to dusky-skinned fifteen-year-old maidens. There were a few dusky-skinned fifteen-year-old maidens on the street today, but not very many. Besides, he didn't know he was going to die.

He came down the street heavily, feeling like Lee J. Cobb minus one sample-case. He wondered whether he'd sell any more brushes today; he needed three more sales before he filled his quota, who the hell wanted to buy hairbrushes when Spring was holding a dance in the street? Sighing, he climbed the stoop of the nearest tenement, passing a pimply-faced sixteen-year-old blonde girl wearing dungarees and a white blouse, and wondering whether she knew how to hula hula. He entered the dim and foul-smelling vestibule, walking past the mail-boxes with their broken locks and hanging

11

flaps, and then past the open and miraculously intact frosted-glass inner door. Garbage cans were stacked alongside the staircase wall on the ground floor. They were empty, but their stench permeated the hallway. He sniffed in discomfort, and then began to climb the steps towards the natural light coming from the air-shaft window on the first floor.

He had three minutes to live.

The sample-case was heavier when you climbed. The more you climbed, the heavier it got. He had noticed that. He was a particularly astute human being, he felt, intelligent and observant, and he had noticed over the years that there was a direct correlation between the physical act of climbing and the steadily increasing weight of his sample-case during the ascent. He was pleased when he gained the first-floor landing. He put the sample-case down, reached for his handkerchief, and mopped his brow.

He had a minute and a half to live.

He folded the handkerchief carefully and put it back into his pocket. He looked up at the metal numerals on the door ahead of him. Apartment 1A. The A was hanging slightly askew. Time was running out.

He located the bell button set into the door jamb.

He reached out with his forefinger.

Three seconds.

He touched the button.

The sudden blinding explosion ripped away the front wall of the apartment, tore the salesman in half, and sent a cascade of hairbrushes and burnt human flesh roaring into the air and down the stairwell.

Spring was really here.

2.

DETECTIVE 2ND/GRADE COTTON Hawes had served aboard a P.T. boat during the last great war for democracy, and his battle experience had therefore been limited to sea engagements alone. He had, to be fair, once participated in the shore bombardment of a tiny Pacific island, but he had never seen the results of his vessel's devastating torpedo attack on a Japanese dock installation. Had he been a foot soldier in Italy, the chaos in the tenement hallway would not have surprised him very much. But he had had a clean bed to sleep in, and three squares a day, as the saying goes, and so the ruin confronting him just inside the vestibule door was something of a shock.

The hallway and the staircase were littered with plaster, lath, wallpaper, wooden beams, kitchen utensils, hairbrushes, broken crockery, human flesh, blood, hair, and garbage. A cloud of settling plaster dust hovered in the air, pierced by the afternoon sunlight which slanted through the air-shaft window. The window itself had been shattered by the explosion, a skeleton of its former self, with broken glass shards covering the first-floor landing. The walls surrounding the window and the staircase were blackened and blistered. Every milk bottle resting in the hallway outside the other two apartments on the landing had been shattered by the blast. Fortunately, the seductress Spring had lured the other first-floor tenants into the street, and so the only loss of human life that April afternoon had been in the hallway and in apartment 1A itself.

Following a coughing, choking patrolman up the littered staircase, Hawes covered his face with a hand-kerchief and tried not to realize he was climbing past the blood-soaked, squishy remains of what had once been a human being. He followed a trail of hairbrushes to the shattered wall and demolished doorway of the apartment; it had rained hairbrushes that day, it had rained hairbrushes and blood. He entered the apart-ment. Smoke still billowed from the kitchen, and there was the unmistakable aroma of gas in the air. Hawes had not thought he would need the mask which had been pressed into his hand by the patrolman down-stairs, but one whiff of the stench changed his mind. He pulled the facepiece over his head, checked the inlet tube connected to the canister, and followed the patrol-man into the kitchen, cursing the fact that the glass eyeholes on the mask were beginning to fog up. A man in overalls was busily working in the kitchen behind the demolished stove, trying to cut off the steady leakage of illuminating gas into the apartment. The explosion had ripped the stove from the wall, severing its connexion with the pipes leading to the main, and the new steady flow of gas into the apartment threat-ened a build-up which could lead to a second explosion. The man in overalls — undoubtedly sent by either the Department of Public Works or the Gas and Electric Company — didn't even look up when Hawes and the patrolman entered the room. He worked busily and quickly. There had been one explosion, and he damn well didn't want another, not while he was on the

14

premises. He knew that a mixture of one part carbon monoxide to one-half part of oxygen, or two-and-a-half parts air, was enough to cause an explosion in the presence of a flame or a spark. He had opened every window in the joint when he'd arrived – even the one in the bedroom where what was on the bed didn't particularly appeal to his aesthetic sense. He had then gone immediately to work on the bent and twisted pipes, trying to stop the flow of gas. He was a devout Catholic, but even if the Pope himself had walked into that kitchen, he would not have stopped work on the pipes. Hawes and the patrolman didn't even rate a nod.

Through the fogged eyepieces of his mask, Hawes watched the man working on the pipes and then glanced around the demolished kitchen. It did not take a mastermind to determine that this was the room where the explosion had taken place. Even without the presence of the up-ended stove and the stench of illuminating gas, the room itself was a shambles – it had to be the nucleus of the blast. Every pane of glass had been shattered, every pot and pan hurled through the air and peppered with holes. The curtains had gone up in instant flame – happily, there had not been a major conflagration. The table and chairs had been tossed into the room closest to the kitchen, and even in that room, the sofa had been blasted out of place and rested up-ended against one damaged wall.

The bedroom, in contrast to the other rooms, had been almost untouched. The window had been opened by the gasman, and the spring breeze touched the curtains, played idly with them. The blanket had been drawn back to the foot of the bed. There were two people lying on the clean white bedsheet. One was a man, the other was a woman; that's the way it is in the spring. The man was wearing undershorts and nothing else. The undershorts were striped in blue. The woman was wearing only her panties.

They were both dead.

Hawes did not know very much about pathology, but the man and woman on the bed – even when viewed through his fogging mask – were both a bright cherry-red colour, and he was willing to bet his shield they had died of acute carbon monoxide poisoning. He was further willing to speculate that the death was either accidental or suicidal. He was too good a cop to rule out homicide immediately, but he nonetheless began a methodical search for a suicide note.

He did not have to look very far.

The note was on the dresser opposite the bed. It had been placed flat on the dresser top, and then a man's wrist-watch had been put on top of it to hold it down. Without touching either the wrist-watch or the note, Hawes bent over to read what had been written.

The note had been typed. He automatically glanced around the room to see if he could locate the machine and saw it resting on a small end-table near the bed. He turned his attention back to the note.

Dear God, forgive us for this terrible thing. We are so much in love, and the world is all against us. There is no other way. Now we can end the suffering of ourselfs and others. Please understand.

Tommy and Irene

Hawes nodded once, in silent understanding, and then made a memo to pick up both note and wristwatch as soon as the photographers were finished with the room. He walked across the room and filled out a tag which he would later affix to the typewriter for delivery to the laboratory where Lieutenant Sam Grossman's boys would perform their comparison tests.

He walked back to the bed.

The man and woman appeared to be in their early twenties. The man had involuntarily soiled himself, probably after sinking into a deep coma and once the gas had really taken hold. The woman had vomited into her pillow. He stood at the foot of the bed and wondered what they had thought it would be like. A nice, quiet, peaceful death? Something like going to sleep? He wondered how they had felt when the headache appeared and they began to get drowsy and faint and unable to move themselves off that bed even if they'd changed their minds about dying together. He wondered how they'd felt just when their bodies had begun to twitch, just before they passed into a stupor where vomiting and evacuation were things beyond their control. He looked at this dead man and woman in their early twenties – Tommy and Irene – and he shook his head and thought. *You poor stupid boobs, what did you hope to find? What made you think a painful death was the answer to a painful life?*

He turned his eyes away from the bed.

Two empty whisky bottles were on the floor. One of them had spilled alcohol onto the scatter rug on the woman's side of the bed. He didn't know whether or not they had drunk themselves into insensibility after turning on the gas jet, but that seemed to be a standard

17

part of the gas-pipe routine. He knew there were people who felt that suicide was an act of extreme bravery, but he could never look upon it as anything but utter cowardice. The empty whisky bottles gave conviction to his thoughts. He made out the tags for each bottle, again postponing the actual tagging until photographs had been made.

The woman's clothes were hung over the back and resting on the seat of a straight-backed chair alongside the bed. Her blouse was hanging, and her brassière was folded over it; her skirt, garter belt, nylons, and leather belt were folded on the seat. A pair of high-heeled black leather pumps were neatly placed at the foot of the chair.

The man's clothes were over and on an easy chair at the other end of the room. Trousers, shirt, undershirt, tie, socks, and belt. His shoes were placed to one side of the chair. Hawes made a note to have the technicians pick up the clothing, which they would place in plastic bags for transmission to the laboratory. He also noted the man's wallet, tie-clip, and loose change lying on the dresser top, together with the woman's ear-rings and an imitation pearl necklace.

By the time he'd finished his search of the apartment, the gas leak had been plugged, the laboratory boys, police photographers, and assistant medical examiner had arrived, and there was nothing to do but go downstairs again and talk to the patrolman who had reported the explosion to the precinct. The patrolman was new and green and terrified. But he had managed to pull his wits together long enough to find a charred and tattered wallet in the hallway rubble, and he turned this over to Hawes as if he were very anxious to get rid of it. Hawes almost wished the patrolman hadn't found it. The wallet gave an identity to the remains of a human being that had been spattered down the staircase and over the walls.

He called on the salesman's wife later that day, after he had spoken to the lab. The salesman's wife said, 'Why did it have to be Harry?'

He explained that the lab's supposition was that her husband had probably approached the door of apartment 1A and pressed the buzzer and this in turn had caused an electrical spark which had precipitated the explosion.

'Why did it have to be Harry?' the salesman's wife asked.

Hawes tried to explain that these things happened sometimes, that they were nobody's fault, that her husband was simply doing his job and had no idea the apartment behind that door was full of illuminating gas. But the woman only stared at him blankly and said again, 'Why did it have to be Harry?'

He went back to the squad-room with a weary ache inside him. He barely said hello to Carella, who was at his own desk typing up a report. Both men left the squad-room at eight-fifteen that night, two-and-a-half hours after they were officially relieved. Carella was in a rotten mood. He ate a cold supper, snapped viciously at his wife, didn't even go in to peek at the sleeping twins, and went straight to bed, where he tossed restlessly all night long. Hawes called Christine Maxwell, a girl he had known for a long time, and asked her to go to a movie with him. He watched the screen with increasing

19

annoyance because something was bugging him about that apparent suicide and he couldn't quite figure out what.

3.

DEAD PEOPLE DO not sweat.

It was very warm in the morgue, and a light sheen of perspiration covered the faces of Carella and Hawes, clung to the upper lip of the man with them, stained the armpits of the attendant who looked at the three men bleakly for a moment and then pulled out the drawer.

The drawer moved almost soundlessly on its rollers. The girl Irene lay naked and dead on the slab; they had found her in her panties, but these had been shipped immediately to the lab, and she lay naked and cool and unsweating while the attendant and the three men looked down at her. In a little while, she would be shipped to another part of the hospital, where an autopsy would be performed. For now, her body was intact. All it lacked was life.

'Is that her?' Carella asked.

The man standing between the two detectives nodded. He was a tall, thin man with pale blue eyes and blond hair. He wore a grey gaberdine suit, and a white button-down shirt with a striped tie. He did not say anything. He simply nodded, and even the nod was a brief one, as if motion were an extravagance.

'And she's your wife, sir?' Hawes asked.

The man nodded again.

'Could you give us her full name, sir?'

'Irene,' the man said.

'Middle name?'

'That *is* her middle name.'

'What do you mean?'

'Her name is Margaret Irene Thayer.' The man paused. 'She didn't like the name Margaret, so she used her middle name.'

'She called herself Irene, is that right?'

'That's right.'

'And your address, Mr Thayer?'

'One-one-three-four Bailey Avenue.'

'You were living there with your wife?'

'Yes.'

Carella and Hawes glanced at each other. Homicide at its best stinks to high heaven because everyone walking this earth has a closet he'd prefer leaving closed and homicide rarely knocks before entering. The girl Margaret Irene Thayer had been found on a bed wearing only her panties, and she'd been lying alongside a man in his undershorts. The man who had just positively identified her was named Michael Thayer, and he was her husband, and one of those little closets had just been opened, and everyone was staring into it. Carella cleared his throat.

'Were . . . er . . . you and your wife separated or . . . ?'

'No,' Thayer said.

'I see,' Carella answered. He paused again. 'You know, Mr Thayer, that . . . that your wife was found with a man.'

'Yes. Their pictures were in the paper. That's why I called the police. I mean, when I saw Irene's picture in the paper. I figured it was some kind of mistake. Because I thought . . . you see, she'd told me she was

22

going out to visit her mother and I never suspected . . . so you see, I thought it was a mistake. She was supposed to be spending the night at her mother's, you see. So I called her mother, and her mother said no, Irene hadn't been there, and then I thought . . . I don't know what I thought. So I called the police and asked if I could . . . could see . . . could see the body of the girl they'd found.'

'And this *is* your wife, Mr Thayer? You have no doubts about that?'

'She . . . she's my wife,' Thayer said.

'Mr Thayer, you said you saw pictures of both your wife and the man in the newspa . . .'

'Yes.'

'Did you happen to recognize the man?'

'No.' Thayer paused. 'Is . . . is he here, too?'

'Yes, sir.'

'I want to see him.'

'If you didn't recognize him, there's no need to . . .'

'I want to see him.' Thayer repeated.

Carella shrugged and then nodded at the attendant. They followed him across the long, high-ceilinged room. Their footsteps echoed across the tiled floor. The attendant consulted a typewritten list on a cupboard, moved down the aisle, stooped, and pulled open a second drawer. Thayer stared down into the face of the man they'd found with his wife.

'He's dead,' he said, but the words did not seem intended for anyone.

'Yes,' Carella said.

Thayer nodded. He nodded again. 'I want to keep looking at him. That's strange, isn't it? I want to find out what was so . . . *different* about him.'

23

'You still don't recognize him?' Hawes asked.

'No. Who is he?'

'We don't know. There was no driver's licence or other identification in his wallet. But one of the names on the suicide note was Tommy. Did your wife ever mention anyone named Tommy?'

'No.'

'And you've never seen him before?'

'Never.' Thayer paused. 'There's something I don't understand. The apartment. Where . . . where you found them. Wasn't . . . couldn't you ask the landlady? Wouldn't she know his name?'

'She might. But that wasn't Tommy's apartment.'

'What do you mean?'

'The landlady told us that apartment was rented by a man named Fred Hassler.'

'Well, perhaps he was using another name,' Thayer suggested.

Carella shook his head. 'No. We brought the landlady down here for a look. This isn't Fred Hassler.' He nodded to the attendant, and the attendant shoved the drawer back into place. 'We're trying to locate Hassler now, but so far we haven't had any luck.' Carella paused. He wiped his forehead and then said, 'Mr Thayer, if it's all right with you, we'd like to get out of here. There are some questions we have to ask you, but we'd prefer doing it over a cup of coffee, if that's all right with you.'

'Yes, of course,' Thayer said.

'You need me any more?' the attendant asked.

'No. Thanks a lot, Charlie.'

'Yeah,' Charlie said, and went back to reading *Playboy*.

*

24

They found a diner three blocks from the hospital, and they sat in a seat near the window and watched the girls going by outside in their thin spring cottons. Carella and Thayer ordered coffee. Hawes was a tea-drinker. They sat sipping from hot mugs and listening to the whir of the overhead fans. It was spring, and the pretty girls were passing by outside, and no one wanted to discuss treachery and sudden death. But there had been sudden death, and the wife of Michael Thayer had been revealed by death in a compromising and apparently treacherous attitude, and so the questions had to be asked.

'You said your wife told you she was going to spend the night with her mother, is that right, Mr Thayer?'

'Yes.'

'What's her mother's name?'

'Mary Tomlinson. My wife's maiden name was Margaret Irene Tomlinson.'

'Where does your mother-in-law live, Mr Thayer?'

'Out on Sands Spit.'

'Did your wife visit her frequently?'

'Yes.'

'How often, Mr Thayer?'

'At least once every two weeks. Sometimes more often.'

'Alone, Mr Thayer?'

'What?'

'Alone? Without you?'

'Yes. My mother-in-law and I don't get along.'

'So you don't visit her, is that right?'

'That's right.'

'But you did call her this morning after you saw Irene's picture in the paper.'

'Yes. I called her.'

'Then you do speak to her.'

'I speak to her, but we don't get along. I told Irene if she wanted to see her mother, she'd have to do it without me. That's all.'

'Which is what she did,' Hawes said, 'on the average of once every two weeks, sometimes more often.'

'Yes.'

'And yesterday she told you she was going to her mother's and would spend the night there?'

'Yes.'

'Did she often spend the night at her mother's?'

'Yes. Her mother is a widow, you see, and Irene felt she was alone and so she spent . . .' Thayer hesitated. He sipped at his coffee, put down his cup, and then looked up. 'Well, now . . . now I don't know. I just don't know.'

'What is it you don't know, Mr Thayer?'

'Well, I used to think . . . well, the woman *is* alone, you know, and even if I don't like her, I didn't think I should stop her daughter from spending time with her. Irene, I mean.'

'Yes.'

'But now . . . after . . . after what's happened. I just don't know. I mean, I don't know whether Irene really spent all that time with her mother or if . . . if . . . if . . .' Thayer shook his head. Quickly, he picked up his coffee cup and gulped at the steaming liquid.

'Or if she spent it with this man Tommy,' Carella said.

Thayer nodded.

'What time did she leave the house yesterday, Mr Thayer?' Hawes asked.

26

'I don't know. I went to work at eight. She was still there when I left.'

'What sort of work do you do?'

'I write greeting-card verse.'

'Freelance, or for some company?'

'Freelance.'

'But you said you left the house yesterday to go to work. Does that mean you don't work at home?'

'That's right,' Thayer said. 'I have a little office downtown.'

'Downtown where?'

'In the Brio Building. It's just a small office. A desk, a typewriter, a filing cabinet, and a couple of chairs. That's all I need.'

'Do you go to that office every morning at eight?' Hawes asked.

'Yes. Except on week-ends. I don't usually work on week-ends. Once in a while, but not usually.'

'But Monday to Friday, you get to your office at eight in the morning, is that right?'

'I don't *get* there at eight. I leave my house at eight. I stop for breakfast, and *then* I go to my office.'

'What time do you get there?'

'About nine.'

'And what time do you quit?'

'About four.'

'And then do you go straight home?' Carella asked.

'No. I usually stop for a drink with the man who has the office across the hall. He's a song writer. There's a lot of song writers in the Brio Building.'

'What's his name?'

'Howard Levin.'

'Did you go for a drink with him yesterday afternoon?'

27

'Yes.'

'At four o'clock?'

'Around that time. I guess it was closer to four-thirty.'

'May I give a recap on this, Mr Thayer?' Hawes asked. 'Yesterday you left your home at eight o'clock in the morning, went for breakfast . . .'

'Where was that?' Carella asked.

'I eat at the R and N Restaurant. That's two blocks from my house.'

'You ate breakfast at the R and N,' Hawes said, 'and arrived at your office in the Brio Building at nine o'clock. Your wife was still at home when you left, but you knew she was going out to visit her mother on Sands Spit, or at least that's what she had told you.'

'Yes, that's right.'

'Did you talk to your wife at any time during the day?'

'No,' Thayer said.

'Is there a telephone in your office?'

'Yes, of course.' Thayer frowned. Something seemed to be bothering him all at once. He did not say what it was, not immediately, but his brows lowered, and his mouth hardened.

'But you didn't call her, nor did she call you.'

'No,' Thayer said, his voice taking on a curiously defensive tone. 'I knew she was going to her mother's. Why would I call her?'

'What time did you go to lunch, Mr Thayer?' Carella asked.

'One o'clock. I think it was one, anyway. Around that time. What is this?' he said suddenly.

'What is *what*, Mr Thayer?'

'Never mind.'

'Where'd you have lunch, Mr Thayer?'

'At an Italian restaurant near the office.'

'The name?'

'Look . . .' Thayer started, and then shook his head.

'Yes?'

'What is this?'

'Mr Thayer,' Hawes said flatly, 'your wife was playing around with another man. It looks as if they committed suicide together, but a lot of things aren't always what they look like.'

'I see.'

'So we want to make sure . . .'

'I see,' Thayer said again. 'You think I had something to do with it, is that it?'

'Not necessarily,' Carella said. 'We're simply trying to find out how and where you spent your time yesterday.'

'I see.'

The table went silent.

'Where *did* you have lunch, Mr Thayer?'

'Am I under arrest?' Thayer asked.

'No, sir.'

'I have a feeling you can get me in trouble,' Thayer said. 'I don't think I want to answer any more questions.'

'Why not?'

'Because I had nothing to do with this thing, and you're trying to make it sound as if . . . as if . . . goddammit, how do you think I feel?' he shouted suddenly. 'I see my wife's picture in the paper, and the story tells me she's dead and . . . and . . . and was was was . . . you lousy bastards, how do you think I feel?'

He put down his coffee cup and covered his face with one hand. They could not tell whether or not he was crying behind that hand. He sat silently and said nothing.

'Mr Thayer,' Carella said gently, 'our department investigates every suicide exactly the way it would a homicide. The same people are notified, the same reports are . . .'

'The hell with you *and* your department,' Thayer said from behind his hand. 'My wife is dead.'

'Yes, sir, we realize that.'

'Then leave me alone, can't you? I thought . . . you said we would have a cup of coffee and . . . now it's . . . this is a third degree.'

'No, sir, it's not a third degree.'

'Then what the hell is it?' Thayer said. His hand suddenly dropped from his face. His eyes flashed. 'My wife is *dead*!' he shouted. 'She was in bed with another man! What the hell is it you want from me?'

'We want to know where you were all day yesterday,' Hawes said. 'That's all.'

'I went to lunch at a restaurant called Nino's. It's on the Stem, two blocks from my office. I got back to the office at about two or two-thirty. I worked until . . .'

'Did you have lunch alone?'

'No. Howard was with me.'

'Go on.'

'I worked until about four-thirty. Howard came in and said he was knocking off, and would I like a drink. I said yes I would. We went to the bar on the corner, it's called Dinty's. I had two Rob Roys, and then Howard and I walked to the subway. I went straight home.'

'What time was that?'

'About five-thirty.'

'Then what?'

'I read the papers and I watched the news on television, and then I made myself some bacon and eggs and then I got into my pyjamas and read a while, and then I went to bed. I got up at seven-thirty this morning. I left the house at eight. I bought a paper on the way to the R and N. While I was having breakfast, I saw Irene's picture. I called my mother-in-law from the restaurant, and then I called the police.' Thayer paused. Sarcastically, he added, 'They were kind enough to provide me with you two gentlemen.'

'Okay, Mr Thayer,' Hawes said.

'Is that all?'

'That's all. I'm sorry we upset you, but there are questions we have to ask and . . .'

'May I go now?'

'Yes, sir.'

'Thank you.' Thayer paused. 'Would you do me a favour?'

'What's that?'

'When you find out who the man was . . . Tommy, the man she was in . . . in bed with . . . would you let me know?'

'If you want us to.'

'Yes, I want you to.'

'All right. We'll call you.'

'Thank you.'

They watched as he walked away from the booth, and out of the diner, a tall thin man who walked with a slouch, his head slightly bent.

'What the hell,' Hawes said, 'we *have* to ask the questions.'

'Yeah,' Carella answered.

'And you've got to admit, Steve, the guy sounds so damn innocent it's implausible.'

'What do you mean?'

'Well, for God's sake, his wife is trotting out to see her mother every other week, and spending the night there, and he never even calls to check up? I don't buy it.'

'You're not married,' Carella said simply.

'Huh?'

'I don't ask Teddy to give me a written report on her whereabouts. You either trust somebody or you don't.'

'And he trusted her, huh?'

'It sounds that way to me.'

'She was a fine one to trust,' Hawes said.

'There are more things in heaven and hell, Horatio,' Carella misquoted, 'than are dreamt of in your philosophy.'

'Like what?' Hawes asked.

'Like love,' Carella answered.

'Exactly. And you have to admit this thing has all the earmarks of a love pact.'

'I don't know.'

'Unless, of course, it's a homicide.'

'I don't know. I don't know what to accept or reject. All I know is it makes me itchy to have to talk to a guy who's grief-stricken when I'm not really sure . . .'

'*If* he's really grief-stricken,' Hawes said. '*If* he didn't happen to turn on that gas jet himself.'

'We don't know,' Carella said.

'That's exactly why we have to ask the questions.'

'Sure. And sometimes give the answers.' He paused, his face suddenly very serious. 'I gave an answer to a girl on a ledge yesterday, Cotton. There was a puzzled, frightened little girl on a ledge, and she was looking for the big answer, and I gave it to her. I told her to jump.'

'Oh, for Christ's sake . . .'

'I told her to jump, Cotton.'

'She'd have jumped no matter what you told her. A girl who gets out on a ledge twelve storeys above the street . . .'

'Were you around last April, Cotton? Do you remember Meyer's heckler, the guy we called the Deaf Man? Combinations and permutations, remember? The law of probability. Remember?'

'What about it?'

'I like to think of what might have happened if I'd said something different to that girl. Suppose, instead of saying, "Go ahead, jump," I'd looked at her and said, "You're the most beautiful girl in the world, and I love you. Please come inside." Do you think she'd have jumped, Cotton?'

'If she wanted to jump, then no matter . . .'

'Or I wonder what would have happened if you, or Pete, or Bert, or Meyer, or anyone on the squad – anyone but me – had been at that window. Would she have liked your voice better than mine? Maybe Pete could have convinced her to come inside. Maybe . . .'

'Steve, Steve, what the hell are you doing?'

'I don't know. I guess I didn't enjoy questioning Michael Thayer.'

'Neither did I.'

'It looks very much like a suicide, Cotton.'

'I know it does.'

'Sure.' Carella nodded. 'But, of course, we can't be

positive, can we? So we have to bully and con and bluff and . . .'

'Come on!' Hawes said sharply, and in the next instant he almost added, 'Why the hell don't you go back to the office and hand in your resignation?' But he looked across the table at Carella and saw that his eyes were troubled, and he remembered what had happened only yesterday when Carella had angrily told a young girl to jump. He caught the words before they left his mouth; he did not tell Carella to resign, he did not tell him to jump. Instead, and with great effort, he smiled and said, 'Tell you what we'll do. Let's hold up a bank and then go down to South America and live on the beach like millionaires, okay? Then we won't have to worry about *asking* questions, only answering them. Okay?'

'I'll ask Teddy,' Carella said, and he smiled thinly.

'Think about it,' Hawes said, 'Meanwhile, I'll call the squad.'

He left the table and went to the phone booth at the far end of the diner. When he returned, he said, 'Good news.'

'What?' Carella asked.

'They just picked up Fred Hassler.'

4.

FRED HASSLER WAS enjoying himself immensely. He was a rotund little man wearing a plaid jacket and a bright blue Italian sports shirt. His eyes were bright and blue, too, and they flashed around the squad-room in obvious enjoyment, his feet jiggling in excitement.

'This is the first time in my life I've ever been in a police station,' he said. 'Jesus, what colour! What atmosphere!'

The colour and atmosphere at the moment consisted of a man who was bleeding profusely from a knife wound on his left arm which Detective Meyer Meyer was patiently trying to dress while Detective Bert Kling was calling for an ambulance. In addition, the colour and atmosphere included a sixty-year-old man who was gripping the meshed wire of the cage – a small locked enclosure in one corner of the squad-room – and shouting, 'Let me *kill* the bastard! Let me kill him!' while alternately spitting at anyone who came anywhere near the compact mesh prison. And the colour and atmosphere included, too, a fat woman in a flowered house dress who was complaining to Hal Willis about a stickball game outside her ground-floor apartment, and it included several ringing telephones, and several clattering typewriters, and the contained smell of the squad-room, a delicate aroma compounded of seven-tenths essence of human sweat, one-tenth percolating coffee, one-tenth stench of urine from the old man in the cage, and one-tenth cheap perfume from the fat lady in the flowered house dress.

Carella and Hawes walked into all this atmosphere and colour by negotiating the iron-runged steps that led from the ground floor of the old building, coming down the corridor past the Interrogation Room, the Men's Room, and the Clerical Office, pushing through the gate in the slatted rail divider, spotting Andy Parker talking to a rotund little man in a straight-backed chair, assuming the man was Fred Hassler, and going directly to him.

'It stinks in here,' Carella said immediately. 'Can't someone open a window?'

'The windows are open,' Meyer said. His hands were covered with blood. He turned to Kling and asked, 'Are they on the way?'

'Yeah,' Kling answered. 'Why didn't a patrolman handle this, Meyer? He should have got a meat wagon right on the beat. What the hell does he think this is? An emergency ward?'

'Don't ask me about patrolmen,' Meyer said. 'I'll never understand patrolmen as long as I live.'

'He brings a guy up here with his arm all cut to ribbons,' Kling said to Carella. 'Somebody ought to talk to the captain about that. We got enough headaches without blood all over the floor.'

'What happened?' Carella asked.

'The old *cockuh* in the cage stabbed him,' Meyer said.

'Why?'

'They were playing cards. The old man says he was cheating.'

'Let me out of here!' the old man screamed suddenly from the cage. 'Let me *kill* the bastard!'

'They got to stop playing ball outside my window,' the fat lady said to Willis.

'You're absolutely right,' Willis told her. 'I'll send a patrolman over right away. He'll get them to go to a playground.'

'There ain't no playground!' the fat lady protested.

'He'll send them to the park. Don't worry, lady, we'll take care of it.'

'You said you'd take care of it last time. So they're *still* playing stickball right outside my window. And using dirty language!'

'Where the hell's that ambulance?' Meyer asked.

'They said they'd be right over,' Kling told him.

'Turn on that fan, will you, Cotton?' Carella said.

'It smells like a Chinese whorehouse, don't it?' Parker said. 'The old man peed his pants when Genero made the collar. He's sixty years old, you know that? But he sure done a job on that arm.'

'Who's going to question him, that's what I'd like to know,' Hawes said. 'That cage smells like the zoo.'

'Genero brought him in,' Parker said, 'we'll get Genero to do the questioning.' He laughed heartily at his own outrageous suggestion, and then abruptly said, 'This is Fred Hassler. Mr Hassler, Detectives Carella and Hawes. They're working on that suicide.'

'How do you do?' Hassler said, rising immediately and grasping Carella's hand. 'This is *mar*-vellous,' he said, 'just *mar*-vellous!'

'Yeah, it's marvellous,' Parker said. 'I'm getting out of this madhouse. If the boss asks for me, tell him I'm in the candy store on Culver and Sixth.'

37

'Doing what?' Carella asked.

'Having an egg cream,' Parker answered.

'Why don't you stick around until the ambulance gets here,' Kling suggested. 'We've got our hands full.'

'You've got more cops in this room than they got at the Academy,' Parker said, and he left. The fat lady followed him down the corridor, muttering under her breath about the 'lousy police in this lousy city'. A patrolman came upstairs to take the old man from the cage to the detention cells on the ground floor. The old man swung at him the moment they unlocked the cage door, and the patrolman instantly clubbed him with his billet and dragged him limp and unprotesting from the squad-room. The ambulance arrived not five minutes later. The man with the slashed arm told the ambulance attendants that he could walk down the steps and out to the waiting ambulance, but they insisted on putting him onto a stretcher. Meyer washed his hands at the corner sink and sat down wearily at his desk. Kling poured himself a cup of coffee. Carella took off his holster, put it into the top drawer of his desk, and sat down beside Fred Hassler. Hawes sat on the edge of the desk.

'Is it like this all the time?' Hassler asked, his eyes bright.

'Not all the time,' Carella said.

'Boy, what excitement!'

'Mmm,' Carella said. 'Where have you been, Mr Hassler?'

'I was out of town. I had no idea you guys were looking for me. When I got back to the apartment this morning – *brother*! What a mess! The landlady told me I'd better call you guys. So I did.'

'Have you got any idea what happened in your apartment while you were gone?' Hawes asked.

'Well, it blew up, that much I know.'

'Do you know who was in it when it blew up?'

'The guy, yeah. The broad, no.'

'Who was the guy?'

'Tommy Barlow.'

'That his full name?' Hawes asked, beginning to write.

'Thomas Barlow, yeah.'

'Address?'

'He lives with his brother someplace in Riverhead. I'm not sure of the address.'

'Do you know the street?'

'No, I don't know that, either. I've never been there.'

'How do you know Tommy, Mr Hassler?'

'We work together in the same place.'

'Where's that?'

'Lone Star Photo-Finishing.'

'In this city?'

'Yeah. Four-one-seven North Eighty-eighth.' Hassler paused. 'You wondering about the "Lone Star"? A guy from Texas started the outfit.'

'I see. How long have you been working there, Mr Hassler?'

'Six years.'

'You know Tommy Barlow all that time?'

'No, sir. Tommy's been with the company no more'n two years.'

'Were you good friends?'

'Pretty good.'

'Is he married?'

39

'Nope. I told you. He lives with his brother. He's a cripple guy, his brother. I met him once down the place. He walks with a cane.'

'Do you know his name?'

'Yeah, wait a minute, Andy . . . ? no, wait a minute . . . Angelo . . . ? something like that, just a minute. Amos! Amos, that's it. Amos Barlow. Yeah.'

'All right, Mr Hassler, what was Tommy Barlow doing in your apartment?'

Hassler grinned lewdly. 'Well, like what do you think he was doing?'

'I meant . . .'

'They found him with a naked broad, what do you think he was doing?'

'I meant how'd he happen to be there, Mr Hassler?'

'Oh. He asked me for the key. He knew I was going out of town, so he asked me if he could use the place. So I said sure. Why not? Nothing wrong with that.'

'Did you know he was going there with a married woman?'

'Nope.'

'Did you know he was going there with a *woman*?'

'I figured.'

'Did he tell you as much?'

'Nope. But why else would he want the key?'

'Would you say he was a good friend of yours, Mr Hassler?'

'Yeah, pretty good. We been bowling together a couple of times. And also, he helps me with my movies.'

'Your movies?'

'Yeah, I'm a movie nut. You know, where I work, we don't process movie film. That's all done by Kodak and

Technicolor and like that. We just develop and print stills, you know. Black and white, colour, but no movies. Anyway, I got this urge to make movies, you see? So I'm always shooting pictures and then I edit them and splice them and Tommy used to help me sometimes. I got this Japanese camera, you see . . .'

'Help you with *what*? The picture-taking or the editing?'

'That, and the acting, too. I've got a reel almost three hundred feet long that's practically all Tommy. You should see some of my stuff. I'm pretty good. That's why this place knocked me on my ass when I walked in here. What colour! What atmosphere! *Mar*-vellous! Just *mar*-vellous!' Hassler paused. 'You think I could come in here and take some pictures sometime?'

'I doubt it,' Carella said.

'Yeah, what a shame,' Hassler said. 'Can you picture that guy's arm bleeding in colour? *Boy!*'

'Can we get back to Tommy for a minute, Mr Hassler?'

'Oh sure. Sure. Listen, I'm sorry if I got off the track. But I'm a nut on movies, you know? I got the bug, you know?'

'Sure, we know,' Hawes said. 'Tell us, Mr Hassler, did Tommy seem despondent or depressed or . . . ?'

'Tommy? Who, Tommy?' Hassler burst out laughing. 'This is the original good-time kid. Always laughing, always happy.'

'When he asked you for the key, did he seem sad?'

'I just told you. He was always laughing.'

'Yes, but when he asked you for the key . . .'

'He asked me, wait a minute, it musta been three days ago. Because he knew I had to go out of town, you

41

see. The reason I had to go out of town is I've got this old aunt who lives upstate and I'm hoping someday when she drops dead she'll leave me her house. She hasn't been feeling too good, and I got a cousin who's got his eye on that house, too, so I figured I better get up there and hold her hand a little before she leaves it to him, you know? So I went up there yesterday, took the day off. Today's Saturday, right?'

'That's right.'

'You guys work on Saturdays?'

'We try to, Mr Hassler,' Carella said. 'Can we get back to Tommy for a minute?'

'Oh, sure. Sure. Listen, I'm sorry if I got off the track. But that house is important to me, you know? Not that I want the old lady to drop dead or anything, but I sure would like to get my hands on that house. It's a big old place, you know? With lilacs all around . . .'

'About Tommy,' Carella cut in. 'As I understand it, when he asked you for the key, he seemed his usual self, is that right? Happy, laughing?'

'That's right.'

'When did you see him last?'

'Thursday, At work.'

'Did he take Friday off, too?'

'Gee, I don't know. Why do you ask?'

'We were just wondering what time he and the girl met. He didn't mention anything about that, did he?'

'No. You'd have to check with the boss, I guess. See whether or not Tommy was off on Friday. That's what I'd do if I was you.'

'Thanks,' Carella said.

'She was married, huh? The broad?'

'Yes.'

'Tough break. Her being married, I mean. I got a rule, you know? I never fool around with married women. The way I figure it, there's plenty of lonely single girls in this city who're just ready to . . .'

'Thanks a lot, Mr Hassler. Where can we reach you if we need you?'

'At the apartment, where do you think?'

'You're going to be staying there?' Hawes asked incredulously.

'Sure. The bedroom's in fine shape. You'd never even know anything happened. The living-room's not too bad, either. That's where I keep all my film. Man, if I'da had it stored in the kitchen, *brother*!'

'Well, thanks again, Mr Hassler.'

'Sure, any time,' Hassler said. He shook hands with both detectives, waved at Meyer Meyer, who acknowledged the wave with a sour nod of his head, and then walked out of the squad-room and down the corridor.

'What's *he* doing?' Meyer asked. 'Running for mayor?'

'We could use a mayor in this city,' Kling answered.

'What do you think?' Carella asked Hawes.

'One thing,' Hawes said. 'If Tommy Barlow was planning to commit suicide, why would he use a friend's apartment? People don't go around causing trouble for their friends, especially when they're ready to take the pipe.'

'Right,' Carella said. 'And since when do potential suicides go around happy and laughing?' He shook his head. 'It doesn't sound as if Tommy was planning a funeral.'

'No,' Hawes said. 'It sounds as if he was planning a party.'

*

It would have been very simple to call the damn thing a suicide and have done with it. Neither Carella nor Hawes was particularly anxious to whip a dead horse, and there was certainly enough evidence around to indicate that Tommy Barlow and Irene Thayer had done the Endsville bit. There was, after all, a suicide note; there was, after all, the presence of enough illuminating gas to have caused an explosion. In addition, there were two empty whisky bottles in the room, and the nearly naked condition of the bodies seemed to strongly indicate this was a true love pact, the doomed lovers perhaps indulging themselves in a final climactic embrace before the gas rendered them unconscious and then dead. All these things in combination, made it very easy to reach a conclusion. And the conclusion, of course, should have been suicide.

Carella and Hawes, though, were fairly conscientious cops who had learned through years of experience that every case has a feel to it. This 'feel' is something intuitive, and impervious to either logic or reasoning. It is something close to insight, something close to total identification with victim and killer alike. When it comes, you listen to it. You can find whisky bottles on the floor, and clothing stacked in neat little piles, and a typewritten suicide note, and an apartment full of illuminating gas; you can add up all these pieces of evidence and come up with an obvious suicide, and the feel tells you it ain't. It's as simple as that.

It was equally simple for the toxicologist attached to the Chief Medical Examiner's office to arrive at his conclusions. Milt Anderson, Ph.D., was not a lazy man, nor was he being particularly negligent. He was, in all fairness, a man who had been practising legal toxicology

44

for more than thirty years, and who was a professor of forensic toxicology at one of the city's finest universities. He knew his work well, and he performed it with accuracy and dispatch. The detectives wanted to know only three things:

1. The cause of death.
2. Whether or not the couple were intoxicated prior to death.
3. Whether or not the couple had engaged in sexual intercourse prior to death.

No one had asked him to speculate on whether the deaths were accidental, suicidal, or homicidal. He did exactly what he was asked. He examined the victims and reported, as requested, on the three areas of concern to the detectives. But he had also been filled in on the circumstances surrounding the deaths, and these were firmly in his mind as he performed his tests.

Anderson knew there had been an explosion of illuminating gas. He knew that the jets on the gas range in Fred Hassler's apartment had been left open. He looked at the bright cherry-red colour of the body tissues, blood, and viscera and was willing right then and there to call it death by acute carbon monoxide poisoning. But he was being paid to do a job, and he knew that the most accurate and incontestable method for the determination of carbon monoxide in blood was the Van Slyke Manometric Method. Since his laboratory equipment included the Van Slyke apparatus, he went to work immediately on the blood of both victims. In both cases, he found that the carbon monoxide saturation was close to 60 per cent, and he knew that as low a saturation as 31 per cent could have caused fatal poisoning. He drew his conclusion. His conclusion was absolutely correct. Both Irene Thayer and Tommy Barlow had died of acute carbon monoxide poisoning.

Anderson knew that whisky bottles had been found in the apartment bedroom. He concluded, as he knew the detectives would have, that the couple had been drinking before they turned on the gas. But the detectives specifically wanted to know whether or not the couple had been intoxicated, and Anderson was grateful for the fact that the bodies had been delivered to him with reasonable dispatch. Alcohol is a funny poison. It feels very nice going down, and it can make you very gay and happy – but it is oxidized very rapidly in the system and will disappear entirely from the body during the first twenty-four hours after its ingestion. Anderson received both bodies almost immediately after Michael Thayer had identified his wife, less than twenty hours after the deaths had occurred. He realized this was cutting it dangerously close, but if the pair *had* been intoxicated, he was certain he would still find a sizeable percentage of alcohol in their brains. Happily, the brain tissue of both bodies was intact and available for testing. If there was one aspect of toxicology (and there were indeed many) that produced the most heated controversy concerning method and results, it was the analysis of ethyl alcohol. The controversy ranged the spectrum from A to Z, and began with that portion or portions of the body which provided the most reliable biological specimen for testing purposes. Anderson was a brain man. He knew there were lexicologists who preferred muscle tissue, or liver tissue, or even samplings from the kidney or spleen, but whenever a brain was available to him, he preferred that as a source for his tissue samplings. Two undamaged brains were available to him in the bodies of Irene Thayer and Tommy Barlow, and he used portions of those first to run a routine steam distillation test in an attempt to isolate and separate any volatile poisons in the bodies. There were none. Then, since he had already recovered alcohol during the distillation process, he used that same sampling for his quantitative determination tests. There were charts and charts and more charts relating to the percentage of alcohol recovered in the brain, and how much alcohol it took to make a man tipsy, or staggering, or reeling, or crocked, or downright fall-down, blind, stoned, inert, dead drunk. He had found only the faintest trace of alcohol in each of the brains, and he knew that *whichever* chart he used, neither of the victims would have come anywhere near to being drunk or even mildly intoxicated. But Anderson preferred using a chart based on the findings of Gettler and Tiber, who had examined the organs of six thousand alcoholic corpses in an attempt to record degrees of drunkenness. Dutifully, he looked at that chart now:

Classification	Percentage of Alcohol in the Brain	Physiologic Effects
1. Trace	0.005 to 0.02	Normal
2. +	0.02 to 0.10	Normal
3. + +	0.10 to 0.25	Less sense of care
4. + + +	0.25 to 0.40	Less sense of equilibrium
5. + + + +	0.40 to 0.60	Unbalance, intoxication

Dutifully, he decided that the answer to the second question posed him was a definite, negative, resounding NO. The couple had *not* been intoxicated prior to death.

As conscientious as he was, he didn't even attempt to analyse the body fluids and organs for any traces of non-volatile poisons. He already had his cause of death – acute carbon monoxide poisoning – and the isolation, recovery and identification of another, *and* unknown, poison in the bodies would have been a vast undertaking. Given even a small quantity of any particular drug, given even the tiniest clue to its existence in a corpse, Anderson, who was a competent lexicologist, would have consulted his texts and then chosen the best method of isolating that drug. But drugs, unfortunately, are not catalogued according to their properties. This means that if there is an unknown drug in a corpse, and if the toxicologist has no clue supplied either by the circumstances of the death or by a previous autopsy report, he must run *every* test he can think of in a catch-as-catch-can game of trying to isolate something toxic. The non-volatile organic poisons ranged from glucosides like oleander and scilla and digitalis, to essential oils like nutmeg and cedar and rue, to aliphatic hypnotics like barbiturates and hydantoins, to organic purgatives like oleum ricini and cascara sagrada, and then into the alkaloids like opium and morphine and atropine . . . there were plenty, and Anderson was familiar with all of them, but he had not been asked to run such exhaustive tests, and saw no necessity for doing so. He had been asked to find out three things, and he already had the answers to the first two. He began work on the third immediately.

He couldn't understand why the cops of the 87th

wanted to know whether or not the victims had been making love before they died. He rather suspected the squad contained a horny bastard somewhere in its ranks, a latent necrophile. In any case, they wanted the information, and it was not too difficult to provide it. The situation might have been different if the bodies had reached him later than they did. Sperm, like alcohol, simply isn't present after twenty-four hours have expired. He didn't expect to find any moving cells in Irene Thayer's vaginal tract because he knew this was impossible so many hours after her death. But he could hopefully find immobile spermatozoa even now. He took a wet smear, studied the specimen under a high-power microscope, and found no traces of spermatozoa. Not content to leave it at that (there were too many conditions which could explain the absence of spermatozoa in the vagina even following intercourse) he turned to the body of Tommy Barlow, irrigated the urethal canal with a saline solution, aspirated the fluid back into a syringe, and then studied it under his microscope for traces of sperm. There were none.

Satisfied with his findings, he concluded his report and asked that it be typed up for transmission to the 87th.

The report was couched in medical language, and it explained exactly why Anderson was answering his questions as he answered them, exactly what evidence he had found to back up his opinions. The men of the 87th waded through the language and decided that what it all meant was:

1. Gaspipe.
2. Sober.
3. Unlaid.

The report made them wonder where all that booze had gone, if neither of the victims had drunk it. The report also made them wonder why Tommy and Irene had taken off their clothes, if not euphemistically to 'be together' for the last time. It had been a reasonable assumption, up to then, that the pair had made love, then dressed themselves partially, and then turned on the gas. If they had *not* made love, why had they undressed?

Somehow, the men on the squad almost wished they'd never received Anderson's damn report.

5.

THERE IS SOMETHING about big women that is always a little frightening: a reversal of roles, a destruction of stereotype. Women are supposed to be delicate and fragile; everybody knows that. They're supposed to be soft and cuddly and a little helpless and dependent. They're supposed to seek comfort and solace in the arms of strong, clear-eyed, resolute men.

The two men who rang the doorbell of Mary Tomlinson's house on Sands Spit were strong, clear-eyed, and resolute.

Steve Carella was six feet tall with wide shoulders, narrow hips, thick wrists and big hands. He did not present a picture of overwhelming massiveness because his power was deceptively concealed in the body of a natural athlete, a man who moved easily and loosely, in total control of fine-honed muscularity. His eyes were brown with a peculiar downward slant, combining with his high cheekbones to give his face a curiously oriental look. He was not a frightening man, but when you opened the door to find him on your front step, you knew for certain he wasn't there to sell insurance.

Cotton Hawes weighed a hundred and ninety pounds. He was six feet two inches tall, and his big-boned body was padded with obvious muscle. His eyes were an electric blue, and he had a straight unbroken nose, and a good mouth with a wide lower lip. He carried a white streak in the hair over his left temple, where he had once been stabbed while investigating a burglary. He did not look like the sort of man anyone would want to challenge – even to a game of checkers.

Both men were big, both men were strong. And besides, they were each carrying loaded guns on their hips. But when Mary Tomlinson opened the door of the development house, they both felt slightly inadequate and seemed to shrink visibly on the doorstep.

Mrs Tomlinson had flaming red hair and flashing green eyes. The eyes and the hair alone would have been enough to present her as a woman of force, but they were accompanied by height and girth, and a granite-like, no-nonsense face. She stood at least five feet nine inches tall inside her doorway, a woman with a large bosom and thick arms, her legs and feet planted firmly to the floor, like a wrestler waiting for a charge. She wore a flowered Hawaiian muu-muu, and she was barefoot, and she looked at the detectives with suspicion as they faced her inadequately and timorously showed their shields.

'Come in,' she said. 'I was wondering when you'd get to me.'

She did not deliver the cliché with any sense of un-originality. She seemed not to know that 'I was wondering when you'd get to me' had been spoken by countless fictitious heavies long before she was born, and would probably continue to be spoken so long as heavies existed. Instead, she delivered the line as if she were chairman of the board of General Motors who, having called a meeting, was irritated when some of executives arrived a little late. She had been expecting the police to get to her, and her only question now was what the hell had taken them so long.

She stamped flatfooted into the house, leaving the door for Hawes to close behind him. The house was a typical Sands Spit development dwelling, a small entrance hall, a kitchen on the left, a living-room on the right, and three bedrooms and a bath running along the rear. Mrs Tomlinson had furnished the place with the taste of a miniaturist. The furniture was small, the pictures on the walls were small, the lamps were small, everything seemed to have been designed for a tiny woman.

'Sit down,' she said, and Hawes and Carella found seats in the living-room, two small cane chairs in which they were instantly uncomfortable. Mrs Tomlinson spread her ample buttocks onto the tiny couch opposite them. She sat like a man, her legs widespread; the folds of the muu-muu dropping between her knees, her big-toed feet again planted firmly on the floor. She looked at her visitors unsmiling, waiting. Carella cleared his throat.

'We'd like to ask you a few questions, Mrs Tomlinson,' he said.

'I assume that's why you're here,' she answered.

'Yes,' Carella said. 'To begin with . . .'

'To begin with,' Mrs Tomlinson cut in, 'I'm in the middle of preparations for my daughter's funeral, so I hope you'll make this short and sweet. *Some*body's got to take care of the damn thing.'

'You're handling all the arrangements, are you?' Hawes asked.

'Who's *going* to handle it?' she said, her lip curling. 'That idiot she lived with?'

'Your son-in-law, you mean?'

'My *son*-in-law,' she repeated, and she managed to

give the words an inflection that immediately presented Michael Thayer as a fumbling creature incapable of coping with anything more difficult than tying his own shoelaces. 'Some son-in-law. The poet. Roses are red, violets are blue, let it be said, happy birthday to you. My *son*-in-law.' She shook her massive head.

'I gather you don't like him very much,' Carella said.

'The feelings are mutual. Haven't you talked to him?'

'Yes, we've talked to him.'

'Then you know.' She paused. 'Or do you? If Michael said anything kind about me, he was lying.'

'He said you don't get along, Mrs Tomlinson.'

'That's the understatement of the year. We hate each other's guts. The bully.'

'Bully?' Hawes said. He looked at Mrs Tomlinson in astonishment because the word seemed thoroughly inappropriate coming from her lips.

'Always shoving his weight around. I hate men who take advantage of us.'

'Take advantage?' Hawes repeated, the astonishment still on his face.

'Yes. Women are to be treated with respect,' she said, 'and cared for gently. And with tenderness.' She shook her head. 'He doesn't know. He's a bully.' She paused, and then reflectively added, 'Women are delicate.'

Hawes and Carella looked at her silently for several moments.

'He . . . uh . . . he bullied your daughter, Mrs Tomlinson?'

'Yes.'

'How?'

'Bossing her. He's a boss. I hate men who are bosses.' She looked at Hawes. 'Are you married?'

'No, ma'am.'

She turned instantly to Carella. 'Are you?'

'Yes, I am.'

'Are you a boss?'

'I . . . I don't think so.'

'Good. You seem like a nice boy.' She paused. 'Not Michael. Always bossing. Did you pay the electric bill? Did you do the marketing? Did you do this and that? It's no wonder.'

Again, the room was silent.

'It's no wonder *what*?' Carella asked.

'It's no wonder Margaret was going to leave him.'

'Margaret?'

'My daughter.'

'Oh. Oh, yes,' Carella said. 'You call her Margaret, do you?'

'That's the name she was born with.'

'Yes, but most people called her Irene, isn't that true?'

'Margaret was the name we gave her, and Margaret was what we called her. Why? What's the matter with that name?'

'Nothing, nothing,' Carella said hastily. 'It's a very nice name.'

'If it's good enough for the princess of England, it's good enough for anybody,' Mrs Tomlinson said.

'Certainly,' Carella said.

'Certainly,' Mrs Tomlinson agreed, and she nodded her head vigorously.

'She was going to leave him?' Hawes asked.

'Yes.'

'You mean divorce him?'

'Yes.'

'How do you know?'

'She told me. How do you think I know? Mothers and daughters shouldn't keep secrets from each other. I told Margaret anything she wanted to know, and she did the same with me.'

'When did she plan on leaving him, Mrs Tomlinson?'

'Next month.'

'When next month?'

'On the sixteenth.'

'Why that particular day?'

Mrs Tomlinson shrugged. 'Is something wrong with that day?'

'No, nothing at all. But was there a special reason for picking the sixteenth?'

'I never stuck my nose in my daughter's business,' Mrs Tomlinson said abruptly. Carella and Hawes exchanged a quick glance.

'But yet you're certain about the date,' Hawes said.

'Yes. She told me she would leave him on the sixteenth.'

'But you don't know why the sixteenth?'

'No,' Mrs Tomlinson said. She smiled suddenly. 'Are *you* going to bully me, too?' she asked.

Carella returned the smile. Graciously, he answered, 'No, certainly not, Mrs Tomlinson. We're only trying to get the facts.'

'I can give you all the facts,' Mrs Tomlinson said. 'The first fact is that my daughter didn't commit suicide. That you can count on.'

'How do you know?'

'Because I knew my daughter. She was like me. She loved life. Nobody who loves life is going to take her own life, that's for sure.'

'Well,' Carella said, 'all the indications . . .'

'Indications! Who cares about indications? My daughter was vital, energetic. People like that don't commit suicide. Look, it runs in the family.'

'Energy?' Hawes asked.

'Energy, right! I've got to keep moving all day long. Even sitting here, I'm beginning to feel fidgety, would you believe it? There are nervous types of women, you know. I'm one of them.'

'And your daughter was another?'

'Absolutely. Always on the go! Vital! Energetic! Alive! Listen, do you want to know something? Shall I tell you how I am in bed?'

Carella looked at Hawes uncomfortably.

'When I get in bed at night, I can't sleep. All that energy. My hands twitch, my legs, I just can't sleep. I take pills every night. Only way I can relax. I'm like a motor.'

'And your daughter was that way, too?'

'Positively! So why take her own life? Impossible. Besides, she was going to leave that bully. She was going to start a *new* life.' She shook her head. 'This whole thing stinks. I don't know who turned on that gas, but it wasn't Margaret, you can count on that.'

'Maybe it was Barlow,' Hawes suggested.

'Tommy? Ridiculous.'

'Why?'

'Because they were going to get married, that's why! So would either of them turn on the gas? Or leave a stupid note like the one in the apartment? "There is no other way!" Nonsense! They'd already decided on another way.'

'Now, let me get this straight, Mrs Tomlinson,'

Carella said. 'You *knew* your daughter was seeing Tommy Barlow.'

'Of course I knew.'

'You didn't try to discourage it?'

'Discourage it? Why the hell would I do that?'

'Well . . . well, she *was* married, Mrs Tomlinson.'

'Married! To that bully? *That* was a marriage? Hah!' Mrs Tomlinson shook her head. 'She married Michael when she was eighteen. What does a girl of eighteen know about love?'

'How old was she now, Mrs Tomlinson?'

'Almost twenty-one. A woman. A woman capable of making up her own mind.' She nodded. 'And what she decided to do was to leave Michael and marry Tommy. As simple as that. So why should she kill herself?'

'Are you aware, Mrs Tomlinson, that your daughter told her husband she was coming to visit you on the day she died?'

'Yes.'

'Did she do that often?'

'Yes.'

'In effect, then, you alibied her, is that right?'

'Alibied? I wouldn't call it that.'

'What would you call it?'

'I would call it two sensitive women helping each other against a bully.'

'You keep referring to Mr Thayer as a bully. Did he ever strike your daughter?'

'Strike her? I'd break every bone in his body!'

'Threaten her, then?'

'Never. He's a boss, that's all. Believe me, I was glad she planned to leave him.'

Carella cleared his throat. He was uncomfortable in

58

the presence of this big woman who thought of herself as a small woman. He was uncomfortable in the presence of this mother who condoned her daughter's adultery.

'I'd like to know something, Mrs Tomlinson.'

'What's that?'

'Michael Thayer said he called you after he saw your daughter's picture in the newspaper . . .'

'That's right.'

'. . . and asked you whether she was here.'

'That's right.'

'Mrs Tomlinson, if you approved of your daughter's relationship with Barlow, if you disliked Michael so much, why did you tell him she wasn't here?'

'Because she wasn't.'

'But you knew she was with Barlow.'

'So what?'

'Mrs Tomlinson, did you *want* Michael to know what was going on?'

'Of course not.'

'Then why did you tell him the truth?'

'What was I supposed to do? Lie and say Margaret was here? Suppose he asked to speak to her?'

'You could have invented some excuse. You could have said she'd stepped out for a minute.'

'Why should I lie to that louse? Anything he got was coming to him!'

'What do you mean?'

'The divorce, I mean. Margaret leaving him.'

'Did he know she planned to leave him?'

'No.'

'Did she tell anyone else about this divorce, Mrs Tomlinson?'

'Certainly. She was seeing a lawyer about it.'

'Who?'

'I think that's my daughter's business.'

'Your daughter is dead,' Carella said.

'Yes, I know,' Mrs Tomlinson said.

And then, for no apparent reason, Carella repeated, 'She's dead.'

The room, for the space of a heartbeat, fell silent. Up until that moment, even though Mrs Tomlinson had been in the midst of funeral preparations when they'd arrived, even though the conversation had most certainly dealt with the circumstances of their visit, Carella had had the oddest feeling that Mrs Tomlinson, that Hawes, that he himself were not really talking about someone who was utterly and completely dead. The feeling had been unsettling, a persistent nagging feeling that, despite references in the past tense, despite allusions to suicide, they were all thinking of Margaret Irene Thayer as being *alive*, as a girl who was indeed about to leave her husband next month to begin a new life.

And so, his voice low, Carella repeated, 'She's dead,' and the room went silent, and suddenly there was perspective.

'She was my only daughter,' Mrs Tomlinson said. She sat on the sofa that was too small for her, a huge woman with flat feet and big hands and lustreless green eyes and fading red hair, and suddenly Carella realized that she *was* truly tiny, that the furniture she'd surrounded herself with was bought for a small and frightened woman lurking somewhere inside that huge body, a woman who really did need gentleness and tenderness.

'We're very sorry,' he said. 'Please believe that.'

'Yes. Yes, I know. But you can't bring her back to me, can you? That's the one thing you can't do.'

'No, Mrs Tomlinson. We can't do that.'

'I was looking at all my old pictures of her yesterday,' she said. 'I wish I had some pictures of Tommy, too. I have a lot of Margaret, but none of the man she was going to marry.' She sighed heavily. 'I wonder how many pills I'll take tonight,' she asked. 'Before I can sleep. I wonder.'

In the silence of the living-room, a small porcelain clock, delicately wrought and resting on a small inlaid end table, began chiming the hour. Silently, Carella counted the strokes. One, two, three, four. The echo of the chimes faded. The room was still again. Hawes shifted his position on the uncomfortable cane chair.

'I've made a hundred lists,' Mrs Tomlinson said. 'Of things to do. Michael is of no help, you know, no help at all. I'm all alone in this. If Margaret were only alive to . . .' And then she stopped because the absurdity of what she was about to say suddenly struck her. 'If Margaret were only alive to help with her funeral preparations' were the words in her mind and on her tongue, and she swallowed them at once because the presence of death was suddenly very large in that small room. She shivered all at once. She stared at Carella and Hawes in the deepening silence of the room. Outside on the street, a woman called to her child. The silence lengthened.

'You . . . you wanted the lawyer's name,' Mrs Tomlinson said.

'Yes.'

'Arthur Patterson. I don't know his address.'

'In the city?'

'Yes.' Mrs Tomlinson shivered again. 'I'm telling you the truth, you know. Margaret *was* leaving him.'

'I believe you, Mrs Tomlinson,' Carella said. He rose suddenly and crossed the room. Gently, tenderly, he took her huge hand between both his own and said, 'We appreciate your help. If there's anything we can do, please call us.'

Mrs Tomlinson looked up into the face of the tall man who stood before the couch.

In a very small voice, she said, 'Thank you.'

6.

ARTHUR PATTERSON WAS a man in his middle thirties who had recently shaved off his moustache. Neither Carella nor Hawes knew that Patterson had performed the moustachectomy only two days before, but had they been alert detectives they would have noticed that Patterson touched the area over his upper lip rather frequently. The area looked very much like the stretch of skin above *any* man's upper lip, but it didn't feel that way to Patterson. To Patterson, the tiny stretch of skin felt very large and very naked. He kept touching the area to reassure himself that it wasn't getting any larger or any more naked. He didn't feel at all like himself, sitting there and discussing Margaret Irene Thayer with two men from the police department. If he stared down the sides of his nose, he could see his upper lip protruding and swollen and nude. He felt as if he looked very silly, and he was sure the detectives were smiling at his nakedness. He touched the skin above his mouth again, and then hastily withdrew his hand.

'Yes,' he said, 'Irene Thayer came to me to see about a divorce.'

'Had you ever handled any legal matters for her before, Mr Patterson?' Carella asked.

'I prepared a will. That was all.'

'You prepared a will for Irene Thayer?'

'For both of them actually. The usual thing, you know.'

'What usual thing, Mr Patterson?'

'Oh, you know. "I direct that all my debts and funeral expenses be paid as soon after my death as may be practicable. All the rest, residue and remainder of my estate, whether real or personal, and wherever situate, I give, devise and bequeath to my wife." That sort of thing.'

'Then in the event of Michael Thayer's death, Irene Thayer would have inherited his entire estate?'

'Yes, that's right. And the reverse was, of course, also true.'

'How do you mean?'

'In the event that Michael Thayer survived his wife, well, anything *she* owned would go to him. That was one of the will's provisions.'

'I see,' Carella said. He paused. Arthur Patterson touched his missing moustache. '*Did* she own anything?'

'I don't know. It doesn't seem likely. She seemed concerned about the expense of getting a divorce.'

'She told you this?'

'Yes.' Patterson shrugged. 'I was in a peculiar position here, you understand. It was Thayer who first came to me about drawing the will. And now I was handling a divorce proceeding for his *wife*. It was an odd feeling.'

'You mean, you felt as if you were really *Michael* Thayer's lawyer?'

'Well, not exactly. But . . . let's put it this way . . . I felt as if I were attorney for the Thayer *family*, do you know what I mean? And not for Irene Thayer alone.'

'But she nonetheless came to you?'

'Yes.'

'And said she wanted a divorce.'

'Yes. She was going to Reno next month.'

'In spite of the expense involved?'

'Well, that was a serious consideration. She initially came to me to find out what the Alabama divorce laws were. She had heard it was a good jurisdiction. But I advised her against an Alabama divorce.'

'Why?'

'Well, they've been getting a little rough down there. In many cases, if it appears that a couple came to the jurisdiction only to get a divorce and not to establish bona-fide residence the state will void the divorce of its own volition. I didn't think she wanted to risk that. I suggested Mexico to her, where we can get a divorce ruling in twenty-four hours, but she didn't like the idea.'

'Why not?'

'I'm not sure. A Mexican divorce is as good as any you can get. But the layman has the mistaken impression that Mexican divorces aren't legal or are easy to upset. Anyway, she didn't go for the idea. So, naturally, I suggested Nevada. Are you familiar with the Nevada divorce laws?'

'No,' Carella said.

'Well, they require a six-weeks' residence in the state, and the grounds range from . . . well, adultery, impotence, desertion, non-support, mental cruelty, physical cruelty, habitual drunkenness . . . I could go on, but that'll give you an idea.'

'On what grounds was she suing for divorce?'

'Mental cruelty.'

'Not adultery?'

'No.' Patterson paused. 'She wouldn't have had to go all the way to Reno if she were claiming adultery, would she? I mean . . . after all . . .' He hesitated again. 'I don't know how much of this I should discuss with you. You see, I *did* suggest the possibility of she and her husband seeing a marriage counsellor, but she wasn't at all interested in that.'

'She wanted a divorce.'

'Yes, she was adamant about it.' Patterson stroked his lip, seemed to be deciding whether or not he should reveal *all* the information he had, and finally sighed and said, 'There was another man involved, you see.'

'That would seem obvious, wouldn't it, Mr Patterson?' Hawes said. 'They were found dead together.'

Patterson stared at Hawes, and then activated a voice he usually reserved for the courtroom. 'The fact that they were found dead together needn't indicate they were planning a future life together. Mr Barlow . . . I believe that was his name . . . ?'

'Yes, Mr Barlow, that's right.'

'Mr Barlow may not even have been the man she intended marrying.'

'Irene's mother seems to think he was.'

'Well, perhaps you have information I do not have.'

'Irene never told you the man's name?'

'No. She simply said she was in love with someone and wanted a divorce as quickly as possible so that she could marry him.'

'She definitely said that?'

'Yes.' Patterson dropped his courtroom voice and assumed the tones of a friendly country lawyer dispensing philosophy around a cracker barrel. 'It's been my experience, however, that many women . . . and men too . . . who are contemplating divorce aren't always sure *why* they want the divorce. That is, Irene Thayer may have thought she was in love with this Barlow person and used that as a reason for escaping from a situation that was intolerable to her.'

'Did she *say* it was intolerable?' Hawes asked.

'She indicated that living with Michael Thayer was something of a trial, yes.'

'Why?'

'She didn't say.'

'How did Mr Thayer feel about the divorce?' Carella asked.

'I did not discuss it with him.'

'Why not?'

'Mrs Thayer preferred it that way. She said she wanted to handle it herself.'

'Did she say why?'

'She preferred it that way, that's all. In fact, she was going to serve him by publication, once she got to Nevada and started the proceedings.'

'Why would she want to do that?'

'Well, it's not unusual, you know.' He shrugged. 'She simply wanted to wait until next month. Considering the fact of the other man, I hardly think . . .'

'Next month *when*?' Hawes asked.

'The end of the month sometime.' Patterson tried hard to keep his hands clenched in his lap, but lost the battle. His fingers went up to his mouth, he stroked the stretch of barren flesh, seemed annoyed with himself, and immediately put his hands in his pockets.

'But she was definitely going to Reno next month, is that right?' Carella said.

'Yes.' Patterson paused and added reflectively, 'I saw her several times. I gave her good advice, too. I don't suppose anyone'll pay me for my work now.'

'Doesn't the will say something about settling debts and paying funeral expenses?' Carella said.

'Why, yes,' Patterson answered. 'Yes, it does. I suppose I *could* submit a bill to Mr Thayer, but . . .' His eyes clouded. 'There's a moral issue here, isn't there? Don't you think there's a moral issue?'

'How so, Mr Patterson?'

'Well, I *am* his lawyer, too. He might not understand why I withheld information of the pending divorce. It's touchy.' He paused. 'But I *did* put in all that work. Do you think I should submit a bill?'

'That's up to you, Mr Patterson.' Carella thought for a moment and then said, 'Would you remember when she planned to leave, exactly?'

'I don't remember,' Patterson said. 'If I were sure Mr Thayer wouldn't get upset, I *would* submit a bill. Really, I would. After all, *I* have office expenses, too, and I did give her a lot of my time.'

'Please try to remember, Mr Patterson.'

'What?'

'When she was planning to leave for Reno.'

'Oh, I'm not sure. The fifteenth, the twentieth, something like that.'

'*Was* it the fifteenth?'

'It could have been. Is the fifteenth a Tuesday? I remember she said it would be Tuesday.'

Carella took a small celluloid calendar from his wallet. 'No,' he said, 'the fifteenth is a Monday.'

'Well, there was something about the week-end interfering, I don't remember exactly what it was. But she said Tuesday, that I remember for certain. Is the twentieth a Tuesday?'

'No, the twentieth is a Saturday. Would she have said Tuesday the sixteenth?'

'Yes, she might have.'

'Would there have been any reason for this? Was she waiting for you to prepare papers or anything?'

'No, her counsel in Reno would handle all that.'

'Then leaving on the sixteenth was *her* idea?'

'Yes. But you know, local lawyers don't usually prepare the papers in an out-of-state divorce case. So this wasn't . . .'

'What?'

'I did a lot of work even if it didn't involve the preparation of any legal papers.'

'What did you mean about a week-end interfering, Mr Patterson?' Hawes asked.

'Oh, she said something about having to wait until Monday.'

'I thought you said Tuesday.'

'Yes, she was leaving on Tuesday, but apparently there was something to be done on Monday before she left. I'm sorry I can't be more specific, but it was only a passing reference, and rather vague, as if she were thinking aloud. But she *was* leaving on the sixteenth, I'm fairly certain about that. And naturally, I put all of my time at her disposal.'

'Mr Patterson,' Carella said, 'you don't have to convince *us*.'

'Huh?'

'That you put in a lot of hard work.'

Patterson immediately stroked his upper lip, certain that no one in the world would have dared to talk to him that way if he were still wearing his moustache. 'I wasn't trying to convince anyone,' he said, miffed but trying hard not to show it. 'I *did* do the work, and I *will* submit a bill.' He nodded vigorously, in agreement with himself. 'I hardly think it should upset Mr Thayer. The facts of his wife's indiscretion were all over the newspapers, anyway.'

'Mr Patterson, what do you think of that suicide note?' Hawes asked.

Patterson shrugged. 'The one they ran in the newspapers? Sensationalism.'

'Yes, but did it seem consistent with what Mrs Thayer was planning?'

'That's a leading question,' Patterson said. 'Of *course* not. Why would she kill herself after going through the trouble of arranging for a divorce? Assuming Barlow was the man she planned to marry . . .'

'You still seem in doubt,' Carella said.

'I'm merely exploring the possibilities. If there were yet another man . . .'

'Mr Patterson,' Carella said, 'the *existing* possibilities are confusing enough. I don't think we have to go looking for more trouble than we already have.'

Patterson smiled thinly and said, 'I thought the police were concerned with investigating *every* possibility. Especially in an apparent suicide that stinks of homicide.'

'You *do* believe it was a homicide?'

'Don't you?' Patterson said.

Carella smiled and answered, 'We're investigating *every* possibility, Mr Patterson.'

There are many many possibilities to investigate when

you happen to run the police lab in a large city. Detective-Lieutenant Sam Grossman ran the laboratory at Headquarters downtown on High Street, and he would have been a very busy fellow even if the 87th didn't occasionally drop in with a case or two. Grossman didn't mind being busy. He was fond of repeating an old gipsy proverb that said something about idle hands being the devil's something-or-other, and he certainly didn't want his hands to become idle and the devil's something-or-other. There were times, however, when he wished he had six or seven hands rather than the customary allotment. It would have been different, perhaps, if Grossman were a slob. Slobs can handle any number of jobs at the same time, dispatching each and every one with equal facility, letting the chips fall where they may, as another old gipsy proverb states. But Grossman was a conscientious cop and a fastidious scientist, and he was firmly rooted in the belief that the police laboratory had been devised to help the working stiffs who were out there trying to solve crimes. He took a salary from the city, and he believed that the only way to earn that salary was to do his job as efficiently and effectively as he knew how.

Grossman was a rare man to head a laboratory because in addition to being a trained detective, he was also a damned good chemist. Most police laboratories were headed by a detective without any real scientific training but with a staff of qualified experts in chemistry, physics, and biology. Grossman had his staff, but he also had his own scientific background, and the mind of a man who had long ago wrestled with burglaries, muggings, robberies and anything a precinct detective could possibly encounter in his working day. There were times, in fact, when Grossman wished he were back in a cosy squad-room, somewhere, exchanging crummy jokes with weary colleagues. There were times, like today, when Grossman wished he had stayed in bed.

He never knew what governing law of probabilities caused the laboratory to be swamped with work at times and comparatively idle at other times. He never knew whether a phase of the moon or the latest nuclear test caused a sudden increase in crimes or accidents, whether people declared a holiday for violence at a specific time of the year or month, or whether some Martian mastermind had decided that such and such a day would be a good time to bug Grossman and his hard-pressed technicians. He only knew that there were days, like today, when there was simply too much to do and not enough people to do it.

An amateur burglar had broken into a store on South Fifteenth by forcing the lock on the rear door. Grossman's staff was now involved in comparing the marks found on the lock with specimen marks made with a crude chisel which the investigating detectives had discovered in the room of a suspect.

A woman had been strangled to death in a bedroom on Culver Avenue. Grossman's technicians had found traces of hair on the pillow, and would first have to compare it with the woman's own hair and, in the likelihood that it was not hers, run tests that would tell them whether the hair had been left by an animal or a human, and – if human – which part of the body the hair had come from, whether it had belonged to a man or a woman, whether it had been dyed, bleached, or cut recently, the age of the person who had carelessly left it behind, and whether or not it had been deformed by shooting, burning, or scalding.

A hold-up man, retreating in panic when he'd heard the siren of an approaching squad car, had fired three bullets into the wall of a gasoline station and then escaped. Grossman's technicians were now involved in comparing the retrieved bullets with specimen bullets fired from guns in their extensive file, attempting to determine the make of firearm the criminal had used so that the cops of the 71st could dig into their M.O. file for a possible clue.

A ten-year-old girl had accused the janitor of her building of having lured her into his basement room, and then having forced her to yield to his sexual advances. The child's garments were now being examined for stains of semen and blood.

A forty-five-year-old man was found dead on a highway, obviously the victim of a hit-and-run. The glass splinters embedded in his clothing were now being compared against specimens from the shattered left front headlight of an abandoned stolen car in an effort to identify the automobile as the one which had struck the man down.

Fingerprints, palm prints, fragmentary impressions of sweat pores, footprints, sole prints, sock prints, broken windows, broken locks, animal tracks and tyre tracks, dust and rust and feathers and film, rope burns and powder burns, stains of paint or urine or oil – all were there on that day, all waiting to be examined and compared, identified and catalogued.

And, in addition, there was the apparent suicide the boys of the 87th had dropped into his lap.

Grossman sighed heavily and once again consulted the drawing his laboratory artist had made from an on-the-spot sketch of the death chamber:

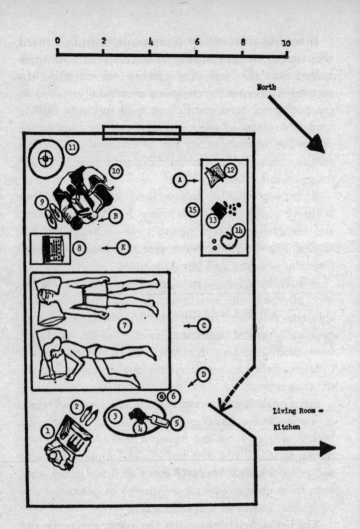

In suicide, as in baseball, it is sometimes difficult to tell who is who or what is what without a scorecard. Grossman turned over the lucite-encased sketch and studied the typewritten key rubber-cemented to its back:

BEDROOM – APARTMENT 1A
1516 South Fifth Street

1. Chair and woman's clothing.
2. Woman's shoes.
3. Scatter rug.
4. Whisky stain.
5. Whisky bottle, up-ended.
6. Whisky bottle, standing.
7. Bed and victims.
8. End table and typewriter.
9. Man's shoes.
10. Easy chair and man's clothing.
11. End table and lamp.
12. Typewritten note and wrist watch.
13. Wallet, tie clip, loose change.
14. String of pearls, earrings.
15. Dresser.

The little circles containing the letters A, B, C, D, and E, Grossman knew, indicated the camera angles of the photographs taken in the bedroom and enclosed in the folder he now held in his hands. The police photographer had taken, in order:

A. A close shot of the suicide note and the wrist-watch holding it down on the dresser top.
B. A medium shot of Tommy Barlow's clothing on the easy chair and his shoes resting beside the chair.
C. A full shot of the bed with the bodies of Irene Thayer and Tommy Barlow lying on it.
D. A medium shot showing the scatter rug and the two whisky bottles, as well as the chair upon and over which were Irene Thayer's clothes, and beside which were her shoes.
E. A close shot of the typewriter resting on an end table beside the bed.

Grossman studied the sketch and the photographs several times more, reread the report one of his technicians had prepared, and then sat down at a long white counter in the lab, took a telephone receiver from its wall bracket, and dialled Frederick 7–8024. The desk sergeant who answered the telephone connected him immediately with Steve Carella in the squad-room upstairs.

'I've got all this junk on your suicide,' Grossman said. 'You want to hear about it?'

'I do,' Carella said.

'Are you guys busy?'

'Moderately so.'

'Boy, this has been a day,' Grossman said. He sighed wearily. 'What'd they give you as cause of death on this one?' he asked.

'Acute carbon monoxide poisoning.'

'Mmm,' Grossman said.

'Why? Did you find some spent discharge shells or something?'

76

'No such luck. It sure *looks* like suicide, from what we've got here, but at the same time . . . I don't know. There's something not too kosher about this.'

'Like what?'

'You'd figure a suicide, wouldn't you?' Grossman said cautiously. 'Whisky bottles, open gas jets, an explosion. It all adds up, right? It verifies the figures.'

'What figures?'

'On deaths from carbon monoxide poisoning in this city every year. I've got a chart here. Shall I read you what the chart says?'

'Read to me,' Carella answered, smiling.

'Eight hundred and forty deaths a year, four hundred and forty of which are suicides. Four hundred and thirty-five of those are from illuminating gas. So it figures, doesn't it? And add the whisky bottles. Suicides of this type will often drink themselves into a stupor after turning on the gas. Or sometimes, they'll take sleeping-pills, anything to make the death nice and pleasant, you know?'

'Yeah, nice and pleasant,' Carella said.

'Yeah. But there's something a little screwy about this set-up, Steve. I'll tell you the truth, I wonder about it.'

'What have you got, Sam?'

'Number one, this whole business of the whisky bottles on the floor. Not near the head of the bed, but near the foot. And one of them knocked over. Why were the bottles near the foot of the bed, where they couldn't be reached if this couple had *really* been drinking?'

'They weren't drunk, Sam,' Carella said. 'Not according to our toxicologist.'

'Then where'd all that booze go to?' Grossman said. 'And something else, Steve. Where are the glasses?'

'I don't know. Where are they?'

'In the kitchen sink. Washed very nicely. Two glasses sitting in the sink all sparkling clean. Funny?'

'Very funny,' Carella said. 'If you've turned on the gas and are trying to get drunk, why get out of bed to wash the glasses?'

'Well, they had to get out of bed anyway, didn't they? To put on their clothes.'

'What do you mean?'

'Look, Steve, the whole thing smells of a love nest, doesn't it? We checked their garments for seminal stains, and there weren't any. So they must have been naked if they . . .'

'They didn't,' Carella said.

'How do you know?'

'Autopsy report. No signs of intercourse.'

'Mmmmm,' Grossman said. 'Then what were they doing with most of their clothes off?'

'Do you want an educated guess?'

'Shoot.'

'They probably planned to go out in a blaze of romantic glory. They got partially undressed, turned on the gas, and then were overcome before anything could happen. That's my guess.'

'It doesn't sound very educated to me,' Grossman said.

'All right, then,' Carella said, 'They were exhibitionists. They wanted their pictures in the paper without clothes on.'

'That not only sounds uneducated, it sounds positively ignorant.'

'Give me a better guess.'

'A third person in that apartment,' Grossman said.

'That's educated, huh?'

'That's highly educated,' Grossman said. 'Considering the fact that three glasses were used.'

'What?'

'*Three* glasses.'

'You said two a minute ago.'

'I said two in the sink. But we went through the cupboard over the sink, and we checked the glassware there, just because we had nothing else to do, you understand. Most of them were shattered by the blast, but . . .'

'Yeah, yeah, go ahead.'

'Light film of dust on all the glasses but one. This one had been recently washed, and then dried with a dish towel we found on a rack under the sink. The lint on the glass compared positive. What do you think?'

'They *could* have used three glasses, Sam.'

'Sure. Then why did they leave two in the sink and put the third one back in the cupboard?'

'I don't know.'

'A third person,' Grossman said. 'In fact, when we consider the last, and, I must admit, very very peculiar phenomenon, I'm almost convinced the third person is much more than just an educated guess.'

'What's the phenomenon, Sam?'

'No latent impressions in the room.'

'What do you mean?'

'No prints.'

'Of a third person, do you mean?'

'Of *any*body, I mean.'

'I don't understand.'

'I'm telling you,' Grossman said. 'Not a finger-print

on *any*thing. Not on the glasses, not on the bottles, not on the typewriter, not even on their *shoes*, Steve. Now how the hell do you type a suicide note and not leave prints all over the keys? How do you take off a pair of shoes – where there's a good wax surface that can pick up some beauties – and not leave *some* kind of an impression? How do you pour yourself a drink, and not leave at least a palm print on the bottle? Uh-uh, Steve, it stinks to high heaven.'

'What's your guess?'

'My guess is somebody went around that room and wiped off every surface, every article that anybody – especially himself – had touched.'

'A man?'

'I didn't say that.'

'You said "himself".'

'Poetic licence. It could have been man, woman, or trained chimpanzee, for all I know. I just finished telling you there's nothing in that apartment, *nothing*. And that's why it stinks. Whoever wiped up the place must have read a lot of stories about how we track down dangerous gunmen because they left behind a telltale print.'

'We won't tell them the truth, huh?'

'No, let 'em guess.' Grossman paused. 'What do you think?'

'Must have been an orgy,' Carella said, smiling.

'You serious?'

'Booze, a naked broad – maybe *two* naked broads, for all we know. What else could it have been?'

'It could have been somebody who found them in bed together, clobbered them, and then set up the joint to look like suicide.'

'Not a mark on either of them, Sam.'

'Well, I'm just telling you what I think. I think there was a third party in that room. Who, or why, you'll have to figure out for yourself.'

'Thanks.'

'Don't mention it. How's the wife and kids?'

'Fine. Sam . . .'

'Mmmm?'

'Sam, not *any* prints? Not a single print?'

'Nothing.'

Carella thought for a moment and then said, 'They could have wiped the place themselves.'

'Why?' Grossman asked.

'Neat. Just as you said. Note neatly typed, clothes neatly stacked, shoes neatly placed. Maybe they were very neat people.'

'Sure. So they went around dusting the place before they took the pipe.'

'Sure.'

'Sure,' Grossman said. 'Would *you* do that?'

'I'm not neat,' Carella said.

7.

THE COMBINATION OF Bert Kling and Michael Thayer
was a curiously trying one. Hawes liked Kling a hell of a
lot, or at least he had liked the Bert Kling he'd known
until last year; the new Bert Kling was someone he
didn't know at all. Being with him for any length of
time was a strange and frustrating experience. This was
surely Bert Kling, the same clean young looks, the blond
hair, the same voice. You saw him coming into the
squad-room or walking down the street, and you wanted
to go up to him with your hand extended and say, 'Hi,
there, Bert, how are you?' You wanted to crack jokes
with him, or go over the details of a perplexing case.
You wanted to sit with him and have a cup of coffee on
days when it was raining outside the squad-room. You
wanted to like this guy who was wearing the face and
body of Bert Kling, you wanted to tell him he was your
friend, you wanted to say, 'Hey, Bert, let's get drunk
together tonight.' You wanted to do all these things and
say all these things because the face was familiar, the
walk was familiar, the voice was familiar – and then
something stopped you dead in your tracks, and you had
the feeling that you were only looking at a plastic mould
of Bert Kling, only talking to the recorded voice of Bert
Kling, that something inside this shell had gone dead,
and you knew what the something was, of course, you
knew that Claire Townsend had been murdered.

There are different ways of mourning.

When a man's fiancée is the victim of a brutal, senseless massacre in a bookshop, he can react in many ways, all of which are valid, none of which can be predetermined. He can cry his eyes out for a week or a month, and then accept the death, accept that life goes on, with or without the girl he was going to marry one day, life is a progression, a moving forward, and death is a cessation. Bert Kling could have accepted the life surrounding him, could have accepted death as a natural part of life.

Or he could have reacted in another manner. He could have refused flatly to acknowledge the death. He could have gone on living with the fantasy that Claire Townsend was alive and well someplace, that the events which had started with a phone call to the squad-room on the thirteenth of October last year, moved into the shocking discovery of Claire among the victims in the bookshop, and culminated in the vicious beating of the man who'd killed her – he could have gone on pretending, indeed believing that none of these things had happened. Everything was just the way it was. He would continue to wait for Claire's return, and when she came he would laugh with her and hold her in his arms and make love to her again, and one day they would be married. He could have kidded himself in that way.

Or he could have accepted the death without a tear, allowing grief to build inside him like a massive monument, stone added to stone, until the smiling outer visage became the ornate façade of a crumbling tomb, vast, and black, and windswept.

It is perhaps simple for an accountant to evaluate the

murder of his fiancée, to go through the tribal custom of mourning, and then to cherish the memory of the girl while philosophically adjusting to the elementary facts of life and death. An accountant adds up columns of figures and decides how much income tax his client owes Uncle Sam. An accountant is concerned with mathematics. Bert Kling was a cop. And being a cop, being involved daily in work which involved crime, he was faced with constant reminders of the girl he had loved and the manner in which she had met her death. It was one thing to walk the streets of the precinct and to cross a six-year-old kid who stood on a street corner waiting for the traffic to pass. It was one thing to be investigating a burglary, or a robbery, or a beating, or a disappearance. It was quite another thing to be investigating a homicide.

The facts of life in the 87th Precinct were too often the facts of death. He had looked into the lifeless eyes of Claire Townsend on October 13th last year, and since that time he had looked into the lifeless eyes of three dozen more victims, male and female, and the eyes were always the same, the eyes always seemed to look beseechingly as if something had been ripped forcibly from them before they were ready, the eyes seemed to be pleading for that something to be put back, the eyes seemed to beg silently, 'Please give it back to me, I wasn't ready.' The circumstances of death were always different. He had walked into a room and found a man with a hatchet embedded in his skull, he had looked down at the eviscerated victim of a hit-and-run, he had opened a closet door and discovered a young girl with a rope knotted about her neck, hanging from the clothes bar, he had found an alcoholic who had drunk himself to death in the doorway of a whorehouse, the circumstances were always different – but the eyes were always the same.

'Please give it back to me,' they said. 'I wasn't ready.'

And each time he looked into a new pair of eyes, he turned away because the image of Claire Townsend on the bookshop floor, her blouse stained a bright red, the book lying open in a tent over her face, his hands lifting the book, his eyes looking into her own dead and staring eyes, this image always and suddenly flared into his mind and left him numb and senseless. He could not think clearly for several moments, he could only turn away from each new corpse and stare at the wall like a man transfixed while a private horror-movie ran in the tight projection-booth of his mind, reel after reel until he wanted to scream aloud and stopped himself from doing so only by clenching his teeth.

Death meant only one thing to Kling. Death meant Claire Townsend. The daily reminders of death were daily reminders of Claire. And with each reminder, his emotions would close like a fist, tightly clenched; he could not open it, he could not afford to let go. He withdrew instead, retreating from each grisly prod, accepting the burden of memory wearily, refusing sympathy, forsaking hope, forseeing a future as bleak and as barren as the present.

The equation that day in the tiny office of Michael Thayer in the Brio Building was a simple one. Hawes examined the equation dispassionately, uncomfortable in the presence of Kling and Thayer, recognizing the source of his discomfort, but finding no solace at all in the recognition. Irene Thayer equalled Death equalled

Claire Townsend. Such was the elementary equation that seemed to electrify the very air in the small room.

The room was on the sixth floor of the building, its single window open to the April breezes. It contained a desk and a file cabinet and a telephone and a calendar and two chairs. Michael Thayer sat in one of the chairs behind the desk. Hawes sat in the chair in front of the desk. Kling stood tensed like a spring coil alongside Hawes, as if ready to unlock and leap across the room and across the desk the moment Thayer said anything contradictory. A stack of completed greeting-card verse rested alongside Thayer's typewriter in a neat, squared pile. A sheet of unfinished doggerel was in the typewriter.

'We work pretty far in advance,' Thayer said. 'I'm already doing stuff for next Valentine's Day.'

'Don't you find it difficult to work so soon after the funeral, Mr Thayer?' Kling asked.

The question seemed so cruel, so heartlessly devised, that Hawes was instantly torn between a desire to gag Kling and a desire to punch him right in the mouth. Instead, he saw the pain flicker in Thayer's eyes for an instant, and he almost felt the pain himself, and then Thayer said very softly, 'Yes, I find it difficult to work.'

'Mr Thayer,' Hawes said quickly, 'we don't mean to intrude at a time like this, believe me, but there are some things we have to know.'

'Yes, you said that the last time I saw you.'

'I meant it then, and I mean it now.'

'Yes, I'm sure.'

'Did you know your wife was going to sue you for divorce?' Kling asked abruptly.

Thayer looked surprised. 'No.' He paused. 'How do you know that?'

'We talked with her lawyer,' Hawes said.

'Her lawyer? Art Patterson, do you mean?'

'Yes, sir.'

'He never said anything to me about it.'

'No, sir, she asked him not to.'

'Why?'

'She wanted it that way, Mr Thayer.'

'Mr Thayer,' Kling said, 'are you sure you had no inkling that your wife was about to divorce you?'

'None whatever.'

'That's a little odd, isn't it? A woman plans to leave you next month, and you haven't got the slightest suspicion that something's in the wind.'

'Irene seemed happy with me,' Thayer said.

'That's not what her mother said.'

'What did her mother say?'

'If I recall the report correctly,' Kling said, 'Mrs Tomlinson referred to you as a bully. And a boss.' Kling paused. 'Did you argue with your wife frequently?'

'Hardly ever.'

'Did you ever strike her?'

'What?'

'Strike her, hit her? Did you ever?'

'Never. Of course not.'

'Bert . . .'

'Just a second, Cotton, will you? Just a second?' He levelled his impatient gaze on Hawes, and then turned back to Thayer. 'Mr Thayer, you're asking us to believe that there was no friction between you and your wife, while all the time she was playing footsie with . . .'

'I didn't say there was no friction!'

'. . . another man and planning to divorce you. Now, either you didn't give a damn about her at all, or else . . .'

'I loved her!'

'. . . or else you were just plain cockeyed and didn't see what was going on right under your nose. Now which one was it, Mr Thayer?'

'I loved Irene, I trusted her!'

'And did she love you?' Kling snapped.

'I thought so.'

'Then why was she going to divorce you?'

'I don't know. I'm just learning about this. I don't even know if it's true. How do I know it's true?'

'Because we're telling you it's true. She planned to leave for Reno on the sixteenth of May. Does that date mean anything to you, Mr Thayer?'

'No.'

'Did you know she was seeing Tommy Barlow regularly?'

'Bert . . .'

'*Did* you?'

'No,' Thayer said.

'Then where did you think she was going every week, every other week?' Kling asked.

'To see her mother.'

'Why did her mother call you a bully?'

'I don't know. She doesn't like me. She could have said anything about me.'

'How old are you, Mr Thayer?'

'Thirty-three.'

'How old was your wife when she died?'

'Twenty. Well, almost twenty-one.'

'How long had you been married?'

'Almost three years.'

'She was eighteen when you married her?'

'Yes. Just eighteen.'

'And you were how old?'

'Thirty.'

'That's a pretty big span, isn't it, Mr Thayer?'

'Not if two people are in love.'

'And you were in love?'

'Yes.'

'And you claim you didn't know anything about your wife's boy friend, or the fact that she was planning to leave you next month?'

'That's right. If I'd known . . .'

'Yes, Mr Thayer? What would you have done if you'd known?'

'I'd have discussed it with her.'

'That's all you'd have done?'

'I'd have tried to talk her out of it.'

'And if that failed?'

'I'd have let her go.'

'You wouldn't have bullied her or bossed her?'

'I *never* bullied or . . . I was always very good to Irene. I . . . I knew she was much younger than I. I cared for her deeply . . . cared for her deeply.'

'How do you feel about her now, Mr Thayer? Now that you know all the facts?'

Thayer hesitated for a long time. 'I wish she would have talked it over with me,' he said at last. He shook his head. 'What she did wasn't the way. She should have talked it over with me.'

'Are you a drinking man, Mr Thayer?' Kling asked suddenly.

'Not . . . well . . . a few drinks every now and then. Not what you'd call a drinking man.'

'Did your wife drink?'

'Socially. A Martini now and then.'

'Scotch?'

'Sometimes.'

'There were two Scotch bottles found in the room with her. Both were empty. One had been knocked over, but the other had apparently been drained. What was the most your wife ever drank?'

'Four drinks. Maybe five. In an evening, I mean. At a party or something.'

'How'd she react to liquor?'

'Well . . . she generally got a little tipsy after two or three drinks.'

'What would a half-bottle of Scotch do to her?'

'Knock her unconscious, I would imagine.'

'Make her sick?'

'Maybe.'

'Did liquor ever make her sick?'

'Once or twice. She really didn't drink that much, so it's difficult to say.'

'The autopsy report showed your wife was not drunk, Mr Thayer. Yet a full bottle of Scotch, or possibly more, was consumed in that apartment on the day she died. Either consumed or poured down the drain. Which do you think it was?'

'I don't know,' Thayer said.

'You just told me your wife didn't drink much. Does killing a bottle of Scotch sound like a thing she would have done?'

'I don't know.' He shook his head again. '*Suicide* doesn't sound to me like a thing Irene would have done. *Adultery* doesn't sound to me . . . *divorce* doesn't sound . . . so how do I know what she would or wouldn't have done? I don't know this woman who supposedly killed herself, who had a lover, who was going to Reno. *I don't know her!* So why are you asking me about her? That's not Irene! That's some . . . some . . . some . . .'

'Some what, Mr Thayer?'

'Some stranger,' he said softly. 'Not my wife. Some stranger.' He shook his head. 'Some stranger,' he repeated.

The lobby of the Brio Building was crowded with musicians and girl vocalists and dancers and arrangers and song writers and agents who filled the air with the musical jargon of Hip. 'Like, man, I told him two bills for the week-end or *adiós*,' a din arising to meet the detectives' ears the moment they stepped from the elevator, 'The jerk went and hocked his ax. So I said, like, man, how you expect to blow if you ditched the horn? So he tells me he can't blow anyway unless he's got junk, so he peddled the ax to buy junk, so now he can't blow anyway, so like what's the percentage?'; bright-eyed girls with bleached-blonde hair and loose-hipped dancers' stances, trombone players with long arms and short goatees, agents with piercing brown eyes behind black-rimmed bop glasses, girl singers with hair falling loose over one eye. 'Like I said to him, like why should I put out for you if I don't put out for anybody else on the band, and he said like this is different, baby. So I said how is it different? So he put his hand under my skirt and said this is like love, baby'; a lonely pusher standing on the edges of the crowd, the Man, waiting for an afternoon appointment with a piano player who'd been an addict since the time he was fourteen; a seventeen-year-old girl with a Cleopatra haircut waiting to meet a trumpet player who had arranged for an audition with his group; the babble of sound hovering in the air, none of which Kling heard, the pretty girls, overly made up, but pretty with a fresh sparkle in their eyes and with tight light dresses stretched taut over comfortable behinds, none of whom Kling saw; the thronged lobby and the newspaper stand with the tabloids black and bold, the headlines no longer carrying the news of the death of Irene Thayer and Tommy Barlow, both of whom had been shoved off the front page by Khrushchev's latest temper tantrum; they shouldered their way through the crowd, two businessmen who had just completed a business call, and came out into the waning light of a late April afternoon.

'You were too rough with him,' Hawes said. He said it suddenly and tersely. He did not turn to look at Kling.

'He may have killed them,' Kling answered tonelessly.

'And maybe he didn't. Who the hell are you? The Lord High Executioner?'

'You want to fight with me, Cotton?' Kling asked.

'No. I'm just telling you.'

'What are you telling me?'

'I'm telling you there are good cops and shitty cops, and I'd hate to see you become one of the shitty ones.'

'Thanks.'

'You'd better watch it, Bert.'

'Thanks.'

They stood on the sidewalk for a moment as the

homeward-bound office workers rushed past them. There didn't seem much else to say for the moment. Like polite strangers, they stood with their coats open and their hands in their pockets.

'You going back uptown?' Kling asked.

'I thought *you* might want to type up the report,' Hawes said. He paused, and then caustically added, '*You* asked all the questions.'

'I guess I did.'

'Sure. So you do the report.'

'You sore?'

'Yes.'

'Screw you,' Kling said, and he walked off into the crowd.

Hawes stared after him for a moment, and then shook his head. He took his hands out of his pockets, hesitated, put his hands back into his pockets again, and then walked towards the subway kiosk on the corner.

He was glad to be away from Kling and away from the squad-room. He was glad to be with Christine Maxwell, who came in from the kitchen of her apartment carrying a tray with a Martini shaker and two iced Martini glasses. He watched her as she walked towards him. She had let her blonde hair grow long since he'd first known her, and it hung loose around the oval of her face now, sleekly reflecting pinpoint ticks of light from the fading sun that filtered through the window. She had taken off her shoes the moment she'd come home from work, but she still wore her stockings and she padded across the room silently, walking with an intuitively feminine grace, insinuatingly female, her straight black

93

skirt tightening over each forward thrust of thigh and leg, the cocktail tray balanced on one long tapered hand, the other hand brushing at an eyelash that had fallen to her cheek. She wore a blue silk blouse that echoed the lilac blue of her eyes, clung loosely to the soft curve of her bosom. She put down the tray and felt his eyes on her and smiled and said, 'Stop it, you make me nervous.'

'Stop what?'

'Looking at me that way.' Quickly, she poured both glasses to the brim.

'What way?'

'You're undressing me.' Christine handed him one of the Martinis and hastily added, 'With your eyes.'

'That would be a most unpractical way to undress you,' Hawes said. 'With my eyes.'

'Yes, but you're doing it, anyway.'

'I'm simply looking at you. I enjoy looking at you.' He lifted his glass in the air, said, 'Here's looking at you,' and swallowed a huge gulp of gin and vermouth.

Christine sat in the chair opposite him, pulling her legs up and under her, sipping at her drink. She looked over the edge of the glass and said, 'I think you ought to marry me. Then you could look at me all day long.'

'I can't marry you,' Hawes said.

'Why not?'

'Because good cops die young.'

'Then you've got nothing to worry about.'

'Are you insinuating I'm not a good cop?'

'I think you're an excellent cop. But you're not exactly young any more.'

'That's true. I'm beginning to creak a little in the joints.' He paused and said, 'But good cops die old, too.

In fact, all cops die, sooner or later. Good ones, bad ones, honest ones, crooked ones . . .'

'Crooked cops? The ones who take bribes?'

'That's right. They die, too.'

Christine shook her head, a mischievous grin on her mouth. 'Crooked cops never die,' she said.

'No?'

'No. They're just paid away.'

Hawes winced and drained his glass. 'I think you went pretty far for that one,' he said.

'I think you went pretty far to avoid discussing our imminent marriage.'

'Our eminent marriage, you mean.'

'I meant imminent, but it'll be eminent, too.'

'You know, I have the feeling I'm drunk,' Hawes said, 'and all I've had is a single drink.'

'I'm an intoxicating woman,' Christine said.

'Come on over here and intoxicate me a little.'

Christine shook her head. 'Nope. I want another drink first.' She drained her glass and poured two fresh Martinis. 'Besides, we were discussing marriage. Are you an honest cop?'

'Absolutely,' Hawes said, picking up his drink.

'Don't you think honest cops should seek honest women?'

'Absolutely.'

'Then why won't you make me an honest woman?'

'You are an honest woman. Only an honest woman could mix a Martini like this one.'

'What's wrong with it, and you're changing the subject again.'

'I was thinking of your legs,' Hawes said.

'I thought you were thinking of my Martinis.'

'That's why it sounded as though I were changing the subject.'

'Now *I* feel a little drunk,' Christine said. She shook her head, as if to clear it. 'How was that again?'

'What's the matter?' Hawes asked. 'Don't you dig Ionesco?'

'I don't only dig him, I also don't understand him.'

'Come over here on the couch, and I'll explain Ionesco.'

'No,' Christine said. 'You'll make advances.'

'That's right.'

'I think a man and a woman should be married before he's permitted to make advances.'

'You do, huh?'

'Sure, I do.'

'Sure.'

'What were you thinking about my legs?' Christine asked.

'How nice they are.'

'Nice? That's a fine word to describe a woman's legs.'

'Shapely.'

'Yes?'

'Well-curved.'

'Yes, go on.'

'Splendid.'

'Splendid?'

'Mmmm. I'd like to take off your stockings,' Hawes said.

'Why?'

'So I can touch your splendid legs.'

'No advances,' Christine said. 'Remember?'

'Right, I forgot. I'd like to take off your stockings so I can see your splendid legs better.'

'You'd like to take off my stockings,' Christine said, 'so you can reach up under my skirt to ungarter them.'

'I hadn't thought of that, but now that you bring it up . . .'

'*You* brought it up.'

'Are you wearing a girdle?'

'Nope.'

'A garter belt?'

'Yep.'

'I like garter belts.'

'All men do.'

'Why should all men like garter belts? And how do *you* know what all men like?'

'Are you jealous?'

'No,' Hawes said.

'If we were married, I wouldn't have any opportunity to know what all men like,' Christine said. 'You'd be the only man in my life.'

'You mean there are other men in your life?'

Christine shrugged.

'Who are they?' Hawes asked. 'I'll arrest them.'

'On what grounds?'

'Obstructing the course of true love.'

'*Do* you love me?' Christine asked.

'Come here, and I'll tell you.'

Christine smiled.

'Come on.'

She smiled again. 'How long would you say we've known each other, Cotton?' she asked.

'Oh, let me see. Four years?'

'Right. How many times would you say we've made love in those four years?'

'Twice,' Hawes said.

'No, seriously.'

'Oh, seriously. *Seriously*, we've made love . . . how much is four times three hundred and sixty-five?'

'Come on, seriously.'

'Gee, I don't know, Christine. Why do you ask?'

'I think we ought to get married.'

'Oh,' Hawes said, with an air of discovery. 'Is *that* what you were leading up to? Ah-ha!'

'Don't you like making love to me?'

'I love making love to you.'

'Then why don't you marry me?'

'Come here, and I'll tell you all about it.'

Christine stood up abruptly. The move surprised him. A serious look had come onto her face suddenly, and it gave a curious purposefulness to her sudden rise. She walked to the window in her stockinged feet and stood there in silhouette for a moment, the dusky sky outside touching her face with the burnished wash of sunset, and then she pulled down the shade and turned towards Hawes with the same serious expression on her face, as if she were about to cry. He watched her and wondered how this had got so serious all at once. Or perhaps it had been serious all along, he wasn't quite sure now. She took a step towards him and then stopped and looked at him with a long deep look, as if trying to resolve something in her own mind, and then gave a quiet sigh, just a short intake of breath, and unbuttoned her blouse. He watched her in the darkened room as she undressed. She hung the blouse over the back of a straight chair, and then unclasped her brassière and put that on the seat of the chair. She pulled back her skirt and ungartered her stockings, and he watched her legs as she rolled the stockings down over the calves and then the ankles and then rose and put them over the back of the chair and stood facing him in her panties and garter belt, and then took off the panties and put them on the seat of the chair, too.

She walked towards him in the dim silence of the room, wearing only the black garter belt, and she stopped before him where he sat on the couch, and she said, 'I do love you, Cotton. You know I love you, don't you?'

She took his face between both slender hands, and she cocked her head to one side, as if seeing his face for the first time, studying it, and then one hand moved gently to the white streak in his red hair, touching it, and then trailing over his temple, and down the bridge of his nose, and then touching his mouth in exploration in the darkness.

'Nothing to say?' she asked. 'Nothing to say, my darling?'

She stood before the couch where he sat, looking down at him with a curiously wistful smile on her mouth. He put his arms around her waist and drew her gently close, cradling his head on her breasts and hearing the sudden frantic beating of her heart, and thinking there really was nothing to say to her, and wondering all at once what love was. He had known her for such a long time, it seemed, had seen her undress in exactly the same way so many times, had held her close to him in just this way, had heard the beating of her heart beneath the full breast. She was Christine Maxwell, beautiful, bright, passionate, exciting, and he enjoyed being with her more than any other person in the world. But holding her close, feeling the beating heart and sensing the wistful smile that still clung to her mouth, and knowing the serious expression was still in her eyes, he wondered whether any of this added up to love, and he suddenly thought of Irene Thayer and Tommy Barlow on the bed in the apartment filled with illuminating gas.

His hands suddenly tightened on Christine's back.

He suddenly wanted to hold her desperately close to him.

She kissed him on the mouth and then sank to the couch beside him and stretched her long legs, and looked at him once more very seriously and then the wistful smile expanded, and she said, 'It's because it makes us look French.'

'What?' he said, puzzled.

'The garter belt,' Christine explained. *'That's* why men like it.'

8.

TOMMY BARLOW HAD been a strapping, well-muscled fellow, six feet and one inch tall, weighing a hundred and seventy-five pounds, with a high forehead and a square jaw and an over-all look of understated power. The understated power had been completely muted by death — there is nothing so powerless as a corpse — but even in death, Tommy Barlow bore very little resemblance to his younger brother.

The brother opened the door for Carella and Meyer four days after the burial of Barlow. Both men were wearing trench coats, but not because they wanted to feel like detectives. They wore them only because a light April drizzle was falling.

'Amos Barlow?' Meyer said.

'Yes?'

Meyer flashed the tin. 'Detectives Carella and Meyer. We'd like to ask you a few questions.'

'Can I see that again, please?' Barlow said.

Meyer, who was the most patient cop in the precinct, if not the entire city, held up his shield again. His patience was an acquired trait, the legacy of his father Max, who'd been something of a practical joker in his day. When Meyer's mother went to Max and told him she was pregnant again, old Max simply couldn't believe it. He thought it was past the time when such miracles of God could happen to his wife, who had already experienced change of life. Unappreciative of the turntable subtleties of a fate that had played a supreme practical joke on the supreme practical joker, he plotted his own gleeful revenge. When the baby was born, he named him Meyer. Meyer was a perfectly good name, and would have fitted the child beautifully if his surname happened to be Schwartz or Goldblatt or even Lipschitz. Unfortunately, his surname was Meyer, and in combination with his given name, the infant emerged like a stutter: Meyer Meyer. Even so, the name wouldn't have been so bad if the family hadn't been orthodox Jews living in a predominantly gentile neighbourhood. Whenever any of the kids needed an excuse for beating up a Jew – and they didn't often need excuses – it was always easiest to find the one with the double-barrelled monicker. Meyer Meyer learned patience: patience towards the father who had inflicted upon him the redundant name, patience towards the kids who regularly sent him home in tatters. Patiently, he waited for the day when *he* could name his *father* Max Max. It never came. Patiently, he waited for the day when he could catch one of the *goyim* alone and beat hell out of him in a fair fight without overwhelming odds. That day came rarely. But Meyer's patience became a way of life, and eventually he adjusted to his father's little gag, and the name he would carry to the end of his days. He adjusted beautifully. Unless one chose to mention the tired old saw about repression leaving its scars. Maybe something *does* have to give, who knows? Meyer Meyer, though he was only thirty-seven years old, was completely bald.

Patiently, he held up the shield.

'Do you have an identification card?'

Meyer dug into his wallet patiently and held up his lucite-encased I.D. card.

'That isn't a very good picture,' Barlow said.

'No,' Meyer admitted.

'But I guess it's you. What did you want to ask me?'

'May we come in?' Meyer said. They were standing outside on the front stoop of the two-storey frame house in Riverhead, and whereas the rain wasn't heavy, it was sharp and penetrating. Barlow studied them for a moment, and then said, 'Of course,' and opened the door wide. They followed him into the house.

He was a short, slight man, no more than five feet eight inches tall, weighing about a hundred and thirty-five pounds. Carella estimated that he was no older than twenty-two or twenty-three, and yet he was beginning to lose the hair at the back of his head. He walked at a slightly crooked angle and with a decided limp. He carried a cane in his right hand, and he used it as though he'd been familiar with it for a long time. The cane was black, Carella noticed, a heavy cane with curving head ornately decorated with silver or pewter, it was difficult to tell which.

'Are you the detectives working on my brother's murder?' Barlow said over his shoulder as he led them towards the living-room.

'Why do you call it that, Mr Barlow?' Meyer said.

'Because that's what it was,' Barlow answered.

He had entered the living-room, walked to the exact centre of it, and then turned to face the detectives squarely. The room was tastefully, if inexpensively, furnished. He shifted his weight to his good leg, raised his cane, and with it gestured towards a couch. Carella and Meyer sat. Meyer took out a small black pad and a pencil.

'What makes you think it was murder?' he said.

'I know it was.'

'How do you know?'

'My brother wouldn't commit suicide,' Barlow said. He nodded at the detectives calmly, his pale blue eyes studying them. 'Not my brother.' He leaned on his cane heavily, and then suddenly seemed tired of standing. Limping, he walked to an easy chair opposite them, sat, looked at them calmly once again, and once again said, 'Not my brother.'

'Why do you say that?' Carella asked.

'Not Tommy.' Barlow shook his head. 'He was too happy. He knew how to enjoy life. You can't tell me Tommy turned on the gas. No. I'll believe a lot of other things, but not that.'

'Maybe the girl talked him into it,' Carella suggested.

'I doubt it,' Barlow said. 'A cheap pick-up? Why would my brother let her . . . ?'

'Just a second, Mr Barlow,' Meyer said. 'This wasn't a casual pick-up, not from the way we understand it.'

'No?'

'No. Your brother and this girl were planning to get married.'

'Who says so?'

'The girl's mother says so, and the girl's lawyer says so.'

'But *Tommy* didn't say so.'

'He never mentioned that he was planning to get married?' Carella asked.

'Never. In fact, he never even mentioned this girl,

104

this Irene Thayer. That's how I know it's all a bunch of lies, the note, everything. My brother probably picked the girl up that very afternoon. Marry her! Kill himself! Who are they trying to kid?'

'Who do you mean by "they", Mr Barlow?'

'What?'

'You said, "Who are *they* trying to . . ."'

'Oh, that's just an expression. I meant, somebody . . . or maybe a couple of people . . .' He shook his head, as if trying to untangle his tongue. 'What I mean is Tommy did *not* plan to marry any girl, and Tommy did *not* kill himself. So somebody must have typed up that note and then turned on the gas and left my brother there to die. To *die. That's* what I mean.'

'I see,' Meyer said. 'Do you have any idea who this "somebody" might be?'

'No. But I don't think you'll have to look very far.'

'Oh?'

'I'm sure a girl like that had a lot of men after her.'

'And you think one of these men might have been responsible for what happened, is that it?'

'That's right.'

'Did you know Irene Thayer was married, Mr Barlow?'

'I read it in the papers.'

'But it's your impression that she was seeing other men besides your brother, is that right?'

'She wasn't *seeing* my brother, that's what I'm trying to tell you. He probably just picked her up.'

'Mr Barlow, we have reason to believe he was seeing her regularly.'

'What reason?'

'What?'

'What reason? What reason to believe . . .'

'We told you, Mr Barlow. The girl's mother and the girl's . . .'

'Sure, the girl, the girl. But if Tommy had been seeing her, wouldn't he have told me? His own brother?'

'Were you very close, Mr Barlow?'

'We certainly were.' Barlow paused. 'Our parents died when we were both very young. In a car crash. They were coming home from a wedding in Bethtown. That was years ago. Tommy was twelve, and I was ten. We went to live with one of my aunts for a while. Then, when we got old enough, we moved out.'

'To this house?'

'No, we only bought this last year. We both worked, you know, from the minute we could get working papers. We've been saving for a long time. We used to live in an apartment about ten blocks from here. But last year, we bought this house. It's nice, don't you think?'

'Very nice,' Carella said.

'We still owe a fortune on it. It's more the bank's than it is ours. But it's a nice little house. Just right for the two of us, not too big, not too small.'

'Will you keep the house now that your brother's dead?' Meyer asked.

'I don't know. I haven't given it much thought. It's a little difficult to get used to, you know, the idea that he's dead. Ever since he died, I've been going around the house looking for traces of him. Old letters, snapshots, anything that was Tommy. We've been together ever since we were kids, you know. Tommy took care of me as if he was my father, I mean it. I wasn't a strong kid, you know. I had polio when I was a kid.'

'I see.'

'Yeah, I had polio. It's funny, isn't it, how polio's almost a thing of the past, isn't it? Kids hardly get polio any more, because of the vaccine. But I had it. I was lucky, I guess. I got off easy. I just limp a little, that's all. Did you notice that I limp a little?'

'Just a little,' Carella said gently.

'Yeah, it's not too noticeable,' Barlow said. He shrugged. 'It doesn't stop me from working or anything. I've been working since the time I was sixteen. Tommy, too. From the minute he was old enough to get working papers. Tommy cried when I got polio. I had this fever, you know, I was only seven years old, and Tommy came into the bedroom, bawling his eyes out. He was quite a guy, my brother. It's gonna be funny around here without him.'

'Mr Barlow, are you sure he never mentioned Irene Thayer to you?'

'Yes, I'm certain.'

'Is it possible he was withholding the information from you?'

'Why would he do that?'

'I don't know, Mr Barlow. Perhaps he might have thought you wouldn't approve of his seeing a married woman.'

'He *wasn't* seeing her, I've already told you that. Besides, since when did Tommy need *my* approval for anything?' Barlow laughed a short mirthless laugh. 'Tommy went his own way, and I went mine. We never even double-dated.'

'Then it's possible he *was* seeing this woman, and you just didn't . . .'

'No.'

'. . . realize it. Maybe the opportunity to discuss it never came up.'

'No.'

'Mr Barlow, we have to believe . . .'

'I'm telling you they're lying. They're trying to cover up for what happened in that room. They're saying my brother was involved with that girl, but it isn't the truth. My brother was too smart for something like . . .' Barlow's eyes suddenly flashed. 'That's right, that's another thing! That's right!'

'What?' Carella asked.

'My brother was no dope, you know. Oh, no. He quit high school to go to work, that's true, but he went to night school afterwards, and he got his diploma. So he was no dope.'

'What are you driving at, Mr Barlow?'

'Well, you saw that phony suicide note, didn't you?'

'We saw it.'

'Did you see how they spelled "ourselves"?'

'How did they spell it, Mr Barlow?'

'O-U-R-S-E-L-F-S.' Barlow shook his head. 'Not my brother. My brother knew how to spell.'

'Maybe the girl typed the note,' Meyer suggested.

'My brother wouldn't have let her type it wrong. Look, my brother just did not commit suicide. That's that. I wish you'd get that into your heads.'

'Someone killed him, is that what you think?' Carella asked.

'Damn right, that's what I think!' Barlow paused, and then studied the detectives slyly. 'Isn't that what *you* think, too?'

'We're not sure, Mr Barlow.'

'No? Then why are you here? If you really thought this was a suicide, why are you going around asking questions? Why don't you just file the case away?'

'We told you, Mr Barlow. We're not sure yet.'

'So there must be something about it that seems a little funny to you, right? Otherwise, you'd forget the whole thing, right? You must get a lot of suicides.'

'Yes, we do, Mr Barlow.'

'Sure. But you know as well as I do that this particular suicide isn't a suicide at all. That's why you're still investigating.'

'We investigate *all* suicides,' Meyer said.

'This is a murder,' Barlow said flatly. 'Who are we kidding? This is a murder, plain and simple. Somebody killed my brother, and you know damn well that's the case.' He had picked up his cane and stabbed it at the air for emphasis, poking a hole into the air each time he said the word 'murder' and again when he said the word 'killed'. He put the cane down now and nodded, and waited for either Carella or Meyer to confirm or deny his accusation. Neither of the men spoke.

'Isn't it? Isn't it murder?' Barlow said at last.

'Maybe,' Carella said.

'No maybes about it. You didn't know my brother. I knew him all my life. There wasn't a man alive who enjoyed living much more than he did. Nobody with that much . . . that much . . . *spirit* yeah, spirit, is going to kill himself. Uh-uh.' He shook his head.

'Well, murder has to be proved,' Meyer said.

'Then prove it. Find something to prove it.'

'Like what, Mr Barlow?'

'I don't know. There must be something in that apartment. There must be a clue there someplace.'

'Well,' Meyer said noncommittally, 'we're working on it.'

'If I can help in any way . . .'

'We'll leave a card,' Carella said. 'If you happen to think of anything your brother mentioned, anything that might give us a lead, we'd appreciate it.'

'A lead to *what*?' Barlow said quickly. 'You *do* think it was murder, don't you?'

'Let's say we're making a routine check, shall we?' Carella said, smiling. 'Where can we reach you if we need you, Mr Barlow?'

'I'm right here every night,' Barlow said, 'from six o'clock on. During the day, you can reach me at the office.'

'Where's that?' Meyer asked.

'Anderson and Loeb. That's downtown, in Isola. Eight-nine-one Mayfair. In the Dock Street section.'

'What sort of a firm is that, Mr Barlow?'

'Optics,' Barlow said.

'And what do you do there?'

'I'm in the mailing room.'

'Okay,' Carella said, 'thanks a lot for your time. We'll keep you posted on any developments.'

'I'd appreciate it,' Barlow said. He rose and began limping towards the door with them. On the front step, he said, 'Find him, will you?' and then closed the door.

They waited until they were in the sedan before they began talking. They were silent as they went down the front walk washed with April rain, silent as they entered the car, silent as Carella started it, turned on the wipers, and pulled the car away from the kerb.

Then Meyer said, 'What do you think, Steve?'

'What do you think?'

Meyer scratched his bald pate. 'Well, nobody thinks it was suicide,' he said cautiously. 'That's for sure.'

'Mmmm.'

'Be funny, wouldn't it?'

'What would?'

'If this thing that everybody's convinced is murder actually turns out to be suicide. That'd be real funny, wouldn't it?'

'Yeah, hilarious.'

'You've got no sense of humour,' Meyer said. 'That's your trouble. I don't mean to bring up personality defects, Steve, but you are essentially a humourless man.'

'That's true.'

'I wouldn't have mentioned it if it weren't true,' Meyer said, his blue eyes twinkling. 'What do you suppose makes you such a serious man?'

'The people I work with, I guess.'

'Do you find them depressing?' Meyer asked, seemingly concerned.

'I find them obnoxious,' Carella confessed.

'Tell me more,' Meyer said gently. 'Did you really hate your father when you were a small boy?'

'Couldn't stand him. Still can't,' Carella said. 'You know why?'

'Why?' Meyer asked.

'Because he's essentially a humourless man,' Carella said, and Meyer burst out laughing.

9.

IN POLICE WORK, 'a routine check' is very often something that can hardly be considered routine. A pair of detectives will kick in the front door of an apartment, be greeted by a screaming, hysterical housewife in her underwear who wants to know what the hell they mean by breaking in like that, and they will answer, 'Just a routine check, ma'am.' A patrolman will pass the stoop of a tenement building and suddenly line up the teenagers innocently standing there, force them to lean against the wall of the building with their palms flat while he frisks them, and when they complain about their rights, will answer, 'Shut up, you punks. This is a routine check.' A narcotics cop will insist on examining a prostitute's thighs for hit marks, even when he knows she couldn't possibly be a junkie, only because he is conducting 'a routine check'.

Routine checks sometimes provide excuses and alibis for anything a cop might feel like doing in the course of an investigation – or even outside the course of one. But there are bona fide routine checks, especially where suicide or homicide is concerned, and Carella was involved in just such a check on the day he discovered Mary Tomlinson was a liar.

Carella never read mystery fiction because he found it a bore, and besides he'd been a cop for a long, long time and he knew that the Means, the Motive, and the

Opportunity were three catchwords that didn't mean a damn when a corpse was staring up at you — or sometimes down at you, as the case might be. He had investigated cases where the motive wasn't a motive at all. A man can push his wife into the river because he thinks he wants to teach her to swim, and you can question him until you're both blue in the face and he'll insist he loved her since they were both in kindergarten and there is simply no motive at all for his having murdered her. The means of murder were always fairly obvious, and he couldn't imagine why anyone outside of a motion-picture cop confronted with exotic and esoteric cases involving rare impossible-to-trace poisons got from pygmy tribes would be overly concerned with what killed a person: usually, you found a guy with a bullet hole in the middle of his forehead, and you figured what killed him was a gun. Sometimes the cause of death was something quite other than what the surface facts seemed to indicate — a girl is found with a knife in her chest, you assume she's been stabbed until the lab tells you someone drowned her in the bathtub first. But usually, if a man looked as if he'd been shot, he'd *been* shot. If a woman looked as if she'd been strangled, she'd *been* strangled. Means and Motive were both crocks to the working cop. Opportunity was the biggest crock of all because every manjack in the U.S. of A., Russia, Madagascar, Japan and the Tasman Sea, Sicily, Greenland, and the Isle of Wight was presented with the opportunity for committing murder almost every waking minute of his life. The consideration of opportunity was only valuable in protecting the innocent. A man who was climbing Fujiyama while a murder was being committed in Naples

113

couldn't very well have had an Opportunity for mayhem. The point was, as Carella saw it, that one million, two hundred and seventy-four thousand, nine hundred and ninety-nine *other* Neapolitans *did* have the Opportunity for pulling off a bit of homicide that day, and the guy who did the deed certainly wasn't going to tell you he just happened to be with the dead man when it happened. The Means, the Motive, and the Opportunity. *Baloney*, Carella thought, but he nonetheless was calling every insurance company in the city in an attempt to find out whether or not either Tommy Barlow or Irene Thayer had carried life insurance.

He had spoken to twelve insurance companies that morning, had knocked off for lunch when his voice and dialling finger showed signs of giving out, and had called six more companies since his return to the squadroom at 1 p.m. He was dialling his nineteenth company when Meyer said, 'What are you doing there on the phone all day?'

'Insurance companies,' Carella answered.

'You're a cop. Forget about insurance. The rates are too high.'

'It's not for me. I'm trying to . . .' Carella waved Meyer aside with his hand, and said into the phone. 'Hello, this is Detective Carella of the 87th Squad. I'd like some information, please.'

'What sort of information, sir?'

'Concerning policy holders.'

'I'll connect you. Just a moment.'

'Thank you.' Carella covered the mouthpiece and said to Meyer, 'I'm trying to find out if Barlow or the girl were insured.'

Meyer nodded, not particularly impressed, and went

back to his typing. Carella waited. In a few moments, a man's voice came onto the line. 'Mr Kapistan, may I help you?'

'Mr Kapistan, this is Detective Carella of the 87th Detective Squad. We're investigating a suicide and are making a routine check of insurance companies in the city.'

'Yes, sir?'

'I wonder if you could tell me whether your firm had ever issued policies for either of the two victims.'

'What are their names, sir?'

Carella was instantly taken with Kapistan. There was a no-nonsense attitude in the man's voice. He could visualize him immediately understanding everything that was said, could see Kapistan's pencil poised over his pad waiting for the victims' names to be spoken.

'Irene Thayer and Thomas Barlow,' Carella said.

'*Miss* Irene Thayer?' Kapistan asked.

'No, that's Mrs. In fact, it's Mrs *Michael* Thayer. But you might check under her maiden name as well. She was only married for a short time.'

'And the maiden name, sir?'

'Irene Tomlinson.'

'Can you hold on a moment, Detective Carella?'

'Certainly,' Carella said his respect for Kapistan soaring. He had met too many people who, confronted with any name that ended in a vowel, automatically stumbled over the pronunciation. There was something psychologically sinister about it, he was sure. The name could be a very simple one, like Bruno, or Di Luca, but the presence of that final vowel always introduced confusion bordering on panic. He had had people call the squad-room and, in desperation, finally say,

'Oh, let me talk to the Italian cop.' Kapistan had only heard the name once, and over a telephone, but he had repeated it accurately, even giving it a distinctive Florentine twist. Good man, Kapistan. Carella waited.

'Mr Carella?' Kapistan said.

'Yes?'

'I've checked both those names. I have nothing for Thomas Barlow and nothing for Irene Thayer or Mrs Michael Thayer.'

'What about Irene Tomlinson?'

'Is that the exact name? We do have a policy owned by Mrs Charles Tomlinson for her daughter Margaret Irene Tomlinson, but . . .'

'That's the one. Margaret Irene. Who did you say owned the policy?'

'Mrs Charles Tomlinson.'

'Do you have her first name there?'

'Just a moment.' Kapistan checked his records. 'Yes, here it is. Mary Tomlinson.'

'What sort of a policy is it?'

'A twenty-year endowment,' Kapistan said.

'In the name of Margaret Irene Tomlinson?'

'That's right. With Mary Tomlinson as payor and beneficiary.'

'How much?' Carella asked.

'Ten thousand dollars.'

'That's not very high.'

'Well, that's the cash surrender value of the policy. In addition, there would be about fifteen hundred dollars in accumulated dividends. Just a moment.' There was another pause. When he came back onto the line, Kapistan said, 'Actually, it's fifteen hundred and fifty dollars.'

'Then, if the policy were held to maturity, the company would give eleven thousand five hundred and fifty dollars to the insured.'

'Yes, that's right.'

'And if the insured died before the policy matured, that money would be paid to the beneficiary, is that right?'

'That's right. Well, not that much money. Only the face value of the policy. Ten thousand dollars.'

'To whom?'

'In this case, to the payor, Mary Tomlinson. You know, of course, that when a child reaches the age of fifteen, ownership of the policy can be transferred to the child. But that wasn't the case here. No one applied for transfer. That's usually best, anyway. The way some kids behave today . . .' Kapistan let the sentence trail.

'Mr Kapistan, as I understand it then, Margaret Irene Tomlinson – Mrs Michael Thayer – was the insured person in a ten-thousand-dollar endowment policy which would have paid her eleven thousand five hundred and fifty dollars upon its maturity, or which will, now that she's dead, pay her mother ten thousand dollars as beneficiary.'

'That is right, sir.' Kapistan paused. 'Detective Carella, I don't mean to impose . . .'

'Go ahead, Mr Kapistan.'

'You are aware, of course, that there isn't a state in the Union where an insurance company will pay a cent in the event the insured was *killed* by the beneficiary.'

'Yes, I know that.'

'I thought I might mention it. Please forgive me.'

'That's quite all right. Can you tell me when this policy would have reached maturity, Mr Kapistan?'

'Just a moment, please.'

There was another pause.

'Mr Carella?'

'Yes, Mr Kapistan?'

'The child was insured on her first birthday. The policy would have matured on her twenty-first birthday.'

'Which is next month some time, right?'

'That's right, sir.'

'*When* next month?'

'The policy matures on May thirteenth.'

Carella had already opened his wallet and pulled out his celluloid calendar. 'That's a Saturday,' he said.

'That's right, sir.'

'Mmm,' Carella said. He paused, and then asked, 'How does the insured usually collect on an endowment policy when it matures?'

'Usually, they'll write to the company, enclosing the policy, and enclosing some form of identification – usually a photostated birth certificate.'

'How long would it take before the company issued a cheque?'

'Oh, a week, ten days. It's simply a matter of paperwork, provided the proof of identity is satisfactory.'

'Suppose the insured were in a hurry? Could it be done sooner?'

'I imagine so.'

'How?'

'Well, I suppose the insured could come directly to our office, with the necessary proof of identity, and with the policy. I suppose that would expedite matters.'

'Would the company give her a cheque that very same day?'

'Presumably, yes. If everything were in order.'

'Are you open on Saturdays, Mr Kapistan?'

'No, sir.'

'Then, if a policy matured on a Saturday the insured would have to wait until at least Monday – that would be the fifteenth in this case – before she could come to the office to ask for her cheque.'

'That's right, sir.'

'That explains the week-end interfering,' Carella said, almost to himself.

'Sir?'

'I was just thinking aloud. Thank you very much, Mr Kapistan. You've been most helpful.'

'Any time at all,' Kapistan answered. 'It was nice talking to you. Good-bye.'

'Good-bye,' Carella said, and he hung up. He sat at his desk for a moment, nodding, smiling, and then he turned to Meyer, 'You want to take a ride to the country?' he asked.

'What country?'

'Sands Spit.'

'Why?'

'To talk to Mary Tomlinson.'

'Why?'

'I want to tell her she's going to be ten thousand dollars richer. I want to see what her reaction is.'

What can your reaction be when two bullies march into your living-room and tell you they know all about an insurance policy on your dead daughter's life, and want to know why you didn't tell them about it? What can your reaction be when these same two bosses tell you they suspect your daughter wasn't leaving for Reno until the 16th of May because the earliest she could collect the policy was the 15th of May?

What do you do?

You cry, that's what you do.

Mary Tomlinson began crying.

Meyer and Carella stood in the middle of the miniature living-room and watched her quiver and shake as sob after sob racked her enormous body.

'All right, Mrs Tomlinson,' Carella said.

'I didn't mean to lie,' she sobbed.

'All right, Mrs Tomlinson, let's cut off the tears, huh? We've got a lot of questions to ask you, and we don't want . . .'

'I didn't mean to lie.'

'Yeah, but you did.'

'I know.'

'Why, Mrs Tomlinson?'

'Because I knew what you'd think.'

'And what would we think?'

'You'd think I did it.'

'Did what?'

'Killed my own daughter. Do you think I'd do that?'

'I don't know, Mrs Tomlinson. Suppose you tell us.'

'I didn't.'

'But she was insured for ten thousand dollars.'

'Yes. Do you think I'd kill my own daughter for ten thousand dollars?'

'Some people would kill their own daughter for ten *cents*, Mrs Tomlinson.'

'No, no,' she said, shaking her head, the tears streaming down her cheeks. 'I *wanted* her to have the money.'

'Then why didn't you just sign the policy over to her?'

'I would have, if she'd asked me. But she didn't make her plans until only recently, and we figured it would be just as simple to wait until the thirteenth of next month, when the policy matured. I wanted her to have the money, don't you think I wanted her to have it? I took out the policy when she was just a year old, my husband had nothing to do with it, God rest his soul. I gave it to her for a first birthday present because I figured she could use the money for her education or whatever she wanted to do with it, when she reached the proper age. So don't you think I wanted her to have it? It cost me four hundred and sixty-two dollars and seventy cents a year. Do you think it was easy to scrape together that kind of money, especially after my husband died, poor man?'

'You seem to have managed it, Mrs Tomlinson.'

'It wasn't always easy. But I did it for her, I did it for Margaret. And now you think I killed her to get the money back? No, no, no, no, no, believe me, no, no, no . . .'

'Take it easy, Mrs Tomlinson.' Carella paused. 'You should have told us the truth from the beginning.'

'You'd have thought the same thing. You'd have thought I killed my own little Margaret.'

'Take it easy, Mrs Tomlinson. *Is* that why she was holding off on the Reno trip? Until she got the policy money?'

'Yes.' Mrs Tomlinson sniffed and nodded.

'Was there any possibility that she *wouldn't* have got that money?'

'What do you mean?'

'Mrs Tomlinson, your daughter *may* have committed suicide, we don't know. And if she did, she must have had a reason. The note we found said there was no other way, but apparently she'd figured out another way and was ready to get ten thousand dollars that would help make the other way possible. I want to know if anything could have happened, if anything could have been said, or implied, to make her think she *wasn't* going to get that money.'

'No.'

'Do you know what I'm driving at?'

'Yes. If she thought the money wasn't coming, she might possibly have felt there was no other way out. No. She knew the money was hers. I'd told her about it since the time she was old enough to understand.'

'Mrs Tomlinson,' Carella said suddenly, 'I'd like to look inside your medicine cabinet.'

'Why?'

'Because our man at the lab casually mentioned that your daughter and Tommy Barlow could have been drugged, and I remember you saying something about taking pills every night, and I want to see just what *kind* of pills you've got in that . . .'

'I didn't do anything. I swear on my dead husband, I swear on my dead daughter, I swear on my own eyes, with God as my witness, I didn't do anything. I swear, I swear.'

'That's fine, Mrs Tomlinson, but we'd like to look through your cabinet, anyway.'

The medicine cabinet was in the bathroom at the rear of the house. Meyer put down the seat and cover of the toilet bowl, sat, crossed his legs, opened his pad, and got ready to write as Carella opened the cabinet.

'Boy,' Carella said.

'What?'

122

'Full to the brim.'

'I'm ready,' Meyer said. 'Shoot.'

'Contents medicine cabinet of Mrs Charles (Mary) Tomlinson, 1635 Federico Drive, Sands Spit. Top shelf: one bottle aspirin, one bottle tincture merthiolate, one bottle Librium, one container adhesive bandages, one packet bobby pins, one bottle sodium chloride and dextrose, one tube hydrocortisone acetate, one letter opener. You got that?'

'I've got it,' Mayer said, writing. 'Shoot.'

'Second shelf: one bottle Esidrix, one tube Vaseline, one bottle insect repellent, one match book, one tube suntan lotion, one bottle Seconal, one toothbrush, one man's razor, six razor blades new, two razor blades used, one black address book trylon and perisphere gold-embossed on cover, one bottle Demerol APG . . .'

'I just thought of something,' Meyer said.

'Yeah, what?'

'If I were J.D. Salinger, listing all this crap in the medicine cabinet would be considered a literary achievement of the highest order.'

'It's a shame you're only Meyer Meyer,' Carella answered. 'Third shelf: one bottle Nytol, three leads from a mechanical pencil, one bottle Fiorinal . . .'

10.

'WHO SAID THEY took sleeping-pills?' Detective-Lieutenant Sam Grossman wanted to know.

'You said they *might* have,' Carella answered. 'You said suicides of this type sometimes took sleeping-pills, anything to make the death nice and pleasant. Isn't that what you said?'

'All right, all right, it's what I said,' Grossman answered impatiently, 'but did I ask you to send me fourteen cockamamie bottles of sleeping-pills?'

'No, but . . .'

'Steve, I'm up to my ears in work here, and you send me all these sleeping-pills. What am I supposed to do with them?'

'I just wanted to know if . . .'

'What'd the necropsy report say, Steve? Did it say anything about sleeping-pills?'

'No,' but I thought . . .'

'Then what are we supposed to do with these fourteen bottles of pills, would you mind telling me? What do you want me to say about them? Can they put you to sleep? Yes, they can put you to sleep. Would an overdose of any or all of them kill you? Yes, some of them could be fatal taken in quantity. Okay? Now, what else?'

'I don't know what else,' Carella said sheepishly.

'You mean you're reaching for straws already, and the case is barely a week old?'

'All right, I'm reaching for straws. Listen, Sam, you were the one who planted the homicide bug in my head, don't you forget it.'

'*Who* planted? You mean you thought it was suicide?'

'I don't know what I thought, but why not? Why can't it be suicide?'

'Don't get sore with me, Steve-oh.'

'I'm not sore.'

'What do you want, magic? Okay! Abra-ca-dabbra, whimmity-wham! I see . . . just a moment, the crystal ball is clearing . . .'

'Go to hell, Sam.'

'I've got nothing to compare any of these damn pills against!' Grossman shouted. 'Who the hell's going to bother looking for nonvolatile poisons when they've got an obvious case of carbon monoxide poisoning? You know how many stiffs are waiting for autopsy at the morgue? Ahh, please.'

'Somebody *should* have bothered,' Carella shouted.

'That's not my department!' Grossman shouted back. 'And you happen to be wrong! *Nobody* should have bothered because it would have taken weeks, for Christ's sake, and what would you have got, anyway? So what if they were drugged?'

'That could indicate homicide!'

'It could indicate balls! It could indicate they went to the drugstore and bought some pills and took them, that's what it could indicate. Don't get me sore, Steve.'

'Don't get *me* sore!' Carella shouted. 'Somebody goofed at the hospital, and you know it!'

'Nobody goofed, and anyway get off my back! Call the goddamn hospital! You want to fight, call them. Did you call me up to fight?'

'I called you up because I sent you fourteen bottles of sleeping pills, and I thought you could help me with them. Obviously, you can't help me, so I'll just say good-bye and let you go back to sleep.'

'Look, Steve . . .'

'Look, Sam . . .'

'Ahhh, the hell with it. The hell with it. There's no talking to a bull. I'll never learn. Miracles. You all want miracles. The hell with it.'

Both men fell silent.

At last Grossman asked, 'What do you want me to do with these bottles?'

'You know what you can do with them,' Carella said.

There was another pause, and then Grossman began laughing. Carella, on the other end of the wire, couldn't suppress his own grin.

'Take my advice,' Grossman said, 'forget about calling the hospital. They did their job, Steve.'

Carella sighed.

'Steve?'

'Yeah, yeah.'

'Forget the pills you sent me, too. They're almost all brand names, anyway. Some of them, you don't even need a prescription. Even if the morgue had done those tests and come up with something, you'd be dealing with a pill anybody in the city could have got hold of. Forget it. Take my advice, forget it.'

'All right,' Carella said. 'I'm sorry I blew my stack.'

'This is a tough one, huh?'

'Very.' Carella paused. 'I'm about to hand in my jock.'

'You'll settle for suicide?'

'I'll settle for disorderly conduct.'

'Not you,' Grossman said simply.

'Not me,' Carella answered. 'Thick-headed. My mother used to call me a thick-headed wop.' He paused. 'Come on, Sam, help me with those pills. Give me an answer.'

'Steve-oh, I don't *have* any.'

'We're even,' Carella said. He sighed. 'You think it was homicide? You still think so?'

Grossman paused for a long time. Then he said, 'Who knows? Throw it in the Open File. Come back to it in a few months, in a year.'

'Would *you* throw it in the Open File?' Carella asked.

'Me? I'm thick-headed,' Grossman said. 'My mother used to call me a thick-headed kike.' He paused again. '*Yes*, I still think it's a homicide.'

'So do I,' Carella said.

By the time he left the squad-room at five forty-five that night, he had called every remaining insurance company on his list in an attempt to find out whether Tommy Barlow had been insured. He had drawn a negative response from each company. As he walked to his car parked across the street from the precinct (the sun visor down, the hand-lettered placard clipped to the visor and announcing that this particular decrepit automobile belonged to a cop; please, officer on the beat, do not tag it) he wondered if Tommy Barlow had been insured by a company outside the city. And then he wondered again whether they simply weren't chasing a suicide right into the ground.

He started the car and began driving home towards Riverhead, reviewing the facts of the case as he drove, driving very slowly and with the windows open because this was April and sometimes – especially in April – Carella felt like seventeen. Jesus, he thought, to die in April. I wonder what the figures on suicide are for April.

Let's examine this thing, he thought. Let's take it from the top for what it obviously is – a suicide. Let's forget there's any such thing as homicide. For the moment, let's consider two people who are about to take their own lives, okay? Let's piece it together that way, because none of the other ways seem to fit.

The first thing they had to do was *decide* they were going to kill themselves, which would seem like an odd thing to decide since they'd already made plans for . . .

No, no, wait a minute, he warned himself. Try to find the good reasons for *suicide*, okay? Try to find the things that spell suicide for Tommy Barlow and Irene Thayer, and not what stinks in this case because the things that stink are already there and suffocating me. Jesus, I wish I could take a deep breath. I wish that poor little girl hadn't jumped, I wish to God I could change it, I wish I could reach out and hold her in my arms and say, Honey, please don't jump, honey, please don't throw it all away.

He stopped for a red light.

He stared at the light for a long time, thinking of the young girl on the ledge twelve storeys above the street, hearing again the scream that had faded down to the gutter, hearing again the dull empty sound of her body striking the pavement.

The light changed to green.

The image of the dead girl lingered in his mind. *That* was a suicide, he thought. *That* was a real suicide. Deserted by a man she loved, no apparent reason for staying alive, she jumped. It has to look black. It has to look so goddam black that there really *is* no other way; it has to appear that death is more comforting than life, it has to be *that* barren and *that* desperate, it has to say exactly what that note in the apartment did say, *there is no other way.*

All right, then, the decision. For some reason – what's the reason? – for some reason, these two, Tommy and Irene, have decided that there is no other way, they must end it, they must . . . what did the note say? . . . now we can end the suffering of ourselfs and others. All right, they had decided to end the suffering. *What* suffering? Nobody *knew* about it, dammit. Michael Thayer is a prime candidate for the cuckold of the year, he lets his wife come and go as she pleases, so who the hell knew about it, who were all these other suffering people? Nobody, that's who. Barlow lived with his brother Amos, and Amos knew nothing at all about Irene, so *he* certainly wasn't suffering. Anyway, why should he have been suffering even if he did know about his brother's girl? And Mary Tomlinson approved of the affair, so *she* wasn't suffering, so nobody was suffering, so let's take another chorus from the top.

Nobody's suffering.

But the note says end the suffering of ourselfs . . . spelled wrong, have to get some information about Tommy and Irene, the way they spelled, maybe look at some of their letters . . . end the suffering of ourselfs and others. But Tommy and Irene weren't suffering because they were meeting every other week like rabbits, maybe more often, and nobody else was suffering, either, so the note doesn't make any sense.

Unless a few people are lying.

Unless, for example, Thayer *did* know all about his wife's little adventure with young Tommy there, and was all broken up about it, and maybe refused a divorce, and maybe *was* suffering a little. In which case, the note would be accurate, no other way out, suffering, good, we'll turn on the gas.

Or maybe young Amos Barlow knew his brother was seeing Irene and didn't like the idea, told him to stay away from a married woman, told him it broke his heart to see Tommy involved in anything as hopeless as this. In which case, the note would again be accurate, Amos would be suffering, no other way out, good, back to the kitchen and the stove.

Or maybe old Mary Tomlinson, the gentle old genial condoner of her daughter's affair, so she says, maybe *she* didn't like the idea, maybe she told her daughter divorce was a rotten thing, no matter how much of a bully and a boss Thayer was, maybe she said, darling daughter, stick it through, work it out, this is senseless and it'll break my heart. In which case, note, suffering, ditto, gas.

And in which case, also, everybody happens to be lying.

Which is unreasonable.

Why lie if there's nothing to cover?

Why insist there's been a homicide if they all know Tommy and Irene had good reason to kill themselves? You don't lie to cover up a suicide.

No, wait a minute, I guess you could. I guess you could figure a suicide is a blot on the family escutcheon, something to live down, maybe something hereditary, maybe something that can rub off on all the relatives and friends. Nobody likes the taint of suicide, so maybe they *are* lying about it. Maybe they figure homicide is a much more socially acceptable way to go, a better status symbol. Yes, my poor daughter and her lover were murdered, don't you know? Yes, my poor wife was killed while having an affair, have you heard? Yes, my beloved brother was done in while making love to his mistress. Very posh. Murder is glamorous. Suicide is a drag.

Well, maybe it was suicide, Carella thought. Maybe they went up there and took off all their clothes – no, not *all* their clothes, they both left their pants on. Propriety. It wouldn't do to be found dead naked, not *stark* naked. They took off some of their clothes, took them off very neatly, stacked them neatly, hung them neatly, of course. Two very neat people. They certainly wouldn't have wanted to be found in a state of nudity. Certainly not. So they left their underwear on for decency's sake. Oh Jesus, I am sick to death of Tommy and Irene, I am sick to death of what I see every time we turn that knob marked homicide and open that rotten goddamn door and find what's inside. I am sick of it. Why can't they keep themselves private? Why must they parade themselves before everyone to see, exhibit themselves as poor pitiful confused human beings who haven't yet mastered the art of living together? Why must they show the world and each other that all they know how to do is *die* together! Go into your room, lock your door, make your love, and leave us alone! Don't confuse it with illuminating gas and explosions, don't muddy it with blood, keep your goddamn privacy *private*!

He stopped for another light, and closed his eyes for a moment.

When he opened them, his mind had clicked shut again.

He was Detective 2nd/Grade Stephen Louis Carella again, shield number 714-56-32.

Tommy got the apartment.

They went up there with two bottles of whisky.

They typed a suicide note.

They turned on the gas.

They took off most of their clothes.

They tried to get drunk, they tried to make love.

The gas reached them before they could accomplish either.

They died.

'This was no goddamn suicide!' Carella said aloud. His own voice startled him. This was no suicide, he repeated silently.

He nodded in the near-darkness of the closed sedan.

This was no suicide.

I want to find out if Tommy Barlow was insured, he thought, and he made an abrupt left turn and began driving towards the house Tommy Barlow had shared with his brother Amos.

The house was dark and deserted when he pulled up to the kerb in front of it. He thought this was odd because Barlow had told him he was home from work every night at six, and it was now six-thirty, but the house seemed empty and lifeless. He got out of the car. There was a silence to the street, and memory suddenly overtook him in a painfully sweet rush, the memory of his own boyhood street, deserted just before suppertime, a young boy walking towards the house his father owned, his mother calling again from the upstairs window,

'Stevie! Supper!' and the slow, smiling nod of his head, April. The buds would be opening. The world would be coming alive. He had once seen a cat run over by an automobile, the guts had been strewn all over the gutter, he had turned away in horror, April and the opening buds, April and a cat lying dead in the gutter, matted fur and blood, and the smell of spring everywhere, green, opening.

Barlow's street was quiet. From another block, Carella could hear the sound of the bells on an ice-cream truck. Too early, he thought. You should hit the street after supper, you're too early. The lawn in front of the Barlow house was turning green. The grass was wet. He wanted to reach down suddenly and touch the wet grass. Up the street, he heard the sound of an automobile turning into the block. He went up the front walk and rang the door-bell. There was no answer. He tried it again. He could hear the chimes sounding somewhere deep inside the silent house. A car door slammed somewhere up the street. He sighed and rang the bell a third time. He waited.

Coming down the front steps, he backed several paces away from the house and looked up at the second-storey windows. He wondered if Barlow hadn't possibly gone directly into the shower upon returning home from work, and he began walking towards the side of the house, looking for a lighted bathroom window upstairs. He kept to the concrete ribbons of the driveway leading to the garage at the back of the house. A high hedge began on the right of the driveway, leading to the fence of the house next door. He went all the way to the back of the house, looking up at the windows. None of them were lighted. Shrugging philosophically, he started back for his car.

The hedge was on his left now, blocking his view of the street, an effective shield screening the back yard.

As he passed the hedge, he was struck.

The blow came suddenly, but with expert precision. He knew it wasn't a fist, he knew it was something long and hard, but he didn't have much time to consider exactly what it was because it struck him across his eyes and the bridge of his nose and sent him stumbling back against the hedge, and then someone shoved at him, pushing him beyond and behind the hedge as he tried to cover his face with one hand, tried to reach for his revolver with the other. Another blow came. There was a soft whistling sound on the early night air, the sound a rapier makes, or a stick, or a baseball bat. The blow struck him on his right shoulder, hard, and then the weapon came back again, and again there was the cutting whistle and he felt the sharp biting blow on his left shoulder, and his right hand suddenly went numb. His gun dropped to the ground. The end of the weapon gouged into his stomach like a battering ram, and then the sharp edge was striking his face again, repeatedly, numbingly. He lashed out at the darkness with his left hand, there was blood in his eyes, and a terrible pain in his nose. He felt his fist connect, and he heard someone shout, and then his assailant was running away from him, his shoes clattering on the concrete driveway strips, and then on the sidewalk. Carella leaned against the hedge. He heard a car door slamming somewhere up the street, and then the sound of an engine, and then the shrieking of tyres as the car pulled away from the kerb.

Licence plate, he thought.

He went around to the other side of the hedge as the car streaked past. He did not see the plate. Instead, he fell forward flat on his face.

11.

THEY PICKED UP Amos Barlow at ten o'clock that night, when he returned to his house in Riverhead. By that time, Carella had been taken to the hospital, where the intern on duty dressed his cuts and insisted, over his protests, that he spend the night there. Barlow seemed surprised by the presence of policemen. Neither of the arresting officers told him why the detectives of the 87th wanted to question him. He went along with the two patrolmen willingly and even agreeably, apparently assuming that something had turned up in connexion with his brother.

Cotton Hawes greeted him in the squad-room and then led him to the small interrogation room off the entrance corridor. Detectives Meyer and Kling were sitting there drinking coffee. They offered Barlow a cup, which he refused.

'Would you prefer some tea?' Hawes asked.

No, thank you,' Barlow said. He watched the three men, waiting for one of them to say something important, but they were seemingly involved in a ritual they had no desire to disturb. They chatted about the weather, and they cracked a joke or two, but they were mostly intent on consuming their beverage. Hawes finished his tea before the other two men finished their coffee. He put down his cup, took the tea-bag from the saucer and dropped it delicately into the cup, and then said, 'Where were you all night, Mr Barlow?'

'Were you trying to reach me?'

'Yes,' Hawes said pleasantly. 'You told detectives Meyer and Carella that you're usually home by six, but you seemed to be a little late tonight.'

'Yes,' Barlow said.

'We called your office, too,' Meyer put in. 'Anderson and Loeb, isn't that right? Eight-nine-one Mayfair?'

'That's right.'

'A cleaning woman answered the phone,' Meyer said. 'Told us everyone had left.'

'Yes, I left the office at about five-thirty,' Barlow said.

'Where'd you go then?' Kling asked.

'I had a date.'

'Who with?'

'A young lady named Martha Tamid.'

'Address?'

'Twelve-double-one Yarley Street. That's in River-head, not far from the Herbert Alexander Oval.'

'What time did you pick her up, Mr Barlow?'

'At about six. Why?'

'Do you drive, Mr Barlow?'

'Yes.'

'Don't you have trouble driving?' Kling asked. 'I notice you use a cane.'

'I can drive,' Barlow said. He picked up the cane and looked at it as if seeing it for the first time. He smiled. 'The leg doesn't hinder me. Not when I drive.'

'May I see that cane, please, sir?' Hawes asked.

Barlow handed it to him 'Nice-looking cane,' Hawes said.

'Yes.'

'Heavy.'

'Yes.'

'Mr Barlow, did you go home at any time this evening?' Meyer asked.

'Yes.'

'When was that?'

'At ten o'clock. Your patrolmen were there. They can verify the time.' Barlow looked suddenly puzzled. 'I'm sorry, but why are you . . . ?'

'Did you go home any time *before* ten o'clock?' Meyer said.

'No.'

'At, say, six-thirty?' Kling asked.

'No. I didn't get home until ten. I went to pick up Martha directly from the office.'

'What'd you do, Mr Barlow? Go out to dinner? A movie?'

'Dinner, yes.'

'No movie?'

'No. We went back to her apartment after dinner.'

'Where'd you eat, Mr Barlow?'

'At a Japanese restaurant in Isola. Tamayuki, something like that. Martha suggested the place.'

'Have you known this Martha Tamid long?'

'Just a short while.'

'And after dinner you went back to her apartment, is that right?'

'That's right.'

'What time was that?'

'About eight or eight-thirty.'

'And you left there at what time?'

'About nine-thirty.'

'You stayed with her for an hour, is that right, Mr Barlow?'

'About an hour, yes.'

'And then you went straight home?'

'That's right,' Barlow said.

'And at no time during the night did you go back to the house. Not to check on anything, not to see if you'd left the gas on . . .'

'Is that supposed to be a joke?' Barlow asked vehemently, turning on Kling.

'What?'

'You *know* how my brother died. If you think talking about gas is funny . . .'

'I'm sorry,' Kling said. 'I wasn't trying to be funny.'

'I didn't go back to the house,' Barlow said. 'I don't know what this is all about. If you don't believe me, call Martha and ask her. She'll tell you anything you want to know. What happened? Was someone else killed?'

'No, Mr Barlow.'

'Then what?'

'Does Miss Tamid have a telephone?' Meyer asked.

'Yes.'

'May we have the number, please?' Hawes said.

Miss Martha Tamid lived five blocks away from the Herbert Alexander Oval in Riverhead, a small grass-covered plot of ground in the exact centre of which stood a statue of General Alexander astride a horse, looking into the wind with his steely penetrating gaze, his strong jaw, his rugged good looks. Hawes drove past the statue, and then turned into the one-way block called Yarley Street, watching the numbers as he drove, and finally pulling up before 1211. It was almost midnight, but they had called Miss Tamid from the office, and she said she wasn't asleep yet and would be happy to tell them anything they wanted to know. They had told Barlow he could go, but Hawes had nodded at Kling, and Kling had followed Barlow the moment he left the squad-room. Then Hawes had clipped on his holster and begun his drive towards Riverhead.

Miss Tamid lived in a six-storey apartment building at the end of the street. She had given Hawes the apartment number on the phone, and he pressed the lobby buzzer of 6C, and then waited for the answering buzz. It came almost instantly. He let himself in and walked to the elevator. The lobby was small and quiet. The entire building seemed to be asleep at this hour. He went up to the sixth floor, found apartment 6C in the centre of the corridor, and rang the bell. He rang it only once, and with a very short ring. The door opened immediately.

Martha Tamid was a tiny girl who looked like an Egyptian belly dancer. Hawes wished he were a private detective because then Miss Tamid would have been in something slinky, or seductive, or both. As it was, she was wearing a blouse and slacks, which was good enough because neither did very much to hide the provocative structure of her tiny body.

'Miss Tamid?' he asked.

'Yes? Detective Hawes?'

'Yes.'

'Please, won't you come in? I was waiting for you.'

'I'm sorry to be calling so late, but we wanted to check this out as soon as possible.'

'That's quite all right. I was watching television. Greta Garbo. She is very good, don't you think?'

'Yes.'

Martha Tamid closed the door behind Hawes and led him into her living-room. The television set was going with an old Greta Garbo – John Gilbert movie. Miss Garbo was seductively gnawing at a bunch of grapes.

'She is very pretty,' Martha said, and then turned off the set. The room was suddenly very still.

'Now then,' Martha said, and she smiled.

The smile was a wide one. It lighted her entire face and touched her dark-brown eyes, setting them aglow. Her hair was black, and she wore it very long, trailing half-way down her back. She had a small beauty mark near the corner of her mouth, and a dusky complexion he had always associated with mediterranean peoples. There was an impish quality to her face, the smile, the ignited brown eyes, the tilt of her head, even the beauty mark. There was something else in her face, too, something about her rich body, an open invitation, a challenge, no, that was ridiculous.

He said, 'Excuse me, are you a belly dancer?'

Martha laughed and said, 'No. I'm a receptionist. Do I look like a belly dancer?'

Hawes smiled. 'Well,' he said.

'But you have not even seen my belly,' Martha said, still laughing, one eyebrow going up just a trifle, just a very slight arching of the brow, but the challenge unmistakable, almost as if she had said, 'But you have not even seen my belly . . . *yet*.'

Hawes cleared his throat. 'Where do you work, Miss Tamid?'

'At Anderson and Loeb.'

'Is that where you met Amos Barlow?'

'Yes.'

'How long have you known him?'

'I'm only new with the firm,' Martha said.

'I'm trying to place your accent,' Hawes said, smiling.

'It's a mélange,' Martha said. 'I was born in Turkey, and then went to Paris, and then to Vienna with my parents. I have only been here in America for six months.'

'I see. When did you begin working for Anderson and Loeb?'

'Last month. I was going to school first. To learn typing and shorthand. Now I know them, so now I am a receptionist.'

'Do you live here with your parents, Miss Tamid?'

'No, I am twenty-three years old. That is old enough to live alone, *n'est-ce pas?* and do what one desires.'

'Yes,' Hawes said.

'You are a very big man,' Martha said. 'Do I make you feel uncomfortable?'

'No, why should you?'

'Because I am so small,' she, said. The radiant challenge came onto her face again. 'Though not all over,' she added.

Hawes nodded abstractedly. 'So then . . . uh . . . you met Mr Barlow when you started working at Anderson and Loeb last month.'

'Yes.' Martha paused. 'Would you like something to drink?'

'No. No, thank you. We're not allowed to on duty.'

'A pity,' she said.

'Yes.'

She smiled briefly, expectantly.

'Did you see Mr Barlow tonight?' Hawes asked.

'Yes.'

'At what time?'

'He picked me up at about six o'clock. Is Mr Barlow in some trouble?'

'No, no, this is just a routine check,' Hawes said. 'What time did you leave the office, Miss Tamid?'

'At five.'

'But *he* didn't leave until five-thirty, is that right?'

'I don't know what time he left. He was still there when I went away, and he arrived at about six.'

'And where did you go then?'

'To a restaurant downtown.'

'Why'd you come all the way up here first? You could have gone directly from the office.'

'But I had to change my clothes, no?'

'Of course,' Hawes said, and he smiled.

'I change my clothes very often,' Martha said. 'I wore to the office a suit, and then I changed to a dress for my date, and when Amos left, I put on a blouse and slacks, because I do not go to bed until very late.'

'I see.' He waited, fully expecting her to say, 'Would you mind if I changed into something more comfortable now?' but she didn't say it, and of course he knew she wouldn't because what the hell, he was only a city detective and not a private eye.

'What time did you come back here from the restaurant?'

'Eight-thirty, nine o'clock. Somewhere like that.'

'And Mr Barlow left at what time?'

'About nine-thirty, nine forty-five.' Martha paused. 'Do you find me unattractive?' she asked.

'What?'

'My looks. Are they bad to you?'

143

'Bad?'

'Not pretty, I mean.'

'No, no. No, no, no, you're very pretty.'

'I think Amos Barlow didn't think so.'

'Why do you say that?'

'I think he was in a hurry to leave me.'

'How do you know?'

'Well, I offered him a drink, and he said no. And then I asked him if he liked to dance, and he said no.' She paused. Reflectively, she said, 'I sometimes don't understand American men.'

'Well, it takes all kinds,' Hawes said philosophically.

'Do *you* like to dance?'

'Sure.'

'But, of course, it's too late to dance now,' Martha grinned. 'The people downstairs would complain.'

'I guess they would,' Hawes said.

Martha sighed, inhaling a deep breath, and then exhaling noisily. 'He must have thought me unattractive,' she said.

'Maybe you're not his type,' Hawes said. 'Does he date many other girls in the office?'

'I don't know. He is a very quiet man.' She shook her head in a delightfully confused way. 'I am very frustrated from him.'

'Well, all we wanted to know, actually,' Hawes said, 'was whether or not he really was with you from six to nine-thirty or so. And I guess he was.'

'Well, he was *with* me,' Martha said, 'but whether he was *really* with me, that is an open question.' She shrugged. 'American men,' she said sadly.

'Thank you very much for your help,' Hawes said, rising. 'I'd better go now. It's getting very late.'

'It is never too late,' Martha Tamid said cryptically,

and she fixed him with a stare so blatant he almost melted. He hesitated for just a moment, wondering, and then walked towards the door.

'Good night, Miss Tamid,' he said. 'Thank you very much.'

'American men,' Martha Tamid said, and closed the door behind him.

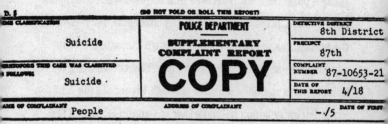

<u>SURVEILLANCE OF AMOS BARLOW BY DETECTIVE</u>
<u>3rd/GRADE BERTRAM KLING:</u>

<u>April 12th:</u>

Followed Barlow from precinct to his home in Riverhead, arrived there 11:08 P.M. Barlow parked car, 1959 Ford sedan in garage at rear of house, entered house through kitchen doorway at back. Kitchen light burned for approximately fifteen minutes. At 11:25, light in second story of house went on. Barlow came to window at front of house, looked out into street, drew shade. At 11:35 P.M., upstairs light went out. Maintained post until 12:30 A.M., at which time I presumed Barlow had gone to sleep. Put in call to 64th Precinct, Riverhead, was relieved on post by Patrolman David Schwartz.

<u>April 13th:</u>

Relieved Schwartz on post at 6:00 A.M. Took up position on corner of Wagner and Fourteenth, shielded by hedges of corner house. No sign of activity in̶ ^at Barlow house until 7:30 A.M. at which time Barlow came from rear of house, walked to garage, pulled car out. Followed him to restaurant nearby on Pike Avenue, place called Family Luncheonette. Parked across the street, Barlow partly visible through plateglass front window. He sat at table alone, ate leisurely breakfast, left luncheonette at 8:22 A.M. Drove through Riverhead via Addison River Parkway which he picked up at Cannon Road and the Avenue (Dover Plains Avenue), joining later with River Harb Highway which he took down to Dock Street section. Got off the highway at Land's End, drove Westerly to Mayfair Avenue, parked the car in open lot on corner of Mayfair and Pickett, walked to office building at 891 Mayfair. No way to continue surveillance into office, so I checked building for rear exits, satisfied there were none, and then stationed myself in lobby near elevator banks. Broke for coffee at 10:15 a̶.̶m̶.̶ ^A.M., but was able to keep watch of elevators from lobby drugstore. Barlow came down again at 12:34 P.M., followed him to a restaurant named Fannie's on Pickett Street where he ate lunch alone, and then walked for about fifteen minutes through small park outside Criminal Courts Building on MacCauley, me following. Then back to office again by 1:25 P.M. I took up position in lobby. Barlow did not emerge from elevators again until 5:10 P.M. He bought an evening newspaper at cigar stand, walked to parking lot, redeemed car, drove directly to River Harb Highway, then onto Addison ~~Parkway~~ River Parkway, exiting at Cannon Road, and then driving from there to his house. Parked car in the garage, went into house, did not come out again all night. I broke for dinner at 6:50 P.M., relieved by Patrolman Gordley of 64th, Riverhead, took up post again at 7:45 P.M., relieved at midnight ~~by~~ again by Gordley.

April 14th:

Barlow followed identical routine as preceding day. There seems to be nothing ~~also~~ at all suspicious about ~~him.~~ His his behavior. habits seem fixed and quiet. Doubt very much if he had anything whatever ~~do~~ do with beating of Carella. to

April 15th:

Saturday morning. Arrived at house earlier than usual (5:30 A.M.) because I thought Barlow's Saturday routine might provide something unusual. Came supplied with coffee and donuts which I had in the car, parked again on corner of Wagner and Fourteenth, ~~sheild~~ by hedges. Had a long wait. shielded Barlow apparently sleeps late on Saturdays. He did not come out of the house until almost twelve noon, by which time I was hungry all over again. Hoped he would stop for lunch

147

somewhere, but he did not. Instead, he once more drove to Cannon Road and then headed North. Thought for a moment he had tipped to the tail when I lost him in traffic for several blocks. But picked him up again just as he made turn east under elevated structure on Martin. Followed him for five blocks East. He pulled up in front of a florist (Konstantinos Brothers, 3451 Martin Avenue) came out bearing a small floral wreath. Drove East another ten blocks, pulled into gates of Cedarcrest Cemetery. He parked the car in the parking lot, walked to the office, remained there for several moments, and then walked into the cemetery carrying the wreath. I followed him on the path winding through the gravestones. He stopped at one of the stones, stood there for a long time with his head bent, just looking down at the stone. Then he knelt and put the wreath on the grave, and clasped his hands and prayed that way, on his knees, with his hands clasped, for what must have been a full half-hour. He rose, brushed at his eyes as if he'd been crying, and then went back to his car. He stopped for lunch at a diner on Cannon Road (Elevated Diner, 867 Cannon) and then went back to the house in Riverhead, ~~via the park~~ via Dover Plains Avenue. Called the 64th and asked for lunch relief, getting a patrolman named Gleason this time. When I got back to the house at 2:35 P.M., Gleason was gone and so was Barlow. The garage doors were open.

Barlow returned at 3:17 P.M. Gleason pulled up a few

minutes later, driving an unmarked sedan. Told me Barlow had only gone to do his weekly marketing, stopping at grocer's, butcher's, hardware store, etc. I thanked Gleason and took up the post again.

Whatever Barlow does with his weekends, he apparently doesn't go out. This was Saturday night, but he didn't leave that house again all day. At 11:00 P.M., all the lights went out. I hung around until one in the morning, and then called the 64th for relief.

<u>April 16th:</u>

I slept late, then checked with Carella at home to find out where brother Tommy Barlow is buried. Confirmed Cedarcrest. I relieved Patrolman Gordley on post at 12:15 P.M. Gordley said Barlow had not been out of the house all morning. At 1:30 P.M., Barlow came out wearing slacks and sweater, carrying cane. He walked to garage, came out pushing power lawn mower, which he started. He mowed front lawn, put mower back in garage, went into house again. At 3:00 P.M., small red compact Chevy II pulled up in front of Barlow's house. Young girl in her twenties, long black hair, got out of car, went up front walk, rang doorbell. I knew Barlow was inside because he hadn't left since mowing the lawn, but the girl stood on the doorstep and rang the bell for a long time, and he didn't answer the door. She finally gave up, walked back to the car, angrily slammed the door, and drove off. Checked immediately with Hawes for description of Martha Tamid, positive identification. Asked for relief from 64th, drove to Miss Tamid's apartment near the Oval. The red compact was parked at the curb, but when I spoke to her she denied having left the apartment, said she'd been in all day, said she had certainly not driven to Barlow's house. She offered me a drink, which I declined. She also asked me if I thought she looked like an Egyptian belly dancer, which I thought was a strange question, but I said yes, now that she mentioned it, I thought she did look like one. She seems like very aggressive and very female person. Can't understand her lying about visit to Barlow.

I took up post again at 6:12 P.M., after dinner. Patrolman said Barlow had not been out. Occurred to me that perhaps Barlow had left house by foot, sneaking out back way, leaving his car in the garage. I called the house from a drugstore two blocks away, hung up when Barlow answered, took up post again. Lights went on at 6:45. Lights went out at 11:00.

I left at 2:00 in the morning, Schwartz relieving. Schwartz wanted to know why we were sticking to this guy. I wish I could tell him.

<u>April 17th:</u>

Monday morning.

Barlow up and off at 7:30 A.M. Identical weekday routine.

Breakfast, office, lunch, office, home, lights out, goodnight.

Time is now 1:30 A.M. I left Barlow house at 1:00 A.M., calling

64th for relief, and getting Gleason who also wanted to know

why we were tailing Barlow.

Request permission to end surveillance.

Bertram Kling

Detective 3rd/Grade Bertram Kling

On the morning of April 18th, which was a bright,
shining Tuesday with the temperature at sixty-three
degrees, and the prevailing winds westerly at two miles
per hour, Detective Steve Carella left his house in
Riverhead and walked towards the elevated structure
some five blocks away. He had been attacked on the
twelfth of the month but time, as the ancient Arab
saying goes, heals all wounds. He had not taken the
beating lightly because nobody in his right mind takes
a beating lightly. A beating hurts. It is not nice to have
someone knock you about the head and the body with
a stick or a cane or a baseball bat. It is not nice to
be carted off to the hospital where interns calmly look
at your bleeding face, and calmly swab the cuts,
and calmly dress them as if they are above all this
petty bleeding, as if you are a page out of a textbook,

elementary stuff, we had this in first-year med, give us something hard, like a duodenal ulcer of the Macedonian canal. It is even worse to have to come home and face your wife with all those bandages and chunks of adhesive plaster clinging to your fine masculine head. Your wife is a deaf-mute and doesn't know how to scream, but the scream is there in her eyes, and you wish with all your might that you could erase that scream, that you hadn't been ambushed by some lousy bastard and beaten to a pulp before you could even get your gun in firing position. You wonder how you are going to explain all this to the children in the morning. You don't want them to start worrying about the fact that you are a cop. You don't want them to begin building anxiety neuroses when they're barely out of diapers.

But time heals all wounds – those Arabs knew how to put it all right – and Carella was aware of another old proverb, an ancient Syrian saying that simply stated, 'Time wounds all heels.' He didn't know who had pounced upon him in the driveway of Barlow's house, but he had every reason to believe that the minions of the law, those stout defenders of the people, those stalwart protectors of the innocent, those relentless tracers of lost persons, those bulwarks of freedom, those citadels of truth and common decency, yeah, he had no doubt the bulls of the 87th would one day pick up some louse who would confess to every crime committed in the past ten years and who would also casually mention he'd happened to beat up a cop named Carella on the night of April twelfth. So Carella was content to bide his time, confident that the odds were on his side. Crime doesn't pay. Everybody knows that. And time is a river.

Time, on that lovely April morning, happened to be a torrential flood, but Carella didn't know that as yet. He was on his way to work, minding his own business on the way to the elevated station, and he hadn't the faintest idea that time was about to reopen a couple of old healed wounds, or that he was about to receive – once again – a few knocks about the head and body. Who expects a beating on a lovely April morning?

The beating came as he was climbing the steps to the elevated platform. The first blow came from behind, and it struck him at the base of the neck, sending him sprawling forward onto the steps. He felt the impact of the sudden shock, felt himself blacking out as he fell forward, and thought only, *Jesus, broad daylight!* and then grasped fumblingly for the steps as he fell. The man with the stick, or the cane, or the baseball bat, or whatever the hell he was using, decided to kick Carella because it was most convenient to kick a man when he was grovelling on his knees, grasping for a hold on the steps. So he kicked him in the face, opening one of the cuts there and releasing a torrent of blood that spilled over Carella's cheek and down his neck, and onto his nice white clean go-to-work shirt. A woman coming down the steps screamed and then ran up the steps again, screaming all the way to the change booth, where the Elevated Transit employee tried to calm her down and find out what had happened, while on the steps the man with the stick or the cane or the baseball bat was striking Carella blow after blow on the head and neck, trying his best, it seemed, to kill him. Carella was aware of the woman's screams, and aware of pounding footsteps, and of a man's voice yelling, 'Stop that! You stop that, do you hear?' but he was mostly aware of blinding flashes of yellow erupting everywhere the goddamned stick fell, and especially aware of his own dizziness as he groped for his revolver, missing it, feeling the cartridges in his belt, groping again for the handle of the gun, feeling his fingers closing around the walnut stock as his attacker again struck him across the bridge of the nose. *Hit me hard enough you bastard and you'll kill me, hit me on the bridge of the nose and I'll drop dead right here at your feet*, the gun was free.

He swung the gun backhanded, clinging to the steps with one hand, swinging the gun without looking in a wide-armed blind sweep at whoever was behind him. The gun connected. Miraculously, he felt it colliding with flesh, and he heard someone grunt in pain, and he whirled instantly, his back to the steps, and he brought back both feet in an intuitive spring-coil action, unleashing them, the soles of his feet colliding with the man's midriff, sending the man pitching back and down the steps; and all the while Carella was itching to pull the trigger of his gun, all the while he was dying to kill this rotten son of a bitch who was an expert at beating up cops. He got to his feet. The man had rolled to the bottom of the steps, and now he crawled to his knees and Carella levelled the .38 and said, 'Stop or I'll shoot!' and he thought, *Go ahead, run. Run, and you're dead*.

But the man didn't run. He sat right where he was at the bottom of the steps while the woman at the top continued screaming and the man from the change booth kept asking over and over again, 'Are you all right, are you all right?'

Carella went down the steps.

He grabbed the man by the chin, holding the gun

muzzle against his chest, and he lifted the man's head and looked into his face.

He had never seen him before in his life.

12.

CARELLA SAID, 'NO hospital!' and the ambulance driver turned to the intern riding in the back, and the intern looked at Carella and said, 'But, sir, you're bleeding rather profusely,' and Carella pinned him with his sternest minion-of-the-law stare and said, 'No goddamn hospital!' and the intern had the distinct impression that if he'd insisted on this going-to-the-hospital routine, he himself might be the one who went. So he shrugged in his very calm, textbook, intern way, wishing they'd be called some morning to pick up a nice timid old lady with a traumatic subdural haemorrhage instead of a bleeding wild man with a gun in his fist, but those were the breaks, and anyway he'd had all this in first-year med. It was better to go to the hospital as a part of the staff, rather than as a patient. So he went.

The man at the bottom of the steps who sat there somewhat sheepishly clutching the area below his stomach, which Carella had kicked with both big feet, wasn't saying very much. His weapon, a sawn-off broom handle, had gone down the steps with him, and Carella picked it up and then bummed a ride from the precinct patrolmen, who had been called – together with the hospital – by the helpful change-booth attendant. The patrolmen dropped Carella and his prisoner at the 87th Precinct. Carella, his gun still in his hand, shoved the man across the sidewalk, and up the front steps, and past the muster desk, and up the iron-ranged stairway leading to the Detective Division, and down the corridor, and through the slatted rail divider, and then pushed him into a straight-backed chair which, it seemed, was immediately surrounded by detectives.

'You're bleeding,' Meyer said to Carella. 'You know that?'

'I know it,' Carella said. To the man seated in the chair with his head bent, Carella said, 'What's your name, mister?'

The man didn't answer.

Carella took the man's jaw between the fingers of one hand, squeezing hard and lifting the man's head, and looking directly into his eyes.

'Your name, mister,' he repeated.

The man didn't answer.

'Get up.'

The man didn't move.

'Get up!' Carella shouted angrily, and he seized the man by the front of the lightweight jacket he was wearing, and then hurled him half-way across the room to the wall alongside the filing cabinets.

'Take it easy, Steve,' Meyer cautioned.

Carella holstered his gun, and went through each of the man's pockets. He found a wallet in one of them, and he turned the man around, shoved him into a chair again, and then sat on the edge of a desk as he went through the wallet. Hawes and Meyer stood on opposite sides of the prisoner, waiting. Meyer glanced at Carella, and then shook his head.

'Miscolo!' he yelled.

'Yo!' Miscolo yelled back from the Clerical Office.

'Bring in some iodine and some Band-Aids, will you?'

'Yo!' Miscolo answered.

Carella looked up from the wallet, 'Richard Bandler,' he said. He looked at the man. 'That your name?'

'You're holding my driver's licence in your hand, who the hell's name do you think it is?'

Carella flipped the licence onto the desk and walked slowly to Bandler and said very slowly and very distinctly, 'Bandler, I don't like you very much. I didn't like you the first time you cold-cocked me, and I don't like you any better after the second time. It's all I can do, Bandler, to keep myself from kicking you clear through next Sunday, so you'd better watch your mouth, Bandler, you dig? You'd just better answer everything I ask you nice and peaceful or you're going to be a cripple before they take you to jail, you understand that, Bandler?'

'It seems plain enough,' Bandler said.

'It *better* be plain enough,' Carella warned. 'Is your name Richard Bandler?'

'That's my name.'

'Get that tone out of your voice!' Carella shouted.

'What tone?'

'Take it easy, Steve,' Hawes said.

Carella clenched his fists, unclenched them, walked back to the desk and picked up the driver's licence again. 'Is this your correct address? Four-one-three South Sixty-fifth, Isola?'

'No. I've moved since.'

'Where to?'

'I'm staying at the Hotel Culbertson downtown.'

'How long have you been staying there?'

'About ten days.'

'You moved from Sixty-fifth Street ten days ago?'

'No. I moved from Sixty-fifth last month.'

'Where to?'

Bandler paused.

'*Where to, Bandler?*'

'The Coast.'

'When did you leave?'

'On March twenty-seventh.'

'Why? Are you wanted in this city?'

'No.'

'Are you wanted *anywhere*?'

'No.'

'We're going to check, you know. If you're wanted . . .'

'I'm not wanted. I'm not a criminal.'

'Maybe you *weren't* a criminal,' Hawes said, 'but you are now, mister. First-degree assault happens to be a big fat felony.'

Bandler said nothing. Miscolo came in from the Clerical Office with the adhesive bandages and the iodine. He took a look at Carella's face, shook his head, clucked his tongue, and then said, 'Jesus, what's the matter with you, anyway?' He took another look and said, 'Go wash your face in the sink there.'

'My face is all right, Alf,' Carella said.

'Go wash your face,' Miscolo said sternly, and Carella sighed and went to the corner sink.

'Have you got a record, Bandler?' Hawes asked.

'No, I told you. I'm not a criminal.'

'All right, why'd you go to California?'

'I've got a job there.'

'What kind of a job?'

'In television.'

'Doing what?'

'I'm an assistant director.'

'What do you direct?' Carella said from the sink. He reached for the white towel hanging on a rack and Miscolo yelled, 'You'll get that full of blood. Use the paper towels.'

'Assistant directors don't direct very much,' Bandier said. 'We maintain quiet on the set, we call actors, we . . .'

'We're not interested in an industry survey,' Hawes said. 'What show do you work on?'

'Well . . . well, you see, I don't actually have a steady job with any one show.'

'Then why did you go to California?' Meyer said. 'You just told us you had a job there.'

'Well, I did.'

'What job?'

'They were shooting a ninety-minute special. So a friend of mine who was directing the show called to see if I'd like to work with him. As assistant, you see. So I went to the Coast.'

Carella came back to the desk and sat on the edge of it. Miscolo picked up the iodine bottle and began swabbing the cuts. 'You're gonna need stitches here,' he said.

'I don't think so.'

'It's the same cut from last week,' Miscolo said, 'It's opened all over again.'

'Why'd you come back from the Coast?' Carella asked.

'The job ended. I looked around for a while, to see if I could get some kind of steady work, but nothing came up. So I came back here.'

'Are you working now?'

'No. I just got back about ten days ago.'

'When was that, Bandler?'

'The eighth.'

'Ow!' Carella said as Miscolo pressed a piece of adhesive in place. 'Why'd you come after me, Bandler?'

'Because . . . I found out what you did.'

'Yeah? What did I do? Ouch! For Christ's sake, Alf . . .'

'I'm sorry, I'm sorry,' Miscolo said. 'I'm not a doctor, you know,' he added petulantly. 'I'm only a lousy clerk. Next time, go to the hospital instead of messing up the whole damn squad-room.'

'What did I do?' Carella asked again.

'You killed my girl,' Bandler said.

'What?'

'You killed my girl.'

For a moment, no one in the room made a connexion. They stared at Bandler in silent amazement, and then Bandler said, 'Blanche. Blanche Mattfield,' and the name still meant nothing to anyone but Carella.

Carella nodded. 'She jumped, Bandler,' he said. 'I had nothing to do with her jumping.'

'You *told* her to jump.'

'I was trying to get her off that ledge.'

'You got her off, all right.'

'How do you know what I said to her?'

'The landlady told me. She was in the room behind you, and she heard you tell her to jump.' Bandler paused and then said, 'Why didn't you just shove her off that ledge? It would have amounted to the same thing.'

'Do you have any idea why she was on that ledge to begin with?' Carella asked.

161

'What difference does it make? She wouldn't have jumped if it hadn't been for you!'

'She wouldn't have been out there if it hadn't been for you!' Carella said.

'Sure,' Bandler said.

'Why'd you leave her?'

'*Who* left her?'

'You did, you did. Come on, Bandler, don't get me sore again! She wanted to die because you left her. 'Good-bye, Blanche, it's been fun.' Those were your exact words.'

'I loved that girl,' Bandler protested. 'She knew I was coming right back. She knew it was just a temporary job. I told her . . .'

'You walked out on her, Bandler.'

'I tell you I didn't. I *loved* her, don't you understand? She knew I was coming back. I told her so. How do I know why she decided to . . . to kill herself?'

'She killed herself because she knew you were finished with her. Do you feel better now?'

'Wh . . . what do you mean?'

'After beating me up? After shoving all the blame onto me?'

'You killed her!' Bandler shouted, and he came out of the chair angrily, and Carella put both hands on his shoulders and shoved him back down again.

'What's the name of this friend of yours on the Coast?'

'Wh . . . what friend?'

'Your director friend. Who was doing the ninety-minute special.'

'It . . . uh . . .'

The room went silent.

'Or *was* there a friend?'

'Ask anybody in the business. I'm one of the best A.D.s around.'

'Did you go out there to work, Bandler? Or did you go out there with a dame?'

'I . . .'

'A dame,' Meyer said, nodding.

'I'm telling you I loved Blanche. Why would I go to California with another woman?'

'Why, Bandler?' Hawes asked.

'I . . .'

'*Why*, Bandler?'

'I . . . *loved* . . . Blanche. I . . . what . . . what the hell was the harm of a little . . . a little innocent fun with . . . with somebody else? She . . . she knew I'd come back to her. She knew that girl meant nothing to me. She knew that.'

'Apparently she didn't.'

Bandler was silent for a long time. Then he said, 'I saw it in the papers out there. Just a little item. About . . . about Blanche jump . . . jumping off that building. I saw it the day after she did it. I . . . I ditched the girl and got a plane back as fast as I could. Saturday. That was the earliest I could book. But she'd been buried by the time I got here and . . . and when I talked to the landlady of her building, she told me what she'd heard you say, so I . . . I figured you had it coming to you. For . . . for killing the girl I loved.'

'You just go on believing that,' Carella said.

'Huh?'

'It'll make the time pass more quickly.'

'Huh?'

'You can get up to ten years for first-degree assault.'
Carella paused. 'What was the harm of a little innocent
fun, huh, Bandler?'

13.

LOVE WAS IN riotous bloom on the day that Fred Hassler came back to the squad-room and set the merry-go-round in violent motion once again. He had no idea he was reactivating the carousel, no knowledge that it had just about run down, or that the Tommy Barlow – Irene Thayer suicide was in danger of being thrown into the Open File. Police work is always a race against time, especially in a precinct like the 87th. A crime is committed, and the bulls go to work on it quickly and efficiently because anything that's likely to turn up is going to turn up *soon* or not at all. They'll go over the ground a hundred times, asking the same questions over and over again in hope of getting a different answer. But a case goes cold too quickly, and in a place like the 87th, there are always new cases, there is always a steady press of crime, there is always a fresh occurrence demanding investigation, there is always the Open File. The Open File is a convenience which allows cops to close a case while keeping it open. Once a case is dumped into the Open File, they can stop thinking about it, and concentrate instead on the three dozen other cases that have miraculously become a part of their working-day routine. The case in the Open File is not officially closed since it hasn't officially been solved – there has been no arrest and conviction. But if it is not officially closed, neither is it truly active; it is simply lying there like a *bagel*. The Tommy Barlow – Irene Thayer case had lost all its momentum, and the cops of the 87th were almost ready to throw it into the Open File on the day Fred Hassler reappeared at the squad-room railing, on the day love was in riotous bloom.

The lovers were fifty-eight and fifty-five years old respectively, and they were standing before Detective Meyer's desk arguing heatedly. The man wore a sports jacket which he had thrown on over his undershirt when the arresting patrolman had knocked on the door. The woman wore a flowered house-dress.

'All right, now who's pressing charges?' Meyer wanted to know.

'*I'm* pressing charges,' the man and woman said together.

'One at a time.'

'*I'm* pressing charges,' the woman said.

'*I'm* pressing charges,' the man said.

Hassler, standing at the slatted railing, tried to catch the attention of someone in the squad-room, but they all seemed to be busy filing or typing, except Meyer who was busy listening to the lovers.

'Who called the police?' Meyer asked.

'*I* called the police,' the woman said.

'Is that true, sir?'

'Sure,' the man said. 'Big mouth called the police.'

'All right, ma'am, why'd you call the police?'

'Because he pinched me,' the woman said.

'Big mouth,' the man said.

'Because he pinched you, huh?' Meyer asked patiently. 'Are you married, folks?'

'We're married,' the man said. 'Big mouth can't

stand a little pinch from her own husband. Right away, she has to yell cop.'

'Shut up, you rotten animal,' the woman said. 'You grabbed a hunk, I thought you were gonna rip it off.'

'I was being friendly.'

'Some friendly.'

'I should have been the one who called the cops,' the man protested. 'But I'm not a big mouth.'

'You pinched me!' she insisted.

'Wash our dirty laundry,' the man muttered. 'Call the cops. Why didn't you call the F.B.I. already?'

'Let's try to calm down,' Meyer said. 'Lady, if your husband pinched you . . .'

'She hit me with a frying-pan!' the man said suddenly.

'Ah!' the woman shouted. 'Ah! Listen! Just listen!'

'That's right, she hit me with a . . .'

'And he calls *me* big mouth! Listen to him!'

'You hit me, Helen, it's the truth!'

'You pinched me, and *that's* the truth.'

'I pinched you 'cause you hit me.'

'I hit you 'cause you pinched me.'

'Look, one at a time,' Meyer warned. 'Now what happened?'

'I was washing the dishes,' the woman said. 'He came up behind me and pinched me.'

'Tell him, tell him,' the man said, shaking his head. 'Nothing sacred between a man and a wife. Blab it all to the police.'

'Then what happened?'

'Then I took a frying-pan from the sink, and I hit him with it.'

'On the head,' the man said. 'You want to see what she done? Here, just feel this lump.'

'Go ahead, tell him everything,' the woman said.

'You were the one who called the police!' the man shouted.

'Because you threatened to kill me!'

'You hit me with the goddamn frying-pan, didn't you?'

'You got me angry, that's why.'

'From a little pinch?'

'It was a big pinch. I got a mark from it. You want to see the mark, officer?'

'Sure, go ahead, show him,' the man said. 'We'll make this a burlesque house. Go ahead, show him.'

'How long have you been married?' Meyer asked patiently.

'Twenty-five years,' the man said.

'Twenty-three years,' the woman corrected.

'It seems more like twenty-five,' the man said, and then burst out laughing at his own wit.

'In addition to beating his wife,' the woman said, 'he's also, as you can see, a comedian.'

'I didn't beat you, I *pinched* you!'

'Why don't you both go home and patch it up?' Meyer asked.

'With him? With this rotten animal?'

'With her? With this loud mouth?'

'Come on, come on, it's springtime, the flowers are blooming, go home and kiss and make up,' Meyer said. 'We got enough troubles around here without having to lock you both up.'

'Lock us up?' the man said indignantly. 'For what? For a little love tap with a frying-pan?'

'For a friendly pinch between husband and wife?' the woman asked.

'We *love* each other,' the man protested.

'I know you do. So go on home, okay?' Meyer winked at the man. 'Okay?'

'Well . . .'

'Sure,' Meyer said, rising, scooping them both in his widespread arms, shoving them towards the gate in the railing. 'Nice young couple like you shouldn't be wasting time arguing. Go on home, it's a beautiful day, how do you do, sir, can I help you?'

'My name's Fred Hassler,' Hassler said. 'I've been here before, but . . .'

'You mean we can just go?' the man asked.

'Yes,' Meyer said, 'go, go. Before I change my mind. Go on, scram.' He turned to Hassler and said, 'Yes, sir, I remember you now. Won't you come in? Don't pinch her any more, mister! And you lay off the frying-pans. Have a seat, Mr Hassler.'

'Thank you,' Hassler said. He did not seem very interested in the colour or atmosphere of the squad-room this time. He seemed very serious, and a trifle angry, and Meyer wondered what had provoked his visit, and then called across the squad-room to where Carella was typing at his own desk.

'Steve, Mr Hassler's here. You remember him, don't you?'

Carella got up from his desk, walked to where Hassler was sitting, and extended his hand. 'Hello, Mr Hassler, how are you?' he asked.

'Fine, thank you,' Hassler said a bit brusquely.

'What can we do for you?' Meyer asked.

'You can get back my stuff,' Hassler replied.

'What stuff?'

'I don't know if it was you or the Forty Thieves who took it, but somebody took it, and I want it back.'

'Is something missing from your apartment, Mr Hassler?' Carella asked.

'Yes, something is missing from my apartment. I'm not saying it was the police. It might have been the firemen. But . . .'

'You think the firemen took it?'

'I'm saying it's possible. They break into an apartment and next thing you know, everything is sticking to their fingers. Well, this time a citizen is complaining. A citizen has a right to complain, hasn't he?'

'Certainly, Mr Hassler. What's missing?'

'To begin with, I'm a good sleeper.'

'Yes, sir.'

'Yes. I don't usually have trouble. But they've begun construction on our block, and last night they were making such a terrible racket that I went to the medicine chest to get some of these sleeping-pills that I had one time when I had the flu, it must have been in nineteen fifty-nine.'

'Yes, sir.'

'Yes, I had this high fever, a hundred and two, almost a hundred and three, and I couldn't sleep, so I got these pills, they're called Barbinal, you take one and it knocks you out like a light for the whole night. I had four of those pills left in a bottle from the time I had the flu in nineteen-fifty-nine.'

'Yes, sir?'

'Yes, well last night I couldn't sleep so I went to the medicine chest figuring I would take one of those

170

Barbinals, and I found the bottle all right, but it was empty.'

'The pills were gone?'

'All four of them. So I knew the firemen had been in the apartment at the time of the explosion, and I also knew the police had been crawling all over it, so I automatically figured. That was the first thing.'

'Something else was missing, Mr Hassler?'

'Mmmm,' Hassler said grimly. 'This morning, when I got up, I thought I'd just make a check of the apartment to see what else had been stolen. Well, a whole reel of film is missing.'

'Film?'

'Movie film. I told you I was a bug on movies. I keep them all stored in my living-room, the reels, in these metal containers, you know? And on the cover of each container, there's a strip of adhesive tape and it gives the date and tells what's on the reel. Well, a reel is missing.'

'Perhaps you misplaced it, Mr Hasler.'

'I didn't misplace it. Those reels are all filed chronologically in a wooden case I made myself, with a space for each reel, and one of those spaces is empty. So, if you don't mind, I'd like my pills back, and also my film.'

'We haven't got either, Mr Hassler.' Carella paused. 'It's possible, you know, that Tommy and Irene took those pills. To put themselves to sleep.'

'I thought they drank themselves to sleep.'

'They may have taken the pills, Mr Hassler.'

'Did they take my film, too? They were both half-naked and dead, and my film wasn't anywhere on them. Besides, Tommy didn't like that particular reel.'

'Tommy saw this reel?'

'Saw it? He was *in* it.'

'What do you mean, Mr Hassler?'

'I told you the first time I was up here that Tommy used to help me with my movies. I got this bug, you know, can I help it? So this one was the story of a guy who's broke, and he's walking in the park and he finds a hundred-dollar bill. So Tommy and I went over to Grover Park one afternoon, and we shot the whole thing, almost three hundred feet in one afternoon. There's only Tommy in it—no, wait a minute, there's also a little kid we found in the park and asked him to be in the picture. The way the plot goes, you see, Tommy finds this bill and then has to decide . . .'

'Tommy *acted* in this film, Mr Hassler, is that right?'

'That's right.' Hassler paused. 'He wasn't a professional actor, you know, but what the hell, we were doing it for kicks, anyway. It came out pretty good.' He shrugged. 'Tommy didn't like it, though. He said he needed a haircut, and it made his face look too thin. Anyway, *I* liked it, and I want it back.'

'But you see, we haven't got it,' Carella said.

'Then the firemen must have it.'

'Mr Hassler, how was this reel of film labelled?'

'The usual way.'

'Which is?'

'First the date on the top line. Then the title of the reel, which in this case was "The Hundred Dollar Bill". Then, after that it said, "with Tommy Barlow and Sammy La Paloma" – that's the name of the kid we discovered in the park. That's all.'

'Then anyone who looked at the cover of the can would know that Tommy Barlow was in this reel of film.'

'That's right.'

'Mr Hassler, thank you very much,' Carella said. 'We'll try our best to get it back for you.'

'It was the Forty Thieves,' Hassler insisted. 'Those louses'll take the sink if it isn't nailed down.'

But Carella wasn't at all sure the firemen were responsible for the theft of Fred Hassler's film. Carella was remembering that Mary Tomlinson had said, 'I wish I had some pictures of Tommy, too. I have a lot of Margaret, but none of the man she was going to marry.' And he was remembering that Michael Thayer had said, 'I want to keep looking at him. That's strange, isn't it? I want to find out what was so . . . *different* about him.' And he was remembering, too, that Amos Barlow had said, 'Ever since he died, I've been going around the house looking for traces of him. Old letters, snapshots, anything that was Tommy.' So whereas he knew that perhaps the firemen had earned their nickname with good reason, he also knew that none of the Forty Thieves would be crazy enough to steal a container of home movies. The carousel music had suddenly started again. The gold ring was once more in sight. The horses were in motion.

Carella went downtown and swore out three search warrants.

Hawes, in the meantime, perhaps motivated by the sudden burst of activity on the case, decided that he wanted to talk to Miss Martha Tamid one more time. They were each, Carella and Hawes, about to gasp their last breath on this case, but they were nonetheless still giving it the old college try. Hawes didn't really believe that Martha Tamid had anything at all to do with the suicide-homicide, but there remained nonetheless the fact that she had lied about going to Amos Barlow's house on the afternoon of April 16. The specific purpose of his visit was to find out why she had lied. She told him immediately and without hesitation.

'Because I was embarrassed.'

'Embarrassed, Miss Tamid?'

'Yes, how would you feel? I knew he was in there. I could see his car in the garage. But he wouldn't answer the doorbell. Well, no matter. It is finished.'

'What do you mean, finished? No, don't answer that yet, Miss Tamid, we'll come back to it. I want to get something else straight first. You're saying that you lied to the police because your feelings were hurt? Is that what you're telling me?'

'Yes.'

'Suppose you tell me why you went there in the first place, Miss Tamid?'

'You are getting harsh with me,' Martha said, her eyes seeming to get larger and a little moist.

'I'm terribly sorry,' Hawes answered. 'Why did you go there?'

Martha Tamid shrugged. 'Because I do not like being ignored,' she said. 'I am a woman.'

'Why did you go there, Miss Tamid?'

'To make love,' she answered simply.

Hawes was silent for several moments. Then he said, 'But Amos Barlow wouldn't open the door.'

'He would not. Of course, he did not know why I was coming there.'

'Otherwise he most certainly *would* have opened the door, is that right?'

'No, he would not have opened the door, anyway. I

174

know that now. But I thought I would mention to you, anyway, that he did not know I was coming to make love.'

'Are you in love with Amos Barlow?' Hawes asked.

'Don't be ridiculous!'

Were you in love with him?'

'Certainly not!'

'But you nonetheless went there that Sunday to . . . to seduce him?'

'Yes.'

'Why?'

'Because I am a woman.'

'Yes, you've already told me that.'

'I do not like to be ignored.'

'You've told me that, too.'

'Then? It's simple, *n'est-ce pas?*' She nodded emphatically. 'Besides, it's finished now. I no longer care.'

'Why is it finished, Miss Tamid? Why do you no longer care?'

'Because he was here, and now I know, and now I do not feel unattractive any more.'

'When was he here?'

'Four nights ago, five nights? I don't remember exactly.'

'He came of his own accord?'

'I invited him.'

'And? What happened?'

'Nothing.'

'Nothing?'

'Nothing.' Martha nodded. 'I am a very patient woman, you know. My patience is endless. But, you know . . . I gave him every opportunity. He is simply . . . he is inexperienced . . . he knows *nothing*, but nothing. And there is a limit to anyone's patience.'

'I'm not sure I follow you, Miss Tamid,' Hawes said.

'You cannot blame a person for being inexperienced. This is not the same thing as being inattentive, you know. So when I tried, and I realized he was . . . *comment dit-on . . . simple? Naïf? Ingénu? . . .* what is there to do? He did not know. He simply did not know.'

'What didn't he know, Miss Tamid?'

'What to do, how to do! He did not know.' She leaned forward suddenly. 'I can trust you, can't I? You are like a *confesseur*, isn't that true? A priest who hears confession? I can tell you?'

'Sure,' Hawes said.

'I took off my blouse,' Martha said, 'because he was fumbling so with the buttons. But then . . . he did not know how to undress me. He simply did not know. He had never been with a woman before, do you understand? He is an innocent.' Martha Tamid sat back in her chair. 'One cannot be offended by innocence,' she said.

The police who went through all those rooms were pretty much offended by all that rampant innocence. They searched Mary Tomlinson's house from basement to attic, and they went through every inch of Michael Thayer's apartment, and they covered Amos Barlow's house like a horde of termites – but they didn't turn up hide or hair of the film that had been stolen from Fred Hassler. They went through Mrs Tomlinson's tiny little Volkswagen, and through Michael Thayer's blue Oldsmobile sedan, and through Amos Barlow's tan Chevrolet, but they found nothing. They searched through Thayer's small office in the Brio Building, and through Barlow's mailing-room at 891 Mayfair – but they did not find the film, and the merry-go-round was slowing to a halt again.

The next day, without realizing how close they'd come to grabbing the gold ring, the detectives held a meeting in the squad-room.

'What do you think?' Hawes asked. 'Have you got any ideas?'

'None,' Carella said.

'Meyer?'

Meyer shook his head.

'Bert?'

Kling hesitated a moment, and then said, 'No.'

'So do we call it suicide and close it out?' Hawes asked.

'What the hell else can we do?' Meyer asked.

'Let's ask Pete for permission to leave it in the Open File,' Carella said.

'That's the same thing as killing it,' Hawes said.

Carella shrugged. 'Something may come up on it some day.'

'When?'

'Who knows? We've run it into the ground. What else can we do?'

Hawes hesitated, unwilling to be the one who officially killed the case. 'You want to vote on it?' he asked. The detectives nodded. 'All those in favour of asking Pete to dump it in Siberia?' None of the men raised their hands.

'Meyer?'

'Dump it,' Meyer said.

'Bert?'

'Dump it.'

'Steve?'

Carella paused for a long time. Then he nodded reluctantly and said, 'Dump it. Dump it.'

The request was placed on Lieutenant Peter Byrnes' desk that afternoon. He glanced at it cursorily, picked up his pen, and then signed it, granting his permission. Before he went home that night, Alf Miscolo, filing a sheaf of papers he'd picked up from all the desks in the squad-room, went to the green cabinet marked OPEN FILE, slid out the drawer, and dropped into it a manila folder containing all the papers on the Tommy Barlow – Irene Thayer case.

For all intents and purposes the case was closed.

14.

THE MAN WAS lying on his back in Grover Park.

They had already traced the outline of his body on the moist grass by the time Carella and Hawes arrived, and the man seemed ludicrously framed by his own ridiculous posture, the white powder capturing the position of death and freezing it. The police photographer was performing his macabre dance around the corpse, choreographing himself into new angles each time his flash-bulb popped. The corpse stared up at him unblinkingly, twisted into the foolish grotesquery of death, one leg bent impossibly beneath him, the other stretched out straight. The sun was shining. It was May, and there was the heady aroma of newly mown grass in the park, the delicious fragrance of magnolia and cornelian cherry and quince. The man had a knife in his heart.

They stood around the body exchanging the amenities, men who were called together only when Death gave a party. The lab boys, the photographer, the assistant medical examiner, the two detectives from Homicide North, the two men from the 87th, they all stood around the man with the knife sticking out of his chest, and they asked each other how they were, and had they heard about Manulus over in the 33rd, got shot by a burglar night before last, what about this moonlighting stuff, did they think the commissioner would stick to his guns, it was a nice day, wasn't it, beautiful weather they'd been having this spring, hardly a drop of rain. They cracked a few jokes – the photographer had one about the first astronaut to reach the moon – and they went about their work with a faintly detached air of busyness. That was a dead man lying in the grass there. They accepted his presence only by performing a mental sleight of hand that in effect denied his humanity. He was no longer a man, he was simply a problem.

Carella pulled the knife from the dead man's chest as soon as the assistant M.E. and the photographer were through with the stiff, carefully lifting the knife with his handkerchief tented over his hand, so as not to smear any latent prints that might be on the handle or blade.

'You going to make out the tag?' one of the laboratory boys asked him.

'Yeah,' Carella answered curtly.

He pulled three or four evidence tags from his back pocket, slid one loose from the rubber-banded stack, returned the others to his pocket, took the cap from his fountain pen, and began writing:

POLICE DEPARTMENT
EVIDENCE

Where Found _Grover Park_
Homicide, male, white Date _5/11_
Found by _Detective Stephen Louis Carella_
In presence of _Detective Cotton Hawes_
Delivered to _Police Laboratory_
_____ Date _5/11_

CASE NUMBER
Det 2nd/Gr. CARELLA, S.L. 714-56-32
RANK   SURNAME   INITIALS   SHIELD

Automatically, he turned over the tag and filled in the information requested on the reverse side:

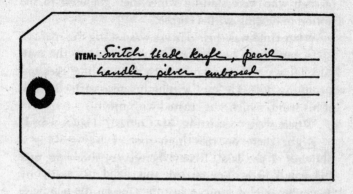

ITEM: Switch blade knife, pearl handle, silver embossed

He looped the strings of the tag over the handle of the knife, fastening the two together where blade joined handle. Then, carrying the knife by the tag, he went over to where the laboratory technician was making a sketch of the body and its location.

'Might as well take this with you,' Carella said.

'Thanks,' the technician said. He accepted the knife and carried it over to his car, which was parked partly on the grass, partly on the road that wound through the park. An ambulance had already arrived, and the attendants were waiting for everyone to finish with the body so they could cart it off to the morgue for autopsy. Hawes, standing some ten feet from where the attendants waited, was questioning a man who claimed he had seen the entire thing. Carella walked over aimlessly. He sometimes felt that all the official rigmarole following the discovery of a corpse was designed to allow a painless adjustment to the very idea of death by violence. The men took their pictures and made their sketches and collected their latent prints and whatever evidence was available, but these were only the motions of men who were stalling while they got used to the notion of dealing with a corpse.

'What time was this?' Hawes was asking the man.

'It must have been about a half-hour ago,' the man said. He was a thin old man with rheumy blue eyes and a running nose. He kept wiping his nose with the back of his hand, which was crusted with mucus.

'Where were you sitting, Mr Coluzzi?' Hawes asked.

'Right there on that high rock. I was making a drawing of the lake. I come here every morning, and I sketch a little. I'm retired, you see. I live with my daughter and my son-in-law on Grover Avenue, just across from the park.'

'Can you tell us what happened, Mr Coluzzi?' Hawes said. He noticed Carella standing beside him and said, 'Steve, this is Mr Dommick Coluzzi. He was an eye-witness to the killing. Mr Coluzzi, this is Detective Carella.'

'How do you do?' Coluzzi said, and then immediately asked, '*Lei è italiano, no?*'

'Yes,' Carella answered.

'*Va bene,*' Coluzzi said, smiling. '*Dicevo a questo suo amico . . .*'

'I don't think he understands Italian,' Carella said gently. 'Do you, Cotton?'

'No,' Hawes answered.

'*Mi scusi,*' Coluzzi said. 'I was telling him that I come here every morning to sketch. And I was sitting up there when the car pulled up.'

'What kind of a car was it, Mr Coluzzi?' Carella asked.

'A Cadillac convertible,' Coluzzi said without hesitation.

'The colour?'

'Blue.'

'Top up or down?'

'Up.'

'You didn't happen to notice the licence plate number, did you?'

'I did,' Coluzzi said, and he wiped his nose with the back of his hand. 'I wrote it down on my pad.'

'You're a very observant person, Mr Coluzzi,' Hawes said, his brows raised in admiration.

Coluzzi shrugged and wiped his nose with the back of his hand. 'It isn't every day you see a man get stabbed to death,' he said. He was plainly enjoying himself. He was perhaps sixty-seven, sixty-eight, a thin old man whose arms were still muscular and wiry, but whose hands trembled slightly, a thin old man who had been let out to pasture, who came to the park each morning to sketch. This morning, which had started out the way all other mornings did for him, something new had come into his life. He had been watching the lake and sketching the section near the dock where the rowboats bobbed in imperfect unison when suddenly a Cadillac had pulled to the side of the winding road, and suddenly murder had been done. And the old man, unnoticed on his high boulder overlooking the lake and the scene of the murder, alert, quick, had watched, and then shouted at the killer, and then had written down the number of the car's licence plate as it drove away. For the first time in a long time, the old man was useful again, and he enjoyed his usefulness, enjoyed talking to these two men who admired his quick thinking, who spoke to him as if they were speaking to an equal, as if they were speaking to another *man*, and not to some child who had to be let out into the sunshine each morning.

'What was the number of the plate, Mr Coluzzi?' Carella asked.

Coluzzi opened his sketch pad. He had been working in charcoal, and a delicately shaded drawing of the boats at the dock filled half of the page. In one corner of the page, in charcoal, he had written:

$$IS\text{-}7146$$

Carella noticed that he had crossed the seven, in the continental manner. He nodded briefly to himself, and then copied the number into his own pad.

'Can you tell us exactly what happened, Mr Coluzzi?' he said.

'The car pulled to the kerb. Down there.' Coluzzi pointed. 'I noticed it right away because it came in with a lot of noise, tyres shrieking, door slamming. And then a man ran up the embankment directly to this other man who was sitting on the bench there. The other man got up right away, and tried to run, but the one who got out of the car was too fast for him. He caught his arm and swung him around, and then he brought his right hand around and at first I thought he was only punching him, do you know, with his right hand, but instead he was stabbing him. I stood up on the rock and yelled at him, and that was when he turned and looked at me, and began running down to the car again. I think he was frightened. I don't think he would have left his knife sticking in the man that way, if he hadn't been frightened.'

'Are *you* frightened, Mr Coluzzi?'

'Me? Of what?'

'Of telling us all this? Of possible reprisal?'

'Reprisal? What's that?'

'*Vendetta*,' Carella said in Italian.

'*Ma che cosa?*' the old man said. '*Vendetta? Che importa?* I'm an old man. What are they going to do with their *vendetta?* Kill me? If this is the worst that can happen to me, I welcome it.'

'We appreciate your help, Mr Coluzzi.'

'The way I figure it, a man is entitled in this country to come to the park and sit on a bench if he wants to. No one has the right to murder him while he is sitting on a bench minding his own business.'

'Thanks again,' Carella said.

'*Prego*,' the old man answered, and went back to sketching the rowboats on the lake.

The old man's eyesight was good, even though he was sixty-seven years old. A call to the Bureau of Motor Vehicles confirmed that a blue 1960 Cadillac convertible bearing the licence plate IS-7146 was registered to a Mr Frank Dumas at 1137 Fairview in, of course, Isola. The 'IS' on the plate made the Isola address mandatory. Carella thanked the clerk at the bureau, turned to Hawes, and said, 'Too easy. It's too damn easy.'

Hawes shrugged and answered, 'We haven't got him yet.'

They checked out a sedan and drove downtown to Fairview Street. Carella was thinking that he had drawn Lineup the next day, and that would mean getting up an hour earlier in order to be all the way downtown on time. Hawes was thinking that he was due in court on Monday to testify in a burglary case. They drove with the windows in the car open. The car was an old Buick, fitted with a police radio and new tyres. It had been a good car in its day, but Carella wondered what it would do in a chase with one of this year's souped-up models. Fairview Street was thronged with people who had come outdoors simply to talk to each other or to catch a breath of spring air. They parked the car at the kerb in front of 1137, and began walking towards the building. The people on the front stoop knew immediately that they were cops. The sedan was unmarked, and both Carella and Hawes were wearing business suits, and shirts and ties, but the people sitting on the front stoop of the tenement knew they were cops and would have known it even if they'd walked up those steps wearing Bermuda shorts and sneakers. A cop has a smell. If you live long enough in an area infested with cops, you get to know the smell. You get to fear it, too, because cops are one thing you can never figure. They will help you one moment and turn on you the next. The people sitting on the front stoop watched Carella and Hawes, two strangers, mount the front steps and walk into the vestibule. The stoop cleared immediately. The two young men standing there immediately decided to go to the candy store for an egg cream. The old man from the building next door decided to go up on the roof and look at his pigeons. The old lady who lived on the ground floor packed up her knitting, picked up her folding chair, and went inside to watch daytime television. Cops almost always spelled trouble, and detectives spelled the biggest kind of trouble.

Carella and Hawes, not unaware of the subtle discrimination taking place behind them, studied the mailboxes and found a listing for Mr Frank Dumas in apartment 44. They went through the vestibule and up the steps. On the second floor, they passed a little girl who was sitting on the steps tightening her skates with a skate key.

'Hello,' she said.

'Hello,' Carella answered.

'Are you coming to my house?' she asked.

'Where's your house?'

'A pommin twenny-one.'

'No, sorry,' Carella said, smiling.

'I thought you was the insurance,' the little girl said, and went back to tightening her skates.

On the fourth-floor landing, they drew their guns. Apartment 44 was in the middle of the hall. They walked silently to the door, listened outside for a moment, and then flanked it. Carella nodded at Hawes, who braced himself for a flatfooted kick at the lock.

He was bringing back his knee when the shots came from within the apartment, shockingly loud, splintering the door.

15.

HAWES DROPPED AT the sound of the first shot, just as the splintered hole appeared in the wooden door. The slug whistled past his head as he fell flat to the floor, and then ricocheted off the wall behind him and went caroming at a crazy angle down the hallway just as the second shot erupted. The wood splintered again, and Carella winced as the slug tore its way across the narrow corridor, inches from his face where he stood to the left of the door, his gun pulled in tight against his chest, his head pulled down into his shoulders. On the floor, Hawes was scrambling away to the right of the door as the third shot came. The next four shots followed almost immediately, ripping wood from the door, ricocheting into the cracked ceiling overhead. He had counted seven shots, an empty automatic if the person inside was firing a certain type of .45. There was a pause. The man could be reloading. Or he could be firing another type of .45 with a magazine capacity of nine cartridges, or a Harrington & Richardson .22 with the same capacity, or . . . there was no time to run through a gun catalogue. He could be reloading, or simply waiting, or even carrying two guns – or he could at this moment be climbing out of the window. Carella took a deep breath. He backed off across the hallway, braced himself against the opposite wall, and unleashed the sole of his foot at the lock on the door.

The door sprang inward, and Carella followed it into a hail of bullets that came from the window. Hawes was immediately behind him. They both dropped flat to the worn linoleum inside the apartment, firing at the window where the figure of a man appeared in silhouette for just a moment, and then vanished. They got to their feet, and rushed across the room. Carella put his head outside the window, and then pulled it back at once as a shot sounded somewhere above him, and a piece of red brick spattered against his cheek.

'He's heading for the roof!' he shouted to Hawes, not turning to look, knowing that Hawes would take the steps up, and knowing that he himself would climb onto the fire-escape in pursuit within the next few moments. He reloaded his gun from the cartridge belt at his waist, and then stepped out onto the fire-escape. He fired a quick shot at the figure two storeys above him, and then began clambering up the iron-runged steps. The man above did not fire again. Instead, as he climbed, he began dropping a barrage of junk collected from the fire-escapes he passed: flower-pots, an iron, a child's toy truck, an old and battered suitcase, all of which crashed around Carella as he made his way steadily up each successive ladder. The barrage stopped when the man gained the roof. Three shots echoed on the still spring air. Hawes had reached the roof.

By the time Carella joined him, the man had leaped the area-way between the two buildings and was out of sight.

'He got away while I was reloading,' Hawes said.

Carella nodded, and then bolstered his .38.

When they got back to the squad-room Meyer was waiting with a report on Frank Dumas.

'No record,' he said, 'not in this city, at least. I'm waiting for word from the Feds.'

'That's too bad,' Carella said. 'It looked like a professional job.'

'Maybe he *is* a pro.'

'You just said he had no record.'

'How do we know Dumas is his right name?'

'The car was registered . . .'

'I talked to MVB a little more,' Meyer said. 'The car was registered only last month. He could have used an alias.'

'That wouldn't have tied with his driver's licence.'

'Since when do thieves worry about driver's licences?'

'Thieves are the most careful drivers in the world,' Carella said.

'I also checked the phone book. There are six listings for Frank Dumas. I'll bet you next month's salary against a *bagel* that Dumas is an alias he picked right out of the directory.'

'Maybe.'

'It's worth checking,' Meyer told them.

He also told Carella and Hawes that Detective Andy Parker's surveillance of a suspected shooting-gallery would be paid off this evening at 7.00 p.m. The lieutenant needed five men for the raid, and the names of Carella and Hawes were on the list. 'We're mustering here at six-thirty,' Meyer said.

'I'd planned to go home at six,' Carella answered.

'The best laid plans,' Meyer said, 'aft get screwed up.'

'Yeah.' Carella scratched his head. 'What do you want to do, Cotton? Go back to Fairview and talk to the landlady or somebody?'

'She ought to know who rented that apartment,' Hawes said.

'You had lunch yet?' Meyer asked.

'No.'

'Get something to eat first. The landlady'll wait.'

They had lunch in a diner near the precinct. Carella was wondering whether the lab would come up with anything positive on that switch-blade knife. He was also wondering why the killer had chosen to use a knife in the park when he obviously owned at least one gun.

'Do you think he saw us pulling up downstairs?' Carella asked.

'He must have. The way that stoop cleared, he'd have to be an idiot not to know we were cops.'

'This doughnut is stale,' Carella said. 'How's yours?'

'It's all right. Here, take half of it.'

'No, go ahead.'

'I won't be able to finish it, anyway.'

Thanks,' Carella said. He sliced Hawes' doughnut in half and began munching on it. 'That's better,' he said. He looked at his watch. 'We'd better get moving. He's got a head start on us already. If we can at least find out whether Dumas is his real name . . .'

'Just let me finish my tea,' Hawes said.

The landlady at 1137 Fairview Street wasn't happy to see cops, and she told them so immediately.

'There's always cops here,' she said. 'I'm fed up to here with cops.'

'That's too bad, lady,' Hawes said, 'but we've got to ask you some questions, anyway.'

'You always come around shooting, and then you ask questions later,' the landlady said angrily.

'Lady, the man in apartment forty-four began shooting first,' Hawes said.

'That's *your* story.'

'Who was he, do you know?'

'Who's going to pay for all that damage to the hallway, can you tell me that?'

'Not us,' Hawes said flatly. 'What's the man's name?'

'John Doe.'

'Come on, lady.'

'That's his name. That's the name he took the apartment under.'

'How long has he been living here?'

'Two months.'

'Did he pay his rent in cash or by cheque?'

'Cash.'

'Didn't you suspect John Doe might not be his real name? Especially since the name Frank Dumas is on his mailbox?'

'I'm not a cop,' the landlady said. 'It's not my job to *suspect* somebody who comes here to rent an apartment. He paid me a month in advance, and he didn't holler about the increase over the last tenant, or the four dollars for the television aerial, so why should I suspect him? I don't care if his name's John Doe or John D. Rockefeller, so long as he pays the rent and doesn't cause trouble.'

'But he's caused a little trouble, hasn't he?'

'*You're* the ones caused the trouble,' the landlady said. 'Coming here with your guns and shooting up the hallway. Do you know there was a little girl sitting on the steps while you were shooting? Do you know that?'

'The little girl was on the second floor, ma'am,' Carella said. 'And besides, we didn't expect shooting.'

'Then you don't know cops the way I do. The minute a cop arrives, there's shooting.'

'We'd like to go through Mr Doe's apartment,' Carella said.

'Then you'd better go get yourself a search warrant.'

'Come on, lady, break your heart,' Hawes said. 'You don't want us to go all the way downtown, do you?'

'I don't care where you go. If you want to search that apartment, you need a warrant. That's the law.'

'You know, of course, that your garbage cans are still on the sidewalk, don't you?' Carella said.

'Huh?'

'Your garbage cans. They're supposed to be taken in by noon. It's one-thirty now.'

'I'll take them in right away,' the landlady said. 'The damn trucks didn't *get* here until noon.'

'That's unfortunate,' Carella said, 'but taking them in now won't change the nature of the misdemeanour. There's a stiff fine involved, you know.'

'What is this? A shakedown?'

'That's exactly what it is, lady,' Hawes said. 'You don't really want us to go all the way downtown for a search warrant, do you?'

'Cops,' the landlady muttered, and she turned her back. 'Go ahead, look through the apartment. Try not to steal anything while you're up there.'

'We'll try,' Carella said, 'but it won't be easy.'

They began climbing the steps to the fourth floor. The same little girl was sitting on the second-floor landing, still adjusting her skates with the skate key.

'Hello,' she said.

'Hello,' Carella answered.

'Are you coming to my house?'

'Apartment twenty-one?' Carella asked.

'That's right.'

'No, I'm sorry.'

'I thought you was the insurance,' the little girl said, and went back to work on the skate.

The door to apartment 44 was open when they reached the fourth-floor landing. Carella's kick had sprung the lock, and the door stood ajar, knifing a wedge of sunlight into the otherwise dark hallway. They walked to the door and casually shoved it open.

A young woman turned swiftly from the dresser where she was going through the drawers. She was perhaps eighteen years old, her hair in curlers, wearing neither make-up nor lipstick, a faded pink robe thrown over her pyjamas.

'Well, hello,' Carella said.

The girl pulled a face, as if she were four years old and had been caught doing something that was strictly forbidden by her parents.

'You're cops, huh?' she said.

'That's right,' Hawes answered. 'What are you doing here, miss?'

'Looking around, that's all.'

'Just browsing, huh?' Carella said.

'Well, sort of, yes.'

'What's your name?'

'Cynthia.'

'Cynthia what?'

'I didn't take anything, mister,' Cynthia said. 'I just came in to look around, that's all. I live right down the hall. You can ask anybody.'

'What do you want us to ask them?'

'If I don't live right down the hall.'

Cynthia shrugged. Her face was getting more and more discouraged, crumbling slowly, the way a very little girl's face will steadily dissolve under the questioning of adults.

'What's your last name, Cynthia?'

'Reilly,' she said

'What are you doing in here, Cynthia?'

Cynthia shrugged.

'Stealing?'

'No!' she said. 'Hey, no! No, I swear to God.'

'Then what?'

'Just looking around.'

'Do you know the man who lives in this apartment?'

'No. I only saw him in the hall once or twice.'

'Do you know his name?'

'No.' Cynthia paused. 'I'm sick,' she said. 'I've got a bad cold. That's why I'm in the bathrobe. I couldn't go to work because I had a fever of a hundred and one point six.'

'So you decided to take a little walk, is that it?'

'Yes, that's it,' Cynthia said. She smiled because she thought at last the detectives were beginning to understand what she was doing in this apartment, but the detectives didn't smile back, and her face returned to its slow crumbling, as if she were ready to burst into tears at any moment.

'And you walked right in here, huh?'

'Only because I was curious.'

'About what?'

'The shooting.' She shrugged. 'Are you going to arrest me? I didn't take anything. I'll die if you take me to prison.' She paused and then blurted, 'I've got a fever!'

'Then you better get back to bed,' Carella said.

'You're letting me go?'

'Go on, get out of here.'

'Thanks,' Cynthia said quickly, and then vanished before they had a chance to change their minds.

Carella sighed. 'You want to take this room? I'll get the other.'

'Okay,' Hawes said. Carella went into the other room. Hawes began looking through the dresser Cynthia had already inspected. He was working on the second drawer when he heard the sound of roller skates in the hallway outside. He looked up as the little girl from the second-floor landing skated into the room.

'Hello,' she said.

'Hello,' Hawes answered.

'Did you just move in?'

'No.'

'Are you going someplace?'

'No.'

'Then why are you taking all your clothes out of the bureau?'

'They're not my clothes,' Hawes said.

'Then you shouldn't be doing that.'

'I guess not.'

'Then why are you?'

'Because I'm trying to find something.'

'What are you trying to find?'

'I'm trying to find the name of the man who lives in this apartment.'

'Oh,' the little girl said. She skated to the other side of the room, skated back, and then asked, 'Is his name in the bureau?'

'Not so far,' Hawes said.

'Do you think his name is in the bureau?'

'It might be. Here, do you see this?'

'It's a shirt,' the little girl said.

'That's right, but I mean here, inside the collar.'

'Those are numbers,' the little girl said. 'I can count to a hundred by tens, would you like to hear me?'

'Not right now,' Hawes said. 'Those numbers are a laundry mark,' Hawes said. 'We may be able to get the man's name by checking them out.'

'Gee,' the girl said and then immediately said, 'Ten, twenty, thirty, fifty . . .'

'Forty,' Hawes corrected.

'. . . *forty*, fifty, sixty, thirty . . .'

'Seventy.'

'I better start all over again. Ten, twenty . . .' She stopped and studied Hawes carefully for a moment. Then she said, 'You don't live here, do you?'

'No.'

'I thought you did at first. I thought maybe you just moved in or something.'

'No.'

'I thought maybe Petie had moved out.'

'No,' Hawes said. He put a pile of shirts onto the dresser and then reached into his back pocket for a tag.

'Why do you need a laundry mark to tell you what Petie's name is?' the little girl asked.

'Because that's the only way we . . .' Hawes paused. 'What did you say, honey?'

'I don't know. What did I say?'

'Something about . . . Petie?'

'Oh, yeah. Petie.'

'Is that his name?'

197

'Whose name?'

'The man who lives here,' Hawes said.

'I don't know. What does it say inside his shirts?'

'Well, never mind his shirts, honey. If you know his name, you can save us a lot of time.'

'Are you a bull?' the little girl asked.

'Now what makes you ask that?'

'My poppa says bulls stink.'

'Is Petie your poppa?'

The little girl began laughing. 'Petie? My poppa is Dave, that's who my poppa is.'

'Well . . . well, what about Petie?'

'What *about* Petie?'

'Is *that* his name?'

'I guess so. If that's what it says inside the shirts, then that must be his name.'

'Petie what?'

'What Petie what?'

'His second name. Petie what?'

'Peter Piper picked a peck of pickled peppers,' the girl said, and she began giggling. 'Do you know how to skate?'

'Yes. Honey, what's Petie's second name?'

'I don't know. *My* second name is Jane. Alice Jane Horowitz.'

'Did he ever *tell* you his second name?'

'Nooooo,' the girl said, drawing out the word cautiously.

'How do you know his first name?'

'Because he showed me how to use a skate key.'

'Yeah? Go ahead.'

'That's all. I was sitting on the steps, and the skate wouldn't open, and he was coming downstairs, and he said, 'Here, Petie'll fix that for you,' and then he fixed it, so that's how I know his name is Petie.'

'Thanks,' Hawes said.

The little girl studied him solemnly for a moment and then said, 'You *are* a bull, aren't you?'

The six bulls who met in the squad-room that night after dinner were not in the mood for a raid on a shooting-gallery. Carella and Meyer wanted to be home with their wives and children. Andy Parker had been trying to get to a movie for the past week, but instead he'd been involved in this surveillance. Bert Kling wanted to finish a book he was reading. Cotton Hawes wanted to be with Christine Maxwell. Lieutenant Byrnes had promised his wife he'd take her to visit her cousin in Bethtown. But nonetheless, the six detectives met in the squad-room and were briefed by Parker on the location and set-up of the apartment he'd had under surveillance for the past three weeks.

'They're shooting up in there, that's for sure,' Parker said. 'But I think something unusual happened last night. A guy came with a suitcase for the first time since I've been on the plant. And he left without it. I think a big delivery was made, and if we hit them tonight, we may be able to nab them with the junk.'

'It's worth a try,' Byrnes said. The least we'll net is a few hopheads.'

'Who'll be out on the street again by tomorrow,' Carella said.

'Depending on how much they're holding,' Hawes said.

'Someday, this city is going to get some realistic laws about narcotics,' Carella said.

'*Aluvai*,' Meyer put in.

'Let's get moving,' Byrnes said.

They travelled in one sedan because they wanted to arrive together, wanted to get out of the car and hit the apartment before the telegraphing grapevine was able to warn of the presence of cops in the neighbourhood. As it was, their margin was a close one. The instant they pulled up in front of the tenement, a man sitting on the front stoop ran inside. Parker ran after him into the hallway and collared the man as he was knocking on a ground-floor door. Parker hit him only once and without hesitation, a sharp rabbit punch at the base of the roan's neck.

'Who's there?' somebody inside the apartment called.

'Me,' Parker said, and by that time the other five detectives were in the hallway.

'Who's me?' the voice inside said, and Parker kicked in the door.

Nobody was shooting up that night. The apartment may have been filled with addicts on the other nights of Parker's surveillance, but tonight there was only a fat old man in an undershirt, a fat old woman in a housedress, and a young kid in a T shirt and dungarees. The trio was standing at the kitchen table, and they were working over what seemed to be eight million pounds of pure heroin. They were cutting it with sugar, diluting the junk for later sale to addicts from here to San Francisco and back again. The old man reached for a Luger in the drawer of the table the moment the door burst inward. He changed his mind about firing the gun because he was suddenly looking at an army of cops armed with everything from riot guns to Thompsons.

'Surprise!' Parker said, and the old man answered, 'Drop dead, you cop bastard.'

Parker, naturally, hit him.

The men got back to the squad-room at about eight-thirty. They all had coffee together, and then Cotton Hawes drove uptown to Christine Maxwell's apartment.

16.

HE LOVED TO watch her strip. He told himself that all he was, after all, was a tired businessman who couldn't afford the price of a musical comedy on his meagre salary, who chose to watch Christine Maxwell rather than a stageful of chorus girls – but he knew he was not the ordinary *voyeur*, knew there was something rather more personal in his joy. He *was* tired, true, and perhaps he *was* only a businessman whose business happened to be crime and punishment. But sitting on the couch across the room from her, a glass of Scotch in his big hands, his bare feet resting on a throw pillow, he watched Christine as she took off her blouse, and he felt something more than simple anticipation. He wanted to hold her naked in his arms, wanted to make love to her, but she was more to him than a promised bed partner; she provided for him a haven, she was someone to whom he returned at the end of a long and difficult day, someone he was always happy to see and who, in turn, always made him feel welcome and wanted.

She reached behind her now and unclasped her brassière, releasing the full globes of her breasts, and then carrying the bra to the chair over whose back she had draped the blouse. She folded the bra in two over the blouse, unzipped her skirt and stepped out of it, folded that onto the seat of the chair, and then stepped out of her half-slip and put that on top of the skirt. She took off her black, high-heeled pumps and put them to one side of the chair, and then ungartered her stockings, rolled them off her legs, and put those on the chair, too. She smiled unselfconsciously at him in the dimness of the room, removed her panties, threw them onto the chair and then, wearing only her garter belt, walked to where he was stretched out on the couch.

'Take that off, too,' he said.

'No,' she said, 'I like to leave something for you.'

'Why?'

'I don't know.' She grinned and kissed him on the mouth. 'I don't like to make it too easy.' She kissed him again. 'What'd you do today?'

'Shot it out with a killer,' he said.

'Did you get him?'

'No.'

'Then what?'

'Went back to talk to his landlady.'

'Any help?'

'Not much. A little girl gave us the guy's first name, though.'

'Good.'

'Petie,' he said. 'How many Peties do you think there are in this city?'

'Two million, I would suspect.'

'Your mouth is nice tonight,' he said, and he kissed her again.

'Mmmm.'

'We went on a dope raid just before I came here. Got a whole suitcase of the stuff, about forty pounds of it, worth something like twelve million bucks.'

'Did you bring some with you?'

'I didn't know you were a junkie,' Hawes murmured.

'I'm a *secret* junkie,' Christine whispered in his ear. 'That's the worst kind.'

'I know.' He paused, grinning in the darkness. 'I've got a few sticks of marijuana in my desk at the office. I'll bring them next time I come.'

'Marijuana,' Christine said. 'That's kid stuff.'

'You're on heroin, huh?'

'Absolutely.' She bit his ear and then said, 'Maybe we can work out something here. You must go on a lot of those raids, don't you?'

'Every now and then. Usually, we leave them to the Narcotics Squad.'

'But you *do* get a certain amount of heroin, don't you?'

'Sure,' Hawes said.

'Maybe we can trade,' Christine said.

'Maybe.' He kissed her on the neck and said, 'Take off your pants.'

'My pants *are* off,' she answered.

'Your thing then, your garter belt.'

'You do it.'

He pulled her to him, his hands going behind her back to the clasps on the flimsy garment. He frowned suddenly and said, 'Now, what the hell?'

'Yes?'

'I thought of something.'

'What?'

'I don't know. It went in my mind, and then right out again. That's funny, isn't it?'

'Do you want me to help you with that?'

'No, I can do it.' He frowned again, 'That's funny, I . . . what are you doing with this thing on, anyway?'

'What?' Christine said, puzzled.

'Well, how . . . ?' He shook his head, 'Never mind,' he said, and he unclasped the garter belt and threw it across the room at the chair, missing.

'Now it's on the floor,' Christine said.

'You want me to go pick it up?'

'No. You stay right here.'

She kissed him, but his mouth was tight and she touched his face in the darkness and felt the frown still there, covering it like a mask.

'What is it?' she asked.

'Must be that guy today. Petie. Whatever his name is.'

'What about him?'

'I don't know.' He hesitated. 'Something . . . I just . . . maybe not him. Something, though.'

'Something about what?'

'I don't *know*. But something just . . . just popped into my mind, and I thought all at once, *Of course!* And then the thing, went away and . . . something . . . something with the work . . . something with murder.'

'Then it *must* be that man today. The one you were shooting at.'

'Sure, it must be, but . . .' He shook his head. 'I'll be damned, to just run out of my mind like that.' He pulled her close and kissed her throat, and then ran his hand down her thigh and then sat up suddenly and said, 'The . . . the . . . the . . .'

'What?' she said. 'What is it?'

'What do you take off?' he blurted.

'What?'

'Come on, Christine!' he said angrily, wanting her to understand immediately, and annoyed when she did not.

'What *is* it?'

'*First!*' he said. 'What do you take off *first?*'

'When? What are you . . . ?'

'Does anybody wear pants *under* a garter belt? Does any woman?'

'Well, no, how could they?'

'Then how the hell . . . ?'

'Unless . . . well, I suppose . . .'

'Unless what?'

'Unless the panties were very brief. But still, it would be terribly awkward, Cotton. I don't see why any woman would . . .'

'They weren't!'

'What?'

'Brief. They weren't. And, dammit, the garter belt was on the chair!'

'What garter belt! It's on the floor, Cotton. You just threw it there yourself a few min . . .'

'Not yours! Irene's!' he shouted, and he rose from the couch suddenly.

'Who?'

'Irene Thayer! Her garter belt was on that chair with the rest of her clothes, but she was wearing her pants, Christine! Now how the hell did she manage that?'

'The suicide, do you mean? The one you were working on last month?'

'Suicide, my foot! How'd she manage to get that garter belt off without taking off her pants first, would you mind telling me?'

'I . . . I don't know,' Christine said. 'Maybe she got undressed and then . . . then felt chilly or something, and put the panties on again. Really, she could have . . .'

206

'Or maybe somebody put them on *for* her! Somebody who didn't know the first thing about dressing or undressing a woman!' He looked at her wildly and then nodded and then punched his fist into the open palm of his other hand. 'Where are my shoes?' he said.

Too much has been said about the guilt complex of the American people. Too much has been said about the Puritan heritage, and a culture seemingly designed to encourage all sorts of anxiety. Hawes didn't know whether the average American male carried guilt around in him like a stone, nor did he much give a damn about the average American male on the night he went to make his arrest. He did know that a guilty criminal is an American who *is* carrying guilt in him like a stone, and he further knew he didn't have a chance in hell of cracking a case that was already in the Open File unless he made use of that guilt. There were probably a hundred easy explanations for why Irene Thayer was found dead with her panties on and her garter belt off. Christine had provided one at the drop of a hat, and a clever murderer could possibly provide another dozen if pressed only slightly. So Hawes didn't go to the house in Riverhead with the idea of thrashing out the correct procedure for removing a woman's undergarments. He went there with a lie as big as the house itself, a lie designed to bring guilt to the surface immediately. He went to that house to make an arrest, and everything in his manner indicated he knew all the facts of the case and wasn't ready to listen to any nonsense. As a start, he rapped on the door of the house with his drawn .38.

He waited in the darkness. He would wait another two minutes, and then he would shoot the lock off the door. He didn't have to wait nearly that long. He heard footsteps approaching the door, and then the door opened and Amos Barlow said, 'Yes?' and Hawes thrust the gun at him and said, 'Get your hat, Mr Barlow. It's all over.'

'What?' Barlow said. A look of complete astonishment crossed his face. He stared out at Hawes with his eyes opened wide.

'You heard me. It's finished. We just got a lab report.'

'What? What lab report? What are you talking about?'

'I'm talking about the fingerprints on the glass you washed and put in the kitchen cabinet,' Hawes lied. 'I'm talking about the murder of your own brother and Irene Thayer. Now get your goddamn hat because this has been a long day, and I'm tired, and I'm just liable to shoot and end it right here and now.'

He waited in the darkness with the gun poised, waited with his heart pounding inside his chest because he didn't know whether or not Barlow would call his bluff. If he did call it, if he said he didn't know what Hawes was talking about, what glass? what kitchen cabinet? what prints? if he did that, Hawes knew there wasn't a chance in hell of ever cracking the case. It would rot in the Open File for ever.

In a very soft voice, Barlow said, 'I thought I'd washed it.'

'You did,' Hawes said quickly, 'You missed a print near the bottom of the glass.'

Barlow nodded, and then sighed.

'I thought I'd been very careful,' he said. 'I went over

the place very carefully.' He shook his head. 'Did you . . . have you known this very long?'

'The lab was backed up with work. We just got the report tonight.'

'Because I thought . . . I thought when you were here the last time looking for the film, I thought that was the end of it. I thought you'd close the case after that.'

'What *did* you do with the film, Mr Barlow?'

'I burned it. I realized it had been a mistake, taking it like that, and I waited a long time before deciding to get rid of it. But . . . I wanted something of Tommy. Do you know? I wanted something to remind me of Tommy.' He shook his head. 'I burned it two days before you came looking for it. I thought that was the end of it, when you came around that time. I thought the case would be closed.'

'Why'd you do it, Mr Barlow?' Hawes asked. 'Why'd you kill them?'

Barlow stared up at him for a moment, a slight man with a lopsided stance, a cane in his right hand. And for that moment, Hawes felt an enormous sympathy for him; he looked at Barlow standing in the doorway of the house he had bought with his brother and tried to understand what had pushed this man into doing murder.

'Why'd you do it?' he asked again.

And Barlow, staring at Hawes, and through Hawes, and past him to a night long ago in April, said simply, The idea just came to me,' and Hawes put the handcuffs onto his wrists.

The idea just came to me. You have to understand that I didn't go up there with the idea of killing them. I didn't even know Irene Thayer existed, you understand, so I couldn't have planned to kill them. You have to realize that. Tommy told me that morning that he had a surprise for me, and he gave me an address and told me to come there on my lunch hour. I go to lunch every day at twelve-thirty. I could hardly wait to know what Tommy's surprise was. I could hardly wait for lunch that day.

So at twelve-thirty I came down from my office and I took a cab uptown to the address he had given me. 1516 South Fifth Street. That was the address. Apartment 1A. That's where I went. I walked upstairs, and I rang the bell and Tommy opened the door with a big smile on his face, he was a happy-go-lucky person, you know, always laughing, and he asked me to come in, and then he took me into the living room, and the girl was there.

Irene.

Irene Thayer.

He looked at me and he said, 'Irene, this is my brother, Amos,' and then with the smile still on his face he said to me, 'Amos, this is Irene Thayer,' and I was reaching for her hand to shake hands with her when he said, 'We're getting married next month.'

I couldn't believe him, do you know? I hadn't even <u>heard</u>

about this girl, and now he'd invited me to this strange apartment on South Fifth and he'd introduced her and told me he was going to marry her next month, and all without ever having even told me he was serious about anybody. I mean, I'm his brother. He could have at least told me.

They . . . they had two bottles of whisky there. Tommy said he had bought them to celebrate. He poured out some whisky, and we drank to the coming marriage, and all the while I was thinking why hadn't he told me before this, why hadn't he told his own brother? We're . . . we were very close, you know. It was Tommy who took care of me after my mother and father died, he was like a father to me, I swear it, there was real love between us, real love. And while we drank, while I was all the time wondering why he hadn't told me about this Irene Thayer, they began to explain that Irene was married and that she would be leaving for Reno and that as soon as she got her divorce Tommy was going to join her there and they planned to spend their honeymoon out West, and then maybe Tommy would take a job out there, he wasn't so sure, but he had heard there were a great many opportunities in California. He might, he said, try to get something in the picture business. He was always fooling around with film, you know, him and this fellow who worked at his place with him.

So we drank, and I began to realize that not only was he getting married to this strange girl I'd just met, but also he was planning on moving out, maybe living in California permanently, after we'd just bought a house for ourselves, well not just that minute, but we'd only been in the new house less than a year, and here he was talking of leaving it, of living in California, all the way on the other end of the country. I began to feel a little sick, and I excused myself and went into the bathroom, feeling nauseated, sick to my stomach, you know, and I looked in the medicine cabinet to see if there was some Alka-Seltzer or something, anything to quiet my stomach, and that was when I saw the sleeping pills, and I guess that was when I got the idea.

I guess so, anyway. I'm not sure. I mean, I don't think I knew then that I was going to turn on the gas or anything, but I _did_ know I was going to put the – pills in their drinks, maybe I thought they'd die _that_ way, do you know what I mean, from an overdose of sleeping pills. When I came out, I had the bottle of pills in my pocket. There were four pills in the bottle. Tommy poured fresh drinks, and I went into the kitchen with them, to put water in them, you know, we were drinking Scotch and water, and that was when I put the pills into their glasses, two pills in each glass, I figured that would be enough to put them to sleep, or maybe to kill them, I don't know what I figured. The pills worked very fast. I was glad they did because my lunch hour was almost over, and I've never been late in all the time I've worked for Anderson and Loeb, never late getting to work in the morning, and not coming back from lunch, either. They were both asleep in maybe fifteen minutes, and I looked at them, and I realized they weren't dead, only asleep, and I guess, yes, that must have been when, yes, I guess that was when I decided that I would have to kill them because, I don't know, because I didn't want Tommy to marry this girl and go to live all the way in California, yes, I suppose that was when I decided to turn on the gas.

I carried them into the bedroom and put them on the bed, and then I saw the typewriter on the stand alongside the bed, and I typed up the note on the machine and put it on the dresser. I don't know why I misspelled the word 'ourselves.' I think it was just a mistake I made, because I don't know how to type, I just pecked the note out with two fingers, but there wasn't any eraser in the room, and besides I thought the mistake made the note look more genuine, so I left it there. I took off Tommy's watch to hold the note down on the dresser, and that was when I got the idea of taking off their clothes. I guess I wanted to make it look as if this had been a love nest, do you know, as if they had just done it, do you know? I mean, before they turned on the gas. So I took off all their clothes, and folded them on the chairs, I tried to make it look the way I thought it would look if they had really taken off their own clothes before doing it. Then I went around the apartment and wiped everything I could remember touching, but I couldn't remember what I'd touched and what I hadn't, so I just wiped everything, with my handkerchief. I found the film in the living room while I was wiping the things off in there. It had Tommy's name on the can, and I remember meeting his friend one time, and I remembered they'd made some movies together, so I put the reel in my coat pocket.

Then I took the whisky bottles into the bedroom, and I opened the second one to make it look as if they'd been drinking a lot, and I spilled it out on the rug to make it look as if they'd got real drunk before turning on the gas, but I still hadn't turned it on, even though the idea was in my head all the time, I knew I was going to do it, but I still hadn't turned it on yet. While I was in the bedroom with the whisky bottles, I looked at the two of them on the bed, and it began bothering me, the two of them on the bed the way they were. I kept thinking about them all the while I was in the kitchen washing out the glasses. I washed and dried all three glasses, and I left two of them in the sink to make it look as if they'd been drinking alone together, and I put the third glass back in the cabinet where all the other glasses were. I thought I'd wiped them all clean. But I guess your lab has ways of finding out, it was silly of me to think they wouldn't find out, with their microscopes and all. But all the while I was washing the glasses, I kept thinking of them on the bed there, and it kept bothering me that they would be found undressed even though

214

I wanted it to look like love. So I went back into the bedroom, and I put their underwear back on, Tommy's and the girl's. I would have put on her . . . her brassiere, but . . . I . . . I didn't know how. So I . . . I did what I could. Then I stood in the doorway and looked into the room for a minute to see if it still looked like love, and I decided that it did, and that was when I went into the kitchen and turned on the gas, and left the apartment.

When the stenographer delivered the typed confession Amos Barlow signed it and went limping out of the room with a patrolman who took him downstairs to the detention cells where he would be kept overnight until his arraignment the next morning. They watched him as he limped out of the squad-room. They could hear the sound of his cane on the iron-runged steps leading to the downstairs level. They listened to it without a sense of triumph, without even a sense of completion.

'You fellows want some coffee?' Miscolo asked, standing just outside the door of the Clerical Office.

'No, thanks, none for me,' Carella said.

'Cotton? Some tea?'

'Thanks, Alf. No.'

The men were silent. The clock on the wall read ten minutes to one. Outside the grilled windows of the squad-room, a light, early morning rain had begun to fall.

Carella sighed heavily and put on his jacket. 'I was just sitting here and wondering how many people commit murder on the spur of the moment, and get away with it. I was just wondering.'

'Plenty,' Hawes said.

Carella sighed again. 'You got any brothers, Cotton?'

'No.'

'Neither have I. How can a man kill his own brother?'

'He didn't want to lose him,' Hawes said.

'He lost him,' Carella answered flatly, and then he sighed again and said, 'Come on, I'll buy you a beer. You want a beer?'

'All right,' Hawes said.

They went down the corridor together. Outside the Clerical Office, they both stopped to say good night to Miscolo. As they came down the iron-runged steps to the first floor, Carella said, 'What time are you coming in tomorrow?'

'I thought I'd get in a little early,' Hawes said.

'Trying for a line on Petie?'

'He's still with us, you know.'

'I know. Anyway, Bert thinks he's got a lead on that numbers bank. We may be hitting it tomorrow, and that'll shoot the whole damn afternoon. Be a good idea to get in early.'

'Maybe we ought to skip the beer.'

'I'd just as soon, if it's okay with you,' Carella said.

It had begun raining harder by the time they came out into the street.

LADY, LADY I DID IT!

This is for Henry Morrison

1.

PATTERNS

The pattern of October sunlight filtering past barred and grilled windows to settle in an amber splash on a scarred wooden floor. Shadows merge with the sun splash – the shadows of tall men in shirt sleeves; this is October, but the squad room is hot and Indian summer is dying slowly.

A telephone rings.

There is the sound of a city beyond those windows. The sudden shriek in unison of children let out from school, the pedlar behind his cart – 'Hot dogs, orange drink' – the sonorous rumble of buses and automobiles, the staccato click of high-heeled pumps, the empty rattle of worn roller skates on chalked sidewalks. Sometimes the city goes suddenly still. You can almost hear a heartbeat. But this silence is a part of the city noise, a part of the pattern. In the stillness, sometimes a pair of lovers will walk beneath the windows of the squad room, and their words will drift upward in a whispered fade. A cop will look up from his typewriter. A city is going by outside.

Patterns.

A detective is standing at the water cooler. He holds the cone-shaped paper cup in his hand, waits until it is filled, and then tilts his head back to drink. A .38 Police Special is resting in a holster which is clipped to the lefthand side of his belt. A typewriter is going across the room, hesitantly, fumblingly, but reports must be

1

typed, and in triplicate; cops do not have private secretaries.

Another phone rings.

'87th Squad, Carella.'

There is a timelessness to this room. There are patterns overlapping patterns, and they combine to form the classic design that is police work. The design varies slightly from day to day. There is an office routine, and an investigatory routine, and very rarely does a case come along which breaks the classic pattern. Police work is like a bullfight. There is always a ring, and always a bull, and always a matador and picadors and chulos, and always, too, the classic music of the arena, the opening trumpet playing *La Virgen de la Macarena*, the ritual music throughout, announcing the various stages of a contest which is not a contest at all. Usually the bull dies. Sometimes, but only when he is an exceptionally brave bull, he is spared. But for the most part he dies. There is no real sport involved here because the outcome is assured before the mock combat begins. The bull will die. There are, to be sure, some surprises within the framework of the sacrificial ceremony – a matador will be gored, a bull will leap the *barrera* – but the pattern remains set and unvaried, the classic ritual of blood.

It is the same with police work.

There are patterns to this room. There is a timelessness to these men in this place doing the work they are doing.

They are all deeply involved in the classic ritual of blood.

'87th Squad, Detective Kling.'

Bert Kling, youngest man on the squad, cradled the telephone receiver between his shoulder and his ear, leaned over the typewriter, and began erasing a mistake. He had misspelled 'apprehended'.

'Who?' he said into the phone. 'Oh, sure, Dave, put her on.' He waited while Dave Murchison, manning the switchboard in the muster room downstairs, put the call through.

From the water cooler, Meyer Meyer filled another paper cup and said, 'He's always got a girl on the phone. The girls in this city, they got nothing else to do, they call Detective Kling and ask him how the crime is going today.' He shook his head.

Kling shushed him with an outstretched palm. 'Hello, honey,' he said into the phone.

'Oh, it's *her*,' Meyer said knowingly.

Steve Carella, completing a call at his own desk, hung up and said, 'It's who?'

'Who do you think? Kim Novak, that's who. She calls here every day. She wants to know should she buy some stock in Columbia Pictures.'

'Will you guys please shut up?' Kling said. Into the phone, he said, 'Oh, the usual. The clowns are at it again.'

Claire Townsend, on the other end of the line, said, 'Tell them to stop kibitzing. Tell them we're in love.'

'They already know that,' Kling said. 'Listen, are we all set for tonight?'

'Yes, but I'll be a little late.'

'Why?'

'I've got a stop to make after school.'

'What kind of a stop?' Kling asked.

'I have to pick up some texts. Stop being suspicious.'

'Why don't you stop being a schoolgirl?' Kling asked. 'Why don't you marry me?'

'When?'

'Tomorrow.'

3

'I can't tomorrow. I'll be very busy tomorrow. Besides, the world needs social workers.'

'Never mind the world. *I* need a wife. I've got holes in my socks.'

'I'll darn them when I get there tonight,' Claire said.

'Well, actually,' Kling whispered, 'I had something else in mind.'

'He's whispering,' Meyer said to Carella.

'Shut up,' Kling said.

'Every time he gets to the good part, he whispers,' Meyer said, and Carella burst out laughing.

'This is getting impossible,' Kling said, sighing. 'Claire, I'll see you at six-thirty, OK?'

'Seven's more like it,' she said. 'I'm wearing a disguise, by the way. So your nosy landlady won't recognize me when she peeks into the hall.'

'What do you mean? What kind of a disguise?'

'You'll see.'

'No, come on. What are you wearing?'

'Well . . . I've got on a white blouse,' Claire said, 'open at the throat, you know, with a strand of very small pearls. And a black skirt, very tight, with a wide black belt, the one with the silver buck . . .'

As she spoke, Kling smiled unconsciously, forming a mental picture of her in the university phone booth. He knew she would be leaning over very close to the mouthpiece. She was five feet seven inches tall, and the booth would seem too small for her. Her hair, as black as sin, would be brushed back from her face, her brown eyes intensely alive as she spoke, perhaps with a faint smile on her mouth. The full white blouse would taper to a narrow waist, the black skirt hanging on wide hips, dropping in a straight line over her thighs and her long legs.

4

'. . . no stockings because the weather's so damn hot,' Claire said, 'and high-heeled black pumps, and that's it.'

'So, where's the disguise?'

'Well, I bought a new bra,' Claire whispered.

'Oh?'

'You should see what it does for me, Bert.' She paused. 'Do you love me, Bert?'

'You know I do,' he said.

'She just asked him does he love her,' Meyer said, and Kling pulled a face.

'Tell me,' Claire whispered.

'I can't right now.'

'Will you tell me later?'

'Mmmm,' Kling said, and he glanced apprehensively at Meyer.

'Wait until you see this bra,' Claire said.

'Yes, I'm looking forward to it,' Kling said, watching Meyer, phrasing his words carefully.

'You don't sound very interested,' Claire said.

'I am. It's a little difficult, that's all.'

'It's called "Abundance",' Claire said.

'What is?'

'The bra.'

'That's nice,' Kling said.

'What are they doing up there? Standing around your desk and breathing down your neck?'

'Well, not exactly, but I think I'd better say good-bye now. I'll see you at six-thirty, honey.'

'Seven,' Claire corrected.

'OK. 'Bye, doll.'

'Abundance,' she whispered, and she hung up. Kling put the receiver back into the cradle.

'OK,' he said, 'I'm going to call the telephone company and ask them to put in a phone booth.'

5

'You're not supposed to make private calls on the city's time,' Carella said, and he winked at Meyer.

'I didn't *make* this call. I *received* it. Also, a man is entitled to a certain amount of privacy, even if he works with a bunch of horny bastards. I don't see why I can't talk to my fiancée without—'

'He's sore,' Meyer said. 'He called her his fiancée instead of his girl. Look, talk to her. Call her back and tell her you sent all us gorillas out of the room and now you can talk to her. Go ahead.'

'Go to hell,' Kling said. Angrily, he turned back to his typewriter, forgetting that he'd been in the middle of an erasure. He began typing again and then realized he was overscoring what he'd already typed. Viciously, he ripped the almost-completed report from the machine. 'See what you made me do?' he shouted impotently. 'Now I have to start all over again!' He shook his head despairingly, took a white, a blue, and a yellow Detective Division Report from his top drawer, separated the three sheets with carbon paper, and began typing again, banging the keys with a vengeance.

Steve Carella walked to the window and looked down to the street below. He was a tall man, and he stood in slender deceptive grace by the meshed grille, the late afternoon sunlight washing over him, his angular body giving no clue to the destructive power in his muscular arms and chest. In profile, he looked slightly oriental, the sun limning high cheekbones and eyes that slanted curiously downward.

'This time of day,' he said, 'I feel like going to sleep.'

Meyer looked at his watch. 'That's because we'll be relieved soon,' he said.

Across the room, Kling kept battering the typewriter keys.

There were sixteen detectives, not counting Lieutenant Byrnes, attached to the 87th Squad. Of those sixteen, four were usually on special assignment somewhere or other, leaving a twelve-man squad, which was divided into four duty sections of three-man teams. Unlike patrolmen, the detectives worked out their own schedules, and the pattern, though arbitrary, was consistent. There were two shifts, the eight a.m. to six p.m. and the six p.m. to eight a.m. The graveyard shift was the longer of the two, and none of the detectives particularly enjoyed it, but they nonetheless drew it every fourth day. They were also 'off duty' every fourth day, a term which didn't mean very much since all cops are technically 'on duty' twenty-four hours a day, every day of the year. Besides, most of the detectives on the squad found that they *needed* those off-duty days to accomplish vital legwork. The schedule was a complicated thing to keep, because the special-assignment cops kept changing, and because Lineup was held every day from Monday to Thursday and the detectives were required to put in appearances there in order to acquaint themselves with the men who were committing crimes throughout the city, and because detectives had to appear in court to testify at trials, and because – the schedule was a difficult one to keep. Teams kept changing, men kept coming and going, there were often eight cops in the squad room instead of three. The schedule was posted each week, but following it was impossible.

In any case, one thing remained constant. The relieving detectives, by unwritten agreement, always arrived at the squad room fifteen minutes before the hour, a carry-over from their patrolman days. The graveyard shift, not due until six p.m., would undoubtedly straggle in any time between five-thirty and five forty-five.

It was five-fifteen p.m. when the telephone rang.

Meyer Meyer lifted the receiver and said '87th Squad. Detective Meyer.' He moved a pad into place on his desk. 'Yeah, go ahead,' he said. He began writing on the pad. 'Yep,' he said. He wrote down an address. 'Yep.' He continued writing. 'Yep, right away.' He hung up. 'Steve, Bert,' he said, 'you want to take this?'

'What is it?' Carella asked.

'Some nut just shot up a bookstore on Culver Avenue.' Meyer said. 'There're three people lying dead on the floor.'

The crowd had already gathered around the bookshop. A sign out front read 'GOOD BOOKS, GOOD READING'. There were two uniformed cops on the sidewalk, and a squad car was pulled up to the kerb across the street. The people pulled back instinctively when they heard the wail of the siren on the police sedan. Carella got out first, slamming the door behind him. He waited for Kling to come around the car, and then both men started for the shop. At the door, the patrolman said. 'Lot of dead people in there, sir.'

'When'd you get here?'

'Few minutes ago. We were just cruising when we took the squeal. We called back the minute we saw what it was.'

'Know how to keep a timetable?'

'Yes, sir.'

'Come along and keep it then.'

'Yes, sir.'

They started into the shop. Not three feet from the door they saw the first body. The man was partially slumped against one of the bookstalls, partially sprawled on the floor. He was wearing a blue seersucker suit, and

8

his hand was still holding a book, and a line of blood had run down his arm, and stained his sleeve, and continued down over the hand holding the book. Kling looked at him and knew instantly that this was going to be a bad one. Just how bad, he did not yet realize.

'Here's another one,' Carella said.

The second body was some ten feet away from the first, another man coatless, his head twisted and fitting snugly into the angle formed by the bookstall and the floor. As they approached, he moved his head slightly, trying to raise it from its uncomfortable position. A new flow of blood spilled on to his shirt collar. He dropped his head again. The patrolman, his throat parched, his voice containing something like awe, said, 'He's alive.'

Carella stooped down beside the man. The man's neck had been ripped open by the force of the bullet which had struck him. Carella looked at torn flesh and muscle, and for an instant he closed his eyes, the action coming as swiftly as the clicking shutter of a camera, the eyes opening again at once, a tight hard mask claiming his face.

'Did you call for a meat wagon?' he asked.

'The minute I got here,' the patrolman said.

'Good.'

'There are two others,' a voice said.

Kling turned away from the dead man in the seersucker suit. The man who'd spoken was a small, birdlike man with a bald head. He stood crouched against one of the bookstalls, his hand to his mouth. He was wearing a shabby brown sweater open over a white shirt. There was abject terror on his face and in his eyes. He was sobbing low, muted sobs which accompanied the tears that flowed from his eyes, oddly channelling themselves along either side of his nose. As Kling approached him,

9

he thought, Two others. Meyer said there were three. But it's four.

'Are you the owner of this shop?' he asked.

'Yes,' the man said. 'Please look at the others. Back there. Is an ambulance coming? A wild man, a wild man. Look at the others, please. They may be alive. One of them is a woman. Please look at them.'

Kling nodded and walked to the back of the shop. He found the third man bent double over one of the counters, an open book beside him; he had undoubtedly been browsing when the shots were loosed. The man was dead, his mouth open, his eyes staring sightlessly. Unconsciously, Kling's hands went to the man's eyelids. Gently he closed them.

The woman lay on the floor beside him.

She was wearing a red blouse.

She had undoubtedly been carrying an armful of books when the bullets took her. She had fallen to the floor, and the books had fallen around her and upon her. One book lay just under her extended right hand. Another, open like a tent, covered her face and her black hair. A third leaned against her curving hip. The red blouse had pulled free from the woman's black skirt as she had fallen. The skirt had risen over the backs of her long legs. One leg was bent, the other rigid and straight. A black high-heeled pump lay several inches away from one naked foot. The woman wore no stockings.

Kling knelt beside her. Oddly, the titles of the books registered on his mind: *Patterns of Culture* and *The Sane Society* and *Interviewing: Its Principles and Methods*. He saw suddenly that the blouse was not a red blouse at all. A corner that had pulled free from the black skirt showed white. There were two enormous holes in the girl's side, and the blood had poured steadily from those wounds,

10

staining the white blouse a bright red. A string of tiny pearls had broken when she had fallen, and the pearls lay scattered on the floor now, tiny luminescent islands in the sticky coagulation of her blood. He felt pain looking at her. He reached for the book which had fallen open over her face. He lifted the book, and the pain suddenly became a very personal, very involved thing.

'Oh my Jesus Christ!' he said.

There was something in his voice which caused Steve Carella to run towards the back of the shop immediately. And then he heard Kling's cry, a single sharp anguished cry that pierced the dust-filled, cordite-stinking air of the shop.

'Claire!'

He was holding the dead girl in his arms when Carella reached him. His hands and his face were covered with Claire Townsend's blood, and he kissed her lifeless eyes and her nose and her throat, and he kept murmuring over and over again, 'Claire, Claire,' and Steve Carella would remember that name and the sound of Kling's voice as long as he lived.

2.

DETECTIVE-LIEUTENANT PETER Byrnes was having dinner with his wife and his son when Carella called him. Harriet, who had been a policeman's wife for a long time, knew immediately that it was someone from the squad. The men of the 87th called only when the family was in the middle of dinner. No, that wasn't quite true. They sometimes called in the middle of the night, when everyone was asleep.

She said, 'I'll get it,' and she rose from the table and walked into the foyer, where the telephone rested on the hall table. When she recognized Carella's voice, she immediately smiled. She could still remember clearly a time not so long ago when Carella had been very personally involved in a situation that had threatened the entire Byrnes family. While investigating the case, Carella had been shot in Grover Park by a narcotics pedlar, and she could remember that long Christmas Eve vigil when it seemed he would die. He had lived, and now when she heard his voice she smiled immediately and unconsciously, as if constantly pleased and surprised and grateful for his presence.

'Harriet,' he said, 'may I talk to Pete, please?'

There was an undertone of urgency to his voice. She said simply, 'Of course, Steve,' and walked instantly from the phone and into the dining room. She said, 'It's Steve.'

Byrnes pushed back his chair. He was a compact man who moved economically, his movements seeming to be a direct translation of thought into energy. The chair went back, his napkin came down on to the table, he moved briskly and rapidly to the phone, picked up the receiver, spoke the instant it was close to his mouth.

'Yeah, Steve?'

'Pete, I . . . I . . .'

'What's the matter?'

'Pete . . .'

'What is it, Steve?'

There was a silence on the other end of the line. For a moment Byrnes thought Carella was . . . crying? He held the phone close to his ear, listening, waiting. A slight tic began near his left eye.

'Pete, I'm . . . I'm at a bookshop on Culver and . . . and . . .'

There was a pause. Byrnes waited. He could hear Carella asking someone where the bookshop was. He could hear a muffled voice giving Carella the information.

'North Forty-ninth,' Carella said into the phone. 'The name is The Brow . . . The Browser. That's the name of the shop, Pete.'

'All right, Steve,' Byrnes said. Still he waited.

'Pete, I think you better come down here.'

'All right, Steve,' Byrnes said. Still he waited.

'Pete, I . . . I can't handle this right now. Kling is . . . Pete, this is a terrible thing.'

'What happened?' Byrnes asked gently.

'Somebody came in . . . and . . . sh . . . shot up the store. Kl . . . Kl . . . Kl . . . Kl . . .'

He could not get the word out. The stammering filled the line like subdued machine-gun fire. *Click, click, click, click*, and Byrnes waited. There was silence.

In a rush, Carella said, 'Kling's girl was here. She's dead.'

Byrnes caught his breath in a quick, small rush. 'I'll be right there,' he said, and he hung up rapidly. For a moment, he felt only intense relief. He had expected worse: he had expected injury to Carella's wife or children. But the relief was short-lived because it was followed immediately by guilt. Kling's girl, he thought, and he tried to construct an image of her; but he'd never met her. And yet she seemed real to him because he had heard the squad-room jokes about Kling's romance with the young social worker, the corny goddamn squad-room jokes . . . she was dead . . . Kling . . .

There.

There was the thing. His first concern had been for Carella, because he looked upon him as the eldest son in a family business. But now he thought of Kling, young and blond and wide-eyed in a business where you could not flinch.

Byrnes did not want to think this way. I'm a cop, he told himself; I run a squad, I'm the boss, I'm the skipper, I'm the old man, they call me the old man. I can't, I can't, I *can't* get involved with the personal lives of the men on that squad, I am not their father, goddamn it!

But he strapped on his gun, and he put on his hat, and he kissed Harriet and touched his real son, Larry, on the shoulder, and there was a troubled and concerned look on his face as he went out of the house because he *was* involved with these men, had been involved with them for a long time now, and maybe this involvement did not make him a better cop, but it most certainly made him a better man.

There were six detectives from the 87th waiting outside the bookshop when Byrnes got there. Meyer Meyer had been relieved and had brought two men from the on-coming graveyard shift with him. Cotton Hawes and Andy Parker had been off duty, but the catcher on the graveyard shift had called to tell them what had happened, and they had rushed over to the bookstore. Bob O'Brien had been on special assignment in a barber's shop four blocks away when a patrolman had brought him the news. He had run all the way to the bookstore.

The men stood on the sidewalk uneasily as Byrnes got out of his car. Two of the men had every right to be there since they were technically manning the squad room. The rest were there voluntarily, and they stood in the slightly stupid posture of volunteers everywhere, not sure why they were there, waiting for someone to tell them what to do. Two Homicide cops were outside with them, smoking, chatting with the police photographer. An ambulance was at the kerb and four patrol cars blocked the street. A dozen patrolmen were on the sidewalk, trying to keep back curious onlookers. A few reporters who had been hanging out in the wire room opposite Headquarters downtown had got the flash from the dispatcher manning the police radio and had come racing uptown to see what all the shouting was about.

Meyer broke away from the knot of men the moment he saw the lieutenant. He walked to him quickly and fell into step beside him.

'Where's Steve?' Byrnes asked.

'Inside.'

'And Bert?'

'I sent him home.'

'How is he?'

'How would you be?' Meyer asked, and Byrnes nodded. 'I had to force him to leave. I sent two patrol-men with him. The girl . . . ah, Pete, this is a mess.'

They stood to one side as a pair of ambulance attendants went past with a man on a stretcher.

'That's the last one,' Meyer said. 'One of them was still alive when they got here. Don't know how long he'll be that way. The M.E. thinks his spine was shattered.'

'How many altogether?' Byrnes asked.

'Four. Three dead.'

'Was . . . was Kling's girl . . . ?'

'Yeah. Dead when they got here.'

Byrnes nodded briefly. Before he went into the bookstore, he said, 'Tell O'Brien he's supposed to be in that barber's shop. Tell the others to go home; we'll call them if we need them. Whose squeal is this, Meyer?'

'It came in about a half hour before relief. You want us to stay on it?'

'Who relieved?'

'Di Maeo, Brown, and Willis.'

'Where's Di Maeo?'

'Back at the squad, catching.'

'Tell Willis and Brown to stick around. Did you have anything important for tonight?'

'No. I'd like to call Sarah, though.'

'Can you stay around for a while?'

'Sure.'

'Thanks,' Byrnes said, and he went into the shop.

The bodies were gone. Only their chalked outlines remained on the floor and on the bookstalls. Two men from the police laboratory were dusting the shop for latent prints. Byrnes looked around for Carella and then thought of something. He went quickly to the door of the shop.

'Willis!' he said.

Hal Willis moved away from the men on the sidewalk. He was a small man, barely clearing the five-foot-eight

16

height requirement for policemen. He walked with grace-
ful precision, a small-boned man who had devoted half
his life to the study and practice of judo, a man constantly
aware of weight and balance, an awareness which showed
in every move he made. He came up alongside the
lieutenant and said, 'Yeah, Pete?'

'I want you to get over to the hospital. Take Brown
with you. See if you can get anything from that man
who's still alive.'

'Right, Pete.'

'He's in a bad way,' Byrnes said. 'A dying declaration
is admissible in court – remember that.'

'Yeah,' Willis said. 'Which hospital?'

'Meyer knows. Ask him.'

'Anything else?'

'Not for now. If they won't let you see him, raise a
stink. Call me at the squad if you get anything. I'll be
there.'

'Right.'

Byrnes went into the shop again. Steve Carella was
sitting on a high stool in one corner of the shop. His
hands, clasped together, were dangling between his knees.
He was staring at the floor when Byrnes approached him.

'Steve?'

He nodded.

'You all right?'

He nodded again.

'Come on.'

'What?'

'Come on; snap out of it.'

Carella raised his head. His eyes were dead. He looked
straight at Byrnes, and straight through him.

'This is a lousy rotten job,' he said.

'All right, it's—'

DETECTIVE DIVISION REPORT	SQUAD	PRECINCT	PRECINCT REPORT NUMBER	DETECTIVE DIVISION REPORT NUMBER
PDCN 360 REV. 25M	87	87°	32-41	D.D. 74 R-11

NAME AND ADDRESS OF PERSON REPORTING	DATE OF REPORT
Fennerman, Martin (N.M.I.)	October 13

SURNAME GIVEN NAME INITIALS	
Browser Bookshop 2680 Culver Avenue	Isola

NUMBER STREET	CITY SECTION

Details

Martin Fennerman is owner and operator of The Browser, a bookstore located at address above. Home address 375 Harris Street in Riverhead. Fennerman is forty-seven years old, divorced; two children living with remarried wife, Olga (Mrs Ira) Trent in Bethtown. Fennerman has owned and operated bookshop at above location for twelve years. Store was held up in 1954, thief apprehended, see D.D. Report #41 F-38, sentenced Castleview, released good behaviour January, 1956, returned to home in Denver, respectably employed there.

Mr Fennerman states as follows:

The shop is open every day but Sunday. He comes to work at nine in the morning, closes at six except on Saturday when he stays open until eight p.m. Except for the holdup in 1954, he has never had any trouble at this location, even though neighbourhood is not ideal for bookshop. There were seven people in the shop this evening when the killer entered. Mr Fennerman keeps count of the people as they come in. He sits behind a high counter just inside the entrance

18

doorway, checks out purchases as customers leave. There is a cash register on the counter, paper bags for wrapping purchases under the counter. Fennerman's system of keeping count was designed to avoid petty theft, he says. In any case, there were seven people in the store when the killer came in. Fennerman says this was at five-ten p.m. One of the stray bullets shattered clock on rear wall of shop, stopping it at five-seven p.m. According to Fennerman, the killer began shooting the moment he entered the shop, so ETA would be five-five or five-six.

The man was tall, perhaps six feet, perhaps more. He was wearing a tweed overcoat, a grey fedora, sunglasses, black gloves. Fennerman especially remembers the black gloves. He thinks the overcoat may have been blue, but he is not certain. The killer came into the store with his hands in his pockets, stopped just beyond the cash register, pulled his hands from his pockets, and began firing. He carried two guns. He kept shooting into the aisle of the shop until both guns were empty, Fennerman says, and then turned and ran out. He said nothing to Fennerman and nothing to any of the patrons. The four people he shot were standing in the aisle running back from the cash register. The other three people in the store were in the other aisle, to the left of the entrance. Fennerman says none of them even knew what was happening until it was all over. One of the women fainted as the killer ran out. Names and disposition of the seven people in the store at time of killing follow, exclusive of Fennerman.

Claire Townsend	DOA
Anthony La Scala	DOA
Herbert Land	DOA
Joseph Wechsler	Hospitalized – Neck Wound
Myra Klein	Hospitalized – Shock
Barbara Deering	Returned to residence
James Woody	Returned to residence

DATE OF THIS REPORT

October 13

| Det-Lt. | Byrnes | P. A. | 681 | 87th Squad |
| RANK | SURNAME | INITIALS | SHIELD NUMBER | COMMAND |

Detective - Lieutenant Peter A. B

SIGNATURE OF COMMANDING OFFICER

'I don't want it, I don't *want* it,' Carella said, his voice rising. 'I want to go home and touch my kids and not have blood on my hands.'

'All right—'

'I don't want the stink of it!' Carella shouted.

'Nobody does! Snap out of it!'

'Snap out of *what*? Of seeing that poor damn girl lying twisted and broken and bleeding on the floor? Of Bert holding her in his arms, covered with blood, and rocking her, rocking her . . . Jesus *Christ*!'

'Nobody asked you to be a cop,' Byrnes said.

'You're goddamn right, nobody asked me! OK. *OK!* Nobody asked.' His eyes had filled with tears. He sat on the high stool with his hands clasped tightly together, as if he were clinging to his sanity with them. 'Bert kept . . . kept saying her name over and over again, rocking her. And I touched his arm and tried to . . . to let him know I was there. Just *there*, do you know? And he turned to me, but he didn't know who I was. He just turned to me and asked, "Claire?" As if he was asking me to deny it, to tell him that this . . . this *dead* person he held in his arms wasn't his girl, do you know, Pete? Pete, do you know?' He began sobbing. 'Oh, that son of a bitch, that rotten son of a bitch.'

'Come on,' Byrnes said.

'Leave me alone.'

'Come on, Steve, I need you,' Byrnes said.

Carella was silent.

'I can't use you this way,' Byrnes said.

Carella sighed deeply. He pulled a handkerchief from his pocket and blew his nose. He put the handkerchief back into his pocket, his eyes avoiding Byrnes's, and he nodded and got off the stool, and then he sighed again.

'How . . . how's Bert?' he asked.

'Meyer sent him home.'

Carella nodded.

'Did you question anybody?' Byrnes asked.

Carella shook his head.

'I think we ought to,' Byrnes said.

3.

BYRNES WAS IN the middle of signing his name to the report he had typed himself when the telephone rang. He lifted the receiver. '87th Squad, Byrnes here.'

'Pete, this is Hal. I'm still at the hospital.'

'Get anything?' Byrnes asked.

'The guy just died,' Willis said.

'Did he say anything?'

'Only one word, Pete. He repeated it several times.'

'What was the word?'

'Carpenter. He kept saying it, maybe four, five times before he died. Carpenter.'

'That's all he said?'

'That's all.'

'All right,' Byrnes said; 'see if they'll let you talk to the woman they have there. Name's Myra Klein. She's the one who fainted in the shop. They're treating her for shock.'

'Right,' Willis said, and he hung up.

Byrnes completed his signature.

Myra Klein was wearing a white hospital gown and complaining bitterly about the city's public servants when Willis came into her room. Apparently the police had sent Miss Klein off to the hospital against her wishes, and apparently she was being kept there now against her wishes. She swore at the nurse who was trying to administer a sedative, turned to the door as Willis opened it, and shouted, 'What do *you* want?'

'I'd like to—'

'Are you a doctor?'

'No, ma'am . . .'

'How do I get *out* of this madhouse?' Miss Klein shouted. 'Who are you?'

'Detective 3rd Grade Harold Will . . .'

'Detective?' Miss Klein shouted. 'Detective? Get him out of here!' she yelled at the nurse, 'You're the ones who *sent* me here!'

'No, ma'am, I just—'

'Is there a crime against passing out?'

'No, but—'

'I told them I was all right. I *told* them.'

'Well, ma'am, I—'

'Instead they stick me in an ambulance. Unconscious, when I can't defend myself.'

'But, ma'am, if you were unconscious, then how—'

'Don't tell *me* what I was,' Miss Klein shouted. 'I can take care of myself. I told them I was all right. They had no right sticking me in an ambulance, unconscious.'

'Who'd you tell, Mrs Klein?'

'It's *Miss* Klein – and what do you care who I told?'

'Well, Miss Klein, the point is—'

'Get him out of here. I don't want to talk to any cops.'

'—if you were unconscious—'

'I said get him out of here!'

'—how could you have possibly told anyone you were all right?'

Myra Klein stared at Willis in total silence for the space of two minutes. Then she said, 'What are you, one of these smart-assed cops?'

'Well—'

'I'm laying here prostrate in shock,' Miss Klein said, 'and they send me Sherlock Holmes.'

23

'Will you take this pill now, Miss Klein?' the nurse asked.

'Get out of here, you miserable panhandler, before I—'

'It'll calm you!' the nurse protested.

'Calm me? *Calm* me? What makes you think I need calming?'

'Leave the pill, nurse,' Willis said gently. 'Maybe Miss Klein will feel more like taking it later.'

'Yeah, leave the pill and get out, and take Mr Holmes with you.'

'No, I'm staying,' Willis said softly.

'Who sent for you? Who needs you?'

'I want to ask you some questions, Miss Klein,' Willis said.

'I don't want to answer any questions. I'm a sick woman. I'm in shock. Now get the hell out of here.'

'Miss Klein,' Willis said evenly, 'four people were killed.'

Myra Klein stared at him. Then she nodded her head. 'Leave the pill, nurse,' she said. 'I'll talk to Mr – what was your name?'

'Willis.'

'Yes. Leave the pill, nurse.' She waited until the door closed behind the nurse. Then she said, 'All I could think of was my brother's dinner. He gets home from work at seven o'clock, and it's past that now, and he's very fussy about his dinner being on the table when he gets home. So here I am laying in a hospital. That's all I could think of.' She paused. 'Then you said, "Four people were killed," and all at once I'm one of the lucky ones.' She nodded expressively. 'What do you want to know, Mr Willis?'

'Can you tell me what happened in that bookshop. Miss Klein?'

24

'Sure, I put on the roast about four-thirty — it's a shame to make roast when there's only myself and my brother, so much goes to waste, you know, but he likes roast beef, so every now and then I make it. I put it on at four thirty — I have one of these automatic ranges, you can set it to go off when the thing is done. I had the potatoes on, too, and the string beans wouldn't take a minute once I got home. There was a book I wanted to get. They have a lending library at that bookstore, you see, over on the left — where I was standing when the man started shooting.'

'It was a man, Miss Klein?'

'Yes. I think so. I only got a quick look. I was standing at the place where Mr Fennerman has the lending library when all of a sudden I heard this loud noise. So I turned around, and I saw this man with two guns in his hands, shooting. At first, I didn't know what it was, I don't know what I thought — a stunt, I guess I thought — I don't know what. Then I saw a nice young man, he was wearing a seersucker suit, he suddenly collapsed on the counter, and he's covered all over with blood, and then I knew it wasn't a stunt, it couldn't be a stunt.'

'What happened then, Miss Klein?'

'I guess I passed out. I could never stand the sight of blood.'

'But you saw the man shooting before you passed out?'

'Yes, I did.'

'Can you tell me what he looked like?'

'Yes, I think so.' She paused. 'Where do you want me to start?'

'Well, was he a tall man? Short? Average height?'

'Average, I think.' She paused again. 'What do you mean by average?'

'Five-nine, five-ten.'

'Yes, about that.'

'He wasn't what you'd call a tall man?'

'No, I mean, he wasn't as short as . . .' She stopped.

'He wasn't as short as me?' Willis said, smiling.

'No. He was taller than you.'

'But not a really tall man. All right, Miss Klein, what was he wearing?'

'A raincoat,' Miss Klein said.

'What colour?'

'Black.'

'Belted or loose?'

'I didn't notice.'

'Any hat?'

'Yes.'

'What kind of hat?'

'A cap,' Miss Klein said.

'The colour?'

'Black, Like the raincoat.'

'Was he wearing gloves?'

'No.'

'Anything else you noticed about him?'

'Yes. He was wearing sunglasses.'

'From where you were standing, could you see any identifying scars or marks?'

'No.'

'Any deformities?'

'No.'

'Was this a white man or a coloured man, Miss Klein?'

'White.'

'Do you know anything about guns?'

'No.'

'Then you couldn't guess what kind of guns he was holding.'

'Kind?'

'Well, yes. The calibre, or whether they were revolvers or automatics or . . . well, were they small guns, Miss Klein?'

'They looked very big to me.'

'Do you know what a .45 looks like?'

'No, I'm sorry.'

'That's all right, Miss Klein; you're being very helpful. Can you tell me how old this man was?'

'About thirty-eight.'

'How old would you say I am, Miss Klein?'

'Thirty-six. Am I close?'

'Ill be thirty-four next month.'

'Well, that's pretty close.'

'Yes, you're a very observant witness, Miss Klein. I wonder if I could sum this up for us. You say you saw a white man of about thirty-eight, average height, and he was wearing a black raincoat, a black cap, and sunglasses. He wore no gloves, he was holding a big gun in each hand, and you noticed no scars or deformities. Is that about it?'

'That's it exactly,' Miss Klein said.

Now, obviously, Miss Klein's 'exactly' and Mr Fennerman's 'exactly' did not exactly add up to a picture of exactness. Willis had not yet read the report typed up by Lieutenant Byrnes and therefore had no way of knowing that the two descriptions of the same man – while agreeing on certain points – varied on a few essentials. For example, Mr Fennerman had said the killer was a tall man, perhaps six feet, perhaps more. Miss Klein, on the other hand, described the killer as being of average height, five-nine or five-ten. Fennerman had said that the killer was wearing a tweed overcoat and that the overcoat may have been blue. Miss Klein said he was

27

wearing a black raincoat. Fennerman: grey fedora. Klein: black cap. Fennerman: black gloves. Klein: no gloves.

Willis knew nothing as yet of the discrepancies, but had he known he would not have been overly surprised. He had been questioning people about the details of committed crimes for a long time now and had discovered rather early in the game that most eyewitnesses had only the faintest notion of what had really taken place. Whatever the reason — the excitement of the moment, the speed of the action, the theory that participation blurred objectivity — whatever the reason an eye-witness description of any chosen event had a peculiar way of leaping into that rarefied atmosphere bordering on fantasy. He had heard the most bizarre contradictions during his years on the police force. He had heard housewives describing in total inaccuracy the clothing their husbands had worn when leaving the house that morning. He had heard pistols described as shotguns, razor blades described as knives, blondes described as brunettes, tall men as short men, fat men as thin men, and, in at least one case, a voluptuous eighteen-year-old red-headed girl described as a dark-haired man in his early twenties.

Willis still asked the questions because it was all part of the game. The game was something like parlour analysis, where the cops listened to each fantastic report and tried to piece together from the subjective dreamlike accounts a picture of objective reality. This picture was often impossible to obtain from the fragmentary distortions. Even when the criminal was finally apprehended, *his* account of the actual crime was tainted by the same subjective distortion. It made things a little difficult. It sometimes made a thoughtful cop like Willis wonder about the reality of a bullet-riddled body on a bookshop floor.

He thanked Miss Klein for her courtesy and her time and left her alone to take her pill and worry about her brother's dinner.

By the end of that day, Friday, October 13, all four survivors of the bookshop massacre had been questioned concerning the event itself and the identity of the killer. In the unaccustomed silence of the squad room, Detective Steve Carella sat down with the four typewritten reports and tried to make some sort of sensible correlation. He worked in pencil on the back of a D.D. report, listing first the names of the witnesses and then their descriptions of the killer. When he finished his list, he looked at it sourly, scratched his head, and then read it over again.

Fennerman	Klein	Deering	Woody
Male	Male	Male	Male
White	White	White	White
20–25	38	30	45
Tall	Average	Average	Tall
Overcoat, blue tweed	Raincoat, black	Overcoat, brown tweed	Overcoat, brown tweed
Grey fedora	Black cap	Grey fedora	Grey fedora
Sunglasses	Sunglasses	Sunglasses	Sunglasses
Black gloves	No gloves	Didn't notice	Gloves (not sure of colour)
No comment on	No scars, etc.	Scar on right cheek	No scars
Two guns	Two guns, big	One gun	Two guns .22 calibre

The witnesses seemed to agree wholeheartedly on only three points: the killer was male, and white, and wearing sunglasses. From their varying estimates of the man's

29

age, Carella found it impossible to make an intelligent guess. Two of the witnesses thought the killer was tall, and two thought he was of average height – so Carella safely reasoned that, at least, the man was not short. Only one of the witnesses, Miss Klein, thought he was wearing a raincoat, whereas the other three agreed it was an overcoat. They could not get together on the colour of the coat, but two of them were certain it was brown. In any case, it was reasonable to assume the coat was dark. Carella was willing to buy the grey fedora since three of the four witnesses claimed this was what they had seen. The gloves were a toss-up. The scar seemed to have been invented by Miss Deering; two of the other witnesses said there had been no scars, and Mr Fennerman hadn't commented at all, a curious circumstance if there *had* been any scars. No, Carella was willing to rule out the possibility of the man's carrying a scar. Concerning the number of guns he'd carried, the majority of the witnesses seemed to agree it was two. Again, Miss Deering's imagination had taken hold, this time in understatement. Miss Klein said the guns were big, and Mr Woody – who himself owned a .22, for which he had a premises permit – claimed both guns were .22s.

Carella put a clean sheet of paper into his typewriter and began typing from his penciled notes.

SUSPECT
Male
White
Not short

Sunglasses
Dark overcoat
Grey fedora

Gloves (?)
No scars, marks; deformities
Two guns

That was a lot to go on.
Sure.
That was a whole hell of a lot to go on.

4.

HE COULD REMEMBER the day they met . . .

He was waiting in the hallway outside apartment 47, after having pressed the bell button. The door opened suddenly. He had heard no approaching footsteps, and the sudden opening of the door surprised him. Unconsciously, he looked first to the girl's feet. She was barefoot.

'My name is Bert Kling,' he said. 'I'm a cop.'

'You sound like the opening to a television show,' she answered.

She stared at Kling levelly. She was a tall girl. Even barefoot she reached to Kling's shoulder. In high heels she would give the average American male trouble. Her hair was black. Not brunette, not brownette, but black, a total black, the black of a starless, moonless night. Her eyes were a deep brown, arched with black brows. Her nose was straight and her cheeks were high, and there wasn't a trace of make-up on her face, not a tint of lipstick on her wide mouth. She wore a white blouse and black toreador pants, which tapered down to her naked ankles and feet. Her toenails were painted a bright red.

She kept staring at him. At last, she said, 'Why'd they send you here?'

'They said you knew Jeannie Paige.'

That was the beginning of Claire Townsend, or at least the beginning of her for him. He was still a patrolman at the time, and he had gone to her in plain clothes and on his own time to ask questions about a dead girl named Jeannie Paige, the sister-in-law of an old friend. She

32

answered all his questions graciously and easily, and at last, when there were no more questions to ask, he rose and said, 'I'd better be going. That *is* dinner I smell, isn't it?'

'My father'll be home soon,' Claire said. 'Mom is dead. I whip something up when I get home from school.'

'Every night?' Kling asked.

'What? I'm sorry . . .'

He didn't know whether to press it or not. She hadn't heard him, and he could easily have shrugged his comment aside. But he chose not to.

'I said, "Every night?"'

'Every night what?'

She certainly was not making it easy for him. 'Do you prepare supper every night? Or do you occasionally get a night off?'

'Oh, I get nights off,' Claire said.

'Maybe you'd enjoy dinner out some night?'

'With you, do you mean?'

'Well, yes. Yes, that's what I had in mind.'

Claire Townsend looked at him long and hard. At last, she said, 'No, I don't think so. I'm sorry. Thanks. I couldn't.'

'Well . . . uh . . .' Quite suddenly, Kling felt like a horse's ass. 'I . . . uh . . . guess I'll be going then. Thanks for the cognac. It was very nice.'

'Yes,' she said, and he remembered her discussing people who were there and yet not there, and he knew exactly what she meant, because she was not there at all. She was somewhere far away, and he wished he knew where. With sudden, desperate longing, he wished he knew where she was because, curiously, he wanted to be there with her.

'Good-bye,' he said.

33

She smiled in answer and closed the door behind him . . .

He could remember.

He sat alone now in the furnished room that was his home. The windows were open. October lay just outside, alive with the sounds of the night-time city. He sat in a hard straight-backed chair and looked out past the curtains, gently stirring in a breeze far too mild for October. He looked beyond the curtains, and through the window, and into the city itself, into the lighted window slashes in the distance, and a klieg light going against the velvet sky, and an aeroplane blinking red and green, all the light of the city streets and the city buildings and the air above the city, all the lights, alive.

He could remember the SPRY sign . . .

Their first date was going badly. They had spent the afternoon together, and now they sat in a restaurant high atop one of the city's better-known hotels, and they looked through the huge windows which faced the river – and across the river there was a sign.

The sign first said: SPRY.

Then it said: SPRY FOR FRYING.

Then it said: SPRY FOR BAKING.

Then it said again: SPRY.

'What'll you drink?' Kling asked.

'A whisky sour, I think,' Claire said.

'No cognac?'

'Later maybe.'

The waiter came over to the table. 'Something to drink, sir?' he asked.

'A whisky sour and a Martini.'

'Lemon peel, sir?'

'Olive,' Kling said.

'Thank you, sir. Would you care to see a menu now?'

'We'll wait until after we've had our drinks, thank you. All right, Claire?'

'Yes, fine,' she said.

They sat in silence. Kling looked through the windows.

SPRY FOR FRYING.

'Claire?'

'Yes?'

SPRY FOR BAKING.

'It's been a bust, hasn't it?'

'Please, Bert.'

'The rain . . . and that lousy movie. I didn't want it to be this way. I wanted—'

'I knew this would happen, Bert. I tried to tell you, didn't I? Didn't I try to warn you off? Didn't I tell you I was the dullest girl in the world? Why did you insist, Bert? Now you make me feel like a . . . like a—'

'I don't want you to feel *any* way,' he said. 'I was only going to suggest that we . . . we start afresh. From now. Forgetting everything that's . . . that's happened.'

'Oh, what's the use?'

'Claire,' he said evenly, 'what the hell's the matter with you?'

'Nothing.'

'Where do you go when you retreat?'

'What?'

'Where do you—'

'I didn't think it showed. I'm sorry.'

'It shows,' Kling said. 'Who was he?'

Claire looked up sharply. 'You're a better detective than I realized.'

'It doesn't take much detection,' he said. There was a sad undertone to his voice, as if her confirmation of his suspicions had suddenly taken all the fight out of him. 'I don't mind your carrying a torch. Lots of girls—'

35

'It's not that,' she interrupted.

'Lots of girls do,' he continued. 'A guy drops them cold, or else it just peters out the way romances sometimes—'

'It's not that!' she said sharply, and when he looked across the table at her, her eyes were filmed with tears.

'Hey, listen, I—'

'Please, Bert, I don't want to—'

'But you said it *was* a guy. You said—'

'All right,' she answered. 'All right, Bert.' She bit down on her lip. 'All right, there was a guy. And I was in love with him. I was seventeen – just like Jeannie Paige – and he was nineteen. We hit it off right away . . . do you know how such things happen, Bert? It happened that way with us. We made a lot of plans, big plans. We were young, and we were strong, and we were in love.'

'I . . . I don't understand,' he said.

'He was killed in Korea.'

Across the river, the sign blared: SPRY FOR FRYING.

The tears. The bitter tears, starting slowly at first, forcing their way past clenched eyelids, trickling silently down her cheeks. Her shoulders began to heave, and she sat as still as a stone, her hands clasped in her lap, her shoulders heaving, sobbing silently while the tears coursed down her face. He had never seen such honest misery before. He turned his face away. He did not want to watch her. She sobbed steadily for several moments, and then the tears stopped as suddenly as they had begun, leaving her face looking as clean as a city street after a sudden summer storm.

'I'm sorry,' she said.

'Don't be.'

'I should have cried a long time ago.'

'Yes.'

The waiter brought the drinks. Kling lifted his glass. 'To a new beginning,' he said.

Claire studied him. It took her a long lime to reach for the drink before her. Finally her hand closed around the glass. She lifted it and touched the rim of Kling's glass. 'To a new beginning,' she said. She threw off the drink quickly.

She looked across at him as if she were seeing him for the first time. The tears had put a sparkle into her eyes. 'It . . . it may take time, Bert,' she said. Her voice came from a long way off.

'I've got all the time in the world,' he said. And then, almost afraid she would laugh at him, he added, 'All I've been doing is killing time, Claire, waiting for you to come along.'

She seemed ready to cry again. He reached across the table and covered her hand with his. 'You're . . . you're very good, Bert,' she said, her voice growing thin, the way a voice does before it collapses into tears. 'You're good, and kind, and gentle, and you're quite beautiful, do you know that? I . . . I think you're very beautiful.'

'You should see me when my hair is combed,' he said, smiling, squeezing her hand.

'I'm not joking,' she said. 'You always think I'm joking, and you really shouldn't, because I'm . . . I'm a serious girl.'

'I know.'

'Bert,' she said. 'Bert.' And she put her other hand over his, so that three hands formed a pyramid on the table. Her face grew very serious. 'Thank you, Bert. Thank you so very, very much.'

He didn't know what to say. He felt embarrassed and stupid and happy and very big. He felt about eighty feet tall.

She leaned forward suddenly and kissed him, a quick sudden kiss that fleetingly touched his mouth and then was gone. She sat back again, seeming very unsure of herself, seeming like a frightened little girl at her first party. 'You . . . you must be patient,' she said.

'I will,' he promised.

The waiter suddenly appeared. The waiter was smiling. He coughed discreetly. 'I thought,' he said gently, 'perhaps a little candlelight at the table, sir? The lady will look even more lovely by candlelight.'

'The lady looks lovely just as she is,' Kling said.

The waiter seemed disappointed. 'But . . .'

'But the candlelight, certainly,' Kling said. 'By all means, the candlelight.'

The waiter beamed. 'Ah, yes, sir. Yes, sir. And then we will order, yes? I have some suggestions, sir, whenever you're ready.' He paused, his smile lighting his face. 'It's a beautiful night, sir, isn't it?'

'It's a wonderful night,' Claire answered . . .

Alone in the night, alone in the light-blinking silence of his furnished room, he tried to tell himself she was not dead. He had spoken to her this afternoon. She had told him about her new bra. She was not dead. She was still alive and vibrant. She was still Claire Townsend.

She was dead.

He sat staring through the window.

He felt numb and cold. There was no feeling in his hands. If he moved his fingers, he knew they would not respond. He sat heavily, shivering in the warm October breeze, staring through the window at the myriad lights of the city, how gently the curtain rustled in the caressing wind, he felt nothing but an empty coldness, something hard and rigid and frighteningly cold at the pit of

38

his stomach, he could not move, he could not cry, he could not feel.

She was dead.

No, he told himself, and he allowed a faint smile to turn the corners of his mouth; no, don't be ridiculous. Claire dead? Don't be ridiculous. I spoke to her this afternoon. She called me at the squad room, the way she always calls. Meyer was making jokes about it. Carella was there – he could tell you. He remembers. She called me, and they were both there, so I know I wasn't dreaming, and if she called me she must be alive, isn't that so? That's only logical. She called me, so I know she's alive. Carella was there. Ask Carella. He'll tell you. He'll tell you Claire is alive.

He could remember talking to Carella once not too long ago in a diner, the plate-glass window splashed with rain. There had been an intimacy to the place, a rained-in snugness as they had discussed the case they were working, as they had lifted steaming coffee mugs. And into the intimate mood of the moment, into the rain-protected comfort of the room, Carella had said, 'When are you going to marry that girl?'

'She wants to get her master's degree before we get married.' Kling said.

'Why?'

'How do I know? She's insecure. She's psychotic. How do I know?'

'What does she want after the master's? A doctorate?'

'Maybe.' Kling had shrugged. 'Listen, I ask her to marry me every time I see her. She wants the master's. So what can I do? I'm in love with her. Can I tell her to go to hell?'

'I suppose not.'

'Well, I can't.' Kling had paused. 'You want to know something, Steve?'

'What?'

'I wish I could keep my hands off her. You know, I wish we didn't have to . . . well, you know, my landlady looks at me cockeyed every time I bring Claire upstairs. And then I have to rush her home because her father is the strictest guy who ever walked the earth. I'm surprised he's leaving her alone this weekend. But what I mean is . . . well, damn it, what the hell does she need that master's for, Steve? I mean, I wish I could leave her alone until we were married, but I just can't. I mean, all I have to do is to be with her, and my mouth goes dry. Is it that way with . . . well, never mind, I didn't mean to get personal.'

'It's that way,' Carella had said.

She's alive, Kling reasoned.

Of course, she's alive. She's going for her master's degree. She's already doing social field work. Why, just today, on the telephone, she told me she'd be a little late: *I have to pick up some texts.*

Interviewing: Its Principles and Methods, he thought.

Patterns of Culture, he thought.

The Sane Society, he thought.

She's dead, he thought.

'NO!'

He screamed the word aloud into the silence of the room. The scream brought him physically out of the chair, as if the force of its explosion had lifted him.

'*No,*' he said again, very softly, and he walked to the window, and he rested his head against the curtain, and he looked down into the street, looking for Claire. She should have been here by now. It was almost . . . what time was it? What time? He knew her walk. He would recognize her the moment she turned into the block – a white blouse, she had said; that and a black skirt – yes, he would know her instantly. He wondered abruptly what the bra looked like, and again he smiled, the curtain soft and reassuring against his cheek, the lights of the restaurant across the way staining his face in alternating red and green neon.

I wonder what's keeping her, he thought.

Well, she's dead, you know, he thought.

He turned away from the window. He walked to the bed, and he looked at it unseeingly, and then he walked to the dresser, and he stared down at its cluttered top, and picked up the hairbrush, and saw strands of her black hair tangled in its bristles, and put down the brush, and looked at his watch, and did not see the time.

It was almost midnight.

He walked back to the window and stared down into the street again, waiting for her.

By six a.m. the next morning he knew she was not coming.

He knew he would never see her again.

5.

A POLICE PRECINCT is a small community within a community. There were one hundred and eighty-six patrolmen attached to the precinct and sixteen detectives attached to the squad. The men of the precinct and the squad knew each other the way people in a small town do: there were close friendships, and nodding acquaint-anceships, and minor feuds, and strictly formal business relationships. But all of the men who used the station house as their office knew each other by sight, and usually by name, even if they had never worked a case together.

By seven forty-five the next morning, when a third of the precinct patrolmen were relieved on post, when the three detectives upstairs were officially relieved, there was not a single man in the precinct – uniformed or plainclothes – who did not know that Bert Kling's girl had been killed in a bookstore on Culver Avenue.

Most of the cops didn't even know her name. To them, she was a vague image, real nonetheless, a person some-what like their own wives or sweethearts, a young girl who took on personality, who became flesh and blood only by association with their own loved ones. She was Bert Kling's girl, and she was dead.

'Kling?' some of the patrolmen asked. 'Which one is he?'

'Kling's girl?' some of the detectives asked. 'You're kidding! You mean it?'

'Man, that's a lousy break,' some of them said.

A police precinct is a small community within a community.

The cops of the 87th Precinct – uniformed and plainclothes – understood that Kling was one of them. There were men among the patrolmen who knew him only as the blond bull who had answered a squeal while they were keeping a timetable. If they'd met him in an official capacity, they would have called him 'sir'. There were other men who had been patrolmen when Kling was still walking a beat, and who were still patrolmen, and who resented his promotion somewhat because he seemed to be just a lucky stiff who'd happened to crack a murder case. There were detectives who felt Kling would have made a better shoe clerk than a detective. There were detectives who felt Kling was indispensable on a case, combining a mature directness with a boyish humility, a combination which could pry answers from the most stubborn witness. There were stool pigeons who felt Kling was tight with a buck. There were prostitutes on *La Via de Putas* who eyed Kling secretly and who admitted among themselves that for this particular cop they wouldn't mind throwing away a free one. There were shop owners who felt he was too strict about city ordinances concerning sidewalk stands. There were kids in the precinct who knew that Kling would look the other way if they turned on a fire hydrant during the summer. There were other kids in the precinct who knew that Kling would break their hands if he caught them fiddling with narcotics, even with something as harmless as mootah. There were traffic cops who called him 'Blondie' behind his back. There was one detective on the squad who hated to read any of Kling's reports because he was a lousy typist and a worse speller. Miscolo, in the Clerical Office, had a suspicion that Kling didn't like the coffee he made.

But all of the cops of the 87th, and many of the citizens who lived in the precinct territory, understood that Kling was one of them.

Oh, there was none of that condolence-card sentiment about their understanding, none of that 'your loss is my loss' horse manure. Actually, Kling's loss was not their loss, and they knew it. Claire Townsend was only a name to most of them, and not even that much to some of them. But Kling was a policeman. Every other cop in the precinct knew that he was a part of the club, and you didn't go around hurting club members or the people they loved.

And so, whereas none of them agreed to it, whereas all of them discussed the crime but none of them discussed what he personally was going to do about it, a curious thing happened on October 14. On October 14 every cop in the precinct stopped being a cop. Well, he didn't turn in his badge and his service revolver – nothing as dramatic as that. But being a cop in the 87th meant being a lot of things, and it meant being them *all* of the time. On October 14 the cops of the 87th still went about their work, which happened to be crime prevention, and they went about it in much the same way as always. Except for one difference.

They arrested muggers, and pushers, and con men, and rapists, and drunks, and junkies, and prostitutes. They discouraged loitering and betting on the horses and unlawful assembly and crashing red lights and gang warfare. They rescued cats and babies and women with their heels caught in grates. They helped schoolchildren across the street. They did everything just the way they always did it. Except for the difference.

The difference was this: their ordinary daily chores, the things they did every day of the week – their *work* –

became a hobby. Or an avocation. Or call it what you will. They were doing it, and perhaps they did it well, but under the guise of working at all the petty little infractions that bugged cops everywhere, they were *really* working on the Kling Case. They didn't call it The Bookstore Case, or The Claire Townsend Case, or The Massacre Case, or anything of the sort. It was The Kling Case. From the moment their day started to the moment their day ended, they were actively at work on it, listening, watching, waiting. Although only four men were officially assigned to the case, the man who'd done that bookshop killing had two hundred and two policemen looking for him.

Steve Carella was one of those policemen.

He had gone home at midnight the night before. At two o'clock, unable to sleep, he had called Kling.

'Bert?' he had said. 'How are you?'

'I'm fine,' Kling had answered.

'Did I wake you?'

'No,' Kling had said. 'I was up.'

'What were you doing, kid?'

'Watching. Watching the street.'

They had talked a while longer, and then Carella had said good-bye and hung up. He had not fallen asleep until four o'clock that morning. The image of Kling in his room, alone, watching the street, had kept drifting in and out of his dreams. At eight o'clock he had awakened, dressed and driven down to the squad room.

Meyer Meyer was already there.

'I want to try something on you, Steve,' Meyer said.

'Go ahead.'

'Do you buy this guy as a fanatic?'

'No,' Carella said immediately.

45

'Me neither. I've been up all night, thinking about what happened in that bookstore. I couldn't sleep a wink.'

'I didn't sleep well either,' Carella said.

'I figured if the guy is a fanatic, he's going to do the same thing tomorrow, right? He'll walk into a supermarket tomorrow and he'll shoot four more people at random, am I right?'

'That's right,' Carella said.

'But that's only if he's a lunatic. And it sounds like a madman, doesn't it? The guy walks into a store and starts blasting? He's got to be nuts, right?' Meyer nodded. 'But I don't buy it.'

'Why not?'

'Instinct. Intuition. I don't know why. I just know this guy is not a madman. I think he wanted somebody in that store dead. I think he knew his victim was going to be in that store, and I think he walked in and began blasting and didn't give a damn who else he killed, so long as he killed the person he was after. That's what I think.'

'That's what I think, too,' Carella said.

'Good. So, assuming he got who he was after, I think we ought to—'

'Suppose he didn't, Meyer?'

'Didn't what?'

'Get who he was after.'

'I thought of that, too, Steve, but I ruled it out. It suddenly came to me in the middle of the night – Jesus, suppose he was after one of the survivors? We'd better get police protection to them right away. But then I ruled it out.'

'I did, too,' Carella said.

'How do you figure?'

'There were three areas in that shop,' Carella said. 'The two aisles, and the high counter where Fennerman was sitting. If our killer wanted Fennerman, he'd have shot directly at him, at the counter. If he'd wanted somebody in the far aisles, where the other three survivors were standing, he'd have blasted in that direction. But, instead, he walked into the shop and began shooting immediately into the nearest aisle. The way I figure it, his victim is dead, Meyer. He *got* who he was after.'

'There're a few other things to consider, Steve,' Meyer said.

'What?'

'We don't know who he was after, so we'll have to start asking questions. But remember, Steve . . .'

'I know.'

'What?'

'Claire Townsend was killed.'

Meyer nodded. 'There's a possibility,' he said, 'that *Claire* was the one he was gunning for.'

The man in the seersucker suit was named Herbert Land.

He taught philosophy at the university on the fringes of the precinct territory. He often went to The Browser because it was close to the school and he could pick up secondhand *Plato* and *Descartes* there at reasonable prices. The man in the seersucker suit was dead because he had been standing in the aisle closest to the door when the killer had cut loose with his barrage.

Herbert Land . . . . DOA

Land had lived in a development house in the nearby suburb of Sands Spit. He had lived there with his wife and two children. The oldest of the kids was six. The youngest was three. Herbert Land's widow, a woman named Veronica, was twenty-eight years old. The moment Meyer

47

and Carella saw her standing in the doorway of the development house they realized she was pregnant. She was a plain woman with brown hair and blue eyes, but she stood in the doorway with a quiet dignity that belied the tear-streaked face and the red-rimmed eyes. She stood and asked them quietly who they were, and then asked to see their identification, standing in the classic posture of the pregnant woman, her belly extended, one hand resting almost on the small of her back, her head slightly tilted. They showed their shields and their ID cards, and she nodded briefly and allowed them to enter her home.

The house was very still. Veronica Land explained that her mother had come to take the children away for a few days. The children did not yet know their father had been killed. She would have to tell them, she knew, but she wanted to be composed when she did, and she had not yet adjusted to the fact herself. She spoke in a low, controlled voice, but the tears sat just behind her eyes, waiting to be released, and the detectives picked through the conversation delicately and cautiously, not wanting to release the torrent. She sat very stiffly in an easy chair, carrying her unborn child like a huge medicine ball in her lap. She did not take her eyes from the detectives as they spoke. Carella had the feeling that every shred of her being was furiously concentrated on what they were saying. He had the feeling that she was clinging to the conversation for support, that if she once lost its thread she would burst into uncontrollable tears.

'How old was your husband, Mrs Land?' Meyer asked.

'Thirty-one.'

'And he was a teacher at the university, is that right?'

'An instructor, yes. As assistant professor.'

'He commuted daily from Sands Spit?'

'Yes.'

'What time did he leave the house, Mrs Land?'

'He caught the eight-seventeen each morning.'

'Do you own a car, Mrs Land?'

'Yes.'

'But your husband took the train?'

'Yes. We have only one car, and I'm . . . well, as you can see, I'm going to have a baby. Herbie . . . Herbie felt I should have the car here. In case . . . well . . .'

'When is the baby due, Mrs Land?' Carella asked.

'It's supposed to come this month,' she answered. 'Sometime this month.'

Carella nodded. The house went still again.

Meyer cleared his throat. 'What time does the eight-seventeen reach the city, would you know, Mrs Land?'

'Nine o'clock, I think. I know his first class was at nine-thirty, and he had to take a subway uptown from the terminal. I think the train got in at nine, yes.'

'And he taught philosophy?'

'He was in the philosophy department, yes. Actually he taught philosophy and ethics and logic and aesthetics.'

'I see. Mrs Land . . . did . . . uh . . . did your husband seem worried about anything? Did he mention anything that might have seemed . . .'

'Worried? What do you mean, worried?' Veronica Land said. 'He was worried about his salary, which is six thousand dollars a year, and he was worried about our mortgage payments, and worried about the one car we have which is about to fall apart. What do you mean "worried"? I don't know what you mean by "worried".'

Meyer glanced at Carella. For a moment the tension in the room was unbearable. Veronica Land fought for control, clasped her hands in her lap just below the bulge of her stomach. She sighed heavily.

49

In a very low voice she said, 'I'm sorry, I don't know what you mean by "worried",' but she had regained control, and the edge of hysteria was gone now. 'I'm sorry.'

'Well, did . . . did he have any enemies that you know of?'

'None.'

'Any instructors at the university with whom he may have . . . well . . . argued . . . or . . . well, I don't know. Any departmental difficulties?'

'No.'

'Had anyone threatened him?'

'No.'

'His students perhaps? Had he talked about any difficulties with students? Had he failed anyone who might possibly have—'

'No.'

'—carried a grudge against—'

'Wait, yes.'

'What?' Carella said.

'Yes, he failed someone. But that was last semester.'

'Who?' Carella asked.

'A boy in his logic class.'

'Do you know his name?'

'Yes. Barney . . . something. Just a minute. He was on the baseball team, and when Herbie failed him he wasn't allowed to . . . Robinson, that was it. Barney Robinson.'

'Barney Robinson,' Carella repeated. 'And you say he was on the baseball team?'

'Yes. They play in the spring semester, you know. That was when Herbie failed him. Last semester.'

'I see. Do you know why he failed him. Mrs Land?'

'Why, yes. He . . . he wasn't doing his work. Why else would Herbie have failed him?'

'And because he failed he wasn't allowed to play on the team, is that right?'

'That's right.'

'Did your husband seem to think Robinson was carrying any resentment?'

'I don't know. You asked me if I could think of someone, and I just thought of this Robinson because . . . Herbie didn't *have* any enemies, Mr – what was your name?'

'Carella.'

'Mr Carella, Herbie didn't have any enemies. You didn't know my husband so . . . so . . . you wouldn't know what . . . what kind of a person he . . .'

She was about to lose control again. Quickly Carella said, 'Did you ever meet this Robinson?'

'No.'

'Then you wouldn't know whether he was tall or short or—'

'No.'

'I see. And your husband discussed him with you, is that right?'

'He only told me he'd had to fail Barney Robinson, and that it meant the boy wouldn't be able to . . . pitch, I think it was.'

'He's a pitcher, is that right?'

'Yes,' she paused. 'I think so. Yes. A pitcher.'

'That's a very important person on a team, Mrs Land. The pitcher.'

'Is he?'

'Yes. So there's the possibility that, in addition to Robinson himself, any number of students could have been resentful of your husband's actions. Isn't that so?'

'I don't know. He never mentioned it except that once.'

'Did any of his colleagues ever mention it?'

'Not that I know of.'

'Did you know any of his colleagues socially?'

'Yes, of course.'

'But they never mentioned Barney Robinson or the fact that your husband had failed him?'

'Never.'

'Not even jokingly?'

'Not at all.'

'Had your husband ever received any threatening letters, Mrs Land?'

'No.'

'Calls?'

'No.'

'But yet you thought of Robinson instantly when we asked if anyone might have a grudge against your husband.'

'Yes. I think it troubled Herbie. Having to fail him, I mean.'

'Did he *say* it troubled him?'

'No. But I know my own husband. He wouldn't have mentioned it if it wasn't troubling him.'

'But he told you about it *after* he'd failed the boy?'

'Yes.'

'How old is Robinson, do you know?'

'I don't know.'

'Do you have any idea what class he was in?'

'What do you mean?'

'Well, would he have graduated already? Or is he still at the school?'

'I don't know.'

'All you know, then, is that your husband failed a boy named Barney Robinson, a baseball player in his logic class.'

'Yes, that's all I know,' Veronica said.

'Thank you very much, Mrs Land. We appreciate—'

'And I know my husband is dead,' Veronica Land said tonelessly. 'I know that, too.'

The university buildings rose in scholastic splendour in the midst of squalor, a tribute to the vagaries of city development. Those many years back, when the university was planned and executed, the surrounding neighbourhood was one of the best in the city, containing several small parks, and rows of dignified brownstones, and apartment buildings with doormen. A slum grows because it has to have some place to go. In this case, it grew towards the university, and around the university, ringing it with poverty and contained hostility. The university remained an island of culture and learning, its green grass providing a moat which defied further encroachment Student and professor alike came out of the subway each morning and walked book-laden through a neighbourhood where *The Razor's Edge* was not a novel by Somerset Maugham but a fact of life. Oddly, there were few incidents between the people of the neighbourhood and the university people. Once a student was mugged on his way to the subway, and once a young girl was almost raped, but a sort of undeclared truce existed, a *laissez faire* attitude which enabled citizen and scholar to pursue separate lives with a minimum of interference.

One of those scholars was Barney Robinson.

They found him on a campus bench, talking to a young brunette who had escaped from a Kerouac novel. They explained who they were and the girl excused herself. Robinson didn't seem particularly pleased by the intrusion, or by the girl's sudden disappearance.

'What's this all about?' he asked. He had blue eyes and

53

a square face, and he was wearing a sweat shirt emblazoned with the name of the university. He straddled the bench and squinted into the sun, looking up at Meyer and Carella.

'We didn't expect to find you here today.' Carella said, 'Do you always have classes on Saturday?'

'What? Oh, no. Practice.'

'What do you mean?'

'Basketball.'

'We thought you were on the baseball team.'

'I am. I'm also on the basket . . .' Robinson paused. 'How'd you know that? What is this?'

'Anyway, we're glad we caught you,' Carella said.

'*Caught* me?'

'That's just an expression.'

'Yeah, I hope so,' Robinson said glumly.

'How tall are you, Mr Robinson?' Meyer asked.

'Six-two.'

'How old are you?'

'Twenty-five.'

'Mr Robinson, did you once take a class with Professor Land?'

'Yeah.' Robinson kept squinting up at the detectives, trying to understand what they were driving at. His tone was cautious but not overly wary. He seemed only to be extremely puzzled.

'When was this?'

'Last semester.'

'What was the class?'

'Logic.'

'How'd you make out?'

'I flunked.'

'Why?'

Robinson shrugged.

'Do you think you deserved to flunk?'

Robinson shrugged again.

'Well, what do you say?' Meyer asked.

'I don't know. I flunked, that's all.'

'Were you doing the work?'

'Sure I was doing the work.'

'Did you understand what you were doing?'

'Yeah, I thought so,' Robinson said.

'But you flunked anyway.'

'Yeah.'

'Well, how'd you feel about that?' Meyer asked. 'You were doing the work, and you say you understood it, but still you flunked. How about that? How'd it make you feel?'

'Lousy – how do you think?' Robinson said. 'Would you mind telling me what this is all about? Since when do detectives—'

'This is just a routine investigation,' Carella said.

'Into what?' Robinson asked.

'How'd you feel about flunking?'

'I told you. Lousy. An investigation into what?'

'Well, that's not important, Mr Robinson. The only—'

'What is it? Is there a fix in or something?'

'A fix?'

'Yeah. The team, is that it? Is somebody trying to fix a game?'

'Why? Have you been approached?'

'Hell, no. If there's something going on, I don't know anything about it.'

'Are you a good basketball player, Mr Robinson?'

'Fair. Baseball's my game.'

'You pitch, is that right?'

'Yeah, that's right. You know an awful lot about me, don't you? For a routine investigation—'

'Are you a good pitcher?'

'Yes,' Robinson answered without hesitation.

'What happened when Land flunked you?'

'I got benched.'

'For how long?'

'For the rest of the season.'

'How'd this affect the team?'

Robinson shrugged. 'I don't want to blow my own horn . . .'

'Go ahead,' Meyer said, 'blow it.'

'We lost eight out of twelve.'

'Think you'd have won them if you were pitching?'

'Let's put it this way,' Robinson said. 'I think we'd have won *some* of them.'

'But, instead, you lost.'

'Yeah.'

'How'd the team feel about this?'

'Lousy. We thought we might cop the city championship. We were unbeaten until I was benched. Then we lost those eight games and we wound up in second place.'

'Well, that's not so bad,' Carella said.

'There's only one first place,' Robinson answered.

'Did the team feel Mr Land had been unfair?'

'I don't know how they felt.'

'How'd *you* feel?'

'Look, those are the breaks,' Robinson said.

'Yes, but how'd you feel?'

'I thought I knew the work.'

'Then why'd he flunk you?'

'Why don't you go ask him?' Robinson said.

This was the place to say 'Because he's dead,' but neither Meyer nor Carella said the words. They watched Robinson squinting up into their faces and into the sun, and Carella said, 'Where were you last night about five o'clock, Mr Robinson?'

'Why?'

'We'd like to know.'

'I don't think that's any of your business,' Robinson said.

'I'm afraid we'll have to be the judge of what's our business or what isn't.'

'Then maybe you better go get a warrant for my arrest.' Robinson said. 'If this is as serious as all that—'

'Nobody said it was serious, Mr Robinson.'

'No?'

'No.' Meyer paused. 'Do you want us to get that warrant?'

'I don't see why I have to tell you—'

'It might help us to clear up a few things, Mr Robinson.'

'What things?'

'Where were you last night at five o'clock?'

'I was . . . I was involved in something personal.'

'Like what?'

'Look, I don't see any reason—'

'What were you involved in?'

'I was with a girl,' Robinson said, sighing.

'From what time to what time?'

'From about four . . . well, a little before four . . . my last class broke at three forty-five . . .'

'Yes, from three forty-five until when?'

'Until about eight.'

'Where were you?'

'At the girl's apartment.'

'Where?'

'Downtown.'

'Where downtown?'

'For Christ's sake . . .'

'Where?'

'On Tremayne Avenue. It's in the Quarter, near Canopy.'

'You were at the apartment at four o'clock?'

'No, we must've got there about four-fifteen, four-thirty.'

'But you *were* there at five?'

'Yes.'

'What were you doing?'

'Well, you know . . .'

'Tell us.'

'I don't *have* to tell you! You figure it out for yourself, goddamn it!'

'OK. What's the girl's name?'

'Olga.'

'Olga what?'

'Olga Wittensten.'

'Was that the girl just sitting here with you?'

'Yeah. What're you gonna do – question her, too? You gonna foul up a good thing?'

'All we want to do is check your story, Mr Robinson. The rest is your problem.'

'This is a very high-strung girl,' Robinson said. 'She's liable to spook. I don't understand what this is all about anyway. Why do you have to check my story? What is it I'm supposed to have done?'

'You're supposed to have been in an apartment on Tremayne Avenue from four-fifteen yesterday afternoon to eight o'clock last night. If you were doing what you're supposed to have been doing, you'll never see us again as long as you live, Mr Robinson.'

'Well, maybe not as long as you live,' Meyer amended.

'Which means you'll be back Monday morning,' Robinson said.

'Why? *Weren't* you in that apartment?'

'I was there. I was there. Go on and check. But the last time there was a basketball scandal, we had detectives and district attorneys and special investigators crawling all over the campus for weeks. If this is the same thing—'

'This isn't the same thing, Mr Robinson.'

'I hope not. I'm clean. I play a clean game. I never took a nickel, and I never will. You just remember that.'

'We will.'

'And when you talk to Olga, for Pete's sake, try not to foul this up, will you? Will you please do me that favour? She's a very high-strung girl.'

They found Olga Wittensten in the student cafeteria drinking a cup of black coffee. She said like man, she had never before seen fuzz up close like this. She said yeah, she had a pad on Tremayne, downtown in the Quarter. She said she like waited for Barney yesterday afternoon, and they cut out to her place and got there about four, four-thirty, something like that. She said they were there all afternoon, like maybe till eight o'clock or so, when they went out to break some bread. Like what was this all about?

Like it was about murder.

6.

BERT KLING ARRIVED at the squad room at two o'clock
that Saturday afternoon, in time to see the report which
had been delivered from Ballistics downtown. He was
unshaven, a blond bristle covering his jowls and his chin.
He was wearing the same suit and shirt he'd worn the
night before, but he had taken off his tie, and his clothes
looked as if he'd worn them to sleep. He accepted a
few condolences in the corridor outside the squad room,
turned down the coffee Miscolo offered him, and went
directly into the lieutenant's office. He stayed with Byrnes
for a half hour. When he came out into the squad room
again, Carella and Meyer had returned from the university, where a promising lead had turned as dead as ashes.
He went to Carella's desk.

'Steve,' he said. 'I'm working on it.'

Carella looked up and nodded. 'Think that's a good
idea?'

'I just spoke to the lieutenant,' Kling said. His voice
was curiously toneless. 'He thinks it'll be all right.'

'I just thought—'

'I want to work on it, Steve.'

'All right.'

'Actually, I . . . I was here when the squeal came in,
so . . . so officially I . . .'

'It's all right with me, Bert. I was only thinking of
you.'

'I'll be all right when we find him,' Kling said.

Carella and Meyer exchanged a silent glance.

'Well . . . well, then, sure. Sure. You . . . you want to see this Ballistics report?'

Kling took the Manila envelope silently, and silently he opened it. There were two reports in the envelope. One described a .45-calibre automatic. The other described a .22. Kling studied each of the reports separately.

There is nothing very mysterious about determining the make of an unknown firearm when one possesses a sample bullet fired from it. Kling, as a working cop, knew this. At the same time, he found the process a little confusing, and he tried not to think about it too much or too often.

He knew that there was a vast working file of revolvers, pistols, and bullets in the Ballistics Bureau, and that all these were classified by calibre, by number of lands and grooves, and by direction of the rifling twist. In addition, he knew that all hand guns in current use had rifled bores which put a fired bullet in rotation as it passed through the barrel. Lands, he had learned by rote, were the smooth surfaces between the spiral grooves in the barrel. Lands and grooves left marks upon a bullet.

When a spent bullet was recovered and sent to Ballistics, it was rolled on a sheet of carbon paper and then compared against the specimen cards in the file. If Ballistics tentatively made a bullet from the file cards, the suspect bullet was put under a microscope with a test bullet from another part of the file and both were accurately compared. Along about then, when twist and angle of twist entered the picture, Kling got a little confused.

That's why he never thought much about it. He knew simply that the same make of pistol or revolver would *always* fire a bullet with the same number and width of grooves and the same spiral direction and twist. So he accepted the Ballistics reports unquestioningly.

'He used two different guns, huh?' Kling said.

'Yes,' Carella answered. 'That explains the conflicting reports from our eyewitnesses. You didn't see those, Bert. They're in the file.'

'Under what?'

'Under . . .' Carella hesitated. 'Under K . . . for Kling.'

Kling nodded briefly. It was difficult to tell what he was thinking in that moment.

'We figured he was after one of the four he got, Bert,' Meyer said. He spoke cautiously and slowly. One of the four had been Claire Townsend.

Kling nodded.

'We don't know which one,' Carella said.

'We questioned Mrs Land this morning, and she gave us what looked like a lead, but it fizzled. We want to hit the others today and tomorrow.'

'I'll take one,' Kling said. He paused. 'I'd rather not question Claire's father, but any of the others . . .'

'Sure,' Carella said.

The men were silent. Both Meyer and Carella knew that something had to be said, and it had to be said now. Meyer was the senior of the two men – in age and in years with the squad – but he looked to Carella pleadingly, and Carella took the cue, cleared his throat, and said, 'Bert, I think . . . I think we ought to get something straight.'

Kling looked up.

'We want this guy. We want him very bad.'

'I know that.'

'We've got almost nothing to go on, and that doesn't make it easy. It'll make it harder if—'

'If *what*?'

'If we don't work this as a team.'

'We're working as a team,' Kling said.

'Bert, are you sure you want in on this?'

'I'm sure.'

'Are you sure you can question somebody and listen to the facts of Claire's death and be able to think of—'

'I can do it,' Kling said immediately.

'Don't cut me off, Bert. I'm talking about a multiple murder in a bookstore, and one of the victims was—'

'I said I can do it.'

'—one of the victims was Claire Townsend. Now can you?'

'Don't be a son of a bitch, Steve. I can do it, and I want to do it, and—'

'I don't think so.'

'Well I think so!' Kling said heatedly.

'You won't even let me mention her name here in the squad room, for Christ's sake! What are you going to do when someone describes the way she was killed?'

'I know she was killed,' Kling said softly.

'Bert . . .'

'I know she's dead.'

'Look, stay off it. Do me a favour and—'

'Friday the thirteenth,' Kling said. 'My mother used to call it a hoodoo jinx of a day. I know she's dead, Steve. I'll be able to . . . to . . . I'll work with you, and I'll be thinking straight, don't worry. You don't know how much I want to catch this guy. You just don't know how much I won't be good for anything else until we get him, believe me. I won't be good for another goddamn thing.'

'There's the possibility,' Carella said evenly, 'that the killer was after Claire.'

'I know.'

'There's the possibility we may find out things about Claire you wouldn't particularly like to know.'

'There's nothing new I can find out about Claire.'

'Homicide opens a lot of closets, Bert.'

'Where do you want me to go?' Kling asked. 'What do you want me to do?'

Carella and Meyer exchanged another long glance. 'OK,' Carella said at last. 'Go home and shave and change your clothes. Here's the address of Mrs Joseph Wechsler. We're trying to find out if any of the victims had any warnings or threats or . . . we want to find exactly *who* he was after, Bert.'

'All right.' Kling picked up the sheet of paper, folded it in two, and slipped it into his jacket pocket. He was starting out of the squad room when Carella called to him.

'Bert?'

Kling turned. 'Yeah?'

'You . . . you know how we feel about this, don't you?'

Kling nodded. 'I think I do.'

'OK.'

The two men stared at each other for a moment. Then Kling turned and walked rapidly out of the room.

The city is a crazy thing of many parts which don't quite fit together. You would think all the pieces would join, like the interlocking pieces of a jigsaw puzzle, but somehow the rivers and streams and bridges and tunnels separate and join areas which, in character and geography, could be foreign countries miles apart and not segments of the same sprawling metropolis.

Isola, of course, was the hub of the city, and the 87th Precinct was smack in the centre of that hub, like a wheel within a wheel, turning. Isola was an island, aptly and literally named by an unimaginative Italian explorer who

64

had stumbled upon America, long after his compatriot had found it and claimed it for Queen Isabella. Columbus notwithstanding, the latterday adventurer had come upon this lovely island, had been struck speechless by its beauty, and had muttered simply, 'Isola'. Not 'Isola *Bella*' or 'Isola *Bellissima*' or 'Isola *la piu bella d'Italia*', but merely 'Isola'.

Island.

He had, since he had been a native Italian, born and raised in the tiny town of San Luigi, pronounced the name in perfect Italian. The name, if not the island itself, had been bastardized over the ensuing centuries, so that it was now pronounced 'Ice-a-luh', or sometimes even 'Ice-luh'. This mispronunciation might have disturbed the island's godfather had he been alive and kicking in the twentieth century, but chances are he wouldn't even have recognized the place. Isola was thronged with skyscrapers above ground, tunnels below the surface. She roared with the thunderous pace of big business. Her ports overflowed with goods from everywhere in the world. Her shores were laced with countless bridges connecting her to the rest of the less frenetic city. Isola had come a long way from San Luigi.

Majesta and Bethtown reflected the English influence on the new world, at least insofar as their names honoured British royalty. Bethtown had been named after the Virgin Queen in a burst of familiarity, the queen's ministers having decided to call the place 'Besstown'. But the man who delivered the new name to the crown colony was a man who'd lisped ever since he learned to talk, and he told the then governor that it was the queen's desire to call this place 'Bethtown'. That's the way it went into the official records. By the time Bess discovered the monumental goof, the name had already gone into familiar usage, and she realized she couldn't very well re-educate the colonists, so she let it stand. Instead, she cut off the lisping messenger's head – but that's show biz.

Majesta had been named after George III, whose advisers at first thought it would be fitting to name the place Georgetown but who then decided there were too many Georgetowns around already. They dug into their Latin texts and came up with the word *majestas*, which meant, 'grandeur' or 'greatness' or 'majesty', and this seemed a proper tribute to their monarch. George later had a little trouble in Boston with some tea-drinkers, his majesty having diminished somewhat, but the name Majesta remained as a reminder of better days.

Calm's Point hadn't been named after anybody. In fact, for a very long time, hardly anyone at all lived on this small island bordering the larger island of Isola. In those days, wild animals foraged through the woods engaging each other in bloody battles – but the rest of the city nonetheless referred to the island across the River Harb as Calm's Point. A few hardy adventurers cleared the woods of beasts, pitched a couple of tents, and began propagating. That's the way to start a suburb, all right. After a while, when the tribe increases, you can petition the city for ferry service. In the event of a real population explosion, you can even hope for a bridge to the mainland.

Bert Kling was heading for Riverhead, where Mrs Joseph Wechsler made her residence. There was, in actuality, no river which had its head – or even its tail – in that part of the city. In the days of the old Dutch settlers the entire part of the city above Isola was owned by a patron named Ryerhert. Ryerhert's Farms was good land interspersed with igneous and metamorphic rock. As the

66

city grew, Ryerhert sold part of his land and donated the rest of it until eventually all of it was owned by the city. Ryerhert was hard to say. Even before 1917, when it became unfashionable for anything to sound even mildly Teutonic, Ryerhert had become Riverhead. There was, to be sure, water in Riverhead. But the water was a brook, really, and it wasn't even called a brook. It was called Five Mile Pond. It was not five miles wide, nor was it five miles long, nor was it five miles from any noticeable landmark. It was simply a brook which was called Five Mile Pond in a community called Riverhead which had no river's head in it.

The city was a crazy thing sometimes.

Mrs Wechsler lived in Riverhead in an apartment building which had a large entrance court flanked by two enormous stone flowerpots without any flowers in them. Kling walked between the pots, and through the entrance court, and into the vestibule. He found a name plate for Joseph Wechsler, apartment 4A, and pressed the bell. There was an answering click on the locked inner vestibule door. He opened the door and walked upstairs to the fourth floor.

He took a deep breath in the hallway outside the Wechsler apartment. Then he knocked.

A woman answered the knock.

She looked at Kling curiously and said, 'Yes?'

'Mrs Wechsler?'

'No?' It was still a question. 'Are you the new rabbi?' the woman asked.

'What?'

'The new . . .'

'No. I'm from the police.'

'Oh.' The woman paused. 'Oh, did you want to see Ruth?'

'Is that Mrs Wechsler?'

'Yes.'

'That's who I'd like to see,' Kling said.

'We . . .' The woman looked confused. 'She . . . you see, we're sitting *shivah*. That's . . . are you Jewish?'

'No.'

'We're in mourning. For Joseph. I'm his sister. I think it would be better if you came back another—'

'Ma'am, I'd appreciate it if I could talk to Mrs Wechsler now. I . . . I can understand . . . but . . .'

He suddenly wanted to leave. He did not want to intrude on mourners. And then he thought, Leave, and the killer gets an edge.

'Could I please see her now?' he asked. 'Would you please ask her?'

'I'll ask her,' the woman said, and she closed the door.

Kling waited in the hallway. He could hear the sounds of an apartment building everywhere around him, the sounds of life. And, beyond the closed door to apartment 4A, the stillness of death.

A young man came up the steps, carrying a book under his arm. He nodded solemnly at Kling, stopped just beside him, and asked, 'This is Wechsler?'

'Yes.'

'Thank you.'

He knocked on the door. While he waited for someone to answer his knock, he touched his fingers to the *mezuzah* fastened to the jamb. They waited together silently in the hallway. From somewhere upstairs a woman shouted to her son in the street. 'Martin! Come upstairs and put on a sweater!' Inside the apartment, there was silence. The young man knocked again. They could hear footsteps beyond the door. Joseph Wechsler's sister opened the door, looked first at Kling and then at the newcomer. 'Are you the rabbi?' she asked.

'Yes,' the man answered.

'Will you come in, please, *rov*?' she said. She turned to Kling. 'Ruth says she will talk to you, Mr – what is your name?'

'Kling.'

'Yes, Mr Kling. Mr Kling, she's just lost her husband. Would you please . . . could you kindly . . . ?'

'I understand,' Kling said.

'Come in then. Please.'

They were sitting in the living room. There was a basket of fruit on the coffee table. The pictures, the mirrors were draped in black. The mourners sat on wooden crates. The men wore black *yomulkas*, the women wore shawls. The young rabbi had entered the room and was beginning to lead a prayer. Ruth Wechsler broke away from the mourners and came to Kling.

'How do you do?' she said. 'I am glad to know you.' She spoke with a thick Yiddish accent, which surprised Kling at first because she seemed like such a young woman and an unfamiliarity with English did not seem to go with youth. And then, looking at her more closely in the dimness of the room, he realized that she was well into her forties, perhaps even in her early fifties, one of those rare Semitic types who never truly age, with jet-black hair and luminous brown eyes, more luminous because they were wet with tears. She took his hand briefly, and he fumblingly shook hands, not knowing what to say, his own grief suddenly swallowed in the eyes of this beautiful pale woman who was ageless.

'Would you come with me, please?' she said. Her accent was really atrocious, almost a burlesque of the Sammy and Abie vaudeville routines, stripped of all amusement by the woman's utter sadness. Kling automatically made an aural adjustment, discounting the thick dialect, translating mentally, hearing still the curious structure of her sentences but cutting through the accent to arrive at the meaning of her words.

She led him to a small room behind the living room. There was a couch and a television set in the room. The screen was blank. Two windows faced the street and the sounds of a city in turbulence. From the living room came the sound of the rabbi's voice raised in the ancient Hebraic mourning prayers. In the small room with the television set Kling sat beside Ruth Wechsler and felt a oneness with the woman. He wanted to take her hands in his own. He wanted to weep with her.

'Mrs Wechsler, I know this is difficult—'

'No, I would like to talk to you,' she said. She pronounced the word 'vould'. She nodded and said, 'I want to help the police. We can't catch the killer unless I help the police.' He looked into the luminous brown eyes and heard the words exactly that way, even though she had actually said, 'Ve ken't ketch d'killuh onless I halp d'police.'

'Then . . . that's very kind of you, Mrs Wechsler. And I'll try not to ask too many questions. I'll try to be as brief as possible.'

'Take what time you need,' she said.

'Mrs Wechsler, would you happen to know what your husband was doing in Isola at that particular bookshop?'

'Nearby there, he has a store.'

'Where is that, Mrs Wechsler?'

'On the Stem and North Forty-seventh.'

'What kind of a store?'

'Hardware.'

'I see, and his store is close to the bookshop. Did he go to the bookshop often?'

'Yes. He was a big reader, Joseph. He doesn't speak too well, Joseph. He has, like me, a terrible accent. But he enjoyed reading. He said this helped him with words, to read it out loud. He would read to me out loud in bed. I think . . . I think he went there to get a book I mentioned last week – that I said it would be nice if we read it.'

'What book was that, Mrs Wechsler?'

'By Herman Wouk, he's a fine man. Joseph read to me out loud *The Caine Mutiny* and *This Is My God*, and I said to him we should get this book, *Marjorie Morningstar*, because when it came out there was some fuss, some Jewish people took offence. I said to Joseph, how could such a fine man like Herman Wouk write a book would offend Jews? I said to Joseph there must be a mistake. There must be too many people, they're too sensitive. I said it must be that Mr Wouk is the offended party, that this man is being misunderstood, that his love is being misunderstood for something else. That's what I said to Joseph. So I asked him to get the book, we should find out for ourselves.'

'I see. And you think he went there to get that book?'

'Yes, I think so.'

'Was this a habit of his? Buying books in that particular store?'

'Buying there, and also using the rental library.'

'I see. But at *that* store? Not at a store in your own neighbourhood, for example?'

'No. Joseph spent a lot of time with his business, you see, and so he would do little errands on his lunch hour, or maybe before he came home, but always in the neighbourhood where he has his business.'

'What sort of errands do you mean, Mrs Wechsler?'

'Oh, like little things. Let me see. Well, like a few weeks ago, there was a portable radio we have, it needed fixing. So Joseph took it with him to work and had it fixed in a neighbourhood store there.'

'I see.'

'Or his automobile, it got a scratch in the fender. Just parked on the street, someone hit him and scraped paint from the fender – isn't there something we can do about that?'

'Well . . . have you contacted your insurance company?'

'Yes, but we have fifty-dollar deductible – you know what that is?'

'Yes.'

'And this was just a small paint job, twenty-five, thirty dollars, I forget. I still have to pay the bill. The car painter sent me his bill last week.'

'I see,' Kling said. 'In other words, your husband made a habit of dealing with businessmen in the neighbourhood where his own business was located. And someone could have known that he went to that bookshop often.'

'Yes. Someone could have known.'

'Is there anyone who . . . who might have had a reason for wanting to kill your husband, Mrs Wechsler?'

Quite suddenly, Ruth Wechsler said, 'You know, I can't get used to he's dead.' She said the words conversationally, as if she were commenting about a puzzling aspect of the weather. Kling fell silent and listened. 'I can't get used to he won't read to me any more out loud. In bed.' She shook her head. 'I can't get used to it.'

The room was silent. In the living room, the litany of the dead rose and fell in melodic, sombre tones.

'Did . . . did he have any enemies, Mrs Wechsler?' Kling asked softly.

Ruth Wechsler shook her head.

'Had he received any threatening notes or telephone calls?'

'No.'

'Had he had any arguments with anyone? Heated words? Anything like that?'

'I don't know. I don't think so.'

'Mrs Wechsler . . . when your husband died . . . at the hospital, the detective who was with him heard him say the word "carpenter". Is that the name of anyone you know?'

'No. Carpenter? No.' She shook her head. 'No, we don't know anybody by that name.'

'Well . . . is it possible your husband was having some woodworking done?'

'No.'

'That he might have contacted a carpenter or a cabinetmaker?'

'No.'

'Nothing like that?'

Kling said, 'Are you sure?'

'I'm positive.'

'Do you have any idea why he would have said that word, Mrs Wechsler? He repeated it over and over. We thought it might have some special meaning.'

'No. Nobody.'

'Do you have any of your husband's letters or bills? Perhaps he was corresponding with someone, or doing business with someone who—'

'I shared everything with my husband. Nobody named Carpenter. No woodworkers. No cabinetmakers. I'm sorry.'

73

'Well, could I have the bills and letters anyway? I'll return them to you in good condition.'

'But please don't take too long with the bills,' Ruth Wechsler said. 'I like to pay bills prompt.' She sighed heavily. 'I have to read it now.'

'I'm sorry, what . . . ?'

'The book. Mr Wouk's book.' She paused. 'My poor husband,' she said. 'My poor darling.'

And though she pronounced the word 'dollink', it did not sound at all amusing.

In the hallway outside the apartment. Kling suddenly leaned back against the wall and squeezed his eyes shut. He breathed heavily and violently for several moments, and then he let out a long sigh, and shoved himself off the wall, and quietly went down the steps to the street.

It was Saturday, and the children were all home from school. A stickball game was in progress in the middle of the street, the boys wearing open shirts in the unaccustomed October balminess. Little girls in bright frocks skipped rope on the sidewalk – 'Double-ee-Dutch, Double-ee-Dutch, catch a rabbit and build a hutch!' Two little boys were playing marbles in the gutter, one of them arguing about the illegal use of a steelie in the game. Further up the street Kling saw three pint-sized conspirators, two boys and a girl, rush up to a doorway on street level, glance around furtively, ring the bell, and then rush across the street to the opposite side. As he passed the doorway, the door opened and a housewife peered out inquisitively. From across the street the three children began chanting. 'Lady, lady, I did it; lady, lady, I did it; lady, lady, I did it; lady, lady, I did it . . .'

The sound of their voices echoed in his ears all the way up the block.

7.

TEDDY CARELLA WAS talking.

She said:

'Yes?' Carella said.

'I'm beginning to get the message,' Carella said.

'Is that the best you can do?' Carella asked. 'That's not very original. So you love me, huh?'

Teddy repeated the three words, her hands rapidly spelling the message. He took her into his arms and kissed the tip of her nose briefly, and then his mouth dropped to hers and he kissed her completely and long-ingly, holding her in his arms after the kiss, her head cradled against his cheek. He released her at last and took off his jacket and then took his service revolver from his right rear pocket, unclipping the holster and putting the gun down on the end table. Teddy frowned and a torrent of words spilled from her hands.

'All right, all right,' Carella answered. 'I won't leave it around where the kids can get at it. Where are they, anyway?'

In the yard, her hands told him. *What happened today? Did you talk—*

But Carella had picked up the revolver and gone into the bedroom of the old Riverhead house, and he could no longer see her hands. She came into the room after him, turned him around to face her, and completed the sentence.

—to Kling? How is he?

Carella unbuttoned his shirt and threw it over one of the chairs. Teddy picked it up and carried it to the hamper. In the back yard he could hear the twins chasing each other, shouting their childish gibberish.

'I talked to Kling, yes,' he said. 'He's working on the case with us.'

Teddy frowned and then shrugged.

'I felt the same way, honey,' Carella answered. He took off his T-shirt, wiped perspiration from his chest and under his arms, and then fired the wadded shirt at the hamper, missing. Teddy cast him a baleful glance and picked up the shirt. 'But he wants in on it, and we can't very well refuse him.' He had turned his back, heading for the bathroom, thoughtlessly. He stopped in his tracks, turned to her, and repeated his words so that she could read his lips. 'We can't very well refuse him.'

Teddy nodded, but she still seemed troubled by the concept. She followed Carella into the bathroom and sat on the edge of the tub while he washed. Through a layer of suds and water, Carella said, 'We figure the killer was after one of the four he got, Teddy. Maybe we're wrong, but that's the way we read it.' His hands had covered his mouth on the last two words as he rinsed away suds.

'Read it,' he repeated, and Teddy nodded. He dried his face and then began speaking again while she watched his lips intently. 'We've been questioning relatives of the deceased. Meyer and I spoke to Mrs Land out on Sands Spit this morning, and Bert went to see Mrs Wechsler this afternoon. So far, there's nothing we can go on. There's Claire's father, of course, and Meyer and I thought we'd go see him tomorrow . . .'

Teddy frowned instantly.

'What is it?' Carella asked.

The folks are coming tomorrow, she told him.

'What time?'

In the afternoon. One or two. For lunch.

'Then Meyer and I . . . well, we'll make it early in the morning. He's got to be talked to, Teddy.'

Teddy nodded.

'We haven't been able to get a line on the third man who was killed in the shop. His name's Anthony La Scala, and his driver's licence gave an address in Isola for him. But Meyer and I checked there a little while ago, and the super told us he'd moved about a month ago. The post office doesn't have a forwarding address for him.'

That might be something, Teddy said.

'It might. I want to do some homework with the phone book later.'

Teddy shook her head.

'Why not?'

He moved a month ago. The phone book . . .

'That's right,' Carella said, nodding. 'His new address and number wouldn't be listed yet. How come you're so smart?' He grinned and held out his hands to her. She took them, and he pulled her from her sitting position and held her close to his naked chest. 'Why don't we have Fanny feed the kids and put them to bed?' he said. 'Then we can go out to dinner and a movie.'

Teddy wiggled her eyebrows.

'Well, yeah, that, too. But I thought later.'

She ran her tongue over her lips and then pulled away from him. He reached out for her, missed, and slapped her on the behind as she went out of the bathroom, laughing soundlessly. When he came into the bedroom, she was taking off her clothes.

'What are you doing?' he asked, puzzled. 'The kids are still awake.'

Teddy let her hands dangle loosely from the wrists and then waggled the fingers.

'Oh, you're gonna take a shower,' he said.

She nodded.

'I think you're just trying to tease me, that's all.'

Teddy shrugged speculatively and then went past him, half naked, into the bathroom. She closed the door, and he heard the lock clicking shut. The door opened again. She cocked her head around the door-frame, grinned mischievously, and then brought her right hand up suddenly. Quickly her fingers moved.

Go talk to your children, she said.

Then, at the end of the sentence, she waved good-bye, her head and hand disappeared, the door clicked shut, the lock snapped. In a moment, Carella heard the shower going. He smiled, put on a fresh T-shirt and went downstairs to find the twins and Fanny.

Fanny was sitting on a bench under the single huge tree in the Carella back yard, a big Irish woman in her early fifties who looked up the moment Carella came out of the house.

'Well,' she said, 'it's himself.'

'Daddy!' Mark yelled, his fist poised to sock his sister

in the eye. He ran across the yard and leaped into Carella's arms. April, a little slower to respond, especially since she'd expected a punch just a moment before, did a small take and then shot across the lawn as if she'd been propelled from a launching pad. The twins were almost two and a half years old, fraternal twins who had managed to combine the best features of their parents in faces that looked similar but not identical. Both had Carella's high cheekbones and slanting oriental eyes. Both had Teddy's black hair and full mouths. At the moment, Mark also had a strangle hold on Carella's neck, and April was doing her best to climb to a sitting position on his waist by clambering up his legs.

'It's himself,' April said, mimicking Fanny, from whom she heard most of her English during the day.

'It's himself indeed,' Carella said. 'How come you weren't waiting at the front door to greet me?'

'Well, who knows when you minions of the law will come home?' Fanny asked smiling.

'Sure, who knows when the minnows,' April said.

'Well, Daddy,' Mark said seriously. 'How was business today?'

'Fine, just fine,' Carella said.

'Did you catch a crook?' April asked.

'No, not yet.'

'Will you catch . . .' She paused and rephrased it. 'Will you catch . . .' Apparently the rephrasing didn't satisfy her either. 'Will you catch . . .' she said, paused again, gave it up, and then completed the sentence. 'Will you catch one tomorrow?'

'Oh, if the weather's good, maybe we will,' Carella said.

'Well, that's good, Daddy,' Mark said.

' "*If* the weather's good," he said,' April put in.

'Well, if you catch one, bring him home,' Mark said.

'Those two are gonna be G men,' Fanny said. She sat in bright, redheaded splendour under the bold autumn foliage of the tree, grinning approval at her brood. A trained nurse who supplemented the meagre salary Carella could afford by taking night calls whenever she could, she had been working for the Carellas ever since the twins were brought home from the hospital.'

'Daddy, what do crooks look like?' Mark asked.

'Well, some of them look like Fanny,' Carella said.

'That's right, teach them,' Fanny said.

'Are there lady crooks?' April asked.

'There are lady crooks and men crooks, yes,' Carella said.

'But no chi'drun,' Mark said. He always had difficulty with the word.

'Children,' Fanny corrected, as she invariably did.

'Chi'drun,' Mark repeated, and he nodded.

'No, no children crooks,' Carella said. 'Children are too smart to be crooks.' He put the twins down and said, 'Fanny, I brought you something.'

'What?'

'A swear box.'

'What in hell is a swear box?'

'I left it in the kitchen for you. You've got to put money in it every time you use a swear word.'

'Like hell I will.'

'Like hell she will,' April said.

'See?' Carella said.

'I don't know where they pick it up.' Fanny answered, shaking her head in mock puzzlement.

'You feel like giving us the night off?' Carella asked.

'It's Saturday, ain't it? Young people have to go out on Saturday.'

'Good,' Mark said.

'Huh?' Carella asked.

'We're young people.'

'Yes, but Fanny's going to feed you and put you to bed, and Mommy and Daddy are going to a movie.'

'Which one?'

'I don't know yet.'

'Go see a monster fimm,' Mark said.

'A what?'

'A monster fimm.'

'Film?'

'Yeah.'

'Why should I? I have two monsters right here.'

'Don't, Daddy,' April said. 'You'll scare us.'

He sat with them in the yard while Teddy showered and dusk claimed the city. He read to them from *Winnie the Pooh* until it was time for their dinner. Then he went upstairs to change his clothes. He and Teddy had a good dinner and saw a good movie. When they got home to the old Riverhead house, they made love. He leaned back against the pillow afterwards and smoked a cigarette in the dark.

And somehow Kling's loss seemed enormously magnified.

8.

728 PETERSON AVENUE was in the heart of Riverhead
in a good middle-class neighbourhood dotted with low
apartment buildings and two-storey frame houses. Ralph
Townsend lived there in apartment number 47. At nine
o'clock on Sunday morning, October 15, Detectives
Meyer Meyer and Steve Carella rang the bell outside the
closed door and waited. Kling had told them the night
before that Claire's father was a night watchman, and
he'd advised them to call at the apartment around nine
o'clock, when the old man would be returning home
from his shift and before he went to bed. As it was, they
caught Townsend in the middle of breakfast. He invited
them into the apartment and then poured coffee for
them. They sat together in the small kitchen, with
sunlight streaming through the window and burnishing
the oilcloth on the table. Townsend was in his middle
fifties, a man with all his hair, as black as his daughter's
had been. He had a huge barrel chest and muscular arms.
He wore a white shirt, the sleeves rolled up over his
biceps. He wore bright-green suspenders. He also wore a
black tie.

'I won't be going to sleep today,' he said, 'I have to go
over to the funeral parlour.'

'You went to work last night, Mr Townsend?' Meyer
asked.

'A man has to work,' Townsend said simply. 'I
mean . . . well, you didn't know Claire, but . . . well,
you see, in this family, we thought . . . her mother died

82

when she was just a little girl, you know, and . . . we . . . we sort of made up between us that what we owed to Mary . . . that was her name, Claire's mother . . . we made up that what we owed to Mary was to *live*, you see. To carry on. To *live*. So . . . I feel I owe the same thing to Claire. I owe it to her to . . . to miss her with all my heart, but to go on living. And working is a part of life.' He fell silent. Then he said, 'So I went to work last night.' And he fell silent again. He sipped at his coffee. 'Last night I went to work, and today I'll go to the funeral parlour where my little girl is lying dead.' He sipped at the coffee again. He was a strong man, and the grief on his face was strong, in keeping with his character. There were no tears in his eyes, but sorrow sat within him like a heavy stone.

'Mr Townsend,' Carella said, 'we have to ask you some questions. I know you'll understand . . .'

'I understand,' Townsend said, 'but I'd like to ask you a question first, if that's all right.'

'Sure,' Carella said.

'I want to know . . . did this have anything to do with Bert?'

'What do you mean?'

'I like Bert,' Townsend said. 'I liked him the minute Claire brought him around. He did wonders for her, you know. She'd been through that thing where her boyfriend was killed, and for a while she . . . she forgot about living, do you know what I mean? I thought . . . I thought we'd agreed on . . . on what to do when her mother died, and then . . . then this fellow she was going with got killed in the war, and Claire just slipped away. Just slipped away. Until Bert came along – and then she changed. She became herself again. She was alive again. Now . . .'

'Yes, Mr Townsend?'

'Now, I . . . I wonder. I mean, Bert's a cop and I like Bert. I like him. But . . . did . . . did Claire get killed because her boyfriend is a cop? That's what I'd like to know.'

'We don't think so, Mr Townsend.'

'Then why did she get killed? I've been over it a hundred times in my mind. And it seems to me that . . . maybe somebody had something against Bert and he took it out on Claire. He killed Claire to get even with Bert. Just because Bert's a cop. Now doesn't that seem to make sense? If anything in this whole damn thing makes sense, doesn't that seem to make the most sense?'

'We haven't overlooked that possibility, Mr Townsend,' Meyer said. 'We've gone back in our files over all the major arrests Bert made. We've eliminated those which were petty offences because they didn't seem to warrant such massive retaliation. We've also eliminated any men or women who are still in prison, since obviously—'

'Yes, I understand.'

'—and also those who were paroled more than a year ago. We figure a vendetta murder would have been committed as soon after—'

'Yes, I see, I see,' Townsend said.

'So we've rounded up recent parolees and men who've completed shorter terms – at least, all those for whom we have known residences. We're still in the process of questioning these people. But, quite frankly, this doesn't seem to be *that* kind of a murder.'

'How do you know?'

'A murder case has a feel to it, Mr Townsend. When you've worked enough of them, you develop a sort of intuition. We don't think Claire's death was connected with the fact that Bert is a cop. We may be wrong, but so far our thinking is going in another direction.'

'What direction is that?' Townsend asked.

'Well, we think the killer was after a specific person in that shop, and that he got the one he was after.'

'Why couldn't it have been Claire? And why couldn't . . . ?'

'It *could* have been Claire, Mr Townsend.'

'Then it also could have been connected to Bert.'

'Yes, but then why didn't the killer go after Bert? Why would he kill Claire?'

'I don't know why. What kind of a crazy twisted bastard would kill four people anyway?' Townsend asked. 'Are you trying to apply logic to this? What logic is there? You just told me he was after only *one* person, for Christ's sake, but he killed *four*!'

Meyer sighed patiently. 'Mr Townsend, we haven't discounted the possibility that someone carrying a grudge against Bert Kling took it out on him by killing your daughter. It's happened before, certainly, and we're investigating that possibility. I'm only trying to say that it doesn't seem to be the most fruitful course we can pursue in this case. That's all. But, of course, we'll continue to explore the possibility until we've exhausted it.'

'I'd like to think Bert had nothing to do with this,' Townsend said.

'Then please think that,' Carella said.

'I'd like to.'

The room was silent.

'In any case,' Meyer said, 'Claire was one of the four people killed. With this in mind—'

'You're wondering whether Claire was the intended victim?'

'Yes, sir. That's what we're wondering.'

'How would I know?'

'Well, Mr Townsend,' Carella said, 'we thought perhaps Claire might have mentioned something that was troubling her. Or—'

'Nothing seemed to be troubling her.'

'Had she received any threatening phone calls? Or letters? Would you know?'

'I work nights,' Townsend said. 'I'm usually asleep during the day while Claire is at school or doing casework. We usually have dinner together, but I don't recall her saying anything about threats. Nothing like that.' He had inadvertently slipped into the present tense in discussing his daughter, casually sidestepping the fact that she was dead.

'What sort of casework did she do?' Carella asked, reverting to the proper tense.

'She works at Buenavista Hospital,' Townsend said.

'What sort of work?'

'Well, you know she's a social worker, don't you?'

'Yes, but—'

'She does . . . well, you *know* what medical social workers do, don't you?'

'Not exactly, Mr Townsend.'

'Well, Claire works—' He stopped suddenly, as if realizing all at once that he had been committing an error in tense. He stared at the detectives, somewhat surprised by his own discovery. He sighed heavily. 'Claire *worked*,' he said, and he hesitated again, giving the word time to set, accepting the knowledge once and for all, 'Claire worked with hospitalized patients. Doctors provide medical care, you know, but very often it takes more than that to make a patient well. Claire provided the something more. She helped the patient towards *using* the medical care, towards *wanting* to be well again.'

'I see,' Carella said. He thought for a moment and then asked, 'Did Claire ever mention any particular patient she was working with?'

'Yes, she mentioned a great many of them.'

'In what way, Mr Townsend?'

'Well, she took a personal interest in *all* the people she worked with. In fact, you might say her work *was* this personal interest, this special attention to a patient's problems.'

'And she would come home and tell you about these people, is that right?'

'Yes. Stories about them . . . or . . . or funny things that happened. You know.'

'Were there times when something happened that wasn't so funny, Mr Townsend?'

'Oh, she had her complaints. She was carrying a very large caseload, and sometimes it got a little difficult. Sometimes her temper wore a little thin.'

'Did she mention any specific trouble?'

'Trouble?'

'With patients? With families of patients? With doctors? With anyone on the hospital staff?'

'No, nothing specific.'

'Anything at all? A slight argument? Anything you can remember?'

'I'm sorry. Claire got along well with people, you see. I guess that's why she was a good social worker. She got along with people. She treated *everyone* like a person. That's a rare talent, Mr Carella.'

'It is,' Carella agreed. 'Mr Townsend, you've been very helpful. Thank you very much.'

'Is . . . is there anything I can tell Bert?' Townsend asked.

'I beg your pardon?'

'Bert. He's sure to be at the funeral parlour.'

On the way downstairs, Meyer asked, 'What do you think?'

'I'd like to hit the hospital,' Carella said. 'What time do you have?'

'Ten-thirty.'

'You game?'

'Sarah said to be home by lunch.' Meyer shrugged.

'Let's do it now, then. It might give us something to go on tomorrow.'

'I don't like hospitals,' Meyer said. 'My mother died in a hospital.'

'If you want me to go alone . . .'

'No, no, I'll come with you. It's just I don't like hospitals, that's all.'

They walked to the police sedan, and Carella slipped in behind the wheel. He started the car and then eased it into the light Sunday morning traffic.

'Let's have a quick run-down while we drive over, OK?' he said.

'OK.'

'What's the other team covering?'

'Di Maeo's checking out the 1954 bookstore holdup. Our records show the thief was released from Castleview in 1956 and returned to Denver. But he wants to make sure the guy didn't come back here. He's checking on some of his buddies, too, to make sure they weren't involved in the Friday shooting.'

'What else?'

'He's going over every arrest Bert ever made, sorting them out, putting a pickup-and-hold on anybody who looks like a possible. He's plenty busy, Steve.'

'OK. What about Willis and Brown?'

'Willis is trying to locate family or friends of the fourth victim. What the hell was his name?'

'La Scala.'

'That's right,' Meyer said. 'Anthony La Scala.'

'How come Italians are always getting shot?' Carella asked.

'They're not.'

'On *The Untouchables* they're always getting shot.'

'Well, that show is stacked,' Meyer said. He grinned slyly and added, 'Did you catch that one?'

'I caught it.'

'Stacked. Robert Sta—'

'I caught it,' Carella said again. 'Has Willis found an address for this La Scala character yet?'

'Not yet.'

'That's pretty peculiar, isn't it?'

'Yeah, pretty peculiar.'

'Makes him sound a little shady.'

'All your countrymen are shady,' Meyer said. 'Didn't you know that? Don't you watch *The Untouchables*?'

'Sure I do. You know what I noticed?'

'What?'

'Robert Stack never smiles.'

'I saw him smile once,' Meyer said.

'When?'

'I forget. He was killing some hood. But I distinctly saw him smile.'

'I never saw him smile,' Carella said seriously.

'Well, a cop's life is a tough one,' Meyer said. 'You know what I noticed?'

'What?'

'Frank Nitti always wears the same striped, double-breasted suit.'

'That's 'cause crime doesn't pay,' Carella said.

'I like that guy who plays Nitti.'

'Yeah, I do, too.' Carella nodded. 'You know something? I don't think I ever saw *him* smile either.'

'What's with you and this smiling business?'

'I don't know. I like to see people smile every now and then.'

'Here,' Meyer said. 'Here's a smile for you.' He grinned from ear to ear.

Carella said, 'Here's the hospital. Save your teeth for the admissions nurse.'

The admissions nurse was charmed to pieces by Meyer's dazzling dental display, and she told them how to reach the ward where Claire Townsend had worked. The intern on duty wasn't quite as thrilled by Meyer's smile. He was underpaid and overworked, and he didn't need a comic vaudeville team lousing up his nice quiet ward on a nice quiet Sunday morning. He was ready to give the itinerant flatfoots a fast brush, but he didn't know he was dealing with Detective Meyer Meyer, scourge of the underworld and the medical profession, the most patient cop and man in the city, if not in the entire United States.

'We're terribly sorry to intrude on your valuable time, Dr McElroy,' Meyer said, 'but—'

McElroy, who was a bit of a sharpshooter himself, quickly said, 'Well, I'm glad you understand, gentlemen. If you'll kindly leave, then, we can all get back to—'

'Yes, we understand,' Meyer sniped, 'and of course you have patients to examine and sedatives to distribute and—'

'You're oversimplifying an intern's work,' McElroy said.

'Naturally I am, and I apologize, because I know how very busy you are, Dr McElroy. But we're dealing with a homicide here—'

'I'm dealing with sick people here,' McElroy interrupted.

'And your job is to keep them from dying. But our job is to find out who killed the ones who are already dead. Anything you can tell us about—'

'I have specific orders from the Chief of Staff,' McElroy said, 'and it's my job to carry them out in his absence. A hospital works by the clock, Detective . . . Meyer, was it?'

'Yes, and I understand—'

'—and I simply haven't the time to answer a lot of questions – not this morning, I haven't. Why don't you wait until Staff comes in, and you can ask—'

'But you worked with Claire Townsend, didn't you?'

'Claire worked with me, and with all the other doctors on this ward, and also with Staff. Look, Detective Meyer—'

'Did you get along well with her?'

'I don't intend to answer any questions, Detective Meyer.'

'I guess he didn't get along with her, Steve,' Meyer said.

'Of *course* I got along with her. Everyone did. Claire was a . . . look, Detective Meyer, you're not going to trick me into a long discussion about Claire. Really! I have work to do. I have patients.'

'I have patience, too,' Meyer said, and he grinned beautifully. 'You were saying about Claire?'

McElroy glared at Meyer silently.

'I guess we could subpoena him,' Carella said.

'Subpoena me? What in hell . . . ? Look,' McElroy said patiently, 'I have to make my rounds at eleven o'clock. Then I have to order medication. Then I have two—'

'Yes, we know you're busy,' Meyer said.

'I have two spinal taps and some intravenouses, not to mention new admissions and personal histories and—'

'Let's go get a warrant,' Carella said.

McElroy's shoulders slumped. 'Why'd I ever become a doctor?' he asked no one in particular.

'How long did you know Claire?'

'About six months,' McElroy said tiredly.

'Did you like working with her?'

'Everyone did. Medical social workers are very valuable to us, and Claire was an unusually conscientious and able person. I was sorry to read about . . . about what happened. Claire was a nice girl. And a good worker.'

'Did she ever have any trouble with anyone on the ward?'

'No.'

'Doctors? Nurses? Patients?'

'No.'

'Now, come on, Dr McElroy,' Meyer said. 'This girl wasn't a saint.'

'Maybe she wasn't a saint,' McElroy said, 'but she was a damn good social worker. And a good social worker doesn't get involved in petty squabbles.'

'*Are* there petty squabbles on this ward?'

'There are petty squabbles everywhere.'

'But Claire never got involved in any of them.'

'Not to my knowledge,' McElroy said.

'How about her patients? You can't tell us all of her patients were ideal, well-adjusted individuals who—'

'No, many of them were quite disturbed.'

'Then, surely, *all* of them didn't readily accept what she was trying to—'

'That's true. Not all of them accepted her at first.'

'Then there *were* problems.'

'At first. But Claire had a wonderful way with people,

and she almost always gained a patient's complete confidence.'

'*Almost* always?'

'Yes.'

'When didn't she?' Carella asked.

'What?'

'Almost isn't always, Dr McElroy. *Did* she have trouble with any of the patients?'

'Nothing serious. Nothing she couldn't work out. I'm trying to tell you that Claire was an unusually dedicated person who had a wonderful way of dealing with her patients. To be quite frank about it, some medical social workers are a severe pain in the ass. But not Claire. Claire was gentle and patient and kind and understanding and . . . she was *good*, period. She knew her job, and she loved her job. She was good at it. That's all I can tell you. Why, she even . . . her work extended beyond this ward. She took a personal interest in the patients' families. She visited homes, helped relatives to make adjustments. She was an unusual person, believe me.'

'Which homes did she visit?'

'What?'

'Which homes did she—'

'Oh, I'm not sure. Several. I can't remember.'

'Try.'

'Really . . .'

'Try.'

'Oh, let me see. There was a man in, several months back, had broken his leg on the job. Claire took an interest in his family, visited the home, helped the children. Or the beginning of last month, for example. We had a woman in with a ruptured appendix. Quite a mess, believe me. Peritonitis, subdiaphragmatic abscess, the works. She was here quite a while – just released last week, as a matter of fact. Claire got very friendly with her young daughter, a girl of about sixteen. Even kept up her interest after the woman was discharged.'

'What do you mean?'

'She called her.'

'The young girl? She called her from here? From the ward?'

'Yes.'

'What did she talk about?'

'I'm sure I don't know. I'm not in the habit of listening to other people's—'

'How often did she call her?'

'Well . . . quite frequently this past week.' McElroy paused. 'In fact, the girl called *her* once. Right here.'

'She did, huh? What's the girl's name?'

'I don't know. I can get you the mother's name. That would be in our records.'

'Yes, would you please?' Carella said.

'This is a little unusual, isn't it?' Meyer asked. 'Keeping up contact with a woman's daughter after the woman's been released?'

'No, not terribly unusual. Most social workers do a follow-up. And as I said, Claire was a very conscientious—'

'But would you say there was a *personal* involvement with this young girl?'

'All of Claire's involvements—'

'Please, Dr McElroy. I think you know what I mean. Was Claire Townsend's interest in this young girl more than the interest she usually expressed in a patient or the family of a patient?'

McElroy thought this one over for a few minutes. Then he said, 'Yes, I would say so.'

'Good. May we look at those records now, please?'

*

Back at the squad, Detective Hal Willis was studying a necropsy report made on the dead body of Anthony La Scala. The report informed him that the cause of death had been three .45-calibre bullets in the lungs and heart and that death had most probably been instantaneous. But the report also mentioned the fact that both of La Scala's arms were scarred around the superficial veins on the flexor surface of the forearm and the bend of the elbow. These scars appeared to be short ropelike thickenings of the dermis from three-eighths of an inch to one inch in length and about three-sixteenths of an inch wide. It was the opinion of the medical examiner, strongly bolstered by a large amount of heroin found in La Scala's blood stream, that the marks on his arms were mainline scars, that La Scala had injected the drug intravenously, and that he had undoubtedly been addicted to the drug for a good long time, judging from the number of scars and the tiny dots arranged seriatim on the thickened areas.

Willis put the report into the Kling Case folder and then said to Brown, who was sitting at the next desk. 'That's great, ain't it? A goddamn hophead. How do we find out where a hophead was living? Probably in Grover Park underneath a goddamn bench! How do we find the friends and relatives of a goddamn hop-head?'

Brown considered this pensively for a moment. Then he said, 'Maybe it's a break, Hal. *This* may have been the one he wanted. Hopheads get mixed up in a lot of crazy things.' He nodded again, emphatically. 'Maybe this is a break.'

And maybe it was.

9.

MONDAY MORNING CAME.

It always does.

On Monday morning you sit back and take a look at things, and things look lousy. That's a part of Monday, the nature of the beast. Monday should be a fresh beginning, a sort of road-company New Year's Day. But, somehow, Monday is only and always a continuation, a familiar awakening to a start which is really only a repetition. There should be laws against Monday morning.

Arthur Brown didn't like Monday morning any more than anyone else did. He was a cop, and only incidentally a Negro, and he lived in a coloured ghetto close to the office. He had a wife named Caroline, and a daughter named Connie, and they shared a four-room flat in a building weary with time. Happily, when Brown got out of bed on the morning of October 16, the floors were not cold. The floors were usually cold around this time of year, despite the city ordinance which made it mandatory to provide steam heat beginning on the fifteenth of October. This year, with Indian summer swinging her hot little behind through the city, the landlords were enjoying a reprieve, and the tenants didn't have to bang on the radiators. Brown was grateful for the warm floors.

He got out of bed quietly, not wanting to wake Caroline, who was asleep beside him. He was a big man with close-cropped black hair and brown eyes and a deep-brown complexion. He had worked on the docks before he joined the force, and his arms and shoulders and chest still bulged with the muscles of his youthful labour. He had been sleeping in his pyjama bottoms, Caroline curled beside him in the over-large top. After he silently slipped out of bed, he walked bare-chested into the kitchen, where he filled a kettle with water and put it on the stove. He turned on the radio very softly and listened to the news broadcast as he shaved. Race riots in the Congo. Sit-in demonstrations in the South. Apartheid in South Africa.

He wondered why he was black.

He often wondered this. He wondered it idly, and with no real conviction that he *was* black. That was the strange part of it. When Arthur Brown looked in the mirror, he saw only himself. Now he knew he was a Negro, yes. But he was also a Democrat, and a detective, and a husband, and a father, and he read *The New York Times* – he was a lot of things. And so he wondered why he was black. He wondered why, being this variety of things besides being black, people would look at him and see Arthur Brown, Negro – and not Arthur Brown, detective, or Arthur Brown, husband, or any of the Arthur Browns who had nothing to do with the fact that he was black. This was not a simple concept, and Brown did not equate it in simple Shakespearian-Shylock terms, which the world had long outgrown.

When Brown looked into his mirror he saw a person.

It was the world who had decided that this person was a black man. Being this person was an extremely difficult thing, because it meant living a life the world had decided upon, and not the life he – Arthur Brown – would particularly have chosen. He, Arthur Brown, did not see a black man or a white man or a yellow man or a chartreuse man when he looked into his mirror.

He saw Arthur Brown.

He saw himself.

But superimposed upon this image of himself was the external concept of black man—white man, a concept which existed and which Brown was forced to accept. He became a person playing a complicated role. He looked at himself and saw Arthur Brown, Man. That's all he wanted to be. He had no desire to be white. In fact, he rather liked the warm, burnished colour of his own skin. He had no desire to go to bed with a creamy-skinned blonde. He had heard coloured friends of his state that white men had bigger sex organs than Negroes, but he didn't believe it, and he felt no envy. He had encountered prejudice in a hundred and one subtle and unsubtle ways from the moment he was old enough to understand what was being said and done around him, but the intolerance never left him feeling angry – it only confused him.

You see, he thought, I'm me, Arthur Brown. Now what is all this white man—black man crap? I don't understand what you want me to be. *You* are saying I'm a Negro, *you* are telling me this is so, but *I* don't know what Negro means, I don't know what this whole damn discussion is all about. What do you want from me, exactly? If I say, why yes, that's right, I'm a Negro, well, *then* what? What the hell is it you want, that's what I'd like to know.

Arthur Brown finished shaving, rinsed his face, and looked into the mirror.

As usual, he saw himself.

He dressed quietly, drank some orange juice and coffee, kissed his daughter as she lay sleeping in her crib, woke Caroline briefly to tell her he was off to work, and then went cross town to the neighbourhood where Joseph Wechsler had run a hardware store.

*

It was purely by chance that Meyer Meyer went to see Mrs Rudy Glennon alone that Monday morning, the chance having been occasioned by the fact that Steve Carella had drawn Lineup duty. Things might have worked out differently had Carella been along, but the police commissioner felt it was necessary to acquaint his working dicks with criminals every Monday to Thursday inclusive. Carella, being a working dick, took the Lineup duty like a man and sent Meyer to Mrs Glennon's apartment alone.

Mrs Glennon was the name supplied by Dr McElroy at Buenavista Hospital, the woman with whose family Claire Townsend had been personally involved. She lived in one of the worst slum sections in Isola, some five blocks from the station house. Meyer walked over, found the apartment building, and climbed the steps to the third floor. He knocked on the door to the apartment and waited.

'Who is it?' a voice called.

'Police,' Meyer called.

'What do you want? I'm in bed.'

'I'd like to talk to you, Mrs Glennon,' Meyer said.

'Come back next week. I'm sick. I'm in bed.'

'I'd like to talk to you now, Mrs Glennon.'

'What about?'

'Mrs Glennon, would you open the door, please?'

'Oh, for the love of Mary, it's open,' she shouted. 'Come in, come in.'

Meyer turned the knob and stepped into the apartment. The shades were drawn and the room he entered was dim. He peered into the apartment.

'I'm in here,' Mrs Glennon said. 'The bedroom.'

He followed the voice into the other room. She was

99

sitting in the middle of a large double bed, propped against the pillows, a small faded woman wearing a faded pink robe over her nightgown. She looked at Meyer as if even the glance sapped all her energy. Her hair was stringy, threaded with grey strands. Her cheeks were gaunt.

'I told you I was sick,' Mrs Glennon said. 'What is it you want?'

'I'm sorry to bother you, Mrs Glennon,' Meyer said. 'The hospital told us you'd been released. I thought—'

'I'm convalescing,' she interrupted. She said the word proudly, as if she had learned it at great expense.

'Well, I'm awfully sorry. But if you feel you can answer a few questions, I'd appreciate it,' Meyer said.

'You're here now. I might as well.'

'You have a daughter, Mrs Glennon?'

'*And* a son. Why?'

'How old are the children?'

'Eileen is sixteen and Terry is eighteen. Why?'

'Where are they now, Mrs Glennon?'

'What's it to you? They haven't done anything wrong.'

'I didn't say they had, Mrs Glennon. I simply—'

'Then why do you want to know where they are?'

'Actually, we're trying to locate—'

'I'm here, Mom,' a voice behind Meyer said. The voice came suddenly, startling him. His hand automatically went for the service revolver clipped to his belt on the left – and then stopped. He turned slowly. The boy standing behind him was undoubtedly Terry Glennon, a strapping youth of eighteen, with his mother's piercing eyes and narrow jaw.

'What do you want, mister?' he said.

'I'm a cop,' Meyer told him before he got any wild ideas. 'I want to ask your mother a few questions.'

'My mother just got out of the hospital. She can't answer no questions,' Terry said.

'It's all right, son,' Mrs Glennon said.

'You let me handle this, Mom. You better go, mister.'

'Well, I'd like to ask—'

'I think you better go,' Terry said.

'I'm sorry, sonny,' Meyer said, 'but I happen to be investigating a homicide, and I think I'll stay.'

'A homi . . .' Terry Glennon swallowed the information silently. 'Who got killed?'

'Why? Who do you *think* got killed?'

'I don't know.'

'Then why'd you ask?'

'I don't know. You said a homicide, so I naturally asked—'

'Uh-huh,' Meyer said. 'You know anyone named Claire Townsend?'

'No.'

'I know her,' Mrs Glennon said. 'Did she send you here?'

'Look, mister,' Terry interrupted, apparently making up his mind once and for all, 'I told you my mother's sick. I don't care *what* you're investigating – she ain't gonna—'

'Terry, now stop it,' his mother said. 'Did you buy the milk I asked you to?'

'Yeah.'

'Where is it?'

'I put it on the table.'

'Well, what good is it gonna do me on the table, where I can't get at it? Put some in a pot and turn up the gas. Then you can go.'

'What do you mean, go?'

'Downstairs. With your friends.'

'What do you mean, my *friends*? Why do you always say it that way?'

'Terry, do what I tell you.'

'You gonna let this guy tire you out?'

'I'm not tired.'

'You're sick!' Terry shouted. 'You just had an operation, for Christ's sake!'

'Terry, don't swear in my house,' Mrs Glennon said, apparently forgetting that she had profaned Christ's mother earlier, when Meyer was standing in the hallway. 'Now go put the milk on to heat and go downstairs and find something to do.'

'Boy, I don't understand you,' Terry said. He shot a petulant glare at his mother, some of it spilling on to Meyer, and then walked angrily out of the room. He picked up the container of milk from the table, went into the kitchen, banged around a lot of pots, and then stormed out of the apartment.

'He's got a temper,' Mrs Glennon said.

'Mmmmm,' Meyer commented.

'*Did* Claire send you here?'

'No, ma'am. Claire Townsend is dead.'

'What? What are you saying?'

'Yes, Ma'am.'

'Tch,' Mrs Glennon said. She tilted her head to one side and then repeated the sound again. 'Tch.'

'Were you very friendly with her, Mrs Glennon?' Meyer asked.

'Yes.' Her eyes seemed to have gone blank. She was thinking of something, but Meyer didn't know what. He had seen this look a great many times before, a statement triggering off a memory or an association, the person being interrogated simply drifting off into a private thought. 'Yes, Claire was a nice girl,' Mrs Glennon said, but her mind was on something else, and Meyer would have given his eyeteeth to have known what.

'She worked with you at the hospital, isn't that right?'

'Yes,' Mrs Glennon said.

'And with your daughter, too.'

'What?'

'Your daughter. I understand Claire was friendly with her.'

'Who told you that?'

'The intern at Buenavista.'

'Oh,' Mrs Glennon nodded. 'Yes, they were friendly,' she admitted.

'Very friendly?'

'Yes. Yes, I suppose so.'

'What is it, Mrs Glennon?'

'Huh? What?'

'What are you thinking about?'

'Nothing. I'm answering your questions. When . . . when did . . . when was Claire killed?'

'Friday evening,' Meyer said.

'Oh, then she—' Mrs Glennon closed her mouth.

'Then she what?' Meyer asked.

'Then she . . . she was killed Friday evening,' Mrs Glennon said.

'Yes.' Meyer watched her face carefully. 'When was the last time you saw her, Mrs Glennon?'

'At the hospital.'

'And your daughter?'

'Eileen? I . . . I don't know when she saw Claire last.'

'Where is she now, Mrs Glennon? At school?'

'No, No, she . . . she's spending a few . . . uh . . . days with my sister. In Bethtown.'

'Doesn't she go to school, Mrs Glennon?'

103

'Yes, certainly she does. But I had the appendicitis, you know, and . . . uh . . . she stayed with my sister while I was in the hospital . . . and . . . uh . . . I thought I ought to send her there for a while now, until I can get on my feet. You see?'

'I see. What's your sister's name, Mrs Glennon?'

'Iris.'

'Yes. Iris what?'

'Iris . . . why do you want to know?'

'Oh, just for the record,' Meyer said.

'I don't want you to bother her, mister. She's got troubles enough of her own. She doesn't even know Claire. I wish you wouldn't bother her.'

'I don't intend to, Mrs Glennon.'

Mrs Glennon frowned. 'Her name is Iris Mulhare.'

Meyer jotted the name into his pad. 'And the address?'

'Look, you said—'

'For the record, Mrs Glennon.'

'1131 Fifty-sixth Street.'

'In Bethtown?'

'Yes.'

'Thank you. And you say your daughter Eileen is with her, is that right?'

'Yes.'

'When did she go there, Mrs Glennon?'

'Saturday. Saturday morning.'

'And she was there earlier, too, is that right? While you were in the hospital.'

'Yes.'

'Where did she meet Claire, Mrs Glennon?'

'At the hospital. She came to visit me one day while Claire was there. That's where they met.'

'Uh-huh,' Meyer said, 'And did Claire visit her at your sister's home? In Bethtown?'

104

'What?'

'I said I suppose Claire visited her at your sister's home.'

'Yes, I . . . I suppose so.'

'Uh-huh,' Meyer said. 'Well, that's very interesting, Mrs Glennon, and I thank you. Tell me, haven't you seen a newspaper?'

'No, I haven't.'

'Then you didn't know Claire was dead until I told you, is that right?'

'That's right.'

'Do you suppose Eileen knows?'

'I . . . I don't know.'

'Well, did she mention anything about it Saturday morning? Before she left for your sister's?'

'No.'

'Were you listening to the radio?'

'No.'

'Because it was on the air, you know. Saturday morning.'

'We weren't listening to the radio.'

'I see. And your daughter didn't see a newspaper before she left the house?'

'No.'

'But, of course, she must know about it by now. Has she said anything about it to you?'

'No.'

'You've spoken to her, haven't you? I mean, she does call you. From your sister's?'

'Yes, I . . . I speak to her.'

'When did you speak to her last, Mrs Glennon?'

'I . . . I'm very tired now. I'd like to rest.'

'Certainly. When did you speak to her last?'

'Yesterday,' Mrs Glennon said, and she sighed deeply.

'I see. Thank you, Mrs Glennon, you've been very helpful. Shall I get you that milk? It's probably warm enough by now.'

'Would you?'

Meyer went into the kitchen. The stove was set alongside a cabinet and a wall. A small cork bulletin board was nailed to the wall. A telephone rested on the cabinet. He took the pot of milk from the stove just as it was ready to overboil. He poured a cupful and then called. 'Do you want a lump of butter in this?'

'Yes, please.'

He opened the refrigerator, took out the butter dish, found a knife in the cabinet drawer, and was slicing off a square when he saw the hand-lettered note pinned to the bulletin board. The note read:

CLAIRE
SATURDAY
271 SOUTH FIRST STREET

He nodded once, briefly, silently copied the address into his pad, and then carried the buttered milk to Mrs Glennon. She thanked him for his kindness, asked him again not to bother her sister, and then began sipping at the cup.

Meyer left the apartment, wondering why Mrs Glennon had lied to him. He was still wondering about it when he reached the first-floor landing.

The attack came swiftly and silently.

He was totally unprepared for it. The fist came flying out of the darkness as he turned the bend in the banister. It struck him on the bridge of his nose. He whirled to face his attacker, reaching for his holstered revolver at the same moment, and suddenly he was struck from behind with something harder than a fist, something that collided with the base of his skull and sent a fleeting wave of blackness across his eyes. He pulled the gun quickly and easily, something else hit him, there were more than two people, again he was struck, he heard his own revolver going off, but he had no knowledge of pulling the trigger. Something dropped to the floor with a clanging metallic sound, they were using pipes, he felt blood trickling into his eye, a pipe lashed out of the near-darkness, striking his mouth, he felt the gun dropping from his hand, felt himself falling to his knees under the steady silent onslaught of the unrelenting lead pipes.

He heard footsteps, a thousand footsteps, running over him and past him and down the steps, thundering, thundering. He did not lose consciousness. With his face pressed to the rough wooden floor, with the taste of his own blood in his mouth, he idly wondered why private eyes always swam down, down, down, into a pool of blackness, wondered idly why Mrs Glennon had lied to him, wondered why he'd been beaten, wondered where his gun was, and groped for it blindly, his fingers sticky with blood. He crawled towards the steps.

He found the top step and then hurtled headlong down the flight, tumbling, crashing into the banister, cutting his bald scalp on the sharp edge of one of the risers, his legs and arms twisted ludicrously as he rolled and bounced to the ground-floor landing. He could see a bright rectangle of light where the vestibule door was opened to the street outside. He spat blood and crawled through the dim vestibule and on to the front stoop, dripping a trail of blood behind him, blinking blood out of his eyes, his nose running blood, his lips running blood.

He half crawled, half dragged himself down the low flight of steps and on to the sidewalk. He tried to raise himself on one elbow, tried to call out to anyone in the street.

No one stopped to assist him.

This was a neighbourhood where you survived by minding your own business.

Ten minutes later a patrolman found him on the sidewalk, where he had swum down, down, down, into that pool of blackness.

The sign outside the garage read BODY AND FENDER WORK, EXPERT PAINTING AND RETOUCHING. The owner of the garage was a man named Fred Batista, and he came out to gas up Brown's unmarked sedan only to learn that Brown was a detective who had come to ask questions. He seemed to enjoy the idea. He asked Brown to park the car over near the air pump and then invited him into the small garage office. Batista needed a shave, and he was wearing grease-covered overalls, but there was a twinkle in his eyes as he and Brown went through the questioning routine. Maybe he'd never seen a cop up close before. Or maybe business was bad and he was glad for a break in the monotony. Whatever the reason, he answered Brown's questions with verve and enthusiasm.

'Joe Wechsler?' he said. 'Why, sure, I knew him. He's got a little hardware store right down the street. Many's the time we run over there when we needed a tool or something. A fine man, Joe was. And a terrible thing what happened to him in the bookstore.' Batista nodded. 'I know Marty Fennerman, too – guy who runs the store. He had a holdup there once, you know that? Did he tell you that?'

'Yes, sir, he told us,' Brown said.

'Sure, I remember, musta been seven, eight years ago. Sure. You want a cigar?'

'No, thank you, Mr Batista.'

'You don't like cigars?' Batista said, offended.

'Yes, I do,' Brown said. 'But I don't like to smoke them in the morning.'

'Why not? Morning, afternoon, what's the difference?'

'Well, I usually have one after lunch and another after dinner.'

'You mind if I smoke one?' Batista asked.

'Go right ahead.'

Batista nodded and spat the end of the cigar into a barrel of soiled rags near his scarred desk. He lighted the cigar, blew out a great stream of smoke, said 'Ahhhhhh', and then leaned back in his ancient swivel chair.

'I understand Mr Wechsler had some work done by you a little while before the shooting, is that right, Mr Batista?'

'That's right,' Batista said. 'A hundred per cent.'

'What kind of work?

'A paint job.'

'Did you do the job personally?'

'No, no. My body and fender man did it. It wasn't such a big job. Some nut hit Joe while he was parked on the street in front of his store. So he brung the car in here and I—'

'The car was hit?'

'Yeah. But nothing big. You know, just a scratched fender, like that. Buddy took care of it.'

'Buddy?'

'Yeah, my body and fender man.'

'Who paid for the job? Mr Wechsler or the man who hit him?'

'Well, truth is, *nobody* paid for it yet. I just billed Joe last week. 'Course, I didn't know he was gonna get killed. Listen, I can wait for my money. His wife's got enough grief right now.'

'But it was Mr Wechsler you billed?'

'Yeah. Joe didn't know who hit him. Like, you know, he come back from lunch one day, and there was this big scratch in the fender. So he brung the car in here, and we took care of it. Buddy's a good man. Only been with me a month or so, but much better than the last guy I had.'

'I wonder if I could talk to him.'

'Sure, go right ahead. He's out back. He's working on a '56 Ford. You can't miss him.'

'What's his last name?'

'Manners. Buddy Manners.'

'Thanks,' Brown said. He excused himself and walked to the back of the garage.

A tall, muscular man in paint-stained coveralls was spraying the side of a blue Ford convertible. He looked up as Brown approached, decided Brown was no one he knew, and went back to work.

'Mr Manners?' Brown asked.

Manners cut off the spray gun and looked up inquisitively. 'Yeah?'

'I'm from the police,' Brown said. 'I wonder if I could ask you a few questions.'

'Police?' Manners said. He shrugged. 'Sure, go right ahead.'

'You did some work for Joseph Wechsler, I understand.'

'For who?'

'Joseph Wechsler.'

'Wechsler, Wechsler . . . oh, yeah, '59 Chevy, that's

110

right. Spray job on the left front fender. Right. I can only remember them by the cars.' He grinned.

'I guess you don't know what happened to Mr Wechsler then.'

'I only know what happened to his car,' Manners said.

'Well, he was killed Friday night.'

'Gee, that's a shame,' Manners said, his face going suddenly serious. 'I'm sorry to hear that.' He paused. 'An accident?'

'No, he was murdered. Don't you read the papers, Mr Manners?'

'Well, I was kind of busy this weekend, I went up to Boston – that's where I'm from originally – to see this girl I know. So I didn't see no papers from here.'

'Did you know Wechsler pretty well?'

Manners shrugged. 'I think I met him twice. First time was when he brung the car in, and then he come in once while I was painting it. Said the colour was a little off. So I mixed a new batch and sprayed the fender again. That was it.'

'Never saw him again?'

'Never. He's dead, huh? That's a shame. He seemed like a nice little guy. For a kike.'

Brown stared at Manners levelly and then said, 'Why do you say that?'

'Well, he seemed nice,' Manners shrugged.

'I mean, why did you call him a kike?'

'Oh. Why, 'cause that's what he was. I mean, did you ever hear him talk? It was a riot. He sounded like he just got off the boat.'

'This spray job you did for him . . . did you argue about the colour of the paint?'

'Argue? No, he just said he thought the colour was a little off, and I said OK, I'll mix a new batch, and that

111

was it. It's hard to match exactly. You know. So I done my best.' Manners shrugged. 'I guess he was satisfied. He didn't say nothing when he picked up the car.'

'Oh, then you did talk to him again?'

'No, I only saw him those two times. But if he'd have kicked about the work, I'da heard it from the boss. So I guess he was satisfied.'

'When did you go to Boston, Mr Manners?'

'Friday afternoon.'

'What time?'

'Well, I knocked off work about three o'clock. I caught the four-ten from Union Station.'

'You go alone, or what?'

'Alone, yeah,' Manners said.

'What's the girl's name? The one in Boston?'

'Why?'

'I'm curious.'

'Mary Nelson. She lives in West Newton. If you think I'm lying about being in Boston—'

'I don't think you're lying.'

'Well, you can check anyway.'

'Maybe I will.'

'OK.' Manners shrugged. 'How'd he get killed? The kike?'

'Someone shot him.'

'That's too bad,' Manners said. He shook his head. 'He seemed like a nice little guy.'

'Yeah. Well, thanks, Mr Manners. Sorry to have interrupted your work.'

'That's OK,' Manners said. 'Any time.'

Brown went to the front of the garage again. He found Batista filling a customer's gas tank. He waited until he was through and then asked, 'What time did Manners leave here Friday afternoon?'

'Two-thirty, three, something like that,' Batista said.

Brown nodded, 'This spray job he did for Wechsler. Did Wechsler complain about it?'

'Oh, only about the first colour Buddy put on. It didn't match right. But we fixed it for him.'

'Any static?'

'Not that I know of, I wasn't here the day Joe came in and told Buddy about it. But Buddy's an easy-going guy. He just mixed up a new batch of paint, and that was it.'

Brown nodded again. 'Well, thanks a lot, Mr Batista,' he said.

'Not at all,' Batista said. 'You sure you don't want a cigar? Go ahead, take one,' Batista smiled. 'For after lunch.'

Carella was downtown at Headquarters watching a parade of felony offenders go through the ritual of the Lineup.

Willis was out talking to known junkies in the neighbourhood, trying to get a lead on the addict named Anthony La Scala.

Di Maeo was rounding up two more known criminals who had been arrested by Bert Kling, convicted, and released from prison during the past year.

Kling was at the funeral parlour with Ralph Townsend, making final arrangements for Claire's burial the next day.

Bob O'Brien was alone in the squad room when the telephone rang. He absent-mindedly lifted the receiver, put it to his ear, and said into the mouthpiece, '87th Squad, O'Brien.' He was in the middle of typing up a report on the results of his barber's shop plant. His mind was still on the report when Sergeant Dave Murchison's voice yanked him rudely away from it.

'Bob, this is Dave downstairs. On the desk. I just got a call from Patrolman Oliver on the South Side.'

'Yeah?'

'He found Meyer beat up on a sidewalk there.'

'Who?'

'Meyer.'

'*Our* Meyer.'

'Yeah, our Meyer.'

'Jesus, what is this? Open season on cops? Where did you say he was?'

'I already sent a meat wagon. He's probably on his way to the hospital.'

'Who did it, Dave?'

'I dunno. Patrolman says he was just laying there in his own blood.'

'I better get over to the hospital. Will you call the loot, Dave? And send somebody up here to cover, will you? I'm all alone.'

'You want me to call somebody in?'

'I don't know what to tell you. There should be a detective up here. You'd better ask the skipper about it. I hate to bust in on a guy's day off.'

'Well, I'll ask the loot. Maybe Miscolo can cover till somebody gets back.'

'Yeah, ask him. What hospital did you say?'

'General.'

'I'll get over there. Thanks, Dave.'

'Right,' Murchison said, and he hung up.

O'Brien put the phone back on to the cradle, opened the top drawer of his desk, took his .38 Police Special from the drawer, clipped it to the left side of his belt, put on his jacket and his hat, made a helpless wide-armed gesture to the empty squad room, and then went through the slatted rail divider and down the iron-rusted steps and past the muster desk where he waved at Murchison, and then out into the October sunshine.

The week was starting fine, all right.

The week was starting just fine.

10.

THEY PICKED UP Terry Glennon at four o'clock. By that time a hardy contingent of bulls had returned to the squad room, and they surrounded Glennon in casual deceptiveness as he sat in a straight-backed chair asking why he had been dragged into a police station.

Bob O'Brien, who was a most obliging cop, said, 'We dragged you into a police station because we think you and some of your buddies beat the crap out of a cop this morning. Does that answer your question?'

'I don't know what you're talking about,' Glennon said.

'The cop's name is Detective Meyer Meyer,' O'Brien went on obligingly. 'He is now at General Hospital being treated for cuts and bruises and shock and maybe concussion. Does that make it any clearer?'

'I still don't know what you're talking about.'

'That's OK; play it cool,' O'Brien said. 'We got all the time in the world. I went to the hospital around lunch time and Meyer told me he had paid a little visit to the Glennon household, where a young guy named Terry Glennon got very upset because Meyer was talking to his mother. The mother, according to Meyer, made some sarcastic reference about the young fellow's friends. Does that ring a bell, Glennon?'

'Yeah, I remember that.'

'How about remembering where you vanished to after you and your buddies ganged up on Meyer?'

'I didn't vanish no place. I was around the block. And I didn't gang up on nobody, neither.'

'You weren't around the block, Glennon. We've been looking for you since noon.'

'So I took a walk,' Glennon said. 'So what?'

'So nothing,' Carella said. 'Fellow can take a walk. No law against that.' He paused, smiled, and said, 'Where'd you go when you left your house, Glennon?'

'Downstairs.'

'Where downstairs?' Willis asked.

'The candy store.'

'What candy store?' Brown asked.

'On the corner.'

'How long did you stay there?' Di Maeo asked.

'I don't know. An hour, two hours, who remembers?'

'Somebody better remember,' O'Brien said. 'Why'd you beat up Meyer?'

'I didn't.'

'Who did?' Carella said.

'I don't know.'

'Ever hear of Claire Townsend?'

'Yes.'

'How?'

'My mother spoke of her. And the cop was asking about her.'

'Ever meet her?'

'No.'

'Know anybody named Joe Wechsler?'

'No.'

'Anthony La Scala?'

'No.'

'Herbert Land?'

'No.'

'Why'd you beat up Meyer?'

'I didn't.'

'Why doesn't your mother like your friends?'

'How do I know? Ask her.'

'We will. Right now we're asking you.'

'I don't know why she don't like them.'

'You belong to a gang, Glennon?'

'No.'

'A club then? What do you call it, Glennon? An athletic and social club?'

'I don't belong to nothing. I don't call it nothing 'cause I don't belong to nothing.'

'Did your gang help you beat up Meyer?'

'I don't have a gang.'

'How many of you were there?'

'I don't know what you're talking about. I went downstairs and—'

'What'd you do? Wait for Meyer in the hallway?'

'—and I stood in the candy store for—'

'Beat him up when he left your mother?'

'—for a few hours, and then I took a walk.'

'Where'd you have lunch?'

'What?'

'Where'd you have lunch?'

'I had a hot dog on Barker.'

'Let's see your hands.'

'What for?'

'Show him your hands!' Carella snapped.

O'Brien turned Glennon's hands over in his own. 'That's all we need,' O'Brien said. 'Those cuts on his knuckles'll cinch it.'

Glennon did not take the bait. He remained silent. If he had been one of the people who'd beaten Meyer with lead pipes, he did not offer the information.

'We're gonna lock you up for a little while,' Willis said. 'I think you'll like our detention cells.'

'You can't lock me up,' Glennon said.

'No? Try us,' Willis answered. 'Steve, I think we better hit the old lady again, find out the names of Junior's friends.'

'You leave my mother alone!' Glennon shouted.

'Why? You gonna beat *us* up, too?'

'You just leave her alone, you hear me? I'm the man of that house! When my father died, *I* became the man of the house! You just stay away from her.'

'Yeah, you're some man,' Brown said. 'You wait in the dark with twelve other guys and you cold-cock a—'

'I didn't wait no place! You just stay away from my mother!'

'Lock him up,' O'Brien said.

'And you can't lock me up, either. You got to have grounds.'

'We got grounds.'

'Yeah? What?'

'Suspicion,' Willis said, calling on the old standby.

'Suspicion of what?'

'Suspicion of being a big shit – how's that? Get rid of him, somebody.'

The somebody who got rid of him was Di Maeo. He pulled him out of the chair, yanking on the handcuffs, and then shoved him through the slatted rail divider and took him downstairs to the detention cells.

'You'd better ask the old lady about this, too,' O'Brien said to Carella. 'Meyer gave it to me at the hospital.'

'What is it?'

O'Brien handed him the page torn from Meyer's pad. It read:

CLAIRE
SATURDAY
271 SOUTH FIRST STREET

Carella read the note: 'Where'd Meyer get this?'

'Hanging on a bulletin board in the Glennon apartment.'

'OK, we'll ask her about it. Anybody checking out this address?'

'I'm going there myself right now,' O'Brien said.

'Good. We'll be with Mrs Glennon. If you get anything, call us there.'

'Right.'

'Does Meyer know who wrote the note?'

'He figures it was the young girl. Eileen Glennon.'

'Why don't we get her in here and ask her about it?'

'Well, that's another thing, Steve, Mrs Glennon says she has a sister in Bethtown, woman named Iris Mulhare.'

'What about her?'

'She claims Eileen went there Saturday morning. She also told Meyer the girl had stayed with Mrs Mulhare all the while the old lady was in the hospital.'

'So?'

'So when I got back to the office, I called Mrs Mulhare. She said yes, the kid was with her. So I said let me talk to her. Well, she hemmed and hawed a little and then told me she was sorry, Eileen must've stepped out for a minute. So I asked her where Eileen had stepped out to. Mrs Mulhare said she didn't know. So I said was she sure Eileen was there at all. She said certainly she was sure. So I said then let me talk to her. And she said, I just told you, she stepped out for a minute. So I told her I thought I'd call the local precinct and send a patrolman over to help find Eileen, and then Mrs Mulhare cracked, and all the dirt came out.'

'Let me hear it.'

'Eileen Glennon isn't with her aunt. The Mulhare woman hasn't seen her for maybe six months.'

'Six months, huh?'

'Right. Eileen isn't there now, and she wasn't there when her mother was in the hospital either. I asked Mrs Mulhare why she'd lied to me, and she said her sister had called that morning – must've been right after Meyer left her – to say, in case anyone asked, Eileen was there in Bethtown.'

'Now why would Mrs Glennon want her to say that?'

'I don't know. But it sure looks as if Claire Townsend was mixed up with a real bunch of prize packages.'

The prize package named Mrs Glennon was out of bed when Carella and Willis arrived. She was sitting in the kitchen drinking a second cup of hot buttered milk, which she'd undoubtedly prepared herself. The neighbourhood grapevine had already informed her of her son's arrest, and she greeted the detectives with undisguised hostility. As if to make her anger more apparent, she slurped noisily at the milk as she answered their questions.

'We want to know the names of your son's friends, Mrs Glennon,' Carella said.

'I don't know any of their names. Terry's a good boy. You had no right to arrest him.'

'We think he and his friends attacked a police officer,' Willis said.

'I don't care what you think. He's a good boy.' She slurped at the milk.

'Does your son belong to a street gang, Mrs Glennon?'

'No.'

'Are you sure?'

'I'm sure.'

'What are his friends' names?'

121

'I don't know.'

'They never come up here to the house, Mrs Glennon?'

'Never. I'm not going to turn over my parlour to a bunch of young—' She cut herself short.

'A bunch of young what, Mrs Glennon?'

'Nothing.'

'Young *hoodlums*, Mrs Glennon?'

'No. My son is a good boy.'

'But he beat up a cop.'

'He didn't. You're only guessing.'

'Where's your daughter, Mrs Glennon?'

'Do you think *she* beat up a cop, too?'

'No, Mrs Glennon, but we think she had an appointment to meet Claire Townsend on Saturday at this address.' Carella put the slip of paper on the kitchen table, alongside the cup of milk. Mrs Glennon looked at it and said nothing.

'Know anything about that address, Mrs Glennon?'

'No.'

'*Was* she supposed to meet Claire Saturday?'

'No. I don't know.'

'Where is she now?'

'At my sister's. In Bethtown.'

'She's not there, Mrs Glennon.'

'That's where she is.'

'No. We spoke to your sister. She's not there, and she was never there.'

'She's there.'

'No. Now where is she, Mrs Glennon?'

'If she's not there, I don't know where she is. She said she was going to see her aunt. She's never lied to me, so I have no reason to believe—'

'Mrs Glennon, you know damn well she didn't go to your sister's. You called your sister this morning, right after Detective Meyer left here. You asked her to lie for you. Where's your daughter, Mrs Glennon?'

'I don't know. Leave me alone! I've got enough trouble! Do you think it's easy? Do you think raising two kids without a man is easy? Do you think I like that crowd my son runs with? And now Eileen? Do you think I . . . ? Leave me alone! I'm sick. I'm a sick woman.' Her voice trailed off. 'Please. Leave me alone. Please.' She was talking in a whisper now. 'I'm sick. Please. I just got out of the hospital. Please. Please leave me alone.'

'What *about* Eileen, Mrs Glennon?'

'Nothing, nothing, nothing, nothing,' she said, her eyes squeezed shut, wailing the words, her hands clenched in her lap.

'Mrs Glennon,' Carella said very softly, 'we'd like to know where your daughter is.'

'I don't know,' Mrs Glennon said. 'I swear to God. I don't know. That's the God's honest truth. I don't know where Eileen is.'

Detective Bob O'Brien stood on the sidewalk and looked up at 271 South First Street.

The building was a five-storey brownstone, and a sign in the first-floor window advertised FURNISHED ROOMS FOR RENT BY DAY OR WEEK. O'Brien climbed the front steps and rang the superintendent's bell. He waited for several moments, received no answer, and rang the bell again.

'Hello?' a voice from somewhere inside called.

'Hello!' O'Brien answered.

'Hello?'

'Hello!' He was beginning to feel like an echo when the front door opened. A thin old man wearing khaki trousers and an undershirt looked out at him. He had shaggy greying brows which partially covered his blue eyes and gave him a peering expression.

'Hello,' he said. 'You ring the bell?'

'I did,' O'Brien answered. 'I'm Detective O—'

'Oh-oh,' the old man said.

O'Brien smiled. 'No trouble, sir,' he said. 'I just wanted to ask a few questions. My name's O'Brien, 87th Squad.'

'How do you do? My name's O'Loughlin, South First Street,' the old man said, and he chuckled.

'Up the rebels!' O'Brien said.

'Up the rebels!' O'Loughlin answered, and both men burst out laughing. 'Come on in, lad. I was just about to have a nip to welcome the end of the day. You can join me.'

'Well, we're not allowed to drink on duty, Mr O'Loughlin.'

'Sure, and who's going to tell anyone about it?' the old man said. 'Come on in.'

They walked through the vestibule and into O'Loughlin's apartment at the end of the hall. They sat in a parlour hung with a coloured-glass chandelier and velvet drapes. The furniture was old and deep and comfortable. O'Loughlin went to a cherrywood cabinet and took out an ornate bottle.

'Irish whisky,' he said.

'What else?' O'Brien asked.

The old man chuckled and poured two stiff hookers. He brought one to O'Brien where he sat on the sofa, and then he sat opposite him in a tall upholstered rocker.

'Up the rebels,' he said softly.

'Up the rebels,' O'Brien answered, and both men drank solemnly.

'What was it you wanted to know, O'Brien?' the old man asked.

'That's got a little bit of a kick,' O'Brien said, staring at the whisky glass, his eyes smarting.

'Mild as your dear mother's milk,' O'Loughlin said. 'Drink up, lad.'

O'Brien raised the glass cautiously to his lips. Gingerly he sipped at it. 'Mr O'Loughlin,' he said, 'we're trying to locate a girl named Eileen Glennon. We found an address—'

'You came to the right place, lad,' O'Loughlin said.

'You know her?'

'Well, I don't *know* her. That is to say, not personally. But she rented a room from me, that she did.'

O'Brien sighed. 'Good,' he said. 'What room is that?'

'Upstairs. Nicest room in the house. Looks out over the park. She said she wanted a nice room with sunshine. So I give her that one.'

'Is she here now?'

'No.' O'Loughlin shook his head.

'Do you have any idea when she'll be back?'

'Well, she hasn't *been* here yet.'

'What do you mean? You said—'

'I said she rented a room from me, is what I said. That was last week. Thursday, as I remember. But she said she'd be wanting the room for Saturday. Saturday came around, and she never showed up.'

'Then she hasn't been here since she rented the room?'

'Nossir, I'm afraid she hasn't What is it? Is the poor girl in some trouble?'

'No, not exactly. We just . . .' O'Brien sighed and sipped at the whisky again. 'Was she renting the room on a daily basis? Did she just want it for Saturday?'

'Nossir. Wanted it for a full week. Paid me in advance. Cash.'

'Didn't you think it a little odd . . . I mean . . . well, do you usually rent rooms to such young girls?'

O'Loughlin raised his shaggy brows and peered at O'Brien. 'Well, she wasn't all *that* young, you understand.'

'Sixteen is pretty young, Mr O'Loughlin.'

'Sixteen?' O'Loughlin burst out laughing. 'Oh, now, the young lady was handing somebody a little blarney, lad. She was twenty-five if she was a day.'

O'Brien looked into his whisky glass. Then he looked up at the old man.

'*How* old, sir?'

'Twenty-five, twenty-six, maybe even a little older. But not sixteen. Nossir, not by a long shot.'

'Eileen Glennon? We're talking about the same girl?'

'Eileen Glennon, that's her name. Came here on Thursday, gave me a week's rent in advance, said she'd come by for the key Saturday. Eileen Glennon.'

'Could you . . . could you tell me what she looked like, Mr O'Loughlin?'

'I sure can. She was a tall girl. Very big. Maybe five-seven, five-eight. I remember having to look up at her while I was talking. And she had pitch-black hair, and big brown eyes, and—'

'Claire,' O'Brien said aloud.

'Huh?'

'Sir, did she mention anything about another girl?'

'Nope.'

'Did she say she was going to bring another girl here?'

'Nope. Wouldn't matter to me, anyway. You rent a room, the room's yours.'

'Did you tell this to her?'

'Well, I made it plain to her, I guess. She said she wanted a quiet room with a lot of sunshine. The way I figured it, the sunshine was optional. But when some-body comes in here asking for a quiet room, I understand they don't want to be disturbed, and I let her know she wouldn't *be* disturbed. Not by me, anyway.' The old man paused. 'I'm talking to you man to man, O'Brien.'

'I appreciate it.'

'I don't run a cathouse here, but I don't bother my people either. Privacy's a tough thing to find in this city. The way I figure it, every man's entitled to a door he can close against the world.'

'And you got the feeling Eileen Glennon wanted that door to close?'

'Yes, lad, that's the feeling I got.'

'But she didn't mention anyone else?'

'Who else would she mention?'

'Did she sign for the room?'

'Not one of my rules. She paid a week's rent in advance, and I gave her a receipt. That's all she needed. Harry O'Loughlin's an honest man who keeps a bargain.'

'But she never came back?'

'No.'

'Now think hard, Mr O'Loughlin. On Saturday, the day Eileen Glennon was supposed to have taken the room, did . . . did anyone come here asking for her?'

'Nope.'

'Think, please. Did a sixteen-year-old girl come here asking for her?'

'Nope.'

'Did you see a sixteen-year-old girl hanging around outside?'

'Nope.'

'As if she were waiting for someone?'

'Nope.'

O'Brien sighed.

'I don't get it,' O'Loughlin said.

'I think you rented the room to a woman named Claire Townsend,' O'Brien said. 'I don't know why she used Eileen Glennon's name, but I suspect she was renting the room for the young girl. Why, I don't know.'

'Well, if she was renting it for someone else . . . let me get this straight. The girl who rented the room was named Claire Townsend?'

'I think so, yes.'

'And you say she used this Eileen Glennon's name and was actually renting the room *for* her?'

'I think so, yes. It looks that way.'

'Then why didn't Eileen Glennon come here Saturday? I mean, if the room was for her . . .'

'I think she did come here, Mr O'Loughlin. She came here and waited for Claire to pick up the key and let her in. But Claire never showed up.'

'Why not? If she went to all the trouble of renting the room—'

'Because Claire Townsend was killed Friday night.'

'Oh.' O'Loughlin picked up his glass and drained it. He poured himself another shot, moved the bottle towards O'Brien's glass, and said, 'Some more?'

O'Brien covered the glass with his palm. 'No. No, thanks.'

'Something I don't understand,' O'Loughlin said.

'What's that?'

'Why'd Claire Townsend use the other girl's name?'

'I don't know.'

'Was she trying to hide something?'

'I don't know.'

'I mean, was she in trouble with the police?'

'No.'

'Was she doing something unlawful?'

'I don't know.'

'And where'd the other girl disappear to? If she rented the room for her . . . ?'

'I don't know,' O'Brien said. He paused and looked at his empty glass. 'Maybe you'd *better* give me another shot,' he said.

The Majesta patrolman had come on duty at four forty-five p.m., and it was now close to six o'clock. It was Indian summer, true, but timetables had no respect for unseasonal temperature and dusk came just as if it were truly autumn. He was walking through a small park, cutting diagonally across it over a path which was part of his beat, when he saw the spot of yellow off under the trees. He peered into the fast-falling darkness. The yellow seemed to be the sleeve and skirt of a topcoat, partially hidden by a large boulder and the trunk of a tree. The patrolman climbed the grassy knoll and walked a little closer. Sure enough, that's what it was. A woman's yellow topcoat.

He walked around the boulder to pick it up.

The coat was thrown carelessly on the ground behind the boulder. A girl was lying on her back not three feet from the coat, staring up at the darkening sky. The girl's eyes and mouth were open. She was wearing a grey skirt, and the skirt was drenched with blood. Dried blood had stained her exposed thighs and her legs. She was no more than sixteen or seventeen years old.

The patrolman, who had seen death before, knew he was looking at a corpse.

He had no way of knowing the corpse was named Eileen Glennon.

11.

A CORPSE HAS no rights.

If you are a corpse, they can take your picture from a hundred unflattering angles as you stare up unseeingly at the popping flash guns, your skirt pulled back to reveal the dried and caked blood on the inside of your thighs and legs, the last flies of summer swarming about your open mouth. They can press their thumbs into your eyes at last to close your lids, and they can pull your skirt down over your knees and mark the position of your body on the shelf of flat rock where you lay motionless behind the trees. They can roll you on to a stretcher and carry you down to the waiting ambulance, the stretcher bouncing as they move along; they are not concerned for your comfort – you are beyond feeling. They can put the stretcher down on the floor of the ambulance with a sudden jolt and then cover you with a sheet – your waist, your young breasts, your throat, your face. You have no rights.

If you are a corpse, they can take off your clothing and put it into a plastic bag, and tag it, and send it to the police laboratory. They can place your cold and naked body on a stainless-steel table and dissect you in search of a cause of death. You have no rights. You are a corpse, a stiff, a container of clues perhaps, but no longer a person; you have forfeited your rights – forfeited them to death.

If you are a junkie, you have more rights than a corpse – but not many more.

You can still walk and breathe and sleep and laugh

and cry — which is something. These things are life — they are not things to be discounted — and you can still do these things. But if you are a junkie you are involved in your own brand of living death, and you are not very much better off than a bona fide corpse. Your death is continuous and persistent It starts every morning when you wake up and take that first shot, and it continues throughout the day-long hustle for heroin, punctured by the other death-giving shots, or through the night and into another morning, over and over again, you're a record player spinning the same tired mournful dirge, and the needle is stuck — in your arm. You know you're dead, and everybody else knows it, too.

Especially the cops.

While the corpse named Eileen Glennon was being disrobed and then dissected, a drug addict named Michael Pine was being questioned in the squad room of the 87th Precinct. His questioner was a cop named Hal Willis who could take junkies or leave them alone but whose preference was to leave them alone. A lot has been said about the psychology of the drug addict, but Hal Willis wasn't a psychologist, he was only a cop. He was a disciplined cop who had learned judo because he was only five feet eight inches tall and because he had learned at an early age that big guys like to push around little guys unless little guys learn how to push back. Judo was an exact science and a disciplined one. Drug addiction, so far as Willis was concerned, was the ultimate in lack of discipline. He didn't like junkies, but only because it seemed to him that they didn't *have* to be junkies. He knew with certainty that if he were ever hooked on heroin, he could kick the habit in a week. He would lock himself in a room and puke out his guts, but he would kick it. Discipline. He didn't hate junkies, and he

131

didn't pity them; he simply felt they were lacking in self-control, and this to Willis was unforgivable.

'You knew La Scala, huh?' he said to Pine.

'Yeah,' Pine answered. He delivered the word quickly and curtly. No wise-guy intonation, no enthusiasm, just 'Yeah', like the sharp rap of a knuckle on wood.

'Know him long?'

'Yeah.'

'How long?'

'Two years.'

'He's been a junkie all that time?'

'Yeah.'

'Do you know he's dead?'

'Yeah.'

'Do you know how he died?'

'Yeah.'

'What do you think?'

Pine shrugged. He was twenty-three years old, a blond boy with blue eyes that seemed wide and staring, partially because he'd had a shot before they picked him up and the dilated pupils gave his eyes a weird look and partially because the skin under his eyes was dark, making the blue of the pupils more startling.

'Anybody after him?' Willis asked.

'No.'

'Are you sure?'

'Yeah.'

'Do you know his pusher?'

Pine did not answer.

'I asked you a question. Do you know who La Scala's pusher was?'

'No.'

'That's a lie,' Willis said 'He's probably the same crumb you use.'

Pine still would not answer.

'That's right,' Willis said, 'protect the pusher. That's the smart thing. You scrape together all your nickels and dimes. Go ahead. Make the pusher fat. And then protect him, so he can go right on sucking your blood. You goddamn fool, who's the pusher?'

Pine did not answer.

'OK. Did La Scala owe him any money?'

'No.'

'You sure?'

'You're a cop,' Pine said. 'You know all about how *fat* pushers are, don't you? Then you also know they take cash on the line. No. Tony didn't owe the connection nothing.'

'Got any ideas who killed him?'

'I don't have any ideas,' Pine said.

'You high now?'

'I'm a little drowsy, that's all,' Pine said.

'When did you have your last shot?'

'About an hour ago?'

'Who's your connection, Pine?'

'Aw, come on, cop,' Pine said. 'What's he gonna bother with knocking off a guy like Tony for, huh? That's stupid, ain't it? Would *you* knock off a customer?'

'How bad was Tony hooked?'

'Through the bag and back again.'

'How much did he spend every day?'

'Twenty-five bucks, maybe three bills, maybe more, I don't know. Whatever it was, his connection sure as hell wasn't gonna lose it by knocking him off. Besides, what's the reason?' Pine smiled thinly. 'Pushers *like* hopheads, don't you know that?'

'Yeah, they like 'em,' Willis said dryly. 'All right, tell me everything you know about La Scala. How old was he?'

'About my age. Twenty-three, twenty-four.'

'Married? Single?'

'Single.'

'Parents living?'

'I think so. But not here.'

'Where?'

'The Coast, I think. I think his old man is in pictures.'

'What do you mean, pictures? La Scala's father is a movie star?'

'Yeah, just like *my* father is a movie star,' Pine said. 'My father's Cary Grant. You didn't know that?'

'Don't get wise,' Willis said. 'What does La Scala's father do?'

'Something with the crew. A grip, a shmip, who knows? He works with the crew.'

'Does he know his son is dead?'

'I doubt it. Nobody in LA reads newspapers.'

'How the hell would you know?'

'I been West.'

'On your way to Mexico to pick up some junk?'

'What does it matter where I was on the way to? I been West, and in LA nobody reads newspapers. In LA what they do is complain about the smog and keep their eyes open in case Lana Turner should stop for a traffic light. That's what they do out there.'

'You're the first junkie we had in here who's also a social commentator,' Willis said.

'Well, it takes all kinds,' Pine said philosophically.

'So La Scala was living alone, that it?'

'Yeah,' Pine said.

'No girl?'

'No.'

'Did he have relatives besides his parents?'

134

'A sister, yeah. But she lives on the Coast, too. In Frisco.'

'You think they read the papers there, Pine?'

'Maybe. All I know for sure about Frisco is that all the ladies wear hats.'

'You think his sister knows he's dead?'

'I don't know. Give her a call and ask her. You got plenty of taxpayers' money. Give her a call.'

'You seem to be perking up a little, Pine. You're getting a real sharp edge of a sudden.'

'Yeah. Well, you can't operate on one level all the time, you know.'

'I wouldn't know. In other words, Pine, La Scala was alone in this city, huh? You know anybody who might have wanted him dead?'

'Nope. Why should they? He wasn't bothering nobody.'

'And all his relatives are in California, is that right, too?'

'That's right.'

'Then nobody here'll miss him,' Willis said.

'I got news for you, cop,' Pine answered. 'Even if they *were* here, they would not miss him.'

Paul Blaney was an assistant medical examiner, a short man with a scraggly black moustache and violet eyes. It was Blaney's contention that he, as junior member on the medical examiner's staff, was always given the most gruesome corpses for necropsy, and he was rather surprised and pleased to receive the body of Eileen Glennon. The girl seemed to be in one piece, and there were no signs of undue violence, no stab wounds, no gunshot wounds, no broken skull. Blaney was sure one of his colleagues had made a mistake in assigning this particular cadaver to him, but he was not a man to look a gift horse in the mouth. Instead, he fell to work with dispatch, half afraid they would change their minds and give him another corpse before he was through.

He called the squad room at one-thirty on Tuesday afternoon, ready to give a full necropsy report to whoever was handling the case. Steve Carella took the call. He had spoken to Blaney many times before, and Blaney was glad that Carella and not another of the 87th's cops had answered the phone. Carella was a man who understood the problems of the medical examiner's office. Carella was a man you could talk to.

The men exchanged the pleasantries and amenities and then Blaney said, 'I'm calling about this little girl they sent over. From what I understand, the body was found in Majesta, but it seems to be connected with a case you're working on, and I was asked to deliver my report to you. I'll send this over typed later, Carella, but I thought you might want the findings right away.'

'I'm glad you called,' Carella said.

'Her name's Eileen Glennon,' Blaney said, 'That right?'

'That's right.'

'I wanted to make sure we were talking about the same person before I went through the whole bit.'

'That's OK,' Carella said.

'This was an interesting one,' Blaney said. 'Not a mark on her. Plenty of bloodstains, but no visible wounds. I figure she's been dead a few days, probably since Sunday night sometime. Where was she found, exactly?'

'In a little park.'

'Hidden?'

'No, not exactly. But the park doesn't get much traffic.'

'Well, that might explain it. In any case, I estimate she was lying wherever they found her since Sunday night, if that's any help to you.'

'It might be helpful,' Carella said. 'How'd she die?'

'Well, now, that's what was interesting about this. Does she lived in Majesta?'

'No. She lives with her mother. In Isola.'

'Well, that makes sense, all right. Though I can't understand why she didn't at least *try* to get home. Of course, considering what I found, she probably had a range of symptoms, which could have confused her. Especially after what she'd been through.'

'What kind of symptoms, Blaney?'

'Chills, febrile temperature, vomiting maybe, syncope, weakness, and eventually stupor and delirium.'

'I see,' Carella said.

'The autopsy revealed a slightly distended cervix, tenderness of the lower abdomen, discharge from the external os, and tenacula marks.'

'I see,' Carella said, not seeing at all.

'A septic infection,' Blaney stated simply. 'And, at first, I thought it might have been the cause of death. But it wasn't. Although it certainly ties in with what *did* kill her.'

'And what was that?' Carella asked patiently.

'The bleeding.'

'But you said there were no wounds.'

'I said there were no *visible* wounds. Of course, the tenacula marks were a clue.'

'What are tenacula marks?' Carella asked.

'Tenacula is a plural for tenaculum – Latin,' Blaney said. 'A tenaculum is a surgical tool, a small sharp-pointed hook set in a handle. We use it for seizing and picking up parts. Of the body, naturally. In operations or dissections.'

Carella suddenly remembered that he didn't very often like talking to Blaney. He tried to speed the conversation along, wanting to get at the facts without all the details.

'Well, where *were* these tenacula marks?' he asked pointedly.

'On the cervical lip,' Blaney said. 'The girl had bled profusely from the uterine canal. I also found pieces of pla—'

'What did she die from, Blaney?' Carella asked impatiently.

'I was getting to that. I was just telling you. I found pieces of pla—'

'How did she die?'

'She died of uterine haemorrhage. The septicaemia was a complication.'

'I don't understand. What caused the haemorrhage?'

'I was trying to tell you, Carella, that I also found pieces of placental tissue in the cervix of the uterus.'

'Placental . . . ?'

'The way I figure it, the job was done either Saturday or Sunday some time. The girl was probably wandering around when—'

'What job? What are you talking about, Blaney?'

'The abortion,' Blaney said flatly. 'That little girl had an abortion some time over the weekend. You want to know what killed her? *That*'s what killed her!'

Somebody had to tell Kling what everybody in the squad room decided that Tuesday. Somebody had to tell him, but Kling was at a funeral. So, instead of speculating, instead of hurling theories at a man who was carrying grief inside him, instead of telling him that one of those closets they'd spoken about had finally been opened and, like all closets opened in the investigation of a homicide, it contained something that should have remained hidden – instead of confronting him with something they knew he would disbelieve anyway – they decided to find out a little more about it. Carella and Meyer went back to see the girl's mother, Mrs Glennon, leaving Bert Kling undisturbed at the funeral.

Indian summer was out of place at that cemetery.

Oh, she had charm, that guileful bitch. The trees lining the road to the burial plot were dressed in gaudy brilliance, reds and oranges and burnt yellows and browns and unimaginable hues mixed on a Renaissance palette. Hotly, they danced overhead, whispering secrets to the balmy October breeze, while the mourners marched beneath the branches of the trees, following the coffin in colourless black, their heads bent, their feet drifting through idle fallen leaves, whispering, whispering.

The hole in the earth was like an open wound.

The grass seemed to end abruptly, and the freshly turned earth began in moist rich darkness, its virgin aroma carried on the air. The grave was long and deep. The coffin was suspended over it, held aloft on canvas straps attached to the mechanism which would lower it gently into the earth.

The sky was so blue.

They stood like uneasy shadows against the wide expanse of sky and the gaudy exhibitionism of the autumn trees. They stood with their heads bent. The coffin was poised for disappearance.

He looked at the black shining box and beyond that to where a man was waiting to release the mechanism. Everything seemed to shimmer in that moment because his eyes had suddenly filled with tears. A hand touched his arm. He turned, and through the glaze of tears he saw Claire's father, Ralph Townsend. The grip tightened on his arm. He nodded and tried to hear the minister's words.

'. . . above all,' the minister was saying, 'she goes to God even as she was delivered from Him: pure of heart, clean of spirit, honest and unafraid of His infinite mercy, Claire Townsend, may you rest in eternal peace.'

'Amen,' they said.

12.

MRS GLENNON HAD had it. She had had it up to here. She didn't want to see another cop as long as she lived. She had identified her daughter at the morgue before they had begun the autopsy and then had gone home to put on her widow's weeds, the same black clothing she had worn years ago when her husband had died. And now there were cops again – Steve Carella and Meyer Meyer. Meyer, in true private eye fashion, had swum up out of that pool of blackness, had had his cuts and bruises dressed, and now sat wearing a serious look and a great deal of adhesive plaster. Mrs Glennon faced them in stony silence while they fired questions at her, refusing to answer, her hands clenched in her lap as she sat unflinchingly in a hard-backed kitchen chair.

'Your daughter had an abortion, do you know that, Mrs Glennon?'

Silence.

'Who did it, Mrs Glennon?'

Silence.

'Whoever did it *killed* her, do you know that?'

Silence.

'Why didn't she come back here?'

'Why'd she wander the streets instead?'

'Was the abortionist in Majesta? Is that why she was there?'

'Did you kick her out when you learned she was pregnant?'

Silence.

'OK, Mrs Glennon, let's take it from the top. Did you know she was pregnant?'

Silence.

'How long was she pregnant?'

Silence.

'Goddamn it, your daughter is *dead*, do you know that?'

'I know that,' Mrs Glennon said.

'Did you know where she was going Saturday when she left here?'

Silence.

'Did you know she was going to have an abortion?'

Silence.

'Mrs Glennon,' Carella said, 'we're just going to assume you *did* know. We're going to assume you had foreknowledge that your daughter was about to produce her own miscarriage, and we're going to book you as an accessory before the fact. You better get your coat and hat.'

'She couldn't have the baby,' Mrs Glennon said.

'Why not?'

Silence.

'OK, get your things. We're going to the station house.'

'I'm not a criminal,' Mrs Glennon said.

'Maybe not,' Carella answered. 'But induced abortion is a crime. Do you know how many young girls die from criminal operations in this city every year? Well, this year your *daughter* is one of them.'

'I'm not a criminal.'

'Abortionists get one to four years, Mrs Glennon. The woman who submits to an abortion can get the same prison term. Unless either she or her "quick" child dies. Then the crime is first-degree manslaughter. And even a relative or friend who guided the woman to an abortionist is held guilty of being a party to the crime if it can be shown that the purpose of the visit was known. In other words, an accessory is as guilty as any of the principals. Now how do you feel about that, Mrs Glennon?'

'I didn't take her anywhere. I was here in bed all day Saturday.'

'Then *who* took her, Mrs Glennon?'

Silence.

'Did Claire Townsend?'

'No. Eileen went alone. Claire had nothing to do with any of this.'

'That's not true, Mrs Glennon. Claire rented a room on South First Street, and she used Eileen's name in the transaction. We figure the room was intended for Eileen's convalescence. Isn't that true, Mrs Glennon?'

'I don't know anything about a room.'

'We found the address right here! And the note clearly indicated that Eileen was supposed to meet Claire Saturday. What time were they supposed to meet, Mrs Glennon?'

'I don't know anything about it.'

'Why was it necessary for Eileen to take a furnished room? Why couldn't she come back here? Why couldn't she come home?'

'I don't know anything about it.'

'Did Claire arrange for the abortion?'

Silence.

'She's dead, Mrs Glennon. Nothing you say can hurt her any more.'

'She was a good girl,' Mrs Glennon said.

'Are you talking about Claire or your daughter?'

Silence.

'Mrs Glennon,' Carella said very softly, 'do you think I like talking about abortion?'

Mrs Glennon looked up at him but said nothing.

'Do you think I like talking about pregnancy? Do you think I like invading your daughter's privacy, your daughter's dignity?' He shook his head tiredly. 'A man murdered her, Mrs Glennon. He slaughtered her like a pig. Won't you please help us find him?'

'And do you want more killing?' Mrs Glennon asked suddenly.

'What?'

'Do you want someone else to be killed?'

'What do you mean?'

'You've met my son.' She nodded her head and fell silent again.

'What about him?'

'You see what he did to this fellow here, don't you? And that was only because the man was *questioning* me. What do you think he'd do if he found out Eileen was . . . was—'

'Who are you afraid for, Mrs Glennon?'

'My son. He'd kill him.'

'*Who* would he kill?'

'The . . . the baby's father.'

'Who? Who is he?'

'No.' She shook her head.

'Mrs Glennon, we're cops,' Meyer said angrily. 'We're not gonna go telling your son . . .'

'I know this neighbourhood,' Mrs Glennon said wisely. 'It's like a small town. If the police know, everyone will know. And then my son will find the man and kill him. No.' She shook her head again. 'Take me to jail if you want to; hold me as an access . . . whatever you called it. Do that. Say that I murdered my own daughter because I was trying to help her. Go ahead. But I won't have more blood on my hands. No.'

'Did Claire know all this?'

'I don't know what Claire knew.'

'But she did arrange for your daughter to—'

'I don't know what she did.'

'Wouldn't this guy marry your daughter, Mrs Glennon?' Meyer asked.

Silence.

'I'd like to ask one more question,' Carella said. 'I hope you'll give us the answer. I want you to know, Mrs Glennon, that all this embarrasses me. I don't like to talk about it. I don't like to think about it. But I know you have the answer to this question, and I want it.'

Silence.

'Who performed the abortion?'

Silence.

'Who?'

Silence.

And then, out of the silence, suddenly, 'Dr Madison. In Majesta.'

'Thank you, Mrs Glennon,' Carella said softly.

In the car on the long drive to Majesta over the Majesta Bridge, spanning two parts of the city, a bridge as old as time, black and sooty against the sky, squat and sombre in contrast to its elegant rivals, Meyer and Carella speculated on what it all meant.

'The thing I still can't understand,' Carella said, 'is Claire's involvement.'

'Me neither. It doesn't sound like her, Steve.'

'But she sure as hell rented that room.'

'Yes'.

'And she made plans to meet Eileen, so she obviously knew Eileen was going to have an abortion.'

'That's right,' Meyer said. 'But that's what's so contradictory. She's a social worker . . . and a *good* one. She knows induced abortion is a felony. She knows if she has anything to do with it, she's involved as an accessory. Even if she didn't know it as a social worker, she certainly knew it as a cop's girlfriend.' Meyer paused. 'I wondered if she ever mentioned this to Bert?'

'I don't know. I think we're gonna have to ask him, sooner or later.'

'I'm not looking forward to it.'

'So . . . damn it,' Carella said, 'most social workers *encourage* unwed mothers to have the babies and place them for adoption. Why would Claire . . . ?'

'The son,' Meyer reminded him. 'A hot-tempered little snot who'd go looking for the father of the child.'

'Claire's boyfriend is a cop,' Carella said flatly, 'She could have prepared us for that eventuality. We could have scared hell out of young Glennon with just a warning to keep his nose clean. I don't understand it.'

'Or, for that matter,' Meyer said, 'why didn't Claire try to contact the father – arrange a marriage? I don't get it. I can't believe she'd get involved in something like this. I just can't believe it.'

'Maybe our doctor friend can shed a little light on the subject,' Carella said. 'What'd the phone book tell us?'

'A. J. Madison, MD,' Meyer said. 'Eleven sixty-three Thirty-seventh, Majesta.'

'That's near that park where they found the girl, isn't it?'

'Yes.'

'You think she'd just come from the doctor's office?'

'I don't know.'

146

'That doesn't sound likely. She was supposed to meet Claire in Isola. She wouldn't have hung around Majesta. And I doubt if she was sick that soon. Jesus, Meyer, I'm confused as hell.'

'You're just a lousy detective, that's all.'

'I know. But I'm still confused as hell.'

Thirty-seventh Avenue was a quiet residential street with brownstone houses approached by low white stoop fronts and shielded from the sidewalk by low wrought-iron fences. The impression was one of serenity and dignity. This could have been a street in Boston or Philadelphia, a subdued street hidden from the ravages of time and the pace of the twentieth century. It wasn't. It was a street which housed Dr A. J. Madison, Abortion-ist.

1163 was in the middle of the block, a brownstone, indistinguishable from the brownstones flanking it, the same low iron fence in black, the same white steps leading to the front door, which was painted a subtle green. A rectangular brass plate was set over the brass button. The plate read 'A. J. Madison, MD'. Carella pushed the button. This was a doctor's office, and he didn't have to be told the door would be unlocked. He twisted the huge brass knob and he and Meyer stepped into the large reception room. There was a desk set in one corner before a wall of books. The other two walls were done in an expensive textured wallpaper. A Picasso print hung on one wall, and two Braques were on the other. A low coffee table carried the latest issues of *Life*, *Look*, and *Ellery Queen's Mystery Magazine*.

'Doesn't seem to be anybody home,' Carella said.

'Nurse is probably out back with him,' Meyer said.

They waited. In a moment they heard cushioned foot-steps coming down the long hall leading to the reception room. A smiling blonde entered the room. She wore a white smock and white shoes. Her hair was held tightly at the back of her head in a compact bun. Her face was clean-chiselled, with high cheekbones and a sweeping jawline and penetrating blue eyes. She was perhaps forty years old, but she looked like a young matron, the pleasant smile, the alert blue eyes.

'Gentlemen?' she said.

'How do you do?' Carella said. 'We'd like to see Dr Madison, please.'

'Yes?'

'Is he in?' Carella asked.

The woman smiled. 'You don't have an appointment, do you?'

'No,' Meyer said. 'Is the doctor in?'

The woman smiled again. 'Yes, the doctor is in.'

'Well, would you tell him we're here, please?'

'Can you tell me what this is in reference to?'

'Police business,' Meyer said flatly.

'Oh?' The woman's light eyebrows moved ever so slightly. 'I see.' She paused. 'What . . . *sort* of police business?'

'This is a personal matter we'd like to discuss with the doctor himself, if you don't mind.'

'I'm afraid you're talking to "the doctor himself",' the woman said.

'What?'

'*I'm* Dr Madison.'

'What?'

'Yes.' She nodded. 'What is it you want, gentlemen?'

'I think we'd better go into your office, doctor.'

'Why? My nurse is out to lunch, and my next appointment isn't until two o'clock. We can talk right here. I assume this won't take long, will it?'

'Well, that depends . . .'

'What is it? An unreported gunshot wound?'

'It's a little more than that, Dr Madison.'

'Oh?'

'Yes,' Carella took a deep breath. 'Dr Madison, did you perform a criminal abortion on a girl named Eileen Glennon last Saturday?'

Dr Madison seemed mildly surprised. Her eyebrows moved up an eighth of an inch, and the smile came to her mouth again. 'I beg your pardon,' she said.

'I said, Dr Madison, did you perform a criminal abortion on—'

'Yes, certainly,' Dr Madison replied. 'I perform criminal abortions every Saturday. I have special rates for weekend curettage. Good day, gentlemen.'

She was turning on her heel when Carella said, 'Hold it right there, Dr Madison.'

'Why should I?' Dr Madison said. 'I don't have to listen to these insults! If this is your idea of a—'

'Yeah, well, you're liable to be a little more insulted,' Meyer said. 'Eileen Glennon is dead.'

'I am very sorry to hear that, but I have no idea *who* the girl is or why you should possibly connect me—'

'Her mother gave us your name, Dr Madison. Now she didn't pick the name out of a hat, did she?'

'I have no idea *where* she picked it – or why. I don't know anyone named Eileen Glennon, and I have certainly never performed a criminal abortion in my life. I have a respectable practice and I wouldn't endanger it for—'

'What's your speciality, Dr Madison?'

'I'm a general practitioner.'

'Must be pretty tough, huh? For a woman doctor to make a living?'

'I do very well, thank you. Your solicitude is wasted. If you're finished with me, I have other things to—'

'Hold it, Dr Madison. Stop running for that back room, huh? This isn't gonna be that easy.'

'What do you want from me?' Dr Madison asked.

'We want you to tell us what happened here Saturday morning.'

'Nothing. I wasn't even *here* Saturday morning. Office hours start at two.'

'What time did Eileen Glennon arrive?'

'I have no idea who Eileen Glennon is.'

'She's the girl you operated on last Saturday,' Meyer said. 'She's the girl who dropped dead of a uterine haemorrhage in the park six blocks from here. That's who she is, Dr Madison.'

'I performed no operation last Saturday.'

'What time did she get here?'

'This is absurd, and a waste of time. If she wasn't here, I'm certainly not going to say she *was*.'

'Did you know she was dead?'

'I didn't even know she was *alive*. I'm sure she was a very nice little girl, but—'

'Why do you call her little, Dr Madison?'

'What?'

'You just called her a nice little girl. Why?'

'I'm sure I don't know. *Wasn't* she a nice little girl?'

'Yeah, but how did you know?'

'How did I know *what*?' Dr Madison said angrily.

'That she was only sixteen years old.'

'I didn't, and I don't. I never heard of Eileen Glennon until just a few moments ago.'

'Didn't you read yesterday's paper?'

'No. I rarely have time for anything but the professional journals.'

'When's the last time you did read a newspaper, Dr Madison?'

'I don't remember. Wednesday, Thursday, I don't remember. I just told you—'

'Then you didn't know she was dead.'

'No. I told you that already. Are we finished now?'

'What time did you operate on her, Dr Madison?'

'I didn't. Nor do I see how you can possibly show that I did. You just told me the girl is dead. *She* can't testify to having had an abortion, and—'

'Oh, she came here alone then, huh?'

'She didn't come here at all. She's dead, and that's that. I never saw her or heard of her in my life.'

'Ever hear of Claire Townsend?' Carella snapped.

'What?'

He decided to take a chance. She had just told him she hadn't seen a newspaper since the middle of last week, before Claire was killed. So, out of the blue, and knowing it was a wild gamble, he said, 'Claire Townsend's still alive. She told us she arranged an abortion for Eileen Glennon. With *you*, Dr Madison. Now how about it?'

The room went silent.

'I think you'd better come downtown and discuss this with Claire personally, huh?' Meyer said.

'I didn't think—'

'You didn't think Claire would tell us, huh? Well, she did. Now how about it?'

'I had nothing to do with the girl's death,' Dr Madison said.

'No. Then who committed the abortion?'

'*I had nothing to do with her death!*'

'Where'd you perform the operation?'

'Here.'

'Saturday morning?'

'Yes.'

'What time?'

'She got here at ten.'

'And you operated when?'

'At about ten-fifteen.'

'Who assisted?'

'I don't have to tell you that. There was a nurse and an anaesthetist I don't have to tell you who they were.'

'An anaesthetist? That's a little unusual, isn't it?'

'I'm not a butcher!' Dr Madison said angrily. 'I performed the kind of operation she could have got from a gynaecologist in a hospital. I observed every rule of proper aseptic surgical technique.'

'Yeah, that's very interesting,' Carella said, 'since the girl had a septic infection in addition to the goddamn haemorrhage. What'd you use on her? A rusty hatpin?'

'Don't you *dare*!' Dr Madison shouted, and she rushed at Carella with her hand raised, the fist clenched in a hopelessly female attack, her eyes blazing. He caught her arm at the wrist and held her away from him, trembling and enraged.

'Now take it easy,' he said.

'Let go of me!'

'Take it easy.'

She pulled her wrist from his grasp. She rubbed the wrist with her left hand, glaring at Carella. 'The girl had proper care,' she said. 'She was under general anaesthesia for the dilatation and curettage.'

'But she died,' Carella said.

'That wasn't my fault! I told her to go directly to bed when she left here. Instead, she—'

'Instead she *what*?'

'She came back!'

'Here?'

152

'Yes, *here*.'

'When was this?'

'Saturday night. She told me Miss Townsend hadn't met her where she was supposed to. She said she couldn't go back home, and she begged me to take her in for the night.' Dr Madison shook her head. 'I couldn't do that. I told her to go to a hospital. I gave her the name of a hospital. They would have treated her.' Dr Madison shook her head again.

'She didn't go to any hospital, Dr Madison. She was probably too frightened.' He paused. 'How sick was she when she came here Saturday night?'

'She didn't seem ill. She only seemed confused.'

'Was she haemorrhaging?'

'Of course not! Do you think I'd have let her go if . . . I'm a *doctor*!'

'Yeah,' Carella said dryly. 'Who happens to perform abortions on the side.'

'Have you ever carried an unwanted child?' Dr Madison said slowly and evenly. 'I *have*.'

'And that makes everything all right, does it?'

'I was trying to help that little girl. I was offering her escape from a situation she didn't ask for.'

'You gave her escape, all right,' Meyer said.

'How much did you charge for her murder?' Carella said.

'I didn't *murder*!'

'How much?'

'Fi . . . five hundred dollars.'

'Where would Eileen Glennon get five hundred dollars?'

'I . . . I don't know. Miss Townsend gave me the money.'

'When did you and Claire arrange all this?'

153

'Two . . . two weeks ago.'

'How'd she get on to you?'

'A friend told her about me. Why don't you ask *her*? Didn't *she* tell you all this?'

Carella ignored the question. 'How long was Eileen pregnant?' he asked.

'She was in her second month.'

'Then . . . since the beginning of September, would you say?'

'Yes, I would guess so.'

'All right, Dr Madison, get your coat. You're coming with us.'

Dr Madison seemed suddenly confused. 'My . . . my patients,' she said.

'You can forget all about your patients from now on,' Meyer said.

'Why? What did I do wrong? Try to save a little girl from unwanted misery? Is that so wrong?'

'Abortion is against the law. You knew that, Dr Madison.'

'It shouldn't be!'

'It is. We don't write them, lady.'

'I was helping her!' Dr Madison said. 'I was only . . .'

'You killed her,' Meyer said.

But his voice lacked conviction, and he put the handcuffs on her wrists without another word.

FIRST COUNT

The Grand Jury of Majesta, by this indictment, accuse the defendant, Alice Jean Madison, of the crime of abortion, in violation of Sections 2 and 80 of the Penal Law of this state, committed as follows:

The defendant, on or about October 14 at 1163 Thirty-

seventh Avenue, Majesta, did unlawfully, feloniously, and wilfully use and employ a certain instrument on Eileen Glennon with intent thereby to procure the miscarriage of said Eileen Glennon, the same not being necessary to preserve the life of the said Eileen Glennon or the life of the child with which she was then pregnant.

SECOND COUNT

The Grand Jury of Majesta, by this indictment, accuse the defendant of the crime of manslaughter in the first degree in that the defendant did unlawfully, feloniously, and wilfully use and employ a certain instrument on Eileen Glennon with intent thereby to procure the miscarriage of said Eileen Glennon, the same not being necessary to preserve the life of the said Eileen Glennon or the life of the child with which she was then pregnant as a result of all of which she died on October 15.

Arthur Parkinson,
District Attorney

13.

Indian summer is leaving the city. There is a chill in the squad room even though the thermostat has been turned up and the radiators are beginning to clang.

Autumn has arrived suddenly and seemingly without warning. The men sit with their hands wrapped around mugs of hot coffee.

There is a chill in the squad room.

'Bert, there are some questions we have to ask you.'

'What kind of questions?'

'About Claire.'

The telephone rings.

'87th Squad, Detective Carella. Oh, yes, sir. No, I'm sorry, we haven't been able to locate them as yet. We're making a routine check of all pawnshops. Mr Mendel. Yes, sir, as soon as we have anything. Thank you for calling.'

There was something ludicrous about the scene. Bert Kling sat in the chair facing the desk. Carella replaced the telephone in its cradle and then went to stand beside Kling. Meyer sat on one corner of the desk, leaning over, his elbow cushioned on his knee. Kling's face was drawn and gaunt. He looked for all the world like a harried suspect being grilled by two hardened detectives.

'What do you want to know?' he asked.

'Did she ever mention Eileen Glennon to you?'

Kling shook his head.

'Bert, please try to think back, will you? This might

156

have been in September sometime, when Mrs Glennon was in the hospital. Did Claire mention having met Mrs Glennon's daughter?'

'No. I would have remembered the minute the Glennons came into the case. No, Steve. She never mentioned the girl.'

'Well, did she ever mention *any* girl? I mean, did she seem troubled about any of her patients?'

'No.' Kling shook his head. 'No, I don't remember, Steve.'

'What did you talk about?' Meyer asked.

'What do you mean?'

'When you were together.'

Kling knew exactly what Meyer was trying to do. He was a cop, and he had used the same technique himself, many times before. Meyer was simply trying to start a train of thought, trying to get words flowing in the hope that they would trigger a significant memory. But, even knowing this, he felt a numbing pain. He did not want to talk about Claire. He did not want to repeat aloud the things they had whispered alone together.

'Can you remember?' Meyer said gently.

'We . . . we talked about a lot of things.'

'Well, like what?'

'Well . . . she had a toothache. This was . . . it must have been the early part of September.'

'Yes, go ahead, Bert,' Carella said.

'And she . . . she was going to a dentist. I remember she . . . she hated it. She . . . she met me one night with her jaw numb. From the novocaine. She asked me to hit her. She . . . she said, "Go ahead, strong man! I'll bet you can't hurt me." She was kidding, you know. Because . . . we had a lot of little jokes like that. You know . . . because I'm a cop.'

'Did she ever talk about school, Bert?'

'Oh, sure,' Kling said. 'She was having a little difficulty with one of her teachers. Oh, nothing like that,' Kling said immediately; 'nothing serious. The instructor had certain ideas about social work, and Claire didn't agree with them.'

'What were the ideas, Bert?'

'I don't remember now. You know how it is in a class. Everybody's got their ideas.'

'But Claire was a *working* student.'

'Yeah. Well, most of the people in the class were. She was doing graduate work, you know. She was going for her master's.'

'Did she ever talk about that?'

'Pretty often. Social work was very important to her, you know.' He paused. 'Well, I guess you don't know. But it was. The only reason we . . . we weren't married yet is because . . . well, you know, she wanted to finish her schooling.'

'Where did you go when you went out, Bert? Any place special?'

'No, just around. Movies, plays sometimes. Dancing. She liked to dance. She was a very good dancer.'

The squad room was suddenly still.

'She was . . .' Kling started and then stopped.

The silence persisted.

'Bert, do you remember any of her ideas about social work? Did she ever discuss them with you?'

'Well, not really. I mean, except where it crossed with police work, do you know what I mean?'

'No.'

'Well, where she was puzzled about a legality. Or where she felt we were doing a bad job. Like with street gangs, you know. She thought we handle them wrong.'

'How, Bert?'

'Well, we're more interested in crime, you know. A kid shoots somebody, we're not too damn interested in the fact that his father's an alcoholic. That's where the social work came in. But she felt social workers and cops should work more closely together. We had a lot of jokes about that, too. I mean, about *us* personally.' He paused. 'I told her all about the P.A.L., and about social workers doing work with street gangs already, but she knew all that. What she wanted was a *closer* working relationship.'

'Had she done much work with young people?'

'Only in connection with her own patients. A lot of people she dealt with had families, you know. So she naturally worked with the kids involved.'

'Did she ever mention a furnished room on South First Street?'

'No.' Kling paused. 'A furnished room? What's this?'

'We think she rented one, Bert. In fact, we *know* she did.'

'Why?'

'To take Eileen Glennon to.'

'Why?'

'Because Eileen Glennon had an abortion.'

'What's Claire got to—'

'Claire arranged for it.'

'No,' Kling said immediately. He shook his head. 'You're mistaken.'

'We've checked it, Bert.'

'That's impossible. Claire would never . . . no, that's impossible. She was too aware of the law. No. She was always asking me questions about legal matters. You're wrong. She wouldn't have any part of a thing like that.'

'When she asked about legal matters . . . did she ever ask about abortion?'

'No. Why would she ask—?' Bert Kling stopped talking. A surprised look crossed his face. He shook his head once, disbelievingly.

'What is it, Bert?'

He shook his head again.

'*Did* she ask about abortion?'

Kling nodded.

'When was this?'

'Last month sometime. I thought at first . . . I thought she was . . .'

'Go ahead, Bert.'

'I thought she. . . well, I thought it was for herself, you know. But . . . what it was . . . she wanted to know about *legal* abortions.'

'She asked you that? She asked you when an abortion was considered legal?'

'Yes. I told her only if the life of either the mother or the child was in danger. You know. P.L. 80 – "unless the same is necessary to preserve the life of the woman or of the—" '

'Yeah, go ahead.'

'That's all.'

'Are you sure?'

'No, wait a minute. She asked me a specific question. Just wait a second.'

They waited. Kling's brow knotted. He passed his hand over his face.

'Yeah,' he said.

'What was it?'

'She asked me if the victim of a rape . . . a girl who got pregnant because of a rape . . . she asked me if the abortion would be legal then.'

'That's it!' Meyer said. 'That's what all the goddamn hiding was about! Sure. That's why the furnished room –

and that's why Eileen couldn't go home. If the brother ever found out she'd been raped—'

'Hold it, hold it,' Kling said. 'What do you mean?'

'What did you tell Claire?'

'Well, I told her I wasn't sure. I told her it seemed to me that morally it should be permissable to have an abortion in those circumstances. I just didn't know.'

'And what did she say?'

'She asked me to check it for her. She said she wanted to know.'

'Did you check it?'

'I called the D.A.'s office the next day. Preserve the life of the mother or child, they told me. Period. Any other induced abortion would be criminal.'

'Did you tell that to Claire?'

'Yes.'

'And what did she say?'

'She blew her stack! She said she thought the law was designed to *protect* the innocent, not to cause them more suffering. I tried to calm her down, you know – what the hell, *I* don't write the laws! She seemed to hold me personally responsible for the damn thing. I asked her why she was getting so excited, and she said something about Puritan morality being the most immoral thing in the world – something like that. She said a girl's life could be completely ruined because she was the victim of a crime and of the law both.'

'Did she ever mention it again?'

'No.'

'Did she ever ask you if you knew any abortionists?'

'No,' Kling paused. 'From what I get . . .' He paused again. 'You think Eileen Glennon was raped, is that it?'

'That's our guess,' Meyer said. 'And probably while her mother was in the hospital.'

'And you think Claire knew about this, and knew she was pregnant, and . . . and arranged an abortion for her?'

'Yes. We're *sure* of that, Bert.' Carella paused. 'She even paid for it.'

Kling nodded. 'I suppose . . . I suppose we could check her bank book.'

'We did that yesterday. She withdrew five hundred dollars on the first of October.'

'I see. Then . . . then I guess . . . well, I guess it's what you say it is.'

Carella nodded. 'I'm sorry, Bert.'

'If she did it, you know,' Kling said, and stopped. '*If* she did it, it was only because the girl had been raped. I mean, she . . . she wouldn't have broken the law otherwise. You know that, don't you?'

Carella nodded again. 'I might have done the same thing,' he said. He did not know if he believed this or not, but he said it anyway.

'She only wanted to protect the girl,' Kling said. 'If you . . . if you look at it one way, she . . . she was actually *preserving* the girl's life, just like the Penal Law says.'

'And in the meanwhile,' Meyer said, 'she was also protecting the guy who raped Eileen. Why does he get out of this clean, Steve? Why does that son of a bitch—'

'Maybe he doesn't,' Carella said. 'Maybe he wanted to do a little protecting of his own. And maybe he started by taking care of one of the people who knew about the rape but who wasn't connected in any personal way.'

'What do you mean?'

'I mean Eileen and her mother wouldn't dare tell about it for fear of what young Glennon would do. But maybe he couldn't be sure of Claire Townsend. So maybe he followed her to that bookshop and—'

'Does the mother know who?' Kling asked.

'Yes, we think so.'

Kling nodded once, tightly. There was nothing in his eyes, nothing in his voice, when at last he spoke.

'She'll tell me,' he said.

It was a promise.

The man lived on the floor above the Glennons.

Kling left the Glennon apartment and began climbing the steps. Mrs Glennon stood in her doorway with her hand pressed to her mouth. It was impossible to know what she was thinking as she watched Kling climb those steps. Maybe she was simply wondering why some people never seemed to have any luck.

Kling knocked on the door to apartment 4A and then waited.

A voice inside called, 'Just a second!'

Kling waited.

The door opened a crack, held by a chain. A man peered out. 'Yes?' he said.

'Police,' Kling said flatly. He held up his wallet, open to his detective's shield.

'What is it?'

'Are you Arnold Halsted?'

'Yes?'

'Open the door, Mr Halsted.'

'What? What is it? Why . . . ?'

'Open the door before I bust it in!' Kling answered.

'OK, OK, just a minute.' Halsted fumbled with the chain. As soon as it was loose, Kling shoved the door open and entered the apartment.

'You alone, Mr Halsted?'

163

'Yes.'

'I understand you have a wife and three children, Mr Halsted. Is that right, Mr Halsted?'

There was something frightening in Kling's voice. Halsted, a short thin man wearing black trousers and a white undershirt, backed away from it instinctively. 'Y . . . yes,' he said. 'That's right.'

'Where are they?'

'The children are . . . in school.'

'And your wife?'

'She works.'

'How about you, Mr Halsted? Don't you work?'

'I'm . . . I'm temporarily unemployed.'

'How long have you been "temporarily unemployed"?' There was a biting edge to Kling's words. He spit them out like razor-sharp stilettos.

'Since . . . since last summer.'

'When?'

'August.'

'What did you do in September, Mr Halsted?'

'I—'

'Besides raping Eileen Glennon?'

'Wh . . . what?' Halsted's voice caught in his throat. His face went white. He took a step backwards, but Kling took a step closer.

'Put on a shirt. You're coming with me.'

'I . . . I . . . I didn't do anything. You're mistaken.'

'You didn't do anything, huh?' Kling shouted. 'You son of a bitch, you didn't do anything! You went down-stairs and raped a sixteen-year-old girl! You didn't do anything? *You didn't do anything?*'

'Shhh, shhh, my neighbours,' Halsted said.

'*Your neighbours?*' Kling shouted. 'You've got the gall to . . .'

164

Halsted backed away into the kitchen, his hands trembling. Kling followed him. 'I . . . I . . . I . . . it was *her* idea,' Halsted said quickly. 'She . . . she . . . she wanted to. I . . . I didn't. It was—'

'You're a filthy lying bastard,' Kling said, and he slapped Halsted openhanded across the face.

Halsted made a frightened little sound, a moan that trembled on to his lips. He covered his face with his hands and mumbled, 'Don't hit me.'

'Did you rape her?' Kling said.

Halsted nodded, his face still buried in his hands.

'Why?'

'I . . . I don't know. Her . . . her mother was in the hospital, you see. Mrs Glennon. She's . . . she's a very good friend of my wife, Mrs Glennon. They go to church together, they belong to the same . . . they made novenas together . . . they . . .'

Kling waited. His hands had bunched into fists. He was waiting to ask the big question. Then he was going to beat Halsted to a pulp on the kitchen floor.

'When . . . when she went to the hospital, my wife would . . . would prepare food for the children. For Terry and . . . and Eileen. And . . .'

'Go ahead!'

'I would bring it down to them whenever . . . whenever my wife was working.'

Slowly Halsted took his hands from his face. He did not raise his eyes to meet Kling's. He stared at the worn and soiled linoleum on the kitchen floor. He was still trembling, a thin frightened man in a sleeveless undershirt, staring at the floor, staring at what he had done.

'It was Saturday,' he said. 'I had seen Terry leaving the house. From the window. I had seen him. My wife had gone to work — she does crochet beading; she's a very skilled worker. It was Saturday. I remember it was very hot here in the apartment. Do you remember how hot it was in September?'

Kling said nothing in reply, but Halsted had not expected an answer. He seemed unaware of Kling's presence. There was total communication between him and the worn linoleum. He did not raise his eyes from the floor.

'I remember. It was very hot. My wife had left sandwiches for me to take down to the children. But I knew Terry was gone, you see. I would have taken down the sandwiches anyway, you see, but I knew Terry was gone. I can't say I didn't know he was gone.'

He stared at the floor for a long time, silently.

'I knocked when I got downstairs. There was no answer. I . . . I tried the door, and it was open, so I . . . I went in. She . . . Eileen was still in bed, asleep. It was twelve o'clock, but she . . . she was asleep. The cover . . . the sheet had . . . had got. . . had moved down from . . . I could *see* her. She was asleep and I could *see* her. I don't know what I did next. I think I put down the tray with the sandwiches, and I got into bed with her, and when she tried to scream I covered her mouth with my hands and I . . . I did it.'

He covered his face again.

'I did it,' he said. 'I did it, I did it.'

'You're a nice guy, Mr Halsted,' Kling said in a tight whisper.

'It . . . it just happened.'

'The way the baby just happened.'

'What? What baby?'

'Didn't you know Eileen was pregnant?'

'Preg . . . what are you saying? Who? What do

166

you . . . ? Eileen. No one said . . . why didn't someone . . . ?'

'You didn't know she was pregnant?'

'No. I swear it! I didn't know!'

'How do you think she died, Mr Halsted?'

'Her mother said . . . Mrs Glennon said an accident!
She even told my wife that – her best friend! She wouldn't
lie to my wife.'

'Wouldn't she?'

'An automobile accident! In Majesta. She . . . she was
visiting her aunt. That's what Mrs Glennon told us.'

'That's what she told your wife maybe. That's the
story you both invented to save *your* miserable hide.'

'No, I swear!' Tears had welled up into Halsted's eyes.
He reached forward eagerly now, pleadingly, grasping for
Kling's arm, straining for support. 'What do you mean?'
he said, sobbing. 'What do you mean? Please, oh, please
God, no . . .'

'She died getting rid of your baby,' Kling said.

'I didn't know. I didn't know. Oh, God, I swear I
didn't—'

'You're a lying bastard!' Kling said.

'Ask Mrs Glennon! I swear to God, I knew nothing
about—'

'You knew, and you went after somebody else who
knew!'

'What?'

'You followed Claire Townsend to—'

'Who? I don't know any—'

'—to that bookshop and *killed* her, you son of a bitch!
Where are the guns? What'd you do with them? Tell me
before I—'

'I swear, I swear—'

'Where were you Friday night from five o'clock on?'

167

'In the building! I swear! We went upstairs to the Lessers'! The fifth floor! We had supper with them, and then we played cards. I swear.'

Kling studied him silently. 'You didn't know Eileen was pregnant?' he said at last.

'No.'

'You didn't know she was going for an abortion?'

'No.'

Kling kept staring at him. Then he said. 'Two stops, Mr Halsted. First Mrs Glennon, and then the Lessers on the fifth floor. Maybe you're a very lucky man.'

Arnold Halsted was a very lucky man.

He had been 'temporarily unemployed' since August, but he had a wife who was an expert crochet beader and willing to assume the burden of family support while he sat around in his undershirt and watched the street from the bedroom window. He had raped a sixteen-year-old girl, but neither Eileen nor her mother had reported the incident to the police because, to begin with, Louise Halsted was a very close friend, and – more important – the Glennons knew that Terry would kill Arnold if he ever learned of the attack.

Mr Halsted was a very lucky man.

This was a neighbourhood full of private trouble. Mrs Glennon had been born into this neighbourhood, and she knew she would die in it, and she knew that trouble would always be a part of her life, an indisputable factor. She had seen no reason to bring trouble to Louise Halsted as well – her friend – perhaps her only friend in a world so hostile. Now, with her daughter dead and her son being held for assault, she listened to Bert Kling's questions and, instead of incriminating Halsted in murder, she told the truth.

She said that he had known nothing whatever of the pregnancy or the abortion.

Arnold Halsted was a very lucky man.

Mrs Lesser, on the fifth floor, said that Louise and Arnold had come upstairs at four-forty-five on Friday afternoon. They had stayed for dinner and for cards afterwards. He couldn't possibly have been anywhere near the bookstore where the killings had taken place.

Arnold Halsted was a very lucky man.

All he had facing him was a rape charge — and the possibility of spending twenty years behind bars.

14.

THE CASE WAS as dead as any of its victims.

The case was as dead as November, which came in with bone-chilling suddenness, freezing the city and its inhabitants, suddenly coating the rivers with ice.

They could shake neither the cold nor the case from the squad room. They carried the case with them all day long, and then they carried it home with them at night. The case was dead, and they knew it.

But so was Claire Townsend.

'It has to be connected with her!' Meyer Meyer said to his wife. 'What else could it be?'

'It could be a hundred other things,' Sarah said angrily. 'You're all blind on this case. It's Bert's girl, and so you've all gone blind.'

Meyer rarely lost his temper with Sarah, but the case was bugging him, and besides, she had overcooked the string beans. 'Who are you?' he shouted. 'Sherlock Holmes?'

'Don't shout at Mommy,' Alan, his oldest son said.

'Shut your mouth and eat your string beans!' Meyer shouted. He turned back to Sarah and said, 'There's too much involved in this! The pregnant girl, the—'

Sarah shot a hasty glance at the children and a warning at Meyer.

'All right, all right,' he said. 'If they don't know where babies come from already, it's time they found out.'

'Where *do* babies come from?' Susie asked.

'Shut up and eat your string beans,' Meyer told her.

'Go ahead, tell her where babies come from,' Sarah said angrily.

'Where, Daddy?'

'It's that women are wonderful, understanding, fruitful, magnificent creatures that God provided for men, you see. And he also made it possible for these lovely, intelligent, sympathetic individuals to be able to make babies, so a man could be surrounded by his children when he comes home from the office.'

'Yes, but where do babies come from?' Susie asked.

'Ask your mother.'

'Can I have a baby?' Susie wanted to know.

'Not yet, dear,' Sarah said. 'Some day.'

'Why can't I have one now?'

'Oh, shut up, Susie,' Jeff, her younger brother by two years, said. 'Don't you know nothing?'

'It's you who don't know nothing,' Susie protested. 'You're not supposed to say "nothing". You're supposed to say "anything".'

'Oh, shut up, you moron,' Jeff said.

'Don't talk to your sister that way,' Meyer warned. 'You can't have a baby because you're too young, Susie. You have to be a woman. Like your mother. Who understands what a man's going through and—'

'I'm simply saying none of you are seeing this thing clearly. You're all involved in a stupid kind of revenge, looking for *any* possible stupid way to tie this in with Claire and blinding yourselves to any other possibility.'

'What possibilities are left, would you mind telling me? We've run this thing into the ground. Not just Claire. Everyone concerned. Everyone. All the victims, *and* their families, *and* their relatives, *and* their friends. There's nothing left, Sarah. So we come right back to Claire and the Glennons, and Dr Madison, and—'

'I've heard this all before,' Sarah said.

'Listen again; it won't kill you.'

'Can I be excused, please?' Alan said.

'Don't you want your dessert?'

'I want to watch "Malibu Run".'

' "Malibu Run" will wait,' Sarah said.

'Mom, it goes on at—'

'It'll wait. You'll have dessert.'

'Let him go if he wants to watch his programme,' Meyer said.

'Look, Detective Meyer,' Sarah said angrily, 'you may be a bigshot investigator who's used to bossing around suspects, but this is *my* table, and I happen to have spent three hours this afternoon preparing dinner, and I don't want my family rushing off to—'

'And burned the string beans while you were doing it,' Meyer said.

'The string beans are *not* burned!'

'They're overcooked!'

'But not burned. Sit right where you are, Alan. You're going to eat dessert if you have to choke on it!'

The family finished its meal in silence. The children left the table, and the sound of underwater mischief came from the living room television set.

'I'm sorry,' Meyer said.

'I am, too. I had no right to interfere with your work.'

'Maybe we *are* blind,' Meyer said. 'Maybe it's sitting there right under our noses.' He sighed heavily. 'But I'm so tired, Sarah. I'm so damned tired.'

CARPENTER

Steve Carella printed the word on a sheet of paper and then studied it. Beneath the word, he printed:

172

WOODWORKER
CABINETMAKER
SAWYER
WOODSMAN (?)

'I can't think of any other words that mean carpenter,' he said to Teddy. Teddy came to where he was sitting and looked at the sheet of paper. She took it from him and, in her own delicate hand, she added the words: LUMBER? LUMBERMAN? LUMBER-WORKER?

Carella nodded and then sighed. 'I think we're reaching.'

He put the sheet of paper aside, and Teddy climbed on to his lap. 'It probably has nothing to do with the damn case anyway.'

Teddy, watching his lips, shook her head.

'You think it does?' Carella asked.

She nodded.

'It would seem to, wouldn't it? Why else would a guy mention it with his last breath? But . . . there are so many other things, Teddy. All this business involving Claire. *That* would seem to be—'

Teddy suddenly put her hands over his eyes.

'What?'

She put her hands over her own eyes.

'Well, maybe we are blind,' he said. He picked up the sheet of paper again. 'You think there's a pun in this damn word? But why would a guy pun when he's dying? He'd tell us just what he was thinking, wouldn't he? Oh, Jesus. I don't know. Let's try breaking it down.' He got another sheet of paper and a pencil for Teddy, and together they began working on possible combinations.

CARPENTER

Carp enter
Car penter
Carpen ter
Carpent, R.

'I'm stuck,' Carella said.

Teddy studied the word list for a moment and then counted the letters in 'carpenter'.

'How many?' Carella asked.

She held up her fingers.

'Nine,' Carella said. 'How does that help us?'

Nine, she wrote on her sheet of paper. *Nein?*

'So?'

She shrugged.

'How about trying it backwards?' Carella said. He wrote down the word: RETNEPRAC. 'That mean anything to you?' he asked.

Teddy studied the word and then shook her head.

'Let's take it from the front again. *Carp.* That's a fish, isn't it?'

She nodded.

'Carp enter. Fish enter. Fish enter. Fishenter, For shenter, Force centre. For centre.' He shrugged. 'You get anything?'

Teddy shook her head.

'Maybe he was trying to tell us that a man named Fish entered the shop and fired those bullets.'

Teddy nodded dubiously.

'Fish,' Carella said. 'Fish enter.' He paused. 'Then why would he say "Carp enter"? Why not simply say "Fish enter"?'

Teddy's hands worked quickly. Carella watched her fingers. *Maybe Willis heard him wrong*, her hands said. *Maybe he was saying something else.*

'Like what?' Carella asked.

She wrote the word on her sheet of paper: CARPEN-TER.

'Like a man who lays carpets?'

Teddy nodded.

'Carpeter.' He thought it over for a moment. 'Maybe.' He shrugged. 'But, then, maybe he was saying "carboner", too.' He could tell by the puzzled look on her face that the words looked alike on his lips: *carpenter, carpeter, carboner*. He moved his paper into place and wrote the word:

CARBONER.

What's a carboner? Teddy's hands asked.

'I don't know,' he said. 'A man who puts carbon on things, I guess.'

Teddy shook her head, a wide grin on her face. *No*, her hands said, *that's the way you Italians say carbon.*

'Atsa right!' Carella said. 'Atsa whatta we say! Carbon-a! Only trouble issa Mr Wechsler, he'sa no was Italian.' He smiled and put down his pencil. 'Come here,' he said. 'I want to discuss this guy who lays carpets.'

Teddy came into his arms and on to his lap.

Neither of them knew how close they'd come.

November.

The trees had lost all their leaves.

He walked the streets alone, hatless, his blond hair whipping in the angry wind. There were ninety thousand people in the precinct and eight million people in the city, and one of them had killed Claire.

Who? he wondered.

He found himself staring at faces. Every passer-by became a potential murderer, and he studied them with scrutiny, unconsciously looking for a man who had murder in his eyes, consciously looking for a man who was white, not short, no scars, marks, or deformities, wearing a dark overcoat, grey fedora, and possibly sunglasses.

In November?

Who?

Lady, lady, *I* did it.

Lady, lady, I fired those guns, *I* left those gaping holes in your side, *I* caused your blood to run all over that bookshop floor, *I* took your life, *I* put you in your grave.

Who?

Who, you son of a bitch?

He could hear his own lonely footsteps echoing on the pavement. The neon clatter was everywhere around him, the sounds of traffic, the sound of voices raised in laughter, but he heard only his own footsteps, their own hollow cadence, and somewhere Claire's remembered voice, clear and vital, even whispering, Claire, Claire, 'Well, I bought a new bra.'

Oh?

'You should see what it does for me, Bert. Do you love me, Bert?'

You know I do.

'Tell me.'

I can't right now.

'Will you tell me later?'

Tears suddenly sprang into his eyes. He felt a loss so total, so complete in that moment, that he thought he would die himself, thought he would suddenly fall to the pavement lifeless. He brushed at his eyes.

He had suddenly remembered that he had not told her

he'd loved her, and he would never have the chance to do it again.

It was fortunate that Steve Carella took the call from Mrs Joseph Wechsler. It was fortunate because Bert Kling was very much in sympathy with the woman and had made a few aural adjustments in listening to her. It was fortunate because Meyer Meyer was too accustomed to hearing similar accents and might not have noticed the single important clue she dropped. It was fortunate because Carella had fooled around long enough with the word 'Carpenter' and was ready to pounce on anything that would shed light upon it. The telephone helped. The instrument provided a barrier between the two. He had never met the woman. He heard only the voice that came over the line, and he had to strain to catch every syllable.

'Hallo, dis is Mrs Vaxler,' the voice said.

'Yes, ma'am,' Carella answered.

'From my hosbin is Joseph Vaxler,' she said.

'Oh, yes, Mrs Wechsler. How are you? I'm Detective Carella.'

'Hallo,' she said. 'Mr Carell, I donn like t'bodder you dis way. I know you busy.'

'That's quite all right, Mrs Wechsler. What is it?'

'Vell, ven your d'tectiff was here, I gave him a bonch bills he said he vanted t'look oveh. I need them beck now.'

'Oh, I'm terribly sorry,' Carella said. 'They should have been returned to you long ago.'

'Dot's ull right,' Mrs Wechsler said. 'I vouldn't be boddering you, but I got today a second bill from d'men vot pented the car, and I remembered I didn't pay yet.'

'I'll see that they're sent to you right away,' Carella said. 'Somebody up here must have goofed.'

'Thank you. I vant to pay them as soon as—'

'The what?' Carella said suddenly.

'Pardon?'

'The what? The man who *what?*'

'I donn know vot you mean, Mr Carell.'

'You said something about a man who—'

'Oh, d'car penter. The men vot pented Joseph's car. Dot's right. Dot's who I got d'second bill from. Vot abodd him?'

'Mrs Wechsler, did . . . did your husband talk the way you do?'

'Vot?'

'Your husband. Did he . . . did he sound the way you do?'

'Oh, voise, d'poor men. But he vas good, you know. He vas a dear, good—'

'Bert!' Carella yelled.

Kling looked up from his desk.

'Come on,' Carella said. 'Goodbye, Mrs Wechsler, I'll call you back later.' He slammed the phone on the hook.

Kling was already clipping on his holster.

'What is it?' he said.

'I think we've got him.'

178

15.

THREE COPS WENT to make the collar, but only one was needed.

Brown, Carella, and Kling talked to Batista, the owner of the garage. They talked in quiet whispers in the front office with the scarred swivel chair. Batista listened with his eyes wide, a cigar hanging from one corner of his mouth. Every now and then he nodded. His eyes got wider when he saw the three detectives draw their revolvers. He told them where Buddy Manners was, and they asked him to stay right there in the front office until this was all over, and he nodded and took the cigar out of his mouth and sat in the swivel chair with a shocked expression on his face because television and the movies had suddenly moved into his life and left him speechless.

Manners was working on a car at the back of the garage. He had a spray gun in his right hand, and he was wearing dark glasses, the paint fanning out from the gun, the side of the car turning black as he worked. The detectives approached with guns in their fists, and Manners looked up at them, seemed undecided for a moment, and then went right on working. He was going to play this one cool. He was going to pretend that three big bastards with drawn guns always marched into the garage while he was spraying cars. Brown was the first to speak; he had met Manners before.

'Hello there, Mr Manners,' he said conversationally.

Manners cut off the spray gun, pushed the dark glasses up on to his forehead, and squinted at the three men.

'Oh, hello,' he said. 'Didn't recognize you.' He still made no mention of the hardware, which was very much in evidence.

'Usually wear sunglasses when you're working?' Brown asked conversationally.

'Sometimes. Not always.'

'How come?'

'Oh, you know. Sometimes this stuff gets all over the place. When I've got a small job, I don't bother. But if it's anything big I usually put on the glasses.' He grinned, 'Be surprised how much wear and tear on the eyeballs it saves.'

'Mmm-huh,' Carella said pleasantly. 'Ever wear sunglasses in the street?'

'Oh, sure' Manners answered.

'Were you wearing them on Friday, October 13?' Carella asked pleasantly.

'Gee, who knows? When was that?'

'The middle of last month,' Carella said pleasantly.

'Maybe, who knows? We had a lot of sunshine last month, didn't we? I could've been wearing them.' He paused. 'Why?'

'Why do you think we're here, Mr Manners?'

Manners shrugged. 'I don't know. Stolen car? That it?'

'No, guess again, Mr Manners,' Brown said.

'Gee, I don't know.'

'We think you're a murderer, Mr Manners,' Carella said.

'Huh?'

'We think you went into a bookstore on Culver Avenue on the evening of—'

And Kling suddenly reached for him. He stepped between Brown and Carella, cutting off Carella's words,

180

grabbing Manners by the front of his coveralls and then pushing him backwards against the side of the car, slamming him there with all the strength of his arm and shoulder.

'Let's have it,' Kling said.

'Let's have what? Let go of my—'

Kling hit him. This was not a dainty slap across the cheek nor even a vicious backhanded swipe to the jaw. Kling hit him with the butt of his .38. The gun collided with Manners' forehead, just over his right eye. It opened a cut two inches long which began bleeding immediately. Whatever Manners had expected, it wasn't this. He went dead white. He shook his head to clear it and then stared at Kling, who hulked over him, right hand holding the gun, poised to strike again.

'Let's have it,' Kling said.

'I . . . I don't know what—'

Kling hit him again. He swung up his arm, and then he brought it forward and down in a sharp short blow, hitting the exact same spot, like a boxer working on an opened wound, hitting directly and with expert precision, and then pulling back the gun, and tightening his left hand in Manners' clothes, and saying, 'Talk.'

'You son of a . . . you son of a bitch,' Manners said, and Kling hit him again, breaking the bridge of his nose with the gun this time, the bones suddenly splintering through the skin.

'Talk,' he said.

Manners was bellowing in pain. He tried to bring his hands to his shattered nose, but Kling shoved them away. He stood before the man like a robot, the hand tight in the front of the coveralls, his eyes slitted and dead, the gun ready.

'Talk.'

'I . . . I . . .'

'Why'd you do it?' Kling asked.

'He . . . he . . . oh, Jesus, my nose . . . Jesus, Jesus, Jesus . . .' The pain was excruciating. He gasped with the agony of trying to bear it. His hands kept flitting up to his face, and Kling kept knocking them away. Tears filled his eyes mixed with the blood from the open wound on his forehead, running into the blood that gushed from his mashed nose. Kling brought back the gun a fourth time.

'No!' Manners screamed. '*Don't!*' And then the words came streaming from his mouth in an anxious torrent, tumbling from his lips before the gun descended again, one word piling on to the next, a hysterical outburst from a terrified and wounded animal. 'He came in here the lousy Jew bastard and told me the colour was wrong the lousy kike told me the colour was wrong I wanted to kill him right then and there I had to do the whole job over again the lousy son of a bitch bastard he had no right telling me the kike the louse I told him I warned him I told him he wasn't going to get away with this can't even speak English the bastard I followed him I killed him I killed him I killed him *I killed* him!'

The gun descended.

It hit Manners in the mouth and shattered his teeth, and he collapsed against the car as Kling raised the gun again and fell upon him.

It took both Carella and Brown a full five minutes to pull Kling off the other man. By that time, he was half dead. Carella was already typing up the false report in his head, the report which would explain how Manners had resisted arrest.

Patterns.

Indictment for Murder in the First Degree by Shooting

FIRST COUNT

The Grand Jury of Isola, by this indictment, accuse the defendant of the crime of murder in the first degree, committed as follows:

The defendant in Isola, on or about October 13, wilfully, feloniously and of malice aforethought shot Herbert Land with a pistol and thereby inflicted divers wounds upon said Herbert Land and thereafter and on or about October 13 said Herbert Land died of the wounds.

SECOND COUNT

. . . feloniously and of malice aforethought, shot Anthony La Scala with a pistol and thereby inflicted divers wounds . . .

THIRD COUNT

. . . upon said Joseph Wechsler and thereafter and on or about October 13 . . .

FOURTH COUNT

. . . said Claire Townsend died of the wounds.

Patterns.

The pattern of December sunlight filtering past barred and grilled windows to settle in a dead white smear on a scarred wooden floor. Shadows merge with the sun smear, the shadows of tall men in shirt sleeves; it will be a cold December this year.

A telephone rings.

There is the sound of a city beyond those windows.

'87th Squad, Carella.'

There are patterns to this room. There is a timelessness to these men in this place doing the work they are doing.

They are all deeply involved in the classic ritual of blood.

THE EMPTY HOURS

This is for Howard Melnick –
my brother-in-law

The Empty Hours

1.

THEY THOUGHT SHE was coloured at first.

The patrolman who investigated the complaint didn't expect to find a dead woman. This was the first time he'd seen a corpse, and he was somewhat shaken by the ludicrously relaxed grotesqueness of the girl lying on her back on the rug, and his hand trembled a little as he made out his report. But when he came to the blank line calling for an identification of RACE, he unhesitatingly wrote 'Negro'.

The call had been taken at Headquarters by a patrolman in the central Complaint Bureau. He sat at a desk with a pad of printed forms before him, and he copied down the information, shrugged because this seemed like a routine squeal, rolled the form and slipped it into a metal carrier, and then shot it by pneumatic tube to the radio room. A dispatcher there read the complaint form, shrugged because this seemed like a routine squeal, studied the precinct map on the wall opposite his desk, and then dispatched car eleven of the 87th Precinct to the scene.

The girl was dead.

She may have been a pretty girl, but she was hideous in death, distorted by the expanding gases inside her skin case. She was wearing a sweater and skirt, and she was barefoot, and her skirt had been pulled back when she fell to the rug. Her head was twisted at a curious angle, the short black hair cradled by the rug, her eyes open and brown in a bloated face. The patrolman felt a

3

sudden impulse to pull the girl's skirt down over her knees. He knew, suddenly, she would have wanted this. Death had caught her in this indecent posture, robbing her of female instinct. There were things this girl would never do again, so many things, all of which must have seemed enormously important to the girl herself. But the single universal thing was an infinitesimal detail, magnified now by death: she would never again perform the simple feminine and somehow beautiful act of pulling her skirt down over her knees.

The patrolman sighed and finished his report. The image of the dead girl remained in his mind all the way down to the squad car.

It was hot in the squadroom on that night in early August. The men working the graveyard shift had reported for duty at 6.00 p.m., and they would not go home until eight the following morning. They were all detectives and perhaps privileged members of the police force, but there were many policemen – Detective Meyer Meyer among them – who maintained that a uniformed cop's life made a hell of a lot more sense than a detective's.

'Sure, it does,' Meyer insisted now, sitting at his desk in his shirt sleeves. 'A patrolman's schedule provides regularity and security. It gives a man a home life.'

'This squadroom is your home, Meyer,' Carella said. 'Admit it.'

'Sure,' Meyer answered, grinning. 'I can't wait to come to work each day.' He passed a hand over his bald pate. 'You know what I like especially about this place? The interior decoration. The décor. It's very restful.'

'Oh, you don't like your fellow workers, huh?' Carella said. He slid off the desk and winked at Cotton Hawes, who was standing at one of the filing cabinets. Then he

4

walked towards the water cooler at the other end of the room, just inside the slatted railing that divided squad-room from corridor. He moved with a nonchalant ease that was deceptive. Steve Carella had never been one of those weightlifting goons, and the image he presented was hardly one of bulging muscular power. But there was a quiet strength about the man and the way he moved, a confidence in the way he casually accepted the capabilities and limitations of his body. He stopped at the water cooler, filled a paper cup, and turned to look at Meyer again.

'No, I like my colleagues,' Meyer said. 'In fact, Steve, if I had my choice in all the world of who to work with, I would choose you honourable, decent guys. Sure.' Meyer nodded, building steam. 'In fact, I'm thinking of having some medals cast off, so I can hand them out to you guys. Boy, am I lucky to have this job! I may come to work without pay from now on. I may just refuse my salary, this job is so enriching. I want to thank you guys. You make me recognize the real values in life.'

'He makes a nice speech.' Hawes said.

'He should run the line-up. It would break the monotony. How come you don't run the line-up, Meyer?'

'Steve, I been offered the job,' Meyer said seriously. 'I told them I'm needed right here at the Eighty-seventh, the garden spot of all the precincts. Why, they offered me chief of detectives, and when I said no, they offered me commissioner, but I was loyal to the squad.'

'Let's give *him* a medal,' Hawes said, and the telephone rang.

Meyer lifted the receiver. 'Eighty-seventh Squad, Detective Meyer. What? Yeah, just a second.' He pulled a pad into place and began writing. 'Yeah, I got it. Right. Right. Right. Okay.' He hung up. Carella had walked to his desk. 'A little coloured girl,' Meyer said.

5

'Yeah?'
'In a furnished room on South Eleventh.'
'Yeah?'
'Dead,' Meyer said.

2.

THE CITY DOESN'T seem to be itself in the very early hours of the morning.

She is a woman, of course, and time will never change that. She awakes as a woman, tentatively touching the day in a yawning, smiling stretch, her lips free of colour, her hair tousled, warm from sleep, her body richer, an innocent girlish quality about her as sunlight stains the eastern sky and covers her with early heat. She dresses in furnished rooms in crummy rundown slums, and she dresses in Hall Avenue penthouses, and in the countless apartments that crowd the buildings of Isola and Riverhead and Calm's Point, in the private houses that line the streets of Bethtown and Majesta, and she emerges a different woman, sleek and businesslike, attractive but not sexy, a look of utter competence about her, manicured and polished, but with no time for nonsense, there is a long working day ahead of her. At five o'clock a metamorphosis takes place. She does not change her costume, this city, this woman, she wears the same frock or the same suit, the same high-heeled pumps or the same suburban loafers, but something breaks through that immaculate shell, a mood, a tone, an undercurrent. She is a different woman who sits in the bars and cocktail lounges, who relaxes on the patios or on the terraces shelving the skyscrapers, a different woman with a somewhat lazily inviting grin, a somewhat tired expression, an impenetrable knowledge on her face and in her eyes: she lifts her glass, she laughs gently, the evening sits expectantly on the skyline, the sky is awash with the purple of day's end.

7

She turns female in the night.

She drops her femininity and turns female. The polish is gone, the mechanized competence; she becomes a little scatterbrained and a little cuddly; she crosses her legs recklessly and allows her lipstick to be kissed clear off her mouth, and she responds to the male hands on her body, and she turns soft and inviting and miraculously primitive. The night is a female time, and the city is nothing but a woman.

And in the empty hours she sleeps, and she does not seem to be herself.

In the morning she will awake again and touch the silent air in a yawn, spreading her arms, the contented smile on her naked mouth. Her hair will be mussed, we will know her, we have seen her this way often.

But now she sleeps. She sleeps silently, this city. Oh, an eye open in the buildings of the night here and there, winking on, off again, silence. She rests. In sleep we do not recognize her. Her sleep is not like death, for we can hear and sense the murmur of life beneath the warm bedclothes. But she is a strange woman whom we have known intimately, loved passionately, and now she curls into an unresponsive ball beneath the sheets, and our hand is on her rich hip. We can feel life there, but we do not know her. She is faceless and featureless in the dark. She could be any city, any woman, anywhere. We touch her uncertainly. She has pulled the black nightgown of early morning around her, and we do not know her. She is a stranger, and her eyes are closed.

The landlady was frightened by the presence of policemen, even though she had summoned them. The taller one, the one who called himself Detective Hawes, was a redheaded giant with a white streak in his hair, a horror if she'd seen one. The landlady stood in the apartment where the girl lay dead on the rug, and she talked to the detectives in whispers, not because she was in the presence of death, but only because it was three o'clock in the morning. The landlady was wearing a bathrobe over her gown. There was an intimacy to the scene, the same intimacy that hangs alike over an impending fishing trip or a completed tragedy. Three a.m. is a time for slumber, and those who are awake while the city sleeps share a common bond that makes them friendly aliens.

'What's the girl's name?' Carella asked. It was three o'clock in the morning, and he had not shaved since five p.m. the day before, but his chin looked smooth. His eyes slanted slightly downward, combining with his clean-shaven face to give him a curiously oriental appearance. The landlady liked him. He was a nice boy, she thought. In her lexicon the men of the world were either 'nice boys' or 'louses'. She wasn't sure about Cotton Hawes yet, but she imagined he was a parasitic insect.

'Claudia Davis,' she answered, directing the answer to Carella whom she liked, and totally ignoring Hawes who had no right to be so big a man with a frightening white streak in his hair.

'Do you know how old she was?' Carella asked.

'Twenty-eight or twenty-nine, I think.'

'Had she been living here long?'

'Since June,' the landlady said.

'That short a time, huh?'

'And *this* has to happen,' the landlady said. 'She seemed like such a nice girl. Who do you suppose did it?'

'I don't know,' Carella said.

'Or do you think it was suicide? I don't smell no gas, do you?'

'No,' Carella said. 'Do you know where she lived before this, Mrs Mauder?'

'No, I don't.'

9

'You didn't ask for references when she took the apartment?'

'It's only a furnished room,' Mrs Mauder said, shrugging. 'She paid me a month's rent in advance.'

'How much was that, Mrs Mauder?'

'Sixty dollars. She paid it in cash. I never take cheques from strangers.'

'But you have no idea whether she's from this city, or out of town, or whatever. Am I right?'

'Yes, that's right.'

'Davis,' Hawes said, shaking his head. 'That'll be a tough name to track down, Steve. Must be a thousand of them in the phone book.'

'Why is your hair white?' the landlady asked.

'Huh?'

'That streak.'

'Oh.' Hawes unconsciously touched his left temple. 'I got knifed once,' he said, dismissing the question abruptly. 'Mrs Mauder, was the girl living alone?'

'I don't know. I mind my own business.'

'Well, surely you would have seen . . .'

'I think she was living alone. I don't pry, and I don't spy. She gave me a month's rent in advance.'

Hawes sighed. He could feel the woman's hostility. He decided to leave the questioning to Carella. 'I'll take a look through the drawers and closets,' he said, and moved off without waiting for Carella's answer.

'It's awfully hot in here,' Carella said.

'The patrolman said we shouldn't touch anything until you got here,' Mrs Mauder said. 'That's why I didn't open the windows or nothing.'

'That was very thoughtful of you,' Carella said, smiling. 'But I think we can open the window now, don't you?'

'If you like. It does smell in here. Is . . . is that her? Smelling?'

'Yes,' Carella answered. He pulled open the window. 'There. That's a little better.'

'Doesn't help much,' the landlady said. 'The weather's been terrible – just terrible. Body can't sleep at all.' She looked down at the dead girl. 'She looks just awful, don't she?'

'Yes. Mrs Mauder, would you know where she worked, or if she had a job?'

'No, I'm sorry.'

'Anyone ever come by asking for her? Friends? Relatives?'

'No, I'm sorry. I never saw any.'

'Can you tell me anything about her habits? When she left the house in the morning? When she returned at night?'

'I'm sorry; I never noticed.'

'Well, what made you think something was wrong in here?'

'The milk. Outside the door. I was out with some friends tonight, you see, and when I came back a man on the third floor called down to say his neighbour was playing the radio very loud and would I tell him to shut up, please. So I went upstairs and asked him to turn down the radio, and then I passed Miss Davis' apartment and saw the milk standing outside the door, and I thought this was kind of funny in such hot weather, but I figured it was *her* milk, you know, and I don't like to pry. So I came down and went to bed, but I couldn't stop thinking about that milk standing outside in the hallway. So I put on a robe and came upstairs and knocked on the door, and she didn't answer. So I called out to her, and she still didn't answer. So I figured something must be wrong. I don't know why. I just figured . . . I don't know. If she was in here, why didn't she answer?'

'How'd you know she was here?'

'I didn't.'

'Was the door locked?'

'Yes.'

'You tried it?'

'Yes. It was locked.'

'I see,' Carella said.

'Couple of cars just pulled up downstairs,' Hawes said, walking over. 'Probably the lab. And Homicide South.'

'They know the squeal is ours,' Carella said. 'Why do they bother?'

'Make it look good,' Hawes said. 'Homicide's got the title on the door, so they figure they ought to go out and earn their salaries.'

'Did you find anything?'

'A brand-new set of luggage in the closet, six pieces. The drawers and closets are full of clothes. Most of them look new. Lots of resort stuff, Steve. Found some brand-new books, too.'

'What else?'

'Some mail on the dresser top.'

'Anything we can use?'

Hawes shrugged. 'A statement from the girl's bank. Bunch of cancelled cheques. Might help us.'

'Maybe,' Carella said. 'Let's see what the lab comes up with.'

The laboratory report came the next day, together with a necropsy report from the assistant medical examiner. In combination, the reports were fairly valuable. The first thing the detectives learned was that the girl was a white Caucasian of approximately thirty years of age.

Yes, white.

The news came as something of a surprise to the cops because the girl lying on the rug had certainly looked

12

like a Negress. After all, her skin was black. Not tan, not coffee-coloured, not brown, but black — that intensely black coloration found in primitive tribes who spend a good deal of their time in the sun. The conclusion seemed to be a logical one, but death is a great equalizer not without a whimsical humour all its own, and the funniest kind of joke is a sight gag. Death changes white to black, and when that grisly old man comes marching in there's no question of who's going to school with whom. There's no longer any question of pigmentation, friend. The girl on the floor looked black, but she was white and whatever else she was she was also stone cold dead, and that's the worst you can do to anybody.

The report explained that the girl's body was in a state of advanced putrefaction, and it went into such esoteric terms as 'general distention of the body cavities, tissues, and blood vessels with gas', and 'black discoloration of the skin, mucous membranes, and irides caused by haemolysis and action of hydrogen sulphide on the blood pigment', all of which broke down to the simple fact that it was a damn hot week in August and the girl had been lying on a rug which retained heat and speeded the post-mortem putrefaction. From what they could tell, and in weather like this, it was mostly a guess, the girl had been dead and decomposing for at least forty-eight hours, which set the time of her demise as August first or thereabouts.

One of the reports went on to say that the clothes she'd been wearing had been purchased in one of the city's larger department stores. All of her clothes — those she wore and those found in her apartment — were rather expensive, but someone at the lab thought it necessary to note that all her panties were trimmed with Belgian lace and retailed for twenty-five dollars a pair. Someone else at the lab mentioned that a thorough examination of her

13

garments and her body had revealed no traces of blood, semen, or oil stains.

The coroner fixed the cause of death as strangulation.

3.

IT IS AMAZING how much an apartment can sometimes yield to science. It is equally amazing, and more than a little disappointing, to get nothing from the scene of a murder when you are desperately seeking a clue. The furnished room in which Claudia Davis had been strangled to death was full of juicy surfaces conceivably carrying hundreds of latent fingerprints. The closets and drawers contained piles of clothing that might have carried traces of anything from gunpowder to face powder.

But the lab boys went around lifting their prints and sifting their dust and vacuuming with a Söderman-Heuberger filter, and they went down to the morgue and studied the girl's skin and came up with a total of nothing. Zero. Oh, not quite zero. They got a lot of prints belonging to Claudia Davis, and a lot of dust collected from all over the city and clinging to her shoes and her furniture. They also found some documents belonging to the dead girl – a birth certificate, a diploma of graduation from a high school in Santa Monica, and an expired library card. And, oh, yes, a key. The key didn't seem to fit any of the locks in the room. They sent all the junk over to the 87th, and Sam Grossman called Carella personally later that day to apologize for the lack of results.

The squadroom was hot and noisy when Carella took the call from the lab. The conversation was a curiously one-sided affair. Carella, who had dumped the contents of the laboratory envelope on to his desk, merely grunted or nodded every now and then. He thanked Grossman at last, hung up, and stared at the window facing the street and Grover Park.

'Get anything?' Meyer asked.

'Yeah. Grossman thinks the killer was wearing gloves.'

'That's nice,' Meyer said.

'Also, I think I know what this key is for.' He lifted it from the desk.

'Yeah? What?'

'Well, did you see these cancelled cheques?'

'No.'

'Take a look,' Carella said.

He opened the brown bank envelope addressed to Claudia Davis, spread the cancelled cheques on his desk top, and then unfolded the yellow bank statement. Meyer studied the display silently.

'Cotton found the envelope in her room,' Carella said. 'The statement covers the month of July. Those are all the cheques she wrote, or at least everything that cleared the bank by the thirty-first.'

'Lots of cheques here,' Meyer said.

'Twenty-five, to be exact. What do you think? I know what *I* think,' Carella said.

'What's that?'

'I look at those cheques. I can see a life. It's like reading someone's diary. Everything she did last month is right here, Meyer. All the department stores she went to, look, a florist, her hairdresser, a candy shop, even her shoemaker, and look at this. A cheque made out to a funeral home. Now who died, Meyer, huh? And look here. She was living at Mrs Mauder's place, but here's a cheque made out to a swank apartment building on the South Side, in Stewart City. And some of these cheques are just made out to names, *people*. This case is crying for some people.'

16

'You want me to get the phone book?'

'No, wait a minute. Look at this bank statement. She opened the account on July fifth with a thousand bucks. All of a sudden, bam, she deposits a thousand bucks in the Seaboard Bank of America.'

'What's so odd about that?'

'Nothing, maybe. But Cotton called the other banks in the city, and Claudia Davis has a very healthy account at the Highland Trust on Cromwell Avenue. And I mean *very* healthy.'

'How healthy?'

'Close to sixty grand.'

'What!'

'You heard me. And the Highland Trust lists no withdrawals for the month of July. So where'd she get the money to put into Seaboard?'

'Was that the only deposit?'

'Take a look.'

Meyer picked up the statement.

'The initial deposit was on July fifth,' Carella said. 'A thousand bucks. She made another thousand-dollar deposit on July twelfth. And another on the nineteenth. And another on the twenty-seventh.'

Meyer raised his eyebrows. 'Four grand. That's a lot of loot.'

'And all deposited in less than a month's time. I've got to work almost a full year to make that kind of money.'

'Not to mention the sixty grand in the other bank. Where do you suppose she got it, Steve?'

'I don't know. It just doesn't make sense. She wears underpants trimmed with Belgian lace, but she lives in a crummy room-and-a-half with bath. How the hell do you figure that? Two bank accounts, twenty-five bucks to cover her ass, and all she pays is sixty bucks a month for a flophouse.'

17

'Maybe she's hot, Steve.'

'No.' Carella shook his head. 'I ran a make with CBI. She hasn't got a record, and she's not wanted for anything. I haven't heard from the feds yet, but I imagine it'll be the same story.'

'What about that key? You said . . .'

'Oh, yeah. That's pretty simple, thank God. Look at this.'

He reached into the pile of cheques and sorted out a yellow slip, larger than the cheques. He handed it to Meyer. The slip read:

THE SEABOARD BANK OF AMERICA
ISOLA BRANCH   P 1698

July 5

WE ARE CHARGING YOUR ACCOUNT AS PER ITEMS BELOW. PLEASE SEE THAT THE
AMOUNT IS DEDUCTED ON YOUR BOOKS SO THAT OUR ACCOUNTS MAY AGREE.

FOR	Safe deposit rental #375		5	00
	U.S. Tax			50
	AMOUNT OF CHARGE		5	50

CHARGE	Claudia Davis	ENTERED BY
	1263 South Eleventh	
	Isola	*RPL*

'She rented a safe-deposit box the same day she opened the new chequing account, huh?' Meyer said.

'Right.'

'What's in it?'

'That's a good question.'

'Look, do you want to save some time, Steve?'

'Sure.'

'Let's get the court order *before* we go to the bank.'

4.

THE MANAGER OF the Seaboard Bank of America was a bald-headed man in his early fifties. Working on the theory that similar physical types are *simpático*, Carella allowed Meyer to do most of the questioning. It was not easy to elicit answers from Mr Anderson, the manager of the bank, because he was by nature a reticent man. But Detective Meyer Meyer was the most patient man in the city, if not the entire world. His patience was an acquired trait, rather than an inherited one. Oh, he had inherited a few things from his father, a jovial man named Max Meyer, but patience was not one of them. If anything, Max Meyer had been a very impatient if not downright short-tempered sort of fellow. When his wife, for example, came to him with the news that she was expecting a baby, Max nearly hit the ceiling. He enjoyed little jokes immensely, was perhaps the biggest practical joker in all Riverhead, but this particular prank of nature failed to amuse him. He had thought his wife was long past the age when bearing children was even a remote possibility. He never thought of himself as approaching dotage, but he was after all getting on in years, and a change-of-life baby was hardly what the doctor had ordered. He allowed the impending birth to simmer inside him, planning his revenge all the while, plotting the practical joke to end all practical jokes.

When the baby was born, he called it Meyer, a delightful handle which when coupled with the family name provided the infant with a double-barrelled monicker: Meyer Meyer.

Now that's pretty funny. Admit it. You can split your sides laughing over that one, unless you happen to be a pretty sensitive kid who also happens to be an Orthodox Jew, and who happens to live in a predominantly Gentile neighbourhood. The kids in the neighbourhood thought Meyer Meyer had been invented solely for their own pleasure. If they needed further provocation for beating up the Jew boy, and they didn't need any, his name provided excellent motivational fuel. 'Meyer Meyer, Jew on fire!' they would shout, and then they would chase him down the street and beat hell out of him.

Meyer learned patience. It is not very often that one kid, or even one grown man, can successfully defend himself against a gang. But sometimes you can talk yourself out of a beating. Sometimes, if you're patient, if you just wait long enough, you can catch one of them alone and stand up to him face to face, man to man, and know the exultation of a fair fight without the frustration of overwhelming odds.

Listen, Max Meyer's joke was a harmless one. You can't deny an old man his pleasure. But Mr Anderson, the manager of the bank, was fifty-four years old and totally bald. Meyer Meyer, the detective second grade who sat opposite him and asked questions, was also totally bald. Maybe a lifetime of sublimation, a lifetime of devoted patience, doesn't leave any scars. Maybe not. But Meyer Meyer was only thirty-seven years old.

Patiently he said, 'Didn't you find these large deposits rather odd, Mr Anderson?'

'No,' Anderson said. 'A thousand dollars is not a lot of money.'

'Mr Anderson,' Meyer said patiently, 'you are aware, of course, that banks in this city are required to report to the police any unusually large sums of money deposited at one time. You are aware of that, are you not?'

'Yes, I am.'

'Miss Davis deposited four thousand dollars in three weeks' time. Didn't that seem unusual to you?'

'No. The deposits were spaced. A thousand dollars is not a lot of money, and not an unusually large deposit.'

'To me,' Meyer said, 'a thousand dollars is a lot of money. You can buy a lot of beer with a thousand dollars.'

'I don't drink beer,' Anderson said flatly.

'Neither do I,' Meyer answered.

'Besides, we *do* call the police whenever we get a very large deposit, unless the depositor is one of our regular customers. I did not feel that these deposits warranted such a call.'

'Thank you, Mr Anderson,' Meyer said. 'We have a court order here. We'd like to open the box Miss Davis rented.'

'May I see the order, please?' Anderson said. Meyer showed it to him. Anderson sighed and said, 'Very well. Do you have Miss Davis' key?'

Carella reached into his pocket. 'Would this be it?' he said. He put a key on the desk. It was the key that had come to him from the lab together with the documents they'd found in the apartment.

'Yes, that's it,' Mr Anderson said. 'There are two different keys to every box, you see. The bank keeps one, and the renter keeps the other. The box cannot be opened without both keys. Will you come with me, please?'

He collected the bank key to safe-deposit box number 375 and led the detectives to the rear of the bank. The room seemed to be lined with shining metal. The boxes, row upon row, reminded Carella of the morgue and the refrigerated shelves that slid in and out of the wall on squeaking rollers. Anderson pushed the bank key into a slot and turned it, and then he put Claudia Davis' key

21

into a second slot and turned that. He pulled the long, thin box out of the wall and handed it to Meyer. Meyer carried it to the counter on the opposite wall and lifted the catch.

'Okay?' he said to Carella.

'Go ahead.'

Meyer raised the lid of the box.

There was $16,000 in the box. There was also a slip of note paper. The $16,000 was neatly divided into four stacks of bills. Three of the stacks held $5,000 each. The fourth stack held only $1,000. Carella picked up the slip of paper. Someone, presumably Claudia Davis, had made some annotations on it in pencil.

$$
\begin{array}{rr}
7/5 & 20,000 \\
7/5 & -1,000 \\
\hline
& 19,000 \\
7/12 & -1,000 \\
\hline
& 18,000 \\
7/19 & -1,000 \\
\hline
& 17,000 \\
7/27 & -1,000 \\
\hline
& 16,000 \\
\end{array}
$$

'Make any sense to you, Mr Anderson?'

'No. I'm afraid not.'

'She came into this bank on July fifth with twenty thousand dollars in cash, Mr Anderson. She put a thousand of that into a chequing account and the remainder into this box. The dates on this slip of paper show exactly when she took cash from the box and transferred it to the chequing account. She knew the rules, Mr Anderson. She knew that twenty grand deposited in one lump would bring a call to the police. This way was a lot safer.'

'We'd better get a list of these serial numbers,' Meyer said.

'Would you have one of your people do that for us, Mr Anderson?'

Anderson seemed ready to protest. Instead, he looked at Carella, sighed, and said, 'Of course.'

The serial numbers didn't help them at all. They compared them against their own lists, and the out-of-town lists, and the FBI lists, but none of those bills was hot.

Only August was.

5.

STEWART CITY HANGS in the hair of Isola like a jewelled tiara. Not really a city, not even a town, merely a collection of swank apartment buildings overlooking the River Dix, the community had been named after the British royalty and remained one of the most exclusive neighbourhoods in town. If you could boast of a Stewart City address, you could also boast of a high income, a country place on Sands Spit, and a Mercedes Benz in the garage under the apartment building. You could give your address with a measure of snobbery and pride – you were, after all, one of the élite.

The dead girl named Claudia Davis had made out a cheque to Management Enterprise, Inc, at 13 Stewart Place South, to the tune of $750. The cheque had been dated July nine, four days after she'd opened the Seaboard account.

A cool breeze was blowing in off the river as Carella and Hawes pulled up. Late-afternoon sunlight dappled the polluted water of the Dix. The bridges connecting Calm's Point with Isola hung against the sky awaiting the assault of dusk.

'Want to pull down the sun visor?' Carella said.

Hawes reached up and turned down the visor. Clipped to the visor so that it showed through the windshield of the car was a hand-lettered card that read POLICEMAN ON DUTY CALL – 87TH PRECINCT. The car, a 1956 Chevrolet, was Carella's own.

'I've got to make a sign for my car,' Hawes said. 'Some bastard tagged it last week.'

24

'What did you do?'

'I went to court and pleaded not guilty. On my day off.'

'Did you get out of it?'

'Sure. I was answering a squeal. It's bad enough I had to use my own car, but for Pete's sake, to get a ticket!'

'I prefer my own car,' Carella said. 'Those three cars belonging to the squad are ready for the junk heap.'

'*Two*,' Hawes corrected, 'One of them's been in the police garage for a month now.'

'Meyer went down to see about it the other day.'

'What'd they say? Was it ready?'

'No, the mechanic told him there were four patrol cars ahead of the sedan, and they took precedence. Now how about that?'

'Sure, it figures. I've still got a chit in for the gas I used, you know that?'

'Forget it. I've never got back a cent I laid out for gas.'

'What'd Meyer do about the car?'

'He slipped the mechanic five bucks. Maybe that'll speed him up.'

'You know what the city ought to do?' Hawes said. They ought to buy some of those used taxicabs. Pick them up for two or three hundred bucks, paint them over, and give them out to the squads. Some of them are still in pretty good condition.'

'Well, it's an idea,' Carella said dubiously, and they entered the building. They found Mrs Miller, the manager, in an office at the rear of the ornate entrance lobby. She was a woman in her early forties with a well-preserved figure and a very husky voice. She wore her hair piled on the top of her head, a pencil stuck rakishly into the reddish-brown heap. She looked at the photostated cheque and said, 'Oh, yes, of course.'

'You knew Miss Davis?'

25

'Yes, she lived here for a long time.'

'How long?'

'Five years.'

'When did she move out?'

'At the end of June.' Mrs Miller crossed her splendid legs and smiled graciously. The legs were remarkable for a woman of her age, and the smile was almost radiant. She moved with an expert femininity, a calculated, conscious fluidity of flesh that suggested availability and yet was totally respectable. She seemed to have devoted a lifetime to learning the ways and wiles of the female and now practised them with facility and charm. She was pleasant to be with, this woman, pleasant to watch and to hear, and to think of touching. Carella and Hawes, charmed to their shoes, found themselves relaxing in her presence.

'This cheque,' Carella said, tapping the photostat. 'What was it for?'

'June's rent. I received it on the tenth of July. Claudia always paid her rent by the tenth of the month. She was a very good tenant.'

'The apartment cost seven hundred and fifty dollars a month?'

'Yes.'

'Isn't that high for an apartment?'

'Not in Stewart City,' Mrs Miller said gently. 'And this was a river-front apartment.'

'I see. I take it Miss Davis had a good job.'

'No, no, she doesn't have a job at all.'

'Then how could she afford . . . ?'

'Well, she's rather well off, you know.'

'Where does she get the money, Mrs Miller?'

'Well . . .' Mrs Miller shrugged. 'I really think you should ask *her*, don't you? I mean, if this is something concerning Claudia, shouldn't you . . . ?'

26

'Mrs Miller,' Carella said, 'Claudia Davis is dead.'

'What?'

'She's . . .'

'What? No. No.' She shook her head. 'Claudia? But the cheque . . . I . . . the cheque came only last month.' She shook her head again. 'No. No.'

'She's dead, Mrs Miller,' Carella said gently. 'She was strangled.'

The charm faltered for just an instant Revulsion knifed the eyes of Mrs Miller, the eyelids flickered, it seemed for an instant that the pupils would turn shining and wet, that the carefully lipsticked mouth would crumble. And then something inside took over, something that demanded control, something that reminded her that a charming woman does not weep and cause her fashionable eye make-up to run.

'I'm sorry,' she said, almost in a whisper. 'I am really, really sorry. She was a nice person.'

'Can you tell us what you know about her, Mrs Miller?'

'Yes. Yes, of course.' She shook her head again, unwilling to accept the idea. That's terrible. That's terrible. Why, she was only a baby.'

'We figured her for thirty, Mrs Miller. Are we wrong?'

'She seemed younger, but perhaps that was because . . . well, she was a rather shy person. Even when she first came here, there was an air of – well, lostness about her. Of course, that was right after her parents died, so . . .'

'Where did she come from, Mrs Miller?'

'California. Santa Monica.'

Carella nodded. 'You were starting to tell us . . . you said she was rather well off. Could you . . . ?'

'Well, the stock, you know.'

'What stock?'

'Her parents had set up a securities trust account for

her. When they died, Claudia began receiving the income from the stock. She was an only child, you know.'

'And she lived on stock dividends alone?'

'They amounted to quite a bit. Which she saved, I might add. She was a very systematic person, not at all frivolous. When she received a dividend cheque, she would endorse it and take it straight to the bank. Claudia was a very sensible girl.'

'Which bank, Mrs Miller?'

'The Highland Trust. Right down the street. On Cromwell Avenue.'

'I see,' Carella said. 'Was she dating many men? Would you know?'

'I don't think so. She kept pretty much to herself. Even after Josie came.'

Carella leaned forward. 'Josie? Who's Josie?'

'Josie Thompson. Josephine, actually. Her cousin.'

'And where did *she* come from?'

'California. They both came from California.'

'And how can we get in touch with this Josie Thompson?'

'Well, she . . . Don't you know? Haven't you . . . ?'

'What, Mrs Miller?'

'Why, Josie is dead. Josie passed on in June. That's why Claudia moved, I suppose. I suppose she couldn't bear the thought of living in that apartment without Josie. It is a little frightening, isn't it?'

'Yes,' Carella said.

DETECTIVE DIVISION SUPPLEMENTARY REPORT	SQUAD	PRECINCT	PRECINCT REPORT	DETECTIVE DIVISION REPORT NUMBER
pdcn 360 rev 25m	87	87	32-101	DD 60 R-42

NAME AND ADDRESS OF PERSON REPORTING	DATE ORIGINAL REPORT
Miller Irene (Mrs John) 13 Stewart Place S	8-4-60
SURNAME GIVEN NAME INITIALS NUMBER STREET	

DETAILS

Summary of interview with Irene (Mrs John) Miller at office of Management Enterprises Inc, address above, in re homicide Claudia Davis.

Mrs Miller states:

Claudia Davis came to this city in June of 1955, took $750-a-month apartment above address, lived there alone. Rarely seen in company of friends, male or female. Young recluse type living on substantial income of inherited securities. Parents, Mr and Mrs Carter Davis, killed on San Diego Freeway in head-on collision with station wagon, April 14 1955. LAPD confirms traffic accident, driver of other vehicle convicted for negligent operation. Mrs Miller describes girl as medium height and weight, close-cropped brunette hair, brown eyes, no scars or birthmarks she can remember, tallies with what we have on corpse. Further says Claudia Davis was quiet, unobtrusive tenant, paid rent and all service bills punctually, was gentle, sweet, plain, childlike, shy, meticulous in money matters well liked but unapproachable.

In April or May of 1959, Josie Thompson, cousin of deceased, arrived from Brentwood, California. (Routine check with Criminal Bureau Identification negative, no record. Checking now with LAPD, and FBI.) Described as slightly older than Claudia, rather different in looks and personality. 'They were like black and white,' Mrs Miller says,'but they hit it off exceptionally well.' Josie moved into the apartment with cousin. Words used to describe relationship between two were 'like the closest of sisters' and 'really in tune', and the 'best of friends', etc. Girls did not date much, were constantly in each other's company, Josie seeming to pick up recluse habits from Claudia. Went on frequent trips together. Spent summer of '59 on Tortoise Island in the bay, returned Labor Day. Went away again at Christmas time to ski Sun Valley, and again in March this year to Kingston, Jamaica, for three weeks, returning at beginning of April. Source of income was fairly standard securities-income account. Claudia did not own the stock, but income on it was hers for as long as she lived. Trust specified that upon her death the stock and imcome to be turned over to UCLA (father's alma mater). In any case, Claudia was assured of a very, very substantial lifetime income (see Highland Trust bank account) and was apparently supporting Josie as well, since Mrs Miller claims neither girl worked. Brought up question of possible lesbianism, but Mrs Miller, who is knowledgeable and hip, says no, neither girl was a dike.

On June 3, Josie and Claudia left for another weekend trip. Doorman reports having helped them pack valises into trunk of Claudia's car, 1960 Cadillac convertible. Claudia did the driving. Girls did not return on Monday morning as they had indicated they would. Claudia called on Wednesday, crying

on telephone. Told Mrs Miller that Josie had had a terrible
accident and was dead. Mrs Miller remembers asking Claudia
if she could help in any way. Claudia said, quote, No,
everything's been taken care of already,

unquote.

On June 17, Mrs Miller received a letter from Claudia (letter
attached handwriting compares positive with cheques Claudia
signed) stating she could not possibly return to apartment,
not after what had happened to her cousin. She reminded Mrs
Miller lease expired on July 4, told her that she would send
cheque for June's rent before July 10. Said moving company
would pack and pick up her belongings, delivering all valuables
and documents to her, and storing rest. (see Claudia Davis'
cheque number 010, 7/14, made payable to Allora Brothers Inc.,
in payment for packing, moving and storage) Claudia Davis
never returned to the apartment. Mrs Miller had not seen her
and knew nothing of her whereabouts until we informed her of
the homicide.

DATE OF THIS REPORT

August 6

RANK	SURNAME	INITIALS	SHIELD NUMBER	COMMANDING OFFICER
Det 2/gr	Carella	S.L.	714-50-32	Det/Lt Peter Byrnes

6.

THE DRIVE UPSTATE to Triangle Lake was a particularly scenic one, and since it was August, and since Sunday was supposed to be Carella's day off, he thought he might just as well combine a little business with pleasure. So he put the top of the car down, and he packed Teddy into the front seat together with a picnic lunch and a gallon Thermos of iced coffee, and he forgot all about Claudia Davis on the drive up through the mountains. Carella found it easy to forget about almost anything when he was with his wife.

Teddy, as far as he was concerned – and his astute judgement had been backed up by many a street-corner whistle – was only the most beautiful woman in the world. He could never understand how he, a hairy, corny, ugly, stupid, clumsy cop, had managed to capture anyone as wonderful as Theodora Franklin. But capture her he had, and he sat beside her now in the open car and stole sidelong glances at her as he drove, excited as always by her very presence.

Her black hair, always wild, seemed to capture something of the wind's frenzy as it whipped about the oval of her face. Her brown eyes were partially squinted against the rush of air over the windshield. She wore a white blouse emphatically curved over a full bosom, black tapered slacks form-fitted over generous hips and good legs. She had kicked off her sandals and folded her knees against her breasts, her bare feet pressed against the glove-compartment panel. There was about her, Carella realized, a curious combination of savage and sophisticate.

31

You never knew whether she was going to kiss you or slug you, and the uncertainty kept her eternally desirable and exciting.

Teddy watched her husband as he drove, his big-knuckled hands on the wheel of the car. She watched him not only because it gave her pleasure to watch him, but also because he was speaking. And since she could not hear, since she had been born a deaf mute, it was essential that she look at his mouth when he spoke. He did not discuss the case at all. She knew that one of the Claudia Davis cheques had been made out to the Fancher Funeral Home in Triangle Lake and she knew that Carella wanted to talk to the proprietor of the place personally. She further knew that this was very import-ant or he wouldn't be spending his Sunday driving all the way upstate. But he had promised her he'd combine business with pleasure. This was the pleasure part of the trip, and in deference to his promise and his wife, he refrained from discussing the case, which was really foremost in his mind. He talked, instead, about the scenery, and their plans for the fall, and the way the twins were growing, and how pretty Teddy looked, and how she'd better button that top button of her blouse before they got out of the car, but he never once mentioned Claudia Davis until they were standing in the office of the Fancher Funeral Home and looking into the gloomy eyes of a man who called himself Barton Scoles.

Scoles was tall and thin and he wore a black suit that he had probably worn to his own confirmation back in 1912. He was so much the stereotype of a small-town undertaker that Carella almost burst out laughing when he met him. Somehow, though, the environment was not conducive to hilarity. There was a strange smell hovering over the thick rugs and the papered walls and the hang-ing chandeliers. It was a while before Carella recognized it as formaldehyde and then made the automatic association and, curious for a man who had stared into the eyes of death so often, suddenly felt like retching.

'Miss Davis made out a cheque to you on July fifteenth,' Carella said. 'Can you tell me what it was for?'

'Sure can,' Scoles said. 'Had to wait a long time for that cheque. She give me only a twenty-five-dollar deposit. Usually take fifty, you know. I got stuck many a time, believe me.'

'How do you mean?' Carella asked.

'People. You bury their dead, and then sometimes they don't pay you for your work. This business isn't *all* fun, you know. Many's the time I handled the whole funeral and the service and the burial and all, and never did get paid. Makes you lose your faith in human nature.'

'But Miss Davis finally *did* pay you.'

'Oh, sure. But I can tell you I was sweating that one out. I can tell you that. After all, she was a strange gal from the city, has the funeral here, nobody comes to it but her, sitting in the chapel out there and watching the body as if someone's going to steal it away, just her and the departed. I tell you, Mr Carella . . . Is that your name?'

'Yes, Carella.'

'I tell you, it was kind of spooky. Lay there two days, she did, her cousin. And then Miss Davis asked that we bury the girl right here in the local cemetery, so I done that for her, too – all on the strength of a twenty-five-dollar deposit. That's trust, Mr Carella, with a capital T.'

'When was this, Mr Scoles?'

'The girl drowned the first weekend in June,' Scoles said. 'Had no business being out on the lake so early, anyways. That water's still icy cold in June. Don't really warm up none till the latter part July. She fell over the side of the boat – she was out there rowing, you know –

and that icy water probably froze her solid, or give her cramps or something, drowned her, anyways.' Scoles shook his head. 'Had no business being out on the lake so early.'

'Did you see a death certificate?'

'Yep, Dr Donneli made it out. Cause of death was drowning, all right, no question about it. We had an inquest, too, you know. The Tuesday after she drowned. They said it was accidental.'

'You said she was out rowing in a boat. Alone?'

'Yep. Her cousin, Miss Davis, was on the shore watching. Jumped in when she fell overboard, tried to reach her, but couldn't make it in time. That water's plenty cold, believe me. Ain't too warm even now, and here it is August already.'

'But it didn't seem to affect Miss Davis, did it?'

'Well, she was probably a strong swimmer. Been my experience most pretty girls are strong girls, too. I'll bet your wife here is a strong girl. She sure is a pretty one.'

Scoles smiled, and Teddy smiled, and squeezed Carella's hand.

'About the payment,' Carella said, 'for the funeral and the burial. Do you have any idea why it took Miss Davis so long to send her cheque?'

'Nope. I wrote her twice. First time was just a friendly little reminder. Second time, I made it a little stronger. Attorney friend of mine in town wrote it on his stationery; that always impresses them. Didn't get an answer either time. Finally, right out of the blue, the cheque came, payment in full. Beats me. Maybe she was affected by the death. Or maybe she's always slow paying her debts. I'm just happy the cheque came, that's all. Sometimes the live ones can give you more trouble than them who's dead, believe me.'

They strolled down to the lake together, Carella and

34

his wife, and ate their picnic lunch on its shores. Carella was strangely silent. Teddy dangled her bare feet in the water. The water, as Scoles had promised, was very cold even though it was August. On the way back from the lake Carella said, 'Honey, would you mind if I make one more stop?'

Teddy turned her eyes to him inquisitively.

'I want to see the chief of police here.'

Teddy frowned. The question was in her eyes, and he answered it immediately.

'To find out whether or not there were any witnesses to that drowning. *Besides* Claudia Davis, I mean. From the way Scoles was talking, I get the impression that lake was pretty deserted in June.'

The chief of police was a short man with a pot belly and big feet. He kept his feet propped up on his desk all the while he spoke to Carella. Carella watched him and wondered why everybody in this damned town seemed to be on vacation from an MGM movie. A row of rifles in a locked rack was behind the chief's desk. A host of WANTED fliers covered a bulletin board to the right of the rack. The chief had a hole in the sole of his left shoe.

'Yep,' he said, 'there was a witness, all right.'

Carella felt a pang of disappointment. 'Who?' he asked.

'Fellow fishing at the lake. Saw the whole thing. Testified before the coroner's jury.'

'What'd he say?'

'Said he was fishing there when Josie Thompson took the boat out. Said Claudia Davis stayed behind, on the shore. Said Miss Thompson fell overboard and went under like a stone. Said Miss Davis jumped in the water and began swimming towards her. Didn't make it in time. That's what he said.'

'What else did he say?'

'Well, he drove Miss Davis back to town in her car. 1960 Caddy convertible, I believe. She could hardly speak. She was sobbing and mumbling and wringing her hands, oh, in a hell of a mess. Why, we had to get the whole story out of that fishing fellow. Wasn't until the next day that Miss Davis could make any kind of sense.'

'When did you hold the inquest?'

'Tuesday. Day before they buried the cousin. Coroner did the dissection on Monday. We got authorization from Miss Davis, Penal Law 2213, next of kin being charged by law with the duty of burial may authorize dissection for the sole purpose of ascertaining the cause of death.'

'And the coroner reported the cause of death as drowning?'

'That's right. Said so right before the jury.'

'Why'd you have an inquest? Did you suspect something more than accidental drowning?'

'Not necessarily. But that fellow who was fishing, well, *he* was from the city, too, you know. And for all we knew, him and Miss Davis could have been in this together, you know, shoved the cousin over the side of the boat, and then faked up a whole story, you know. They both coulda been lying in their teeth.'

'Were they?'

'Not so we could tell. You never seen anybody so grief-stricken as Miss Davis was when the fishing fellow drove her into town. Girl would have to be a hell of an actress to behave that way. Calmed down the next day, but you shoulda seen her when it happened. And at the inquest it was plain this fishing fellow had never met her before that day at the lake. Convinced the jury he had no prior knowledge of or connection with either of the two girls. Convinced me, too, for that matter.'

'What's his name?' Carella asked. 'This fishing fellow.'

'Courtenoy.'

'What did you say?'

'Courtenoy. Sidney Courtenoy.'

'Thanks,' Carella answered, and he rose suddenly. 'Come on, Teddy. I want to get back to the city.'

7.

COURTENOY LIVED IN a one-family clapboard house in Riverhead. He was rolling up the door of his garage when Carella and Meyer pulled into his driveway early Monday morning. He turned to look at the car curiously, one hand on the rising garage door. The door stopped, halfway up, halfway down. Carella stepped into the driveway.

'Mr Courtenoy?' he asked.

'Yes?' He stared at Carella, puzzlement on his face, the puzzlement that is always there when a perfect stranger addresses you by name. Courtenoy was a man in his late forties, wearing a cap and a badly fitted sports jacket and dark flannel slacks in the month of August. His hair was greying at the temples. He looked tired, very tired, and his weariness had nothing whatever to do with the fact that it was only seven o'clock in the morning. A lunch box was at his feet where he had apparently put it when he began rolling up the garage door. The car in the garage was a 1953 Ford.

'We're police officers,' Carella said. 'Mind if we ask you a few questions?'

'I'd like to see your badge,' Courtenoy said. Carella showed it to him. Courtenoy nodded as if he had performed a precautionary public duty. 'What are your questions?' he said. 'I'm on my way to work. Is this about that damn building permit again?'

'What building permit?'

'For extending the garage. I'm buying my son a little jalopy, don't want to leave it out on the street. Been having a hell of a time getting a building permit. Can you imagine that? All I want to do is add another twelve feet to the garage. You'd think I was trying to build a city park or something. Is that what this is about?'

From inside the house a woman's voice called, 'Who is it, Sid?'

'Nothing, nothing,' Courtenoy said impatiently. 'Nobody. Never mind, Bett.' He looked at Carella. 'My wife. You married?'

'Yes, sir, I'm married,' Carella said.

'Then you know,' Courtenoy said cryptically. 'What are your questions?'

'Ever see this before?' Carella asked. He handed a photostated copy of the cheque to Courtenoy, who looked at it briefly and handed it back.

'Sure.'

'Want to explain it, Mr Courtenoy?'

'Explain what?'

'Explain why Claudia Davis sent you a cheque for a hundred and twenty dollars.'

'As recompense,' Courtenoy said unhesitatingly.

'Oh, recompense, huh?' Meyer said. 'For what, Mr Courtenoy ? For a little cock-and-bull story?'

'Huh? What are you talking about?'

'Recompense for *what*, Mr Courtenoy?'

'For missing three days' work, what the hell did you think?'

'How's that again?'

'No, what did you *think*?' Courtenoy said angrily, waving his finger at Meyer. 'What did you think it was for? Some kind of payoff or something? Is that what you thought?'

'Mr Courtenoy . . .'

'I lost three days' work because of that damn inquest. I had to stay up at Triangle Lake all day Monday and

Tuesday and then again on Wednesday waiting for the jury decision. I'm a bricklayer. I get five bucks an hour and I lost three days' work, eight hours a day, and so Miss Davis was good enough to send me a cheque for a hundred and twenty bucks. Now just what the hell did you think, would you mind telling me?'

'Did you know Miss Davis before that day at Triangle Lake, Mr Courtenoy?'

'Never saw her before in my life. What is this? Am I on trial here? What is this?'

From inside the house the woman's voice came again sharply, 'Sidney! Is something wrong? Are you all right?'

'Nothing's wrong. Shut up, will you?'

There was an aggrieved silence from within the clapboard structure. Courtenoy muttered something under his breath and then turned to face the detectives again. 'You finished?' he said.

'Not quite, Mr Courtenoy. We'd like you to tell us what you saw that day at the lake.'

'What the hell for? Go read the minutes of the inquest if you're so damn interested. I've got to get to work.'

'That can wait, Mr Courtenoy.'

'Like hell it can. This job is away over in . . .'

'Mr Courtenoy, we don't want to have to go all the way downtown and come back with a warrant for your arrest.'

'*My arrest*! For what? Listen, what did I . . . ?'

'Sidney? Sidney, shall I call the police?' the woman shouted from inside the house.

'Oh, shut the hell up!' Courtenoy answered. 'Call the police,' he mumbled. 'I'm up to my ears in cops, and she wants to call the police. What do you want from me? I'm an honest bricklayer. I saw a girl drown. I told it just the way I saw it. Is that a crime? Why are you bothering me?'

'Just tell it again, Mr Courtenoy. Just the way you saw it.'

'She was out in the boat,' Courtenoy said, sighing. 'I was fishing. Her cousin was on the shore. She fell over the side.'

'Josie Thompson.'

'Yes, Josie Thompson, whatever the hell her name was.'

'She was alone in the boat.'

'Yes. She was alone in the boat.'

'Go on.'

'The other one – Miss Davis – screamed and ran into the water, and began swimming, towards her.' He shook his head. 'She didn't make it in time. That boat was a long way out. When she got there, the lake was still. She dove under and came up, and then dove under again, but it was too late, it was just too late. Then, as she was swimming back, I thought *she* was going to drown, too. She faltered and sank below the surface, and I waited and I thought sure she was gone. Then there was a patch of yellow that broke through the water, and I saw she was all right.'

'Why didn't you jump in to help her, Mr Courtenoy?'

'I don't know how to swim.'

'All right. What happened next?'

'She came out of the water – Miss Davis. She was exhausted and hysterical. I tried to calm her down, but she kept yelling and crying, not making any sense at all. I dragged her over to the car, and I asked her for the car keys. She didn't seem to know what I was talking about at first. "The keys!" I said, and she just stared at me. "Your car keys!" I yelled. "The keys to the car." Finally she reached in her purse and handed me the keys.'

'Go on.'

'I drove her into town. It was me who told the story to

the police. She couldn't talk, all she could do was babble and scream and cry. It was a terrible thing to watch. I'd never before seen a woman so completely off her nut. We couldn't get two straight words out of her until the next day. Then she was all right. Told the police who she was, explained what I'd already told them the day before, and told them the dead girl was her cousin, Josie Thompson. They dragged the lake and got her out of the water. A shame. A real shame. Nice young girl like that.'

'What was the dead girl wearing?'

'Cotton dress. Loafers, I think. Or sandals. Little thin sweater over the dress. A cardigan.'

'Any jewellery?'

'I don't think so. No.'

'Was she carrying a purse?'

'No. Her purse was in the car with Miss Davis.'

'What was Miss Davis wearing?'

'When? The day of the drowning? Or when they pulled her cousin out of the lake?'

'Was she there then?'

'Sure. Identified the body.'

'No, I wanted to know what she was wearing on the day of the accident, Mr Courtenoy.'

'Oh, skirt and a blouse, I think. Ribbon in her hair. Loafers. I'm not sure.'

'What colour blouse? Yellow?'

'No. Blue.'

'You said yellow.'

'No, blue. I didn't say yellow.'

Carella frowned. 'I thought you said yellow earlier.' He shrugged. 'All right, what happened after the inquest?'

'Nothing much. Miss Davis thanked me for being so kind and said she would send me a cheque for the time I'd missed. I refused at first and then I thought, What the hell, I'm a hard-working man, and money doesn't grow on trees. So I gave her my address. I figured she could afford it. Driving a Caddy, and hiring a fellow to take it back to the city.'

'Why didn't she drive it back herself?'

'I don't know. I guess she was still a little shaken. Listen, that was a terrible experience. Did you ever see anyone die up close?'

'Yes,' Carella said.

From inside the house Courtenoy's wife yelled, 'Sidney, tell those men to get out of our driveway!'

'You heard her,' Courtenoy said, and finished rolling up his garage door.

8.

NOBODY LIKES MONDAY morning.

It was invented for hangovers. It is really not the beginning of a new week, but only the tail end of the week before. Nobody likes it, and it doesn't have to be rainy or gloomy or blue in order to provoke disaffection. It can be bright and sunny and the beginning of August. It can start with a driveway interview at seven a.m. and grow progressively worse by nine-thirty that same morning. Monday is Monday and legislation will never change its personality. Monday is Monday, and it stinks.

By nine-thirty that Monday morning, Detective Steve Carella was on the edge of total bewilderment and, like any normal person, he blamed it on Monday. He had come back to the squadroom and painstakingly gone over the pile of cheques Claudia Davis had written during the month of July, a total of twenty-five, searching them for some clue to her strangulation, studying them with the scrutiny of a typographer in a print shop. Several things seemed evident from the cheques, but nothing seemed pertinent. He could recall having said: 'I look at those cheques, I can see a life. It's like reading somebody's diary,' and he was beginning to believe he had uttered some famous last words in those two succinct sentences. For if this was the diary of Claudia Davis, it was a singularly unprovocative account that would never make the nation's bestseller lists.

Most of the cheques had been made out to clothing or department stores. Claudia, true to the species, seemed to have a penchant for shopping and a chequebook that yielded to her spending urge. Calls to the various stores represented revealed that her taste ranged through a wide variety of items. A check of sales slips showed that she had purchased during the month of July alone three baby doll nightgowns, two half slips, a trenchcoat, a wrist-watch, four pairs of tapered slacks in various colours, two pairs of walking shoes, a pair of sunglasses, four bikini swimsuits, eight wash-and-wear frocks, two skirts, two cashmere sweaters, half-a-dozen bestselling novels, a large bottle of aspirin, two bottles of Dramamine, six pieces of luggage, and four boxes of cleansing tissue. The most expensive thing she had purchased was an evening gown costing $500. These purchases accounted for most of the cheques she had drawn in July. There were also cheques to a hairdresser, a florist, a shoemaker, a candy shop, and three unexplained cheques that were drawn to individuals, two men and a woman.

The first was made out to George Badueck.

The second was made out to David Oblinsky.

The third was made out to Martha Fedelson.

Someone on the squad had attacked the telephone directory and come up with addresses for two of the three. The third, Oblinsky, had an unlisted number, but a half-hour's argument with a supervisor had finally netted an address for him. The completed list was now on Carella's desk together with all the cancelled cheques. He should have begun tracking down those names, he knew, but something was still bugging him.

'Why did Courtenoy lie to me and Meyer?' he asked Cotton Hawes. 'Why did he lie about something as simple as what Claudia Davis was wearing on the day of the drowning?'

'How did he lie?'

'First he said she was wearing yellow, said he saw a

patch of yellow break the surface of the lake. Then he changed it to blue. Why did he do that, Cotton?'

'I don't know.'

'And if he lied about that, why couldn't he have been lying about everything? Why couldn't he and Claudia have done in little Josie together?'

'I don't know,' Hawes said.

'Where'd that twenty thousand bucks come from, Cotton?'

'Maybe it was a stock dividend.'

'Maybe. Then why didn't she simply deposit the cheque? This was cash, Cotton, *cash*. Now where did it come from? That's a nice piece of change. You don't pick twenty grand out of the gutter.'

'I suppose not.'

'I know where you can get twenty grand, Cotton.'

'Where?'

'From an insurance company. When someone dies.' Carella nodded once, sharply. 'I'm going to make some calls. Damnit, that money had to come from *some*-place.'

He hit pay dirt on his sixth call. The man he spoke to was named Jeremiah Dodd and was a representative of the Security Insurance Corporation, Inc. He recognized Josie Thompson's name at once.

'Oh, yes,' he said. 'We settled that claim in July.'

'Who made the claim, Mr Dodd?'

'The beneficiary, of course. Just a moment. Let me get the folder on this. Will you hold on, please?'

Carella waited impatiently. Over at the insurance company on the other end of the line he could hear muted voices. A girl giggled suddenly, and he wondered who was kissing whom over by the water cooler. At last Dodd came back on the line.

'Here it is,' he said. 'Josephine Thompson. Beneficiary

was her cousin, Miss Claudia Davis. Oh, yes, now it's all coming back. Yes, this is the one.'

'What one?'

'Where the girls were mutual beneficiaries.'

'What do you mean?'

'The cousins,' Dodd said. 'There were two life policies. One for Miss Davis and one for Miss Thompson. And they were mutual beneficiaries.'

'You mean Miss Davis was the beneficiary of Miss Thompson's policy and vice versa?'

'Yes, that's right.'

'That's very interesting. How large were the policies?'

'Oh, very small.'

'Well, how *small* then?'

'I believe they were both insured for twelve thousand five hundred. Just a moment; let me check. Yes, that's right.'

'And Miss Davis applied for payment on the policy after her cousin died, huh?'

'Yes. Here it is, right here. Josephine Thompson drowned at Lake Triangle on June fourth. That's right. Claudia Davis sent me the policy and the certificate of death and also a coroner's jury verdict.'

'She didn't miss a trick, did she?'

'Sir? I'm sorry, I . . .'

'Did you pay her?'

'Yes. It was a perfectly legitimate claim. We began processing it at once.'

'Did you send anyone up to Lake Triangle to investigate the circumstances of Miss Thompson's death?'

'Yes, but it was merely a routine investigation. A coroner's inquest is good enough for us, Detective Carella.'

'When did you pay Miss Davis?'

'On July first.'

'You sent her a cheque for twelve thousand five hundred dollars, is that right?'

'No, sir.'

'Didn't you say . . . ?'

'The policy insured her for twelve-five, that's correct. But there was a double indemnity clause, you see, and Josephine Thompson's death was accidental. No, we had to pay the policy's limit, Detective Carella. On July first we sent Claudia Davis a cheque for twenty-five thousand dollars.'

9.

THERE ARE NO mysteries in police work.

Nothing fits into a carefully preconceived scheme. The high point of any given case is very often the corpse that opens the case. There is no climactic progression; suspense is for the movies. There are only people and curiously twisted motives, and small unexplained details, and coincidence, and the unexpected, and they combine to form a sequence of events, but there is no real mystery, there never is. There is only life, and sometimes death, and neither follows a rule book. Policemen hate mystery stories because they recognize in them a control that is lacking in their own very real, sometimes routine, sometimes spectacular, sometimes tedious investigation of a case. It is very nice and very clever and very convenient to have all the pieces fit together neatly. It is very kind to think of detectives as master mathematicians working on an algebraic problem whose constants are death and a victim, whose unknown is a murderer. But many of these mastermind detectives have trouble adding up the deductions on their twice-monthly paycheques. The world is full of wizards, for sure, but hardly any of them work for the city police.

There was one big mathematical discrepancy in the Claudia Davis case.

There seemed to be $5,000 unaccounted for.

Twenty-five grand had been mailed to Claudia Davis on July 1, and she presumably received the cheque after the Fourth of July holiday, cashed it someplace, and then took her money to the Seaboard Bank of America, opened a new chequing account, and rented a safe-deposit box. But her total deposit at Seaboard had been $20,000 whereas the cheque had been for $25,000, so where was the laggard five? And who had cashed the cheque for her? Mr Dodd of the Security Insurance Corporation, Inc, explained the company's rather complicated accounting system to Carella. A cheque was kept in the local office for several days after it was cashed in order to close out the policy, after which it was sent to the main office in Chicago where it sometimes stayed for several weeks until the master files were closed out. It was then sent to the company's accounting and auditing firm in San Francisco. It was Dodd's guess that the cancelled cheque had already been sent to the California accountants, and he promised to put a tracer on it at once. Carella asked him to please hurry. Someone had cashed that cheque for Claudia and, supposedly, someone also had one-fifth of the cheque's face value.

The very fact that Claudia had not taken the cheque itself to Seaboard seemed to indicate that she had something to hide. Presumably, she did not want anyone asking questions about insurance company cheques, or insurance policies, or double indemnities, or accidental drownings, or especially her cousin Josie. The cheque was a perfectly good one, and yet she had chosen to cash it *before* opening a new account. Why? And why, for that matter, had she bothered opening a new account when she had a rather well-stuffed and active account at another bank?

There are only whys in police work, but they do not add up to mystery. They add up to work, and nobody in the world likes work. The bulls of the 87th would have preferred to sit on their backsides and sip at gin-and-tonics, but the whys were there, so they put on their hats and their holsters and tried to find some becauses.

Cotton Hawes systematically interrogated each and every tenant in the rooming house where Claudia Davis had been killed. They all had alibis tighter than the closed fist of an Arabian stablekeeper. In his report to the lieutenant, Hawes expressed the belief that none of the tenants was guilty of homicide. As far as he was concerned, they were all clean.

Meyer Meyer attacked the 87th's stool pigeons. There were moneychangers galore in the precinct and the city, men who turned hot loot into cold cash — for a price. If someone had cashed a $25,000 cheque for Claudia and kept $5,000 of it during the process, couldn't that person conceivably be one of the moneychangers? He put the precinct stoolies on the ear, asked them to sound around for word of a Security Insurance Corporation cheque. The stoolies came up with nothing.

Detective Lieutenant Sam Grossman took his laboratory boys to the murder room and went over it again. And again. And again. He reported that the lock on the door was a snap lock, the kind that clicks shut automatically when the door is slammed. Whoever killed Claudia Davis could have done so without performing any locked-room gymnastics. All he had to do was close the door behind him when he left. Grossman also reported that Claudia's bed had apparently not been slept in on the night of the murder. A pair of shoes had been found at the foot of a large easy chair in the bedroom and a novel was wedged open on the arm of the chair. He suggested that Claudia had fallen asleep while reading, had awakened, and gone into the other room where she had met her murderer and her death. He had no suggestion as to just who that murderer might have been.

Steve Carella was hot and impatient and overloaded. There were other things happening in the precinct, things like burglaries and muggings and knifings and assaults and kids with summertime on their hands hitting other kids with ball bats because they didn't like the way they pronounced the word 'señor'. There were telephones jangling, and reports to be typed in triplicate, and people filing into the squadroom day and night with complaints against the citizenry of that fair city, and the Claudia Davis case was beginning to be a big fat pain in the keester. Carella wondered what it was like to be a shoemaker. And while he was wondering, he began to chase down the cheques made out to George Badueck, David Oblinsky, and Martha Fedelson.

Happily, Bert Kling had nothing whatsoever to do with the Claudia Davis case. He hadn't even discussed it with any of the men on the squad. He was a young detective and a new detective, and the things that happened in that precinct were enough to drive a guy nuts and keep him busy forty-eight hours every day, so he didn't go around sticking his nose into other people's cases. He had enough troubles of his own. One of those troubles was the line-up.

On Wednesday morning Bert Kling's name appeared on the line-up duty chart.

10.

THE LINE-UP WAS held in the gym downtown at Headquarters on High Street. It was held four days a week, Monday to Thursday, and the purpose of the parade was to acquaint the city's detectives with the people who were committing crime, the premise being that crime is a repetitive profession and that a crook will always be a crook, and it's good to know who your adversaries are should you happen to come face to face with them on the street. Timely recognition of a thief had helped crack many a case and had, on some occasions, even saved a detective's life. So the line-up was a pretty valuable in-group custom. This didn't mean that detectives enjoyed the trip downtown. They drew line-up perhaps once every two weeks and, often as not, line-up duty fell on their day off, and nobody appreciated rubbing elbows with criminals on his day off.

The line-up that Wednesday morning followed the classic pattern of all line-ups. The detectives sat in the gymnasium on folding chairs, and the chief of detectives sat behind a high podium at the back of the gym. The green shades were drawn, and the stage illuminated, and the offenders who'd been arrested the day before were marched before the assembled bulls while the chief read off the charges and handled the interrogation. The pattern was a simple one. The arresting officer, uniformed or plainclothes, would join the chief at the rear of the gym when his arrest came up. The chief would read off the felon's name, and then the section of the city in which he'd been arrested, and then a number. He

53

would say, for example, 'Jones, John, Riverhead, three.' The 'three' would simply indicate that this was the third arrest in Riverhead that day. Only felonies and special types of misdemeanours were handled at the line-up, so this narrowed the list of performers on any given day. Following the case number, the chief would read off the offence, and then say either 'Statement' or 'No statement', telling the assembled cops that the thief either had or had not said anything when they'd put the collar on him. If there had been a statement, the chief would limit his questions to rather general topics since he didn't want to lead the felon into saying anything that might contradict his usually incriminating initial statement, words that could be used against him in court. If there had been *no* statement, the chief would pull out all the stops. He was generally armed with whatever police records were available on the man who stood under the blinding lights, and it was the smart thief who understood the purpose of the line-up and who knew he was not bound to answer a goddamned thing they asked him. The chief of detectives was something like a deadly earnest Mike Wallace, but the stakes were slightly higher here because this involved something a little more important than a novelist plugging his new book or a senator explaining the stand he had taken on a farm bill. These were truly 'interviews in depth', and the booby prize was very often a long stretch up the river in a cosy one-windowed room.

The line-up bored the hell out of Kling. It always did. It was like seeing a stage show for the hundredth time. Every now and then somebody stopped the show with a really good routine. But usually it was the same old song and dance. It wasn't any different that Wednesday. By the time the eighth offender had been paraded and subjected to the chief's bludgeoning interrogation, Kling was beginning to doze. The detective sitting next to him nudged him gently in the ribs.

'. . . Reynolds, Ralph,' the chief was saying, 'Isola, four. Caught burgling an apartment on North Third. No statement. How about it, Ralph?'

'How about what?'

'You do this sort of thing often?'

'What sort of thing?'

'Burglary.'

'I'm no burglar,' Reynolds said.

'I've got his B-sheet here,' the chief said. 'Arrested for burglary in 1948, witness withdrew her testimony, claimed she had mistakenly identified him. Arrested again for burglary in 1952, convicted for Burglary One, sentenced to ten at Castleview, paroled in '58 on good behaviour. You're back at the old stand, huh, Ralph?'

'No, not me. I've been straight ever since I got out.'

'Then what were you doing in that apartment during the middle of the night?'

'I was a little drunk. I must have walked into the wrong building.'

'What do you mean?'

'I thought it was my apartment.'

'Where do you live, Ralph?'

'Oh . . . uh . . . well . . .'

'Come on, Ralph.'

'Well, I live on South Fifth.'

'And the apartment you were in last night is on North Third. You must have been pretty drunk to wander that far off course.'

'Yeah, I guess I was pretty drunk.'

'Woman in that apartment said you hit her when she woke up. Is that true, Ralph?'

'No. No, hey, I never hit her.'

'She says so, Ralph.'

55

'Well, she's mistaken.'

'Well, now, a doctor's report says somebody clipped her on the jaw, Ralph, now how about that?'

'Well, maybe.'

'Yes or no?'

'Well, maybe when she started screaming she got me nervous. I mean, you know, I thought it was my apartment and all.'

'Ralph, you were burgling that apartment. How about telling us the truth?'

'No, I got in there by mistake.'

'How'd you get in?'

'The door was open.'

'In the middle of the night, huh? The door was open?'

'Yeah.'

'You sure you didn't pick the lock or something, huh?'

'No, no. Why would I do that? I thought it was my apartment.'

'Ralph, what were you doing with burglar's tools?'

'Who? Who me? Those weren't burglar's tools.'

'Then what were they? You had a glass cutter, and a bunch of jimmies, and some punches, and a drill and bits, and three celluloid strips, and some lock-picking tools, and eight skeleton keys. Those sound like burglar's tools to me, Ralph.'

'No. I'm a carpenter.'

'Yeah, you're a carpenter all right, Ralph. We searched your apartment, Ralph, and found a couple of things we're curious about. Do you always keep sixteen wristwatches and four typewriters and twelve bracelets and eight rings and a mink stole and three sets of silverware, Ralph?'

'Yeah. I'm a collector.'

'Of other people's things. We also found four hundred

dollars in American currency and five thousand dollars in French francs. Where'd you get that money, Ralph?'

'Which?'

'Whichever you feel like telling us about.'

'Well, the US stuff I . . . I won at the track. And the other, well, a Frenchman owed me some gold, and so he paid me in francs. That's all.'

'We're checking our stolen-goods list right this minute, Ralph.'

'So check!' Reynolds said, suddenly angry. 'What the hell do you want from me? Work for your goddamn living! You want it all on a platter! Like fun! I told you everything I'm gonna . . .'

'Get him out of here,' the chief said. 'Next, Blake, Donald, Bethtown, two. Attempted rape. No statement . . .'

Bert Kling made himself comfortable on the folding chair and began to doze again.

11.

THE CHEQUE MADE out to George Badueck was numbered 018. It was a small cheque, five dollars. It did not seem very important to Carella, but it was one of the unexplained three, and he decided to give it a whirl.

Badueck, as it turned out, was a photographer. His shop was directly across the street from the County Court Building in Isola. A sign in his window advised that he took photographs for chauffeurs' licences, hunting licences, passports, taxicab permits, pistol permits, and the like. The shop was small and crowded. Badueck fitted into the shop like a beetle in an ant trap. He was a huge man with thick, unruly black hair and the smell of developing fluid on him.

'Who remembers?' he said. 'I get millions of people in here every day of the week. They pay me in cash, they pay me with cheques, they're ugly, they're pretty, they're skinny, they're fat, they all look the same on the pictures I take. Lousy. They all look like I'm photographing them for you guys. You never see any of these official-type pictures? Man, they look like mug shots, all of them. So who remembers this . . . what's her name? Claudia Davis, yeah. Another face, that's all. Another mug shot. Why? Is the cheque bad or something?'

'No, it's a good cheque.'

'So what's the fuss?'

'No fuss,' Carella said. 'Thanks a lot.'

He sighed and went out into the August heat. The County Court Building across the street was white and Gothic in the sunshine. He wiped a handkerchief across

58

his forehead and thought, *Another face, that's all*. Sighing, he crossed the street and entered the building. It was cool in the high vaulted corridors. He consulted the directory and went up to the Bureau of Motor Vehicles first. He asked the clerk there if anyone named Claudia Davis had applied for a licence requiring a photograph.

'We only require pictures on chauffeurs' licences,' the clerk said.

'Well, would you check?' Carella asked.

'Sure. Might take a few minutes, though. Would you have a seat?'

Carella sat. It was very cool. It felt like October. He looked at his watch. It was almost time for lunch, and he was getting hungry. The clerk came back and motioned him over.

'We've got a Claudia Davis listed,' he said, 'but she's already got a licence, and she didn't apply for a new one.'

'What kind of licence?'

'Operator's.'

'When does it expire?'

'Next September.'

'And she hasn't applied for anything needing a photo?'

'Nope. Sorry.'

'That's all right. Thanks,' Carella said.

He went out into the corridor again. He hardly thought it likely that Claudia Davis had applied for a permit to own or operate a taxicab, so he skipped the Hack Bureau and went upstairs to Pistol Permits. The woman he spoke to there was very kind and very efficient. She checked her files and told him that no one named Claudia Davis had ever applied for either a carry or a premises pistol permit. Carella thanked her and went into the hall again. He was very hungry. His stomach was beginning to growl. He debated having lunch and then returning and decided, *Hell, I'd better get it done now*.

The man behind the counter in the Passport Bureau was old and thin and he wore a green eyeshade. Carella asked his question, and the old man went to his files and creakingly returned to the window.

'That's right,' he said.

'What's right?'

'She did. Claudia Davis. She applied for a passport.'

'When?'

The old man checked the slip of paper in his trembling hands. 'July twentieth,' he said.

'Did you give it to her?'

'We accepted her application, sure. Isn't us who issues the passports. We've got to send the application on to Washington.'

'But you did accept it?'

'Sure, why not? Had all the necessary stuff. Why shouldn't we accept it?'

'What was the necessary stuff?'

'Two photos, proof of citizenship, filled-out application, and cash.'

'What did she show as proof of citizenship?'

'Her birth certificate.'

'Where was she born?'

'California.'

'She paid you in cash?'

'That's right.'

'Not a cheque?'

'Nope. She started to write a cheque, but the blamed pen was on the blink. We use ballpoints, you know, and it gave out after she filled in the application. So she paid me in cash. It's not all that much money, you know.'

'I see. Thank you,' Carella said.

'Not at all,' the old man replied, and he creaked back to his files to replace the record on Claudia Davis.

*

The cheque was numbered 007, and it was dated July twelfth, and it was made out to a woman named Martha Fedelson.

Miss Fedelson adjusted her pince-nez and looked at the cheque. Then she moved some papers aside on the small desk in the cluttered office, and put the cheque down, and leaned closer to it, and studied it again.

'Yes,' she said, 'that cheque was made out to me. Claudia Davis wrote it right in this office.' Miss Fedelson smiled. 'If you can call it an office. Desk space and a telephone. But then, I'm just starting, you know.'

'How long have you been a travel agent, Miss Fedelson?'

'Six months now. It's very exciting work.'

'Had you ever booked a trip for Miss Davis before?'

'No. This was the first time.'

'Did someone refer her to you?'

'No. She picked my name out of the phone book.'

'And asked you to arrange this trip for her, is that right?'

'Yes.'

'And this cheque? What's it for?'

'Her airline tickets, and deposits at several hotels.'

'Hotels *where*?'

'In Paris and Dijon. And then another in Lausanne, Switzerland.'

'She was going to Europe?'

'Yes. From Lausanne she was heading to the Italian Riviera. I was working on that for her, too. Getting transportation and the hotels, you know.'

'When did she plan to leave?'

'September first.'

'Well, that explains the luggage and the clothes,' Carella said aloud.

'I'm sorry,' Miss Fedelson said, and she smiled and raised her eyebrows.

61

'Nothing, nothing,' Carella said. 'What was your impression of Miss Davis?'

'Oh, that's hard to say. She was only here once, you understand.' Miss Fedelson thought for a moment, and then said, 'I suppose she *could* have been a pretty girl if she tried, but she wasn't trying. Her hair was short and dark, and she seemed rather – well, withdrawn, I guess. She didn't take her sunglasses off all the while she was here. I suppose you would call her shy. Or frightened. I don't know.' Miss Fedelson smiled again. 'Have I helped you any?'

'Well, now we know she was going abroad,' Carella said.

'September is a good time to go,' Miss Fedelson answered. 'In September the tourists have all gone home.' There was a wistful sound to her voice. Carella thanked her for her time and left the small office with its travel folders on the cluttered desk top.

12.

HE WAS RUNNING out of cheques and running out of
ideas. Everything seemed to point towards a girl in
flight, a girl in hiding, but what was there to hide, what
was there to run from? Josie Thompson had been in that
boat alone. The coroner's jury had labelled it accidental
drowning. The insurance company hadn't contested
Claudia's claim, and they'd given her a legitimate cheque
that she could have cashed anywhere in the world. And
yet there *was* hiding, and there *was* flight – and he
couldn't understand why.

He took the list of remaining cheques from his pocket.
The girl's shoemaker, the girl's hairdresser, a florist, a
candy shop. None of them truly important. And the
remaining cheque made out to an individual, the cheque
numbered 006 and dated July eleventh, and written to a
man named David Oblinsky in the amount of $45.75.
Carella had his lunch at two-thirty and then went downtown. He found Oblinsky in a diner near the bus terminal. Oblinsky was sitting on one of the counter stools,
and he was drinking a cup of coffee. He asked Carella to
join him, and Carella did.

'You traced me through that cheque, huh?' he said.
'The phone company gave you my number and my
address, huh? I'm unlisted, you know. They ain't supposed to give out my number.'

'Well, they made a special concession because it was
police business.'

'Yeah, well, suppose the cops called and asked for
Marlon Brando's number? You think they'd give it out?

Like hell they would. I don't like that. No, sir, I don't like it one damn bit.'

'What do you do, Mr Oblinsky? Is there a reason for the unlisted number?'

'I drive a cab is what I do. Sure there's a reason. It's classy to have an unlisted number. Didn't you know that?'

Carella smiled. 'No, I didn't.'

'Sure, it is.'

'Why did Claudia Davis give you this cheque?' Carella asked.

'Well, I work for a cab company here in this city, you see. But usually on weekends or on my day off I use my own car and I take people on long trips, you know what I mean? Like to the country, or the mountains, or the beach, wherever they want to go. I don't care. I'll take them wherever they want to go.'

'I see.'

'Sure. So in June sometime, the beginning of June it was, I get a call from this guy I know up at Triangle Lake, he tells me there's a rich broad there who needs somebody to drive her Caddy back to the city for her. He said it was worth thirty bucks if I was willing to take the train up and the heap back. I told him, no sir, I wanted forty-five or it was no deal. I knew I had him over a barrel, you understand? He'd already told me he checked with the local hicks and none of them felt like making the ride. So he said he would talk it over with her and get back to me. Well, he called again . . . you know, it burns me up about the phone company. They ain't supposed to give out my number like that. Suppose it was Marilyn Monroe? You think they'd give out her number? I'm gonna raise a stink about this, believe me.'

'What happened when he called you back?'

'Well, he said she was willing to pay forty-five, but

64

like could I wait until July sometime when she would send me a cheque because she was a little short at the moment. So I figured what the hell, am I going to get stiffed by a dame who's driving a 1960 Caddy? I figured I could trust her until July. But I also told him, if that was the case, then I also wanted her to pay the tolls on the way back, which I don't ordinarily ask my customers to do. That's what the seventy-five cents was for. The tolls.'

'So you took the train up there and then drove Miss Davis and the Cadillac back to the city, is that right?'

'Yeah.'

'I suppose she was pretty distraught on the trip home.'

'Huh?'

'You know. Not too coherent.'

'Huh?'

'Broken up. Crying. Hysterical,' Carella said.

'No. No, she was okay.'

'Well, what I mean is . . .' Carella hesitated. 'I assumed she wasn't capable, of driving the car back herself.'

'Yeah, that's right. That's why she hired me.'

'Well, then . . .'

'But not because she was broken up or anything.'

'Then why?' Carella frowned. 'Was there a lot of luggage? Did she need your help with that?'

'Yeah, sure. Both hers and her cousin's. Her cousin drowned, you know.'

'Yes. I know that.'

'But anybody coulda helped her with her luggage,' Oblinsky said. 'No, that wasn't why she hired me. She really *needed* me, mister.'

'Why?'

'Why? Because she don't know how to drive, that's why.'

Carella stared at him. 'You're wrong,' he said.

'Oh, no,' Oblinsky said. 'She can't drive, believe me. While I was putting the luggage in the trunk, I asked her to start the car, and she didn't even know how to do that. Hey, you think I ought to raise a fuss with the phone company?'

'I don't know,' Carella said, rising suddenly. All at once the cheque made out to Claudia Davis' hairdresser seemed terribly important to him. He had almost run out of cheques, but all at once he had an idea.

13.

THE HAIRDRESSER'S SALON was on South Twenty-third, just off Jefferson Avenue. A green canopy covered the sidewalk outside the salon. The words ARTURO MANFREDI, INC, were lettered discreetly in white on the canopy. A glass plaque in the window repeated the name of the establishment and added, for the benefit of those who did not read either *Vogue* or *Harper's Bazaar*, that there were two branches of the shop, one here in Isola and another in 'Nassau, the Bahamas'. Beneath that, in smaller, more modest letters, were the words 'Internationally Renowned'. Carella and Hawes went into the shop at four-thirty in the afternoon. Two meticulously coiffed and manicured women were sitting in the small reception room, their expensively sleek legs crossed, apparently awaiting either their chauffeurs, their husbands, or their lovers. They both looked up expectantly when the detectives entered, expressed mild disappointment by only slightly raising newly plucked eyebrows, and went back to reading their fashion magazines. Carella and Hawes walked to the desk. The girl behind the desk was a blonde with a brilliant shellacked look and an English finishing school voice.

'Yes?' she said. 'May I help you?'

She lost a tiny trace of her poise when Carella flashed his buzzer. She read the raised lettering on the shield, glanced at the photo on the plastic-encased ID card, quickly regained her polished calm, and said coolly and unemotionally, 'Yes, what can I do for you?'

'We wonder if you can tell us anything about the girl

67

who wrote this cheque?' Carella said. He reached into his jacket pocket, took out a folded photostat of the cheque, unfolded it, and put it on the desk before the blonde. The blonde looked at it casually.

'What is the name?' she asked. 'I can't make it out.'

'Claudia Davis.'

'D-A-V-I-S?'

'Yes.'

'I don't recognize the name,' the blonde said. 'She's not one of our regular customers.'

'But she did make out a cheque to your salon,' Carella said. 'She wrote this on July seventh. Would you please check your records and find out why she was here and who took care of her?'

'I'm sorry,' the blonde said.

'What?'

'I'm sorry, but we close at five o'clock, and this is the busiest time of the day for us. I'm sure you can understand that. If you'd care to come back a little later . . .'

'No, we wouldn't care to come back a little later,' Carella said. 'Because if we came back a little later, it would be with a search warrant and possibly a warrant for the seizure of your books, and sometimes that can cause a little commotion among the gossip columnists, and that kind of commotion might add to your international renown a little bit. We've had a long day, miss, and this is important, so how about it?'

'Of course. We're always delighted to cooperate with the police,' the blonde said frigidly. 'Especially when they're so well mannered.'

'Yes, we're all of that,' Carella answered.

'Yes. July seventh, did you say?'

'July seventh.'

The blonde left the desk and went into the back of the

salon. A brunette came out front and said, 'Has Miss Marie left for the evening?'

'Who's Miss Marie?' Hawes asked.

'The blonde girl.'

'No. She's getting something for us.'

'That white streak is very attractive,' the brunette said. 'I'm Miss Olga.'

'How do you do.'

'Fine, thank you,' Miss Olga said. 'When she comes back, would you tell her there's something wrong with one of the dryers on the third floor?'

'Yes, I will,' Hawes said.

Miss Olga smiled, waved, and vanished into the rear of the salon again. Miss Marie reappeared not a moment later. She looked at Carella and said, 'A Miss Claudia Davis was here on July seventh. Mr Sam worked on her. Would you like to talk to him?'

'Yes, we would.'

'Then follow me, please,' she said curtly.

They followed her into the back of the salon past women who sat with crossed legs, wearing smocks, their heads in hair dryers.

'Oh, by the way,' Hawes said, 'Miss Olga said to tell you there's something wrong with one of the third-floor dryers.'

'Thank you,' Miss Marie said.

Hawes felt particularly clumsy in this world of women's machines. There was an air of delicate efficiency about the place, and Hawes – six feet two inches tall in his bare soles, weighing in at a hundred and ninety pounds – was certain he would knock over a bottle of nail polish or a pail of hair rinse. As they entered the second-floor salon, as he looked down that long line of humming space helmets at women with crossed legs and what looked like barbers' aprons covering their nylon

69

slips, he became aware of a new phenomenon. The women were slowly turning their heads inside the dryers to look at the white streak over his left temple. He suddenly felt like a horse's ass. For whereas the streak was the legitimate result of a knifing – they had shaved his red hair to get at the wound, and it had grown back this way – he realized all at once that many of these women had shelled out hard-earned dollars to simulate identical white streaks in their own hair, and he no longer felt like a cop making a business call. Instead, he felt like a customer who had come to have his god-damned streak touched up a little.

'This is Mr Sam,' Miss Marie said, and Hawes turned to see Carella shaking hands with a rather elongated man. The man wasn't particularly tall, he was simply elongated. He gave the impression of being seen from the side seats in a movie theatre, stretched out of true proportion, curiously two-dimensional. He wore a white smock, and there were three narrow combs in the breast pocket. He carried a pair of scissors in one thin, sensitive-looking hand.

'How do you do?' he said to Carella, and he executed a half-bow, European in origin, American in execution. He turned to Hawes, took his hand, shook it, and again said, 'How do you do?'

'They're from the police,' Miss Marie said briskly, releasing Mr Sam from any obligation to be polite, and then left the men alone.

'A woman named Claudia Davis was here on July seventh,' Carella said. 'Apparently she had her hair done by you. Can you tell us what you remember about her?'

'Miss Davis, Miss Davis,' Mr Sam said, touching his high forehead in an attempt at visual shorthand, trying to convey the concept of thought without having to do the accompanying brainwork. 'Let me see, Miss Davis, Miss Davis.'

'Yes.'

'Yes, Miss Davis. A very pretty blonde.'

'No,' Carella said. He shook his head. 'A brunette. You're thinking of the wrong person.'

'No, I'm thinking of the right person,' Mr Sam said. He tapped his temple with one extended forefinger, another piece of visual abbreviation. 'I remember. Claudia Davis. A blonde.'

'A brunette,' Carella insisted, and he kept watching Mr Sam.

'When she left. But when she came, a blonde.'

'What?' Hawes said.

'She was a blonde, a very pretty, natural blonde. It is rare. Natural blondness, I mean. I couldn't understand why she wanted to change the colour.'

'You dyed her hair?' Hawes asked.

'That is correct.'

'Did she say *why* she wanted to be a brunette?'

'No, sir. I argued with her. I said, "You have *beautiful* hair, I can do *mar*-vellous things with this hair of yours. You are a *blonde*, my dear, there are drab women who come in here every day of the week and *beg* to be turned into blondes." No. She would not listen. I dyed it for her.' Mr Sam seemed to become offended by the idea all over again. He looked at the detectives as if they had been responsible for the stubbornness of Claudia Davis.

'What else did you do for her, Mr Sam?' Carella asked.

'The dye, a cut, and a set. And I believe one of the girls gave her a facial and a manicure.'

'What do you mean by a cut? Was her hair long when she came here?'

'Yes, beautiful long blonde hair. She wanted it cut. I cut it.' Mr Sam shook his head. 'A pity. She looked

71

terrible. I don't usually say this about someone I work on, but she walked out of here looking terrible. You would hardly recognize her as the same pretty blonde who came in not three hours before.'

'Maybe that was the idea,' Carella said.

'I beg your pardon?'

'Forget it. Thank you, Mr Sam. We know you're busy.'

In the street outside Hawes said, 'You knew before we went in there, didn't you, Mr Steve?'

'I suspected, Mr Cotton, I suspected. Come on, let's get back to the squad.'

14.

THEY KICKED IT around like a bunch of advertising executives. They sat in Lieutenant Byrnes' office and tried to find out how the cookie crumbled and which way the Tootsie rolled. They were just throwing out a life preserver to see if anyone grabbed at it, that's all. What they were doing, you see, was running up the flag to see if anyone saluted, that's all. The lieutenant's office was a four-windowed office because he was top man in this particular combine. It was a very elegant office. It had an electric fan all its own, and a big wide desk. It got cross ventilation from the street. It was really very pleasant. Well, to tell the truth, it was a pretty ratty office in which to be holding a top-level meeting, but it was the best the precinct had to offer. And after a while you got used to the chipping paint and the soiled walls and the bad lighting and the stench of urine from the men's room down the hall. Peter Byrnes didn't work for BBD & O. He worked for the city. Somehow, there was a difference.

'I just put in a call to Irene Miller,' Carella said. 'I asked her to describe Claudia Davis to me, and she went through it all over again. Short dark hair, shy, plain. Then I asked her to describe the cousin, Josie Thompson.' Carella nodded glumly. 'Guess what?'

'A pretty girl,' Hawes said. 'A pretty girl with long blonde hair.'

'Sure. Why, Mrs Miller practically spelled it out the first time we talked to her. It's all there in the report. She said they were like black and white, in looks and personality. Black and white, sure. A brunette and a goddamn blonde!'

'That explains the yellow,' Hawes said.

'What yellow?'

'Courtenoy. He said he saw a patch of yellow breaking the surface. He wasn't talking about her clothes, Steve. He was talking about her *hair*.'

'It explains a lot of things,' Carella said. 'It explains why shy Claudia Davis was preparing for her European trip by purchasing baby doll nightgowns and bikini bathing suits. And it explains why the undertaker up there referred to Claudia as a pretty girl. And it explains why our necropsy report said she was thirty when everybody talked about her as if she were much younger.'

'The girl who drowned wasn't Josie, huh?' Meyer said. 'You figure she was Claudia.'

'Damn right I figure she was Claudia.'

'And you figure she cut her hair afterwards, and dyed it, and took her cousin's name, and tried to pass as her cousin until she could get out of the country, huh?' Meyer said.

'Why?' Byrnes said. He was a compact man with a compact bullet head and a chunky economical body. He did not like to waste time or words.

'Because the trust income was in Claudia's name. Because Josie didn't have a dime of her own.'

'She could have collected on her cousin's insurance policy,' Meyer said.

'Sure, but that would have been the end of it. The trust called for those stocks to be turned over to UCLA if Claudia died. A college, for God's sake! How do you suppose Josie felt about that? Look, I'm not trying to hang a homicide on her. I just think she took advantage of a damn good situation. Claudia was in that boat alone. When she fell over the side, Josie really tried to rescue

74

her, no question about it. But she missed, and Claudia drowned. Okay. Josie went all to pieces, couldn't talk straight, crying, sobbing, real hysterical woman, we've seen them before. But came the dawn. And with the dawn, Josie began thinking. They were away from the city, strangers in a strange town. Claudia had drowned but no one *knew* that she was Claudia. No one but Josie. She had no identification on her, remember? Her purse was in the car. Okay. If Josie identified her cousin correctly, she'd collect twenty-five grand on the insurance policy, and then all that stock would be turned over to the college, and that would be the end of the gravy train. But suppose, just suppose Josie told the police the girl in the lake was Josie Thompson?' Suppose she said, "I, Claudia Davis, tell you that girl who drowned is my cousin, Josie Thompson"?'

Hawes nodded. 'Then she'd still collect on an insurance policy, and also fall heir to those fat security dividends coming in.'

'Right. What does it take to cash a dividend cheque? A bank account, that's all. A bank account with an established signature. So all she had to do was open one, sign her name as Claudia Davis, and then endorse every dividend cheque that came in exactly the same way.'

'Which explains the new account,' Meyer said. 'She couldn't use Claudia's old account because the bank undoubtedly knew both Claudia *and* her signature. So Josie had to forfeit the sixty grand at Highland Trust and start from scratch.'

'And while she was building a new identity and a new fortune,' Hawes said, 'just to make sure Claudia's few friends forgot all about her, Josie was running off to Europe. She may have planned to stay there for years.'

'It all ties in,' Carella said. 'Claudia had a driver's licence. She was the one who drove the car away from

75

Stewart City. But Josie had to hire a chauffeur to take her back.'

'And would Claudia, who was so meticulous about money matters, have kept so many people waiting for payment?' Hawes said. 'No, sir. That was Josie. And Josie was broke, Josie was waiting for that insurance policy to pay off so she could settle those debts and get the hell out of the country.'

'Well, I admit it adds up,' Meyer said.

Peter Byrnes never wasted words. 'Who cashed that twenty-five-thousand-dollar cheque for Josie?' he said.

There was silence in the room.

'Who's got that missing five grand?' he said.

There was another silence.

'Who *killed* Josie?' he said.

15.

JEREMIAH DODD OF the Security Insurance Corporation, Inc., did not call until two days later. He asked to speak to Detective Carella, and when he got him on the phone, he said, 'Mr Carella, I've just heard from San Francisco on that cheque.'

'What cheque?' Carella asked. He had been interrogating a witness to a knifing in a grocery store on Culver Avenue. The Claudia Davis or rather the Josie Thompson case was not quite yet in the Open File, but it was ready to be dumped there, and was truly the farthest thing from Carella's mind at the moment.

'The cheque that was paid to Claudia Davis,' Dodd said.

'Oh, yes. Who cashed it?'

'Well, there are two endorsements on the back. One was made by Claudia Davis, of course. The other was made by an outfit called Leslie Summers, Inc. It's a regular company stamp marked "For Deposit Only" and signed by one of the officers.'

'Have you any idea what sort of a company that is?' Carella asked.

'Yes,' Dodd said. 'They handle foreign exchange.'

'Thank you,' Carella said.

He went there with Bert Kling later that afternoon. He went with Kling completely by chance and only because Kling was heading downtown to buy his mother a birthday gift and offered Carella a ride. When they parked the car, Kling asked, 'How long will this take, Steve?'

'Few minutes, I guess.'

77

'Want to meet me back here?'

'Well, I'll be at 720 Hall, Leslie Summers, Inc. If you're through before me, come on over.'

'Okay, I'll see you,' Kling said.

They parted on Hall Avenue without shaking hands. Carella found the street-level office of Leslie Summers, Inc., and walked in. A counter ran the length of the room, and there were several girls behind it. One of the girls was speaking to a customer in French and another was talking Italian to a man who wanted lire in exchange for dollars. A board behind the desk quoted the current exchange rate for countries all over the world. Carella got in line and waited. When he reached the counter, the girl who'd been speaking French said, 'Yes, sir?'

'I'm a detective,' Carella said. He opened his wallet to where his shield was pinned to the leather. 'You cashed a cheque for Miss Claudia Davis sometime in July. An insurance-company cheque for twenty-five thousand dollars. Would you happen to remember it?'

'No, sir, I don't think I handled it.'

'Would you check around and see who did, please?'

The girl held a brief consultation with the other girls, and then walked to a desk behind which sat a corpulent, balding man with a razor-thin moustache. They talked with each other for a full five minutes. The man kept waving his hands. The girl kept trying to explain about the insurance-company cheque. The bell over the front door sounded. Bert Kling came in, looked around, saw Carella, and joined him at the counter.

'All done?' Carella asked.

'Yeah, I bought her a charm for her bracelet. How about you?'

'They're holding a summit meeting,' Carella said.

The fat man waddled over to the counter. 'What is the trouble?' he asked Carella.

'No trouble. Did you cash a cheque for twenty-five thousand dollars?'

'Yes. Is the cheque no good?'

'It's a good cheque.'

'It looked like a good cheque. It was an insurance-company cheque. The young lady waited while we called the company. They said it was bona fide and we should accept it. Was it a bad cheque?'

'No, no, it was fine.'

'She had identification. It all seemed very proper.'

'What did she show you?'

'A driver's licence or a passport is what we usually require. But she had neither. We accepted her birth certificate. After all, we *did* call the company. Is the cheque no good?'

'It's fine. But the cheque was for twenty-five thousand, and we're trying to find out what happened to five thousand of . . .'

'Oh, yes. The francs.'

'What?'

'She bought five thousand dollars' worth of French francs,' the fat man said. 'She was going abroad?'

'Yes, she was going abroad,' Carella said. He sighed heavily. 'Well, that's that, I guess.'

'It all seemed very proper,' the fat man insisted.

'Oh, it was, it was. Thank you. Come on, Bert.'

They walked down Hall Avenue in silence.

'Beats me,' Carella said.

'What's that, Steve?'

'This case.' He sighed again. 'Oh, what the hell!'

'Yeah, let's get some coffee. What was all that business about the francs?'

'She bought five thousand dollars' worth of francs,' Carella said.

'The French are getting a big play lately, huh?' Kling said, smiling. 'Here's a place. This look okay?'

'Yeah, fine.' Carella pulled open the door of the luncheonette. 'What do you mean, Bert?'

'With the francs.'

'What about them?'

'The exchange rate must be very good.'

'I don't get you.'

'You know. All those francs kicking around.'

'Bert, what the hell are you talking about?'

'Weren't you with me? Last Wednesday?'

'With you where?'

'The line-up. I thought you were with me.'

'No, I wasn't,' Carella said tiredly.

'Oh, well, that's why.'

'That's why what? Bert, for the love of . . .'

'That's why you don't remember him.'

'Who?'

'The punk they brought in on that burglary pickup. They found five grand in French francs in his apartment.'

Carella felt as if he'd just been hit by a truck.

16.

IT HAD BEEN crazy from the beginning. Some of them are like that. The girl had looked black, but she was really white. They thought she was Claudia Davis, but she was Josie Thompson. And they had been looking for a murderer when all there happened to be was a burglar.

They brought him up from his cell where he was awaiting trial for Burglary One. He came up in an elevator with a police escort. The police van had dropped him off at the side door of the Criminal Courts Building, and he had entered the corridor under guard and been marched down through the connecting tunnel and into the building that housed the district attorney's office, and then taken into the elevator. The door of the elevator opened into a tiny room upstairs. The other door of the room was locked from the outside and a sign on it read NO ADMITTANCE. The patrolman who'd brought Ralph Reynolds up to the interrogation room stood with his back against the elevator door all the while the detectives talked to him, and his right hand was on the butt of his Police Special.

'I never heard of her,' Reynolds said.

'Claudia Davis,' Carella said. 'Or Josie Thompson. Take your choice.'

'I don't know either one of them. What the hell *is* this? You got me on a burglary rap, now you try to pull in everything was ever done in this city?'

'Who said anything was done, Reynolds?'

'If nothing was done, why'd you drag me up here?'

'They found five thousand bucks in French francs in your pad, Reynolds. Where'd you get it?'

'Who wants to know?'

'Don't get snotty, Reynolds! Where'd you get that money?'

'A guy owed it to me. He paid me in francs. He was a French guy.'

'What's his name?'

'I can't remember.'

'You'd better start trying.'

'Pierre something.'

'Pierre what?' Meyer said.

'Pierre La Salle, something like that. I didn't know him too good.'

'But you lent him five grand, huh?'

'Yeah.'

'What were you doing on the night of August first?'

'Why? What happened on August first?'

'You tell us.'

'I don't know what I was doing.'

'Were you working?'

'I'm unemployed.'

'You know what we mean!'

'No. What do you mean?'

'Were you breaking into apartments?'

'No.'

'Speak up! Yes or no?'

'I said no.'

'He's lying, Steve,' Meyer said.

'Sure he is.'

'Yeah, sure I am. Look, cop, you got nothing on me but Burglary One, if that. And that you gotta prove in court. So stop trying to hang anything else on me. You ain't got a chance.'

'Not unless those prints check out,' Carella said quickly.

'What prints?'

'The prints we found on the dead girl's throat,' Carella lied.

'I was wearing . . . !'

The small room went as still as death.

Reynolds sighed heavily. He looked at the floor.

'You want to tell us?'

'No,' he said. 'Go to hell.'

He finally told them. After twelve hours of repeated questioning he finally broke down. He hadn't meant to kill her, he said. He didn't even know anybody was in the apartment. He had looked in the bedroom, and the bed was empty. He hadn't seen her asleep in one of the chairs, fully dressed. He had found the French money in a big jar on one of the shelves over the sink. He had taken the money and then accidentally dropped the jar, and she woke up and came into the room and saw him and began screaming. So he grabbed her by the throat. He only meant to shut her up. But she kept struggling. She was very strong. He kept holding on, but only to shut her up. She kept struggling, so he had to hold on. She kept struggling as if . . . as if he'd really been trying to kill her, as if she didn't want to lose her life. But that was manslaughter wasn't it? He wasn't trying to kill her. That wasn't homicide, was it?

'I didn't mean to kill her!' he shouted as they took him into the elevator. 'She began screaming! I'm not a killer! Look at me! Do I look like a killer?' And then, as the elevator began dropping to the basement, he shouted. 'I'm a burglar!' as if proud of his profession, as if stating that he was something more than a common thief, a trained workman, a skilled artisan. 'I'm not a killer! I'm a burglar!' he screamed. 'I'm not a killer! I'm not a killer!' And his voice echoed down the elevator shaft as the car dropped to the basement and the waiting van.

They sat in the small room for several moments after he was gone.

'Hot in here,' Meyer said.

'Yeah.' Carella nodded.

'What's the matter?'

'Nothing.'

'Maybe he's right,' Meyer said. 'Maybe he's only a burglar.'

'He stopped being that the minute he stole a life, Meyer.'

'Josie Thompson stole a life, too.'

'No,' Carella said. He shook his head. 'She only borrowed one. There's a difference, Meyer.'

The room went silent.

'You feel like some coffee?' Meyer asked.

'Sure.'

They took the elevator down and then walked out into the brilliant August sunshine. The streets were teeming with life. They walked into the human swarm, but they were curiously silent.

At last Carella said, 'I guess I think she shouldn't be dead. I guess I think that someone who tried so hard to make a life shouldn't have had it taken away from her.'

Meyer put his hand on Carella's shoulder. 'Listen,' he said earnestly. 'It's a job. It's only a job.'

'Sure,' Carella said. 'It's only a job.'

'J'

1.

IT WAS THE first of April, the day for fools.

It was also Saturday, and the day before Easter.

Death should not have come at all, but it had. And, having come, perhaps it was justified in its confusion. Today was the fool's day, the day for practical jokes. Tomorrow was Easter, the day of the bonnet and egg, the day for the spring march of finery and frills. Oh, yes, it was rumoured in some quarters of the city that Easter Sunday had something to do with a different sort of march at a place called Calvary, but it had been a long time since death was vetoed and rendered null and void, and people have short memories, especially where holidays are concerned.

Today, Death was very much in evidence, and plainly confused. Striving as it was to reconcile the trappings of two holidays – or perhaps three – it succeeded in producing only a blended distortion.

The young man who lay on his back in the alley was wearing black, as if in mourning. But over the black, in contradiction, was a fine silken shawl, fringed at both ends. He seemed dressed for spring, but this was the fool's day, and Death could not resist the temptation.

The black was punctuated with red and blue and white. The cobbled floor of the alley followed the same decorative scheme, red and blue and white, splashed about in gay spring abandon. Two overturned buckets of paint, one white, one blue, seemed to have ricocheted off the wall of the building and come to disorderly rest on the alley floor. The man's shoes were spattered with

87

paint. His black garment was covered with paint. His hands were drenched in paint. Blue and white, white and blue, his black garment, his silken shawl, the floor of the alley, the brick wall of the building before which he lay – all were splashed with blue and white.

The third colour did not mix well with the others.

The third colour was red, a little too primary, a little too bright.

The third colour had not come from a paint can. The third colour still spilled freely from two dozen open wounds on the man's chest and stomach and neck and face and hands, staining the black, staining the silken shawl, spreading in a bright red pool on the alley floor, suffusing the paint with sunset, mingling with the paint but not mixing well, spreading until it touched the foot of the ladder lying crookedly along the wall, encircling the paintbrush lying at the wall's base. The bristles of the brush were still wet with white paint. The man's blood touched the bristles, and then trickled to the cement line where brick wall touched cobbled alley, flowing in an inching stream downwards towards the street.

Someone had signed the wall.

On the wall, someone had painted, in bright, white paint, the single letter J. Nothing more – only J.

The blood trickled down the alley to the city street.

Night was coming.

Detective Cotton Hawes was a tea drinker. He had picked up the habit from his minister father, the man who'd named him after Cotton Mather, the last of the red-hot Puritans. In the afternoons, the good Reverend Jeremiah Hawes had entertained members of his congregation, serving tea and cakes which his wife Matilda baked in the old, iron, kitchen oven. The boy, Cotton Hawes, had been allowed to join the tea-drinking congregation, thus developing a habit which had continued to this day.

At eight o'clock on the night of April first, while a young man lay in an alleyway with two dozen bleeding wounds shrieking in silence to the passersby on the street below, Hawes sat drinking tea. As a boy, he had downed the hot beverage in the book-lined study at the rear of the parish house, a mixture of Oolong and Pekoe which his mother brewed in the kitchen and served in English bone-china cups she had inherited from her grandmother. Tonight, he sat in the grubby, shopworn comfort of the 87th Precinct squadroom and drank, from a cardboard container, the tea Alf Miscolo had prepared in the clerical office. It was hot tea. That was about the most he could say for it.

The open, mesh-covered windows of the squadroom admitted a mild spring breeze from Grover Park across the way, a warm seductive breeze which made him wish he were outside on the street. It was criminal to be catching up on a night like this. It was also boring. Aside from one wife-beating squeal, which Steve Carella was out checking this very minute, the telephone had been ominously quiet. In the silence of the squadroom, Hawes had managed to type up three overdue DD reports, two chits for gasoline and a bulletin-board notice to the men of the squad reminding them that this was the first of the month and time for them to cough up fifty cents each for the maintenance of Alf Miscolo's improvised kitchen. He had also read a half-dozen FBI fliers, and listed in his little black memo book the licence-plate numbers of two more stolen vehicles.

Now he sat drinking insipid tea and wondering why it was so quiet. He supposed the lull had something to do with Easter. Maybe there was going to be an egg-rolling ceremony down South Twelfth Street tomorrow. Maybe all the criminals and potential criminals in the 87th were home dyeing. Eggs, that is. He smiled and took another sip of the tea. From the clerical office beyond the slatted rail divider which separated the squadroom from the corridor, he could hear the rattling of Miscolo's typewriter. Above that, and beyond it, coming from the iron-runged steps which led upstairs, he could hear the ring of footsteps. He turned towards the corridor just as Steve Carella entered it from the opposite end.

Carella walked easily and nonchalantly towards the railing, a big man who moved with fine-honed athletic precision. He shoved open the gate in the railing, walked to his desk, took off his jacket, pulled down his tie and unbuttoned the top button of his shirt.

'What happened?' Hawes asked.

'The same thing that always happens,' Carella said. He sighed heavily and rubbed his hand over his face. 'Is there any more coffee?' he asked.

'I'm drinking tea.'

'Hey, Miscolo!' Carella yelled. 'Any coffee in there?'

'I'll put on some more water!' Miscolo yelled back.

'So what happened?' Hawes asked.

'Oh, the same old jazz,' Carella said. 'It's a waste of time to even go out on these wife-beating squeals. I've never answered one yet that netted anything.'

'She wouldn't press charges,' Hawes said knowingly.

'Charges, hell. There wasn't even any beating, according to her. She's got blood running out of her nose, and a shiner the size of a half-dollar, and she's the one who screamed for the patrolman – but the minute I get there, everything's calm and peaceful.' Carella shook his head. '"A beating, officer?"' he mimicked in a high, shrill voice. '"You must be mistaken, officer. Why, my husband is a good, kind, sweet man. We've been married for twenty years, and he never lifted a finger to me. You must be mistaken, sir." '

'Then who yelled for the cop?' Hawes asked.

'That's just what I said to her.'

'What'd she answer?'

'She said, "Oh, we were just having a friendly little family argument." The guy almost knocked three teeth out of her mouth, but that's just a friendly little family argument. So I asked her how she happened to have a bloody nose and a mouse under her eye and – catch this, Cotton – she said she got them ironing.'

'What?'

'Ironing.'

'Now, how the hell—'

'She said the ironing board collapsed and the iron jumped up and hit her in the eye, and one of the ironing-board legs clipped her in the nose. By the time I left, she and her husband were ready to go on a second honeymoon. She was hugging him all over the place, and he was sneaking his hand under her dress, so I figured I'd come back here where it isn't so sexy.'

'Good idea,' Hawes said.

'Hey, Miscolo!' Carella shouted, 'Where's that coffee?'

'A watched pot never boils!' Miscolo shouted back cleverly.

'We've got George Bernard Shaw in the clerical office,' Carella said. 'Anything happen since I left?'

'Nothing. Not a peep.'

'The streets are quiet, too,' Carella said, suddenly thoughtful.

'Before the storm,' Hawes said.

'Mmmm.'

The squadroom was silent again. Beyond the meshed window, they could hear the myriad sounds of the city, the auto horns, the muffled cries, the belching of buses, a little girl singing as she walked past the station house.

'Well, I suppose I ought to type up some overdue reports,' Carella said.

He wheeled over a typing cart, took three Detective Division reports from his desk, inserted carbon between two of the sheets and began typing.

Hawes stared at the distant lights of Isola's buildings and sucked in a draught of mesh-filtered spring air.

He wondered why it was so quiet.

He wondered just exactly what all those people were doing out there.

Some of those people were playing April Fool's Day pranks. Some of them were getting ready for tomorrow, which was Easter Sunday. And some of them were celebrating a third and ancient holiday known as Passover. Now that's a coincidence which could cause one to speculate upon the similarity of dissimilar religions and the existence of a single, all-powerful God, and all that sort of mystic stuff, if one were inclined towards speculation. Speculator or not, it doesn't take a big detective to check a calendar, and the coincidence was there, take it or leave it. Buddhist, atheist, or Seventh Day Adventist, you had to admit there was something very democratic and wholesome about Easter and Passover coinciding the way they did, something which gave a festive air to the entire city. Jews and Gentiles alike, because of a chance mating of the Christian and Hebrew calendars, were celebrating important holidays at almost the same time. Passover had officially begun at sunset on Friday, March thirty-first, another coincidence, since Passover did not always fall on the Jewish Sabbath; but this year, it did. And tonight was April first, and the traditional second *seder* service, the annual re-enactment of the Jews' liberation from Egyptian bondage, was being observed in Jewish homes throughout the city.

Detective Meyer Meyer was a Jew.

Or at least, he thought he was a Jew. Sometimes he wasn't quite certain. Because if he was a Jew, he sometimes asked himself, how come he hadn't seen the inside of a synagogue in twenty years? And if he was a Jew, how come two of his favourite dishes were roast pork and broiled lobster, both of which were forbidden by the dietary laws of the religion? And if he was such a Jew, how come he allowed his son Alan – who was thirteen and who had been *barmitzvahed* only last month – to play Post Office with Alice McCarthy, who was as Irish as a four-leaf clover?

Sometimes, Meyer got confused.

Sitting at the head of the traditional table on this night of the second *seder*, he didn't know quite how he felt. He looked at his family, Sarah and the three children, and then he looked at the *seder* table, festively set with a floral centrepiece and lighted candles and the large platter upon which were placed the traditional objects – three matzos, a roasted shankbone, a roasted egg, bitter herbs, charoses, watercress – and he still didn't know exactly how he felt. He took a deep breath and began the prayer.

'And it was evening,' Meyer said, 'and it was morning, the sixth day. Thus the heaven and the earth were finished, and all the host of them. And on the seventh day, God had finished his work which He had made: and He rested on the seventh day from his work which he had done. And God blessed the seventh day, and hallowed it, because that in it He rested from all his work, which God had created in order to make it.'

There was a certain beauty to the words, and they lingered in his mind as he went through the ceremony, describing the various objects on the table and their symbolic meaning. When he elevated the dish containing the bone and the egg, everyone sitting around the table took hold of the dish, and Meyer said, 'This is the bread of affliction which our ancestors ate in the land of Egypt; let all those who are hungry, enter and eat thereof, and all who are in distress, come and celebrate the Passover.'

He spoke of his ancestors, but he wondered who he – their descendant – was.

'Wherefore is this night distinguished from all other nights?' he asked. 'Any other night, we may eat either leavened or unleavened bread, but on this night only unleavened bread; all other nights, we may eat any species of herbs, but on this night only bitter herbs . . .'

The telephone rang. Meyer stopped speaking and looked at his wife. For a moment, both seemed reluctant to break the spell of the ceremony. And then Meyer gave a slight, barely discernible shrug. Perhaps, as he went to the telephone, he was recalling that he was a cop first, and a Jew only second.

'Hello?' he said.

'Meyer, this is Cotton Hawes.'

'What is it, Cotton?'

'Look, I know this is your holiday—'

'What's the trouble?'

'We've got a killing,' Hawes said.

Patiently, Meyer said, 'We've always got a killing.'

'This is different. A patrolman called in about five minutes ago. The guy was stabbed in the alley behind—'

'Cotton, I don't understand,' Meyer said. 'I switched the duty with Steve. Didn't he show up?'

'What is it, Meyer?' Sarah called from the dining room.

'It's all right, it's all right,' Meyer answered. 'Isn't Steve there?' he asked Hawes, annoyance in his voice.

'Sure, he's out on the squeal, but that's not the point.'

'What *is* the point?' Meyer asked. 'I was right in the middle of—'

'We need you on this one,' Hawes said. 'Look, I'm sorry as hell. But there are aspects to – Meyer, this guy they found in the alley—'

'Well, what about him?' Meyer asked.

'We think he's a rabbi,' Hawes said.

2.

THE SEXTON OF the Isola Jewish Centre was named Yirmiyahu Cohen, and when he introduced himself, he used the Jewish word for sexton, *shamash*. He was a tall, thin man in his late fifties, wearing a sombre black suit and donning a skullcap the moment he, Carella and Meyer re-entered the synagogue.

The three had stood in the alley behind the synagogue not a moment before, staring down at the body of the dead rabbi and the trail of mayhem surrounding him. Yirmiyahu had wept openly, his eyes closed, unable to look at the dead man who had been the Jewish community's spiritual leader. Carella and Meyer, who had both been cops for a good long time, did not weep.

There is plenty to weep at if you happen to be looking down at the victim of a homicidal stabbing. The rabbi's black robe and fringed prayer shawl were drenched with blood, but happily, they hid from view the multiple stab wounds in his chest and abdomen, wounds which would later be examined at the morgue for external description, number, location, dimension, form of perforation and direction and depth of penetration. Since twenty-five per cent of all fatal stab wounds are cases of cardiac penetration, and since there was a wild array of slashes and a sodden mass of coagulating blood near or around the rabbi's heart, the two detectives automatically assumed that a cardiac stab wound had been the cause of death, and were grateful for the fact that the rabbi was fully clothed. They had both visited the mortuary and seen naked bodies on naked slabs, no longer bleeding, all blood and all life drained away, but skin torn like the flimsiest cheesecloth, the soft interior of the body deprived of its protective flesh, turned outwards, exposed, the ripe wounds gaping and open, had stared at evisceration and wanted to vomit.

The rabbi now owned flesh, too, and at least a part of it had been exposed to his attacker's fury. Looking down at the dead man, neither Carella nor Meyer wanted to weep, but their eyes tightened a little and their throats went peculiarly dry because death by stabbing is a damn frightening thing. Whoever had handled the knife had done so in apparent frenzy. The only exposed areas of the rabbi's body were his hands, his neck, and his face – and these, more than the apparently fatal, hidden incisions beneath the black robe and the prayer shawl, shrieked bloody murder to the night. The rabbi's throat showed two superficial cuts which almost resembled suicidal hesitation cuts. A deeper horizontal slash at the front of his neck had exposed the trachea, carotids and jugular vein, but these did not appear to be severed – at least, not to the layman eyes of Carella and Meyer. There were cuts around the rabbi's eyes and a cut across the bridge of his nose.

But the wounds which caused both Carella and Meyer to turn away from the body were the slashes on the insides of the rabbi's hands. These, they knew, were the defence cuts. These spoke louder than all the others, for they immediately reconstructed the image of a weaponless man struggling to protect himself against the swinging blade of an assassin, raising his hands in hopeless defence, the fingers cut and hanging, the palms slashed to ribbons. At the end of the alley, the patrolman who'd first arrived on the scene was identifying the body to the medical examiner as the one he'd found. Another patrolman was pushing curious bystanders behind the police barricade he'd set up. The laboratory boys and photographers had already begun their work.

Carella and Meyer were happy to be inside the synagogue again.

The room was silent and empty, a house of worship without any worshippers at the moment. They sat on folding chairs in the large, empty room. The eternal light burned over the ark in which the Torah, the five books of Moses, was kept. Forward of the ark, one on each side of it, were the lighted candelabra, the *menorah*, found by tradition in every Jewish house of worship.

Detective Steve Carella began the litany of another tradition. He took out his notebook, poised his pencil over a clean page, turned to Yirmiyahu, and began asking questions in a pattern that had become classic through repeated use.

'What was the rabbi's name?' he asked.

Yirmiyahu blew his nose and said, 'Solomon. Rabbi Solomon.'

'First name?'

'Yaakov.'

'That's Jacob,' Meyer said. 'Jacob Solomon.'

Carella nodded and wrote the name into his book.

'Are you Jewish?' Yirmiyahu asked Meyer.

Meyer paused for an instant, and then said, 'Yes.'

'Was he married or single?' Carella asked.

'Married,' Yirmiyahu said.

'Do you know his wife's name?'

'I'm not sure. I think it's Havah.'

'That's Eve,' Meyer translated.

'And would you know where the rabbi lived?'

'Yes. The house on the comer.'

'What's the address?'

'I don't know. It's the house with the yellow shutters.'

'How do you happen to be here right now, Mr Cohen?' Carella asked. 'Did someone call to inform you of the rabbi's death?'

'No. No, I often come past the synagogue. To check the light, you see.'

'What light is that, sir?' Carella asked.

'The eternal light. Over the ark. It's supposed to burn at all times. Many synagogues have a small electric bulb in the lamp. We're one of the few synagogues in the city who still use oil in it. And, as *shamash*, I felt it was my duty to make certain the light—'

'Is this an Orthodox congregation?' Meyer asked.

'No. It's Conservative,' Yirmiyahu said.

'There are three types of congregation now,' Meyer explained to Carella. 'Orthodox, Conservative and Reform. It gets a little complicated.'

'Yes,' Yirmiyahu said emphatically.

'So you were coming to the synagogue to check on the lamp,' Carella said. 'Is that right?'

'That's correct.'

'And what happened?'

'I saw a police car at the side of the synagogue. So I walked over and asked what the trouble was. And they told me.'

'I see. When was the last time you saw the rabbi alive, Mr Cohen?'

'At evening services.'

'Services start at sundown, Steve. The Jewish day—'

'Yes, I know,' Carella said. 'What time did services end, Mr Cohen?'

'At about seven-thirty.'

'And the rabbi was here? Is that right?'

'Well, he stepped outside when services were over.'

'And you stayed inside. Was there any special reason?'

'Yes. I was collecting the prayer shawls and the *yarmelkas*, and I was putting—'

'*Yarmelkas* are skullcaps,' Meyer said. 'Those little black—'

'Yes, I know,' Carella said. 'Go ahead, Mr Cohen.'

'I was putting the *rimonim* back on to the handles of the scroll.'

'Putting the what, sir?' Carella asked.

'Listen to the big Talmudic scholar,' Meyer said, grinning. 'Doesn't even know what *rimonim* are. They're these decorative silver covers, Steve, shaped like pomegranates. Symbolizing fruitfulness, I guess.'

Carella returned the grin. 'Thank you,' he said.

'A man has been killed,' Yirmiyahu said softly.

The detectives were silent for a moment. The banter between them had been of the faintest sort, mild in comparison to some of the grisly humour that homicide detectives passed back and forth over a dead body. Carella and Meyer were accustomed to working together in an easy, friendly manner, and they were accustomed to dealing with the facts of sudden death, but they realized at once that they had offended the dead rabbi's sexton.

'I'm sorry, Mr Cohen,' he said. 'We meant no offence, you understand.'

The old man nodded stoically, a man who had inherited a legacy of years and years of persecution, a man who automatically concluded that all Gentiles looked upon a Jew's life as a cheap commodity. There was unutterable sadness on his long, thin face, as if he alone were bearing the oppressive weight of the centuries on his narrow shoulders.

The synagogue suddenly seemed smaller. Looking at the old man's face and the sadness there, Meyer wanted to touch it gently and say, 'It's all right, *tsadik*, it's all right,' the Hebrew word leaping into his mind – *tsadik*, a man possessed of saintly virtues, a person of noble character and simple living.

The silence persisted. Yirmiyahu Cohen began weeping again, and the detectives sat in embarrassment on the folding chairs and waited.

At last Carella said, 'Were you still here when the rabbi came inside again?'

'I left while he was gone,' Yirmiyahu said. 'I wanted to return home. This is the *Pesach*, the Passover. My family was waiting for me to conduct the *seder*.'

'I see.' Carella paused. He glanced at Meyer.

'Did you hear any noise in the alley, Mr Cohen?' Meyer asked. 'When the rabbi was out there?'

'Nothing.'

Meyer sighed and took a package of cigarettes from his jacket pocket. He was about to light one when Yirmiyahu said, 'Didn't you say you were Jewish?'

'Huh?' Meyer said. He struck the match.

'You are going to *smoke* on the second day of *Pesach*?' Yirmiyahu asked.

'Oh. Oh, well . . .' The cigarette felt suddenly large in Meyer's hand, the fingers clumsy. He shook out the match. 'You – uh – you have any other questions, Steve?' he asked.

'No,' Carella said.

'Then I guess you can go, Mr Cohen,' Meyer said. 'Thank you very much.'

'*Shalom*,' Yirmiyahu said, and shuffled dejectedly out of the room.

'You're not supposed to smoke, you see,' Meyer explained to Carella, 'on the first two days of Passover, and the last two, a good Jew doesn't smoke, or ride, or work, or handle money or—'

'I thought this was a Conservative synagogue,' Carella said. 'That sounds like Orthodox practice to me.'

'Well, he's an old man,' Meyer said. 'I guess the customs die hard.'

'The way the rabbi did,' Carella said grimly.

3.

THEY STOOD OUTSIDE in the alley where chalk marks outlined the position of the dead body. The rabbi had been carted away, but his blood still stained the cobblestones, and the rampant paint had been carefully sidestepped by the laboratory boys searching for footprints and fingerprints, searching for anything which would provide a lead to the killer.

'J,' the wall read.

'You know, Steve, I feel funny on this case,' Meyer told Carella.

'I do, too.'

Meyer raised his eyebrows, somewhat surprised. 'How come?'

'I don't know. I guess because he was a man of God.' Carella shrugged. 'There's something unworldly and naïve and – pure, I guess – about rabbis and priests and ministers and I guess I feel they shouldn't be touched by all the dirty things in life.' He paused. 'Somebody's got to stay untouched, Meyer.'

'Maybe so,' Meyer paused. 'I feel funny because I'm a Jew, Steve.' His voice was very soft. He seemed to be confessing something he would not have admitted to another living soul.

'I can understand that,' Carella said gently.

'Are you policemen?'

The voice startled them. It came suddenly from the other end of the alley, and they both whirled instantly to face it.

Instinctively, Meyer's right hand reached for the service revolver holstered in his right rear pocket.

'Are you policemen?' the voice asked again. It was a woman's voice, thick with a Yiddish accent. The street lamp was behind the owner of the voice. Meyer and Carella saw only a frail figure clothed in black, pale white hands clutched to the breast of the black coat, pinpoints of light burning where the woman's eyes should have been.

'We're policemen,' Meyer answered. His hand hovered near the butt of his pistol. Beside him, he could feel Carella tensed for a draw.

'I know who killed the *rov*,' the woman said.

'What?' Carella asked.

'She says she knows who killed the rabbi,' Meyer whispered in soft astonishment.

His hand dropped to his side. They began walking towards the street end of the alley. The woman stood there motionless, the light behind her, her face in shadow, the pale hands still, her eyes burning.

'Who killed him?' Carella said.

'I know the *rotsayach*,' the woman answered. 'I know the murderer.'

'Who?' Carella said again.

'Him!' the woman shouted, and she pointed to the painted white J on the synagogue wall. 'The *sonei Yisroel*! Him!'

'The anti-Semite,' Meyer translated. 'She says the anti-Semite did it.'

They had come abreast of the woman now. The three stood at the end of the alley with the street lamp casting long shadows on the cobbles. They could see her face. Black hair and brown eyes, the classic Jewish face of a woman in her fifties, the beauty stained by age and something else, a fine-drawn tension hidden in her eyes and on her mouth.

'What anti-Semite?' Carella asked. He realized he was whispering. There was something about the woman's face and the blackness of her coat and the paleness of her hands which made whispering a necessity.

'On the next block,' she said. Her voice was a voice of judgement and doom. 'The one they call Finch.'

'You saw him kill the rabbi?' Carella asked. 'You saw him do it?'

'No.' She paused. 'But I know in my heart that he's the one . . .'

'What's your name, ma'am?' Meyer asked.

'Hannah Kaufman,' she said. 'I know it was him. He said he would do it, and now he has started.'

'He said he would do what?' Meyer asked the old woman patiently.

'He said he would kill all the Jews.'

'You heard him say this?'

'*Everyone* has heard him.'

'His name is Finch?' Meyer asked her. 'You're sure?'

'Finch,' the woman said. 'On the next block. Over the candy store.'

'What do you think?' he asked Carella.

Carella nodded. 'Let's try him.'

4.

IF AMERICA IS a melting pot, the 87th Precinct is a crucible. Start at the River Harb, the northernmost boundary of the precinct territory, and the first thing you hit is exclusive Smoke Rise, where the walled-in residents sit in white-Protestant respectability in houses set a hundred feet back from private roads, admiring the greatest view the city has to offer. Come out of Smoke Rise and hit fancy Silvermine Road where the aristocracy of apartment buildings have begun to submit to the assault of time and the encroachment of the surrounding slums. Forty-thousand-dollar-a-year executives still live in these apartment buildings, but people write on the walls here, too: limericks, prurient slogans, which industrious doormen try valiantly to erase.

There is nothing so eternal as Anglo-Saxon etched in graphite.

Silvermine Park is south of the Road, and no one ventures there at night. During the day, the park is thronged with governesses idly chatting about the last time they saw Sweden, gently rocking shellacked blue baby buggies. But after sunset, not even lovers will enter the park. The Stem, further south, explodes the moment the sun leaves the sky. Gaudy and incandescent, it mixes Chinese restaurants with Jewish delicatessens, pizza joints with Greek cabarets offering belly dancers. Threadbare as a beggar's sleeve, Ainsley Avenue crosses the centre of the precinct, trying to maintain a dignity long gone, crowding the sidewalks with austere but dirty apartment buildings, furnished rooms, garages and a sprinkling of sawdust saloons. Culver Avenue turns completely Irish with the speed of a leprechaun. The faces, the bars, even the buildings seem displaced, seem to have been stolen and transported from the centre of Dublin; but no lace curtains hang in the windows. Poverty turns a naked face to the streets here, setting the pattern for the rest of the precinct territory. Poverty rakes the back of the Culver Avenue Irish, claws its way on to the white and tan and brown and black faces of the Puerto Ricans lining Mason Avenue, flops on to the beds of the whores on *La Via de Putas*, and then pushes its way into the real crucible, the city side streets where different minority groups live cheek by jowl, as close as lovers, hating each other. It is here that Puerto Rican and Jew, Italian and Negro, Irishman and Cuban are forced by dire economic need to live in a ghetto which, by its very composition, loses definition and becomes a meaningless tangle of unrelated bloodlines.

Rabbi Solomon's synagogue was on the same street as a Catholic church. A Baptist store-front mission was on the avenue leading to the next block. The candy store over which the man named Finch lived was owned by a Puerto Rican whose son had been a cop – a man named Hernandez.

Carella and Meyer paused in the lobby of the building and studied the name plates in the mailboxes. There were eight boxes in the row. Two had name plates. Three had broken locks. The man named Finch lived in apartment thirty-three on the third floor.

The lock on the vestibule door was broken. From behind the stairwell, where the garbage cans were stacked before being put out for collection in the morning, the stink of that evening's dinner remains assailed the nostrils and left the detectives mute until they had gained the first-floor landing.

On the way up to the third floor, Carella said, 'This seems too easy, Meyer. It's over before it begins.'

On the third-floor landing, both men drew their service revolvers. They found apartment thirty-three and bracketed the door.

'Mr Finch?' Meyer called.

'Who is it?' a voice answered.

'Police. Open up.'

The apartment and the hallway went still.

'Finch?' Meyer said.

There was no answer. Carella backed off against the opposite wall. Meyer nodded. Bracing himself against the wall, Carella raised his right foot, the leg bent at the knee, then released it like a triggered spring. The flat of his sole collided with the door just below the lock. The door burst inwards, and Meyer followed it into the apartment, his gun in his fist.

Finch was a man in his late twenties, with a square crew-cut head and bright green eyes. He was closing the closet door as Meyer burst into the room. He was wearing only trousers and an undershirt, his feet bare. He needed a shave, and the bristles on his chin and face emphasized a white scar that ran from just under his right cheek to the curve of his jaw. He turned from the closet with the air of a man who has satisfactorily completed a mysterious mission.

'Hold it right there,' Meyer said.

There's a joke they tell about an old woman on a train who repeatedly asks the man sitting beside her if he's Jewish. The man, trying to read his newspaper, keeps answering. 'No, I'm not Jewish.' The old lady keeps pestering him, tugging at his sleeve, asking the same question over and over again. Finally the man puts down his newspaper and says, 'All right, all right, damn it! I'm Jewish.'

And the old lady smiles at him sweetly and says, 'You know something? You don't look it.'

The joke, of course, relies on a prejudice which assumes that you can tell a man's religion by looking at his face. There was nothing about Meyer Meyer's looks or speech which would indicate that he was Jewish. His face was round and clean-shaven, he was thirty-seven years old and completely bald, and he possessed the bluest eyes this side of Denmark. He was almost six feet tall and perhaps a trifle overweight, and the only conversation he'd had with Finch were the few words he'd spoken through the closed door, and the four words he'd spoken since he entered the apartment, all of which were delivered in big-city English without any noticeable trace of accent.

But when Meyer Meyer said, 'Hold it right there,' a smile came on to Finch's face, and he answered, 'I wasn't going anyplace, Jewboy.'

Well, maybe the sight of the rabbi lying in his own blood had been too much for Meyer. Maybe the words 'sonei Yisroel' had recalled the days of his childhood when, one of the few Orthodox Jews in a Gentile neighbourhood, and bearing the double-barrelled name his father had foisted upon him, he was forced to defend himself against every hoodlum who crossed his path, invariably against overwhelming odds. He was normally a very patient man. He had borne his father's practical joke with amazing good will, even though he sometimes grinned mirthlessly through bleeding lips. But tonight, this second night of Passover, after having looked down at the bleeding rabbi, after having heard the tortured sobs of the sexton, after having seen the patiently suffering face of the woman in black, the words hurled at him from the other end of the apartment had a startling effect.

Meyer said nothing. He simply walked to where Finch was standing near the closet, and lifted the .38 high above his head. He flipped the gun up as his arm descended, so that the heavy butt was in striking position as it whipped towards Finch's jaw.

Finch brought up his hands, but not to shield his face in defence. His hands were huge, with big knuckles, the imprimatur of the habitual street fighter. He opened the fingers and caught Meyer's descending arm at the wrist, stopping the gun three inches from his face.

He wasn't dealing with a kid; he was dealing with a cop. He obviously intended to shake that gun out of Meyer's fist and then beat him senseless on the floor of the apartment. But Meyer brought up his right knee and smashed it into Finch's groin, and then, his wrist still pinioned, he bunched his left fist and drove it hard and straight into Finch's gut. That did it. The fingers loosened and Finch backed away a step just as Meyer brought the pistol back across his own body and then unleashed it in a backhand swipe. The butt cracked against Finch's jaw and sent him sprawling against the closet wall.

Miraculously, the jaw did not break. Finch collided with the closet, grabbed the door behind him with both hands opened wide and flat against the wood, and then shook his head. He blinked his eyes and shook his head again. By what seemed to be sheer will power, he managed to stand erect without falling on his face.

Meyer stood watching him, saying nothing, breathing hard. Carella, who had come into the room, stood at the far end, ready to shoot Finch if he so much as raised a pinky.

'Your name Finch?' Meyer asked.

'I don't talk to Jews,' Finch answered.

'Then try *me*,' Carella said. 'What's your name?'

110

'Go to hell, you and your Jewboy friend both.'

Meyer did not raise his voice. He simply took a step closer to Finch, and very softly said, 'Mister, in two minutes, you're gonna be a cripple because you resisted arrest.'

He didn't have to say anything else, because his eyes told the full story, and Finch was a fast reader.

'Okay,' Finch said, nodding. 'That's my name.'

'What's in the closet, Finch?' Carella asked.

'My clothes.'

'Get away from the door.'

'What for?'

Neither of the cops answered. Finch studied them for ten seconds, and quickly moved away from the door. Meyer opened it. The closet was stacked high with piles of tied and bundled pamphlets. The cord on one bundle was untied, the pamphlets spilling on to the closet floor. Apparently, this bundle was the one Finch had thrown into the closet when he'd heard the knock on the door. Meyer stooped and picked up one of the pamphlets. It was badly and cheaply printed, but the intent was unmistakable. The title of the pamphlet was 'The Bloodsucker Jew'.

'Where'd you get this?' Meyer asked.

'I belong to a book club,' Finch answered.

'There are a few laws against this sort of thing,' Carella said.

'Yeah?' Finch answered. 'Name me one.'

'Happy to. Section 1340 of the Penal Law – libel defined.'

'Maybe you ought to read Section 1342,' Finch said, '*The publication is justified when the matter charged as libellous is true, and was published with good motives and for justifiable ends.*'

'Then let's try Section 514,' Carella said. ' "*A person*

111

who denies or aids or incites another to deny any person because of race, creed, colour or national origin . . ."'

'I'm not trying to incite anyone,' Finch said, grinning.

'Nor am I a lawyer,' Carella said. 'But we can also try Section 700, which defines discrimination, and Section 1430, which makes it a felony to perform an act of malicious injury to a place of religious worship.'

'Huh?' Finch said.

'Yeah,' Carella answered.

'What the hell are you talking about?'

'I'm talking about the little paint job you did on the synagogue wall.'

'What paint job? What synagogue?'

'Where were you at eight o'clock tonight, Finch?'

'Out.'

'Where?'

'I don't remember.'

'You better *start* remembering.'

'Why? Is there a section of the Penal Law against loss of memory?'

'No,' Carella said. 'But there's one against homicide.'

5.

THE TEAM STOOD around him in the squadroom.

The team consisted of Detectives Steve Carella, Meyer Meyer, Cotton Hawes, and Bert Kling. Two detectives from Homicide South had put in a brief appearance to legitimize the action, and then went home to sleep, knowing full well that the investigation of a homicide is always left to the precinct discovering the stiff. The team stood around Finch in a loose semicircle. This wasn't a movie sound stage, so there wasn't a bright light shining in Finch's eyes, nor did any of the cops lay a finger on him. These days, there were too many smart-assed lawyers around who were ready and able to leap upon irregular interrogation methods when and if a case finally came to trial. The detectives simply stood around Finch in a loose, relaxed semicircle, and their only weapons were a thorough familiarity with the interrogation process and with each other, and the mathematical superiority of four minds pitted against one.

'What time did you leave the apartment?' Hawes asked.

'Around seven.'

'And what time did you return?' Kling asked.

'Nine, nine-thirty. Something like that.'

'Where'd you go?' Carella asked.

'I had to see somebody.'

'A rabbi?' Meyer asked.

'No.'

'Who?'

'I don't want to get anybody in trouble.'

'You're in plenty of trouble yourself,' Hawes said. 'Where'd you go?'

'No place.'

'Okay, suit yourself,' Carella said. 'You've been shooting your mouth off about killing Jews, haven't you?'

'I never said anything like that.'

'Where'd you get these pamphlets?'

'I found them.'

'You agree with what they say?'

'Yes.'

'You know where the synagogue in this neighbourhood is?'

'Yes.'

'Were you anywhere near it tonight between seven and nine?'

'No.'

'Then where were you?'

'No place.'

'Anybody see you there?' Kling asked.

'See me where?'

'The no place you went to.'

'Nobody saw me.'

'You went no place,' Hawes said, 'and nobody saw you. Is that right?'

'That's right.'

'The invisible man,' Kling said.

'That's right.'

'When you get around to killing all these Jews,' Carella said, 'how do you plan to do it?'

'I don't plan to kill anybody,' he said defensively.

'Who you gonna start with?'

'Nobody.'

'Ben-Gurion?'

'Nobody.'

'Or maybe you've already started.'

'I didn't kill anybody, and I'm not gonna kill any-body. I want to call a lawyer.'

'A Jewish lawyer?'

'I wouldn't have—'

'What wouldn't you have?'

'Nothing.'

'You like Jews?'

'No.'

'You hate them?'

'No.'

'Then you like them.'

'No. I didn't say—'

'You either like them or you hate them. Which?'

'That's none of your goddamn business!'

'But you agree with the crap in those hate pamphlets, don't you?'

'They're not hate pamphlets.'

'What do you call them?'

'Expressions of opinion.'

'Whose opinion?'

'*Everybody's* opinion!'

'Yours included?'

'Yes, mine included!'

'Do you know Rabbi Solomon?'

'No.'

'What do you think of rabbis in general?'

'I never think of rabbis.'

'But you think of Jews a lot, don't you?'

'There's no crime about think—'

'If you think of Jews you must think of rabbis. Isn't that right?'

'Why should I waste my time—'

'The rabbi is the spiritual leader of the Jewish people, isn't he?'

'I don't know anything about rabbis.'

'But you must know that.'

'What if I do?'

'Well, if you said you were going to kill the Jews—'

'I never said—'

'—then a good place to start would be with—'

'I never said anything like that!'

'We've got a witness who heard you! A good place to start would be with a rabbi, isn't that so?'

'Go shove your rabbi—'

'Where were you between seven and nine tonight?'

'No place.'

'You were behind that synagogue, weren't you?'

'No.'

'You were painting a J on the wall, weren't you?'

'No! No, I wasn't!'

'You were stabbing a rabbi!'

'You were killing a Jew!'

'I wasn't any place near that—'

'Book him, Cotton. Suspicion of murder.'

'Suspicion of – I'm telling you I wasn't—'

'Either shut up or start talking, you bastard,' Carella said. Finch shut up.

6.

THE GIRL CAME to see Meyer Meyer on Easter Sunday.

She had reddish-brown hair and brown eyes, and she wore a dress of bright persimmon with a sprig of flowers pinned to the left breast. She stood at the railing and none of the detectives in the squadroom even noticed the flowers; they were too busy speculating on the depth and texture of the girl's rich curves.

The girl didn't say a word. She didn't have to. The effect was almost comic, akin to the cocktail-party scene where the voluptuous blonde takes out a cigarette and four hundred men are stampeded in the rush to light it. The first man to reach the slatted rail divider was Cotton Hawes, since he was single and unattached. The second man was Hal Willis, who was also single and a good red-blooded American boy. Meyer Meyer, an old married poop, contented himself with ogling the girl from behind his desk. The word *shtik* crossed Meyer's mind, but he rapidly pushed the thought aside.

'Can I help you, miss?' Hawes and Willis asked simultaneously.

'I'd like to see Detective Meyer,' the girl said.

'Meyer?' Hawes asked, as if his manhood had been maligned.

'Meyer?' Willis repeated.

'Is he the man handling the murder of the rabbi?'

'Well we're *all* sort of working on it,' Hawes said modestly.

'I'm Artie Finch's girlfriend,' the girl said. 'I want to talk to Detective Meyer.'

Meyer rose from his desk with the air of a man who has been singled out from the stag line by the belle of the ball. Using his best radio announcer's voice, and his best company manners, he said, 'Yes, miss, I'm Detective Meyer.'

He held open the gate in the railing, all but executed a bow, and led the girl to his desk. Hawes and Kling watched as the girl sat and crossed her legs. Meyer moved a pad into place with all the aplomb of a General Motors executive.

'I'm sorry, miss,' he said. 'What was your name?'

'Eleanor,' she said. 'Eleanor Fay.'

'F-A-Y-E?' Meyer asked, writing.

'F-A-Y.'

'And you're Arthur Finch's fiancée? Is that right?'

'I'm his girlfriend,' Eleanor corrected.

'You're not engaged?'

'Not officially, no.' She smiled demurely, modestly and sweetly. Across the room, Cotton Hawes rolled his eyes towards the ceiling.

'What did you want to see me about, Miss Fay?' Meyer asked.

'I wanted to see you about Arthur. He's innocent. He didn't kill that man.'

'I see. What do you know about it, Miss Fay?'

'Well, I read in the paper that the rabbi was killed sometime between seven-thirty and nine. I think that's right, isn't it?'

'Approximately, yes.'

'Well, Arthur couldn't have done it. I know where he was during that time.'

'And where was he?' Meyer asked.

He figured he knew just what the girl would say. He had heard the same words from an assortment of molls, mistresses, fiancées, girlfriends and just plain acquaintances of men accused of everything from disorderly

118

conduct to first-degree murder. The girl would protest that Finch was with her during that time. After a bit of tooth-pulling, she would admit that – well – they were alone together. After a little more coaxing, the girl would reluctantly state, the reluctance adding credulity to her story, that – well – they were alone in intimate circumstances together. The alibi having been firmly established, she would then wait patiently for her man's deliverance.

'And where was he?' Meyer asked, and waited patiently.

'From seven to eight,' Eleanor said, 'he was with a man named Bret Loomis in a restaurant called The Gate, on Culver and South Third.'

'What?' Meyer was surprised.

'Yes. From there, Arthur went to see his sister in Riverhead. I can give you the address if you like. He got there at about eight-thirty and stayed a half-hour or so. Then he went straight home.'

'What time did he get home?'

'Ten o'clock.'

'He told us nine, nine-thirty.'

'He was mistaken. I know he got home at ten because he called me the minute he was in the house. It was ten o'clock.'

'I see. And he told you he'd just got home?'

'Yes.' Eleanor Fay nodded and uncrossed her legs. Willis, at the water cooler, did not miss the sudden revealing glimpse of nylon and thigh.

'Did he also tell you he'd spent all that time with Loomis first and then with his sister?'

'Yes, he did.'

'Then why didn't he tell *us*?' Meyer asked.

'I don't know why. Arthur is a person who respects family and friends. I suppose he didn't want to involve them with the police.'

119

'That's very considerate of him,' Meyer said drily, 'especially since he's being held on suspicion of murder. What's his sister's name?'

'Irene Granavan. Mrs Carl Granavan.'

'And her address?'

'Nineteen-eleven Morris Road. In Riverhead.'

'Know where I can find this Bret Loomis?'

'He lives in a rooming house on Culver Avenue. The address is 3918. It's near Fourth.'

'You came pretty well prepared, didn't you, Miss Fay?' Meyer asked.

'If you don't come prepared,' Eleanor answered, 'why come at all?'

7.

BRET LOOMIS WAS thirty-one years old, five feet six inches tall, bearded. When he admitted the detectives to the apartment, he was wearing a bulky black sweater and tight-fitting dungarees. Standing next to Cotton Hawes, he looked like a little boy who had tried on a false beard in an attempt to get a laugh out of his father.

'Sorry to bother you, Mr Loomis,' Meyer said. 'We know this is Easter, and—'

'Oh, yeah?' Loomis said. He seemed surprised. 'Hey, that's right, ain't it? It's Easter. I'll be damned. Maybe I oughta go out and buy myself a pot of flowers.'

'You didn't know it was Easter?' Hawes asked.

'Like, man, who ever reads the newspapers? Gloom, gloom! I'm fed up to here with it. Let's have a beer, celebrate Easter. Okay?'

'Well, thanks,' Meyer said, 'but—'

'Come on, so it ain't allowed. Who's gonna know besides you, me and the bedpost? Three beers coming up.'

Meyer looked at Hawes and shrugged. Hawes shrugged back. Together, they watched Loomis as he went to the refrigerator in one corner of the room and took out three bottles of beer.

'Sit down,' he said. 'You'll have to drink from the bottle because I'm a little short of glasses. Sit down, sit down.'

The detectives glanced around the room, puzzled.

'Oh,' Loomis said, 'you'd better sit on the floor. I'm a little short of chairs.'

The three men squatted around a low table which had obviously been made from a tree stump. Loomis put the bottles on the table top, lifted his own bottle, said 'Cheers,' and took a long drag at it.

'What do you do for a living, Mr Loomis?' Meyer asked.

'I live,' Loomis said.

'What?'

'I *live* for a living. That's what I do.'

'I meant, how do you support yourself?'

'I get payment from my ex-wife.'

'*You* get payments?' Hawes asked.

'Yeah. She was so delighted to get rid of me that she made a settlement. A hundred bucks a week. That's pretty good, isn't it?'

'That's very good,' Meyer said.

'You think so?' Loomis seemed thoughtful. 'I think I coulda boosted it to *two* hundred if I held out a little longer. The bitch was running around with another guy, you see, and was all hot to marry him. He's got plenty of loot. I bet I coulda boosted it to two hundred.'

'How long do these payments continue?' Hawes asked, fascinated.

'Until I get married again – which I will never ever do as long as I live. Drink your beer. It's good beer.' He took a drag at his bottle and said, 'What'd you want to see me about?'

'Do you know a man named Arthur Finch?'

'Sure. He in trouble?'

'Yes.'

'What'd he do?'

'Well, let's skip that for the moment, Mr Loomis,' Hawes said. 'We'd like you to tell us—'

'Where'd you get that white streak in your hair?' Loomis asked suddenly.

'Huh?' Hawes touched his left temple unconsciously. 'Oh, I got knifed once. It grew back this way.'

'All you need is a blue streak on the other temple. Then you'll look like the American flag,' Loomis said, and laughed.

'Yeah,' Hawes said. 'Mr Loomis, can you tell us where you were last night between seven and eight o'clock?'

'Oh, boy,' Loomis said, 'this is like "Dragnet", ain't it? "Where were you on the night of December twenty-first? All we want are the facts."'

'Just like "Dragnet",' Meyer said drily, 'Where were you, Mr Loomis?'

'Last night? Seven o'clock?' He thought for a moment. 'Oh, sure.'

'Where?'

'Olga's pad.'

'Who?'

'Olga Trenovich. She's like a sculptress. She does these crazy little statues in wax. Like she drips the wax all over everything. You dig?'

'And you were with her last night?'

'Yeah. She had like a little session up at her pad. A couple of coloured guys on sax and drums and two other kids on trumpet and piano.'

'You got there at seven, Mr Loomis?'

'No. I got there at six-thirty.'

'And what time did you leave?'

'Gossssshhhhh, who remembers?' Loomis said. 'It was the wee, small hours.'

'After midnight, you mean?' Hawes asked.

'Oh, sure. Two, three in the morning,' Loomis said.

'You got there at six-thirty and left at two or three in the morning? Is that right?'

'Yeah.'

'Was Arthur Finch with you?'

'Hell, no.'

'Did you see him at all last night?'

'Nope. Haven't seen him since – let me see – last month sometime.'

'You were *not* with Arthur Finch in a restaurant called The Gate?'

'When? Last night, you mean?'

'Yes.'

'Nope. I just told you. I haven't seen Artie in almost two weeks.' A sudden spark flashed in Loomis' eyes and he looked at Hawes and Meyer guiltily.

'Oh-oh,' he said. 'What'd I just do? Did I screw up Artie's alibi?'

'You screwed it up fine, Mr Loomis,' Hawes said.

8.

IRENE GRANAVAN, FINCH'S sister, was a twenty-one-year-old girl who had already borne three children and was working on her fourth, in her fifth month of pregnancy. She admitted the detectives to her apartment in a Riverhead housing development, and then immediately sat down.

'You have to forgive me,' she said. 'My back aches. The doctor thinks maybe it'll be twins. That's all I need is twins.' She pressed the palms of her hands into the small of her back, sighed heavily, and said, 'I'm always having a baby. I got married when I was seventeen, and I've been pregnant ever since. All my kids think I'm a fat woman. They've never seen me that I wasn't pregnant.' She sighed again. 'You got any children?' she asked Meyer.

'Three,' he answered.

'I sometimes wish . . .' She stopped and pulled a curious face, a face which denied dreams.

'What do you wish, Mrs Granavan?' Hawes asked.

'That I could go to Bermuda. Alone.' She paused. 'Have you ever been to Bermuda?'

'No.'

'I hear it's very nice there,' Irene Granavan said wistfully, and the apartment went still.

'Mrs Granavan,' Meyer said, 'we'd like to ask you a few questions about your brother.'

'What's he done now?'

'Has he done things before?' Hawes said.

'Well, you know . . .' She shrugged.

125

'What?' Meyer asked.

'Well, the fuss down at City Hall. And the picketing of that movie. You know.'

'We don't know, Mrs Granavan.'

'Well, I hate to say this about my own brother, but I think he's a little nuts on the subject. You know.'

'What subject?'

'Well, the movie, for example. It's about Israel, and him and his friends picketed it and all, and handed out pamphlets about Jews, and . . . You remember, don't you? The crowd threw stones at him and all. There were a lot of concentration-camp survivors in the crowd, you know.' She paused. 'I think he must be a little nuts to do something like that, don't you think?'

'You said something about City Hall, Mrs Granavan. What did your brother—'

'Well, it was when the mayor invited this Jewish assemblyman – I forget his name – to make a speech with him on the steps of City Hall. My brother went down and – well, the same business. You know.'

'You mentioned your brother's friends. What friends?'

'The nuts he hangs out with.'

'Would you know their names?' Meyer wanted to know.

'I know only one of them. He was here once with my brother. He's got pimples all over his face. I remember him because I was pregnant with Sean at the time, and he asked if he could put his hands on my stomach to feel the baby kicking. I told him he certainly could not. That shut *him* up, all right.'

'What was his name, Mrs Granavan?'

'Fred. That's short for Frederick. Frederick Schultz.'

'He's German?' Meyer asked.

'Yes.'

Meyer nodded briefly.

126

'Mrs Granavan,' Hawes said, 'was your brother here last night?'

'Why? Did he say he was?'

'Was he?'

'No.'

'Not at all?'

'No. He wasn't here last night. I was home alone last night. My husband bowls on Saturdays.' She paused. 'I sit at home and hug my fat belly, and he bowls. You know what I wish sometimes?'

'What?' Meyer asked.

And, as if she had not said it once before, Irene Granavan said, 'I wish I could go to Bermuda sometime. Alone.'

'The thing is,' the house painter said to Carella. 'I'd like my ladder back.'

'I can understand that,' Carella said.

'The brushes they can keep, although some of them are very expensive brushes. But the ladder I absolutely need. I'm losing a day's work already because of those guys down at your lab.'

'Well, you see—'

'I go back to the synagogue this morning, and my ladder and my brushes and even my paints are all gone. And what a mess somebody made of that alley! So this old guy who's sexton of the place he tells me the priest was killed Saturday night, and the cops took all the stuff away with them. I wanted to know what cops, and he said he didn't know. So I called Headquarters this morning, and I got a runaround from six different cops who finally put me through to some guy named Grossman at the lab.'

'Yes, Lieutenant Grossman,' Carella said.

'That's right. And he tells me I can't have my god-damn ladder back until they finish their tests on it. Now

127

what the hell do they expect to find on my ladder, would you mind telling me?'

'I don't know, Mr Cabot. Fingerprints, perhaps.'

'Yeah, *my* fingerprints! Am I gonna get involved in murder *besides* losing a day's work?'

'I don't think so,' Carella said, smiling.

'I shouldn't have taken that job, anyway,' Cabot said. 'I shouldn't have even bothered with it.'

'Who hired you for the job, Mr Cabot?'

'The priest did.'

'The rabbi, you mean?' Carella asked.

'Yeah, the priest, the rabbi, whatever the hell you call him.' Cabot shrugged.

'And what were you supposed to do, Mr Cabot?'

'I was supposed to paint. What do you think I was supposed to do?'

'Paint what?'

'The trim. Around the windows and the roof.'

'White and blue?'

'White around the windows, and blue for the roof trim.'

'The colours of Israel,' Carella said.

'Yeah,' the painter agreed. Then he said, 'What?'

'Nothing. Why did you say you shouldn't have taken the job, Mr Cabot?'

'Well, because of all the arguing first. He wanted it done for Peaceable, he said, and Peaceable fell on the first. But I couldn't—'

'Peaceable? You mean Passover?'

'Yeah, Peaceable, Passover, whatever the hell you call it.' He shrugged again.

'You were about to say?'

'I was about to say we had a little argument about it. I was working on another job, and I couldn't get to his job until Friday, the thirty-first. I figured I'd work late into the night, you know, but the priest told me I couldn't

128

work after sundown. So I said, why can't I work after sundown, so he said the Sabbath began at sundown, not to mention the first day of Peace-Passover, and that work wasn't allowed on the first two days of Passover, nor on the Sabbath neither, for that matter. Because the Lord rested on the Sabbath, you see. The seventh day.'

'Yes, I see.'

'Sure. So I said, "Father, I'm not of the Jewish faith," is what I said, "and I can work any day of the week I like." Besides, I got a big job to start on Monday, and I figured I could knock off the church all day Friday and Friday night or, if worse came to worse, Saturday, for which I usually get time and a half. So we compromised.'

'How did you compromise?'

'Well, this priest was of what you call the Conservative crowd, not the Reformers, which are very advanced, but still these Conservatives don't follow all the old rules of the religion is what I gather. So he said I could work during the day Friday, and then I could come back and work Saturday, provided I knocked off at sundown. Don't ask me what kind of crazy compromise it was. I think he had in mind that he holds mass at sundown and it would be a mortal sin if I was outside painting while everybody was inside praying, and on a very special high holy day, at that.'

'I see. So you painted until sundown Friday?'

'Right.'

'And then you came back Saturday morning?'

'Right. But what it was, the windows needed a lot of putty, and the sills needed scraping and sanding, so by sundown Saturday, I still wasn't finished with the job. I had a talk with the priest, who said he was about to go inside and pray, and could I come back after services to finish off the job? I told him I had a better idea. I would come back Monday morning and knock off the little bit that had to be done before I went on to this very big job I got in Majesta — it's painting a whole factory; that's a big job. So I left everything right where it was in back of the church. I figured, who'd steal anything from right behind a church. Am I right?'

'Right,' Carella said.

'Yeah. Well, you know who'd steal them from right behind a church?'

'Who?'

'The cops!' Cabot shouted. 'That's who! Now how the hell do I get my ladder back, would you please tell me? I got a call from the factory today. They said if I don't start work tomorrow, at the latest, I can forget all about the job. And me without a ladder!'

'Maybe we've got a ladder downstairs you can borrow,' Carella said.

'Mister, I need a tall painter's ladder. This is a very high factory. Can you call this Captain Grossman and ask him to please let me have my ladder back? I got mouths to feed.'

'I'll talk to him, Mr Cabot,' Carella said. 'Leave me your number, will you?'

'I tried to borrow my brother-in-law's ladder — he's a paper hanger — but he's papering this movie star's apartment, downtown on Jefferson. So just try to get *his* ladder. Just try.'

'Well, I'll call Grossman,' Carella said.

'The other day, what she done, this movie actress, she marched into the living room wearing only this towel, you see? She wanted to know what—'

'I'll call Grossman,' Carella said.

As it turned out, he didn't have to call Grossman, because a lab report arrived late that afternoon, together with Cabot's ladder and the rest of his working equipment, including his brushes, his putty knife, several cans of linseed oil and turpentine, a pair of paint-stained gloves and two dropcloths. At about the same time the report arrived, Grossman called from downtown, saving Carella a dime.

'Did you get my report?' Grossman asked.

'I was just reading it.'

'What do you make of it?'

'I don't know,' Carella said.

'Want my guess?'

'Sure I'm always interested in what the layman thinks,' Carella answered him.

'Layman, I'll give you a hit on the head!' Grossman answered laughing. 'You notice the rabbi's prints were on those paint-can lids, and also on the ladder?'

'Yes, I did.'

'The ones on the lids were thumb prints, so I imagine the rabbi put those lids back on to the paint cans or, if they were already on the cans, pushed down on them to make sure they were secure.'

'Why would he want to do that?'

'Maybe he was moving the stuff. There's a tool shed behind the synagogue. Had you noticed that?'

'No, I hadn't.'

'Tch-tch, big detective. Yeah, there's one there, all right, about fifty yards behind the building. So I figure the painter rushed off, leaving his junk all over the back yard, and the rabbi was moving it to the tool shed when he was surprised by the killer.'

'Well, the painter did leave his stuff there, that's true. He expected to come back Monday morning.'

'Today, yeah,' Grossman said. 'But maybe the rabbi figured he didn't want his back yard looking like a pigsty, especially since this is Passover. So he took it into his head to move the stuff over to the tool shed. This is just speculation, you understand.'

131

'No kidding?' Carella said. 'I thought it was sound, scientific deduction.'

'Go to hell. Those *are* thumb prints on the lids, so it's logical to conclude he pressed down on them. And the prints on the ladder seem to indicate he was carrying it.'

'This report said you didn't find any prints but the rabbi's,' Carella said. 'Isn't that just a little unusual?'

'You didn't read it right,' Grossman said. 'We found a portion of a print on one of the paintbrushes. And we also—'

'Oh yeah,' Carella said, 'here it is. This doesn't say much, Sam.'

'What do you want me to do? It seems to be a tented-arch pattern, like the rabbi's, but there's too little to tell. The print could have been left on that brush by someone else.'

'Like the painter?'

'No. We've pretty much decided the painter used gloves while he worked. Otherwise, we'd have found a flock of similar prints on all the tools.'

'Then who left that print on the brush? The killer?'

'Maybe.'

'But the portion isn't enough to get anything positive on?'

'Sorry, Steve.'

'So your guess on what happened is that the rabbi went outside after services to clean up the mess. The killer surprised him, knifed him, made a mess of the alley, and then painted that J on the wall. Is that it?'

'I guess so, though—'

'What?'

'Well, there was a lot of blood leading right over to that wall, Steve. As if the rabbi had crawled there after he'd been stabbed.'

'Probably trying to get to the back door of the synagogue.'

'Maybe,' Grossman said. 'One thing I can tell you. Whoever killed him must have been pretty much of a mess when he got home. No doubt about that.'

'Why do you say that?'

'That spattered paint all over the alley,' Grossman said. 'It's my guess that the rabbi threw those paint cans at his attacker.'

'You're a pretty good guesser, Sam,' Carella told him, grinning.

'Thanks,' Grossman said.

'Tell me something.'

'Yeah?'

'You ever solve any murders?'

'Go to hell,' Grossman said, and he hung up.

9.

ALONE WITH HIS wife that night in the living room of their apartment, Meyer tried to keep his attention *off* a television series about cops and *on* the various documents he had collected from Rabbi Solomon's study in the synagogue. The cops on television were shooting up a storm, blank bullets flying all over the place and killing hoodlums by the score. It almost made a working man like Meyer Meyer wish for an exciting life of romantic adventure.

The romantic adventure of *his* life, Sarah Lipkin Meyer, sat in an easy chair opposite the television screen, her legs crossed, absorbed in the fictional derring-do of the policemen.

'Ooooh, *get* him!' Sarah screamed at one point, and Meyer turned to look at her curiously, and then went back to the rabbi's books.

The rabbi kept a ledger of expenses, all of which had to do with the synagogue and his duties there. The ledger did not make interesting reading, and told Meyer nothing he wanted to know. The rabbi also kept a calendar of synagogue events and Meyer glanced through them reminiscently, remembering his own youth and the busy Jewish life centring around the synagogue in the neighbourhood adjacent to his own. *March twelfth*, the calendar read, *regular Sunday breakfast of the Men's Club. Speaker, Harry Pine, director of Commission on International Affairs of American Jewish Congress. Topic: The Eichmann Case.*

Meyer's eye ran down the list of events itemized in Rabbi Solomon's book:

12 March, 7.15 p.m.
Youth Group meeting.

18 March, 9.30 a.m.
Bar Mitzvah services for Nathan Rothman. Kiddush after services. Open invitation to Centre membership.

22 March, 8.45 p.m.
Clinton Samuels, Assistant Professor of Philosophy in Education, Brandeis University, will lead discussion in 'The Matter of Identity for the Jews in Modern America'.

26 March
Eternal Light Radio. 'The Search' by Virginia Mazer, biographical script on Lillian Wald, founder of Henry Street Settlement in New York.

Meyer looked up from the calendar. 'Sarah?' he said.

'Shhh, shhh, just a minute,' Sarah answered. She was nibbling furiously at her thumb, her eyes glued to the silent television screen. An ear-shattering volley of shots suddenly erupted, all but smashing the picture tube. The theme music came up, and Sarah let out a deep sigh and turned to her husband.

Meyer looked at her curiously, as if seeing her for the first time, remembering the Sarah Lipkin of long, long ago and wondering if the Sarah Meyer of today was very much different from that initial exciting image. 'Nobody's lips kin like Sarah's lips kin,' the fraternity boys had chanted, and Meyer had memorized the chant, and investigated the possibilities, learning for the first time in his life that every cliché bears a kernel of folklore. He looked at her mouth now, pursed in puzzlement as she studied his face. Her eyes were blue, and her hair was brown, and she had a damn good figure and splendid

135

legs, and he nodded in agreement with his youthful judgement.

'Sarah, do you feel any identity as a Jew in modern America?' he asked.

'What?' Sarah said.

'I said—'

'Oh, boy,' Sarah said. 'What brought *that* on?'

'The rabbi, I guess.' Meyer scratched his bald pate. 'I guess I haven't felt so much like a Jew since— since I was confirmed, I guess. It's a funny thing.'

'Don't let it trouble you,' Sarah said gently. 'You *are* a Jew.'

'Am I?' he asked, and he looked straight into her eyes.

She returned the gaze. 'You have to answer that one for yourself,' she said.

'I know I— well, I get mad as hell thinking about this guy Finch. Which isn't good, you know. After all, maybe he's innocent.'

'Do you think so?'

'No. I think he did it. But is it *me* who thinks that, Meyer Meyer, Detective Second Grade? Or is it Meyer Meyer who got beat up by the *goyim* when he was a kid, and Meyer Meyer who heard his grandfather tell stories about pogroms, or who listened to the radio and heard what Hitler was doing in Germany, or who nearly strangled a German colonel with his bare hands just outside—'

'You can't separate the two, darling,' Sarah said.

'Maybe you can't. I'm only trying to say I never much felt like a Jew until this case came along. Now, all of a sudden . . .' He shrugged.

'Shall I get your prayer shawl?' Sarah said, smiling.

'Wise guy,' Meyer said. He closed the rabbi's calendar, and opened the next book on the desk. The book was a personal diary. He unlocked it, and began leafing through it.

Friday, 6 January
Shabbat, Parshat Shemot. I lighted the candles at 4.24.
Evening services were at 6.15. It has been a hundred
years since the Civil War. We discussed the Jewish
Community of the South, then and now.

18 January
It seems odd to me that I should have to familiarize the
membership about the proper blessings over the Sabbath
candles. Have we come so far towards forgetfulness?

*Baruch ata adonai elohenu melech haolam asher kidshanu
b'mitzvotav vitzivanu l'hadlick ney shel shabbat.*

Blessed are Thou O Lord our God, King of the
universe who hast sanctified us by Thy laws and com-
manded us to kindle the Sabbath Light.

Perhaps he is right. Perhaps the Jews are doomed.

20 January
I had hoped that the Maccabean festival would make us
realize the hardships borne by the Jews 2,000 years ago
in comparison to our good and easy lives today in a
democracy. Today, we have the freedom to worship as we
desire, but this should impose upon us the responsibility
of enjoying that freedom. And yet Hanukkah has come
and gone, and it seems to me The Feast of Lights taught
us nothing, gave us nothing more than a joyous holiday
to celebrate.

The Jews will die, he says.

2 February
I believe I am beginning to fear him. He shouted threats
at me today, said that I, of all the Jews, would lead the
way to destruction. I was tempted to call the police, but
I understand he has done this before. There are those in
the membership who have suffered his harangues and

who seemed to feel he is harmless. But he rants with the fervour of a fanatic, and his eyes frighten me.

12 February
A member called today to ask me something about the dietary laws. I was forced to call the local butcher because I did not know the prescribed length of the *hallof*, the slaughtering knife. Even the butcher, in jest, said to me that a real rabbi would know these things. I *am* a real rabbi. I believe in the Lord, my God, I teach His will and His law to His people. What need a rabbi know about *shehitoh*, the art of slaughtering animals? Is it important to know that the slaughtering knife must be twice the width of the throat of the slaughtered animal, and no more than fourteen finger breadths in length? The butcher told me that the knife must be sharp and smooth, with no perceptible notches. It is examined by passing finger and fingernail over both edges of the blade before and after slaughtering. If a notch is found, the animal is then unfit. Now I know. But is it necessary to know this? Is it not enough to love God, and to teach His ways?

His anger continues to frighten me.

14 February
I found a knife in the ark today, at the rear of the cabinet behind the Torah.

8 March
We had no further use of the Bibles we replaced, and since they were old and tattered, but nonetheless ritual articles containing the name of God, we buried them in the back yard, near the tool shed.

I must see about contacting a painter to do the outside of the synagogue. Someone suggested a Mr Frank Cabot who lives in the neighbourhood. I will call him tomorrow, perhaps. Passover will be coming soon, and I would like the temple to look nice.

The mystery is solved. It is kept for trimming the wick in the oil lamp over the ark.

The telephone rang. Meyer, absorbed in the diary, didn't even hear it. Sarah went to the phone and lifted it from the cradle.

'Hello?' she said. 'Oh, hello, Steve. How are you?' She laughed and said, 'No, I was watching television. That's right.' She laughed again. 'Yes, just a minute, I'll get him.' She put the phone down and walked to where Meyer was working. 'It's Steve,' she said. 'He wants to speak to you.'

'Huh?'

'The phone. Steve.'

'Oh,' Meyer nodded. 'Thanks.' He walked over to the phone and lifted the receiver. 'Hello, Steve,' he said.

'Hi. Can you get down here right away?'

'Why? What's the matter?'

'Finch,' Carella said. 'He's broken jail.'

10.

FINCH HAD BEEN kept in the detention cells of the precinct house all day Sunday where, it being Easter, he had been served turkey for his midday meal. On Monday morning, he'd been transported by van to Headquarters downtown on High Street where, as a felony offender, he participated in that quaint police custom known simply as 'the line-up'. He had been mugged and printed afterwards in the basement of the building, and then led across the street to the Criminal Courts Building where he had been arraigned for first-degree murder and, over his lawyer's protest, ordered to be held without bail until trial. The police van had then transported him crosstown to the house of detention on Canopy Avenue where he'd remained all day Monday, until after the evening meal. At that time, those offenders who had committed, or who were alleged to have committed, the most serious crimes, were once more shackled and put into the van, which carried them uptown and south to the edge of the River Dix for transportation by ferry to the prison on Walker Island.

He'd made his break, Carella reported, while he was being moved from the van to the ferry. According to what the harbour police said, Finch was still handcuffed and wearing prison garb. The break had taken place at about ten p.m. It was assumed that it had been witnessed by several dozen hospital attendants waiting for the ferry which would take them to Dix Sanitarium, a city-owned-and-operated hospital for drug addicts, situated in the middle of the river about a mile and a half from

140

the prison. It was also assumed that the break had been witnessed by a dozen or more water rats who leaped among the dock pilings and who, because of their size, were sometimes mistaken for pussy cats by neighbourhood kids who played near the river's edge. Considering the fact that Finch was dressed in drab grey uniform and handcuffs – a dazzling display of sartorial elegance, to be sure, but not likely to be seen on any other male walking the city streets – it was amazing that he hadn't yet been picked up. They had, of course, checked his apartment first, finding nothing there but the four walls and the furniture. One of the unmarried detectives on the squad, probably hoping for an invitation to go along, suggested that they look up Eleanor Fay, Finch's girl. Wasn't it likely he'd head for her pad? Carella and Meyer agreed that it was entirely likely, clipped their holsters on, neglected to offer the invitation to their colleague, and went out into the night.

It was a nice night, and Eleanor Fay lived in a nice neighbourhood of old brownstones wedged in between new, all-glass apartment houses with garages below the sidewalk. April had danced across the city and left her subtle warmth in the air. The two men drove in one of the squad's sedans, the windows rolled down. They did not say much to each other, April had robbed them of speech. The police radio droned its calls endlessly; radio motor patrolmen all over the city acknowledged violence and mayhem.

'There it is,' Meyer said. 'Just up ahead.'

'Now try to find a parking spot,' Carella complained.

They circled the block twice before finding an opening in front of a drugstore on the avenue. They got out of the car, left it unlocked, and walked briskly in the balmy night. The brownstone was in the middle of the block. They climbed the twelve steps to the vestibule, and studied the name plates alongside the buzzers. Eleanor Fay was in apartment 2B. Without hesitation, Carella pressed the buzzer for apartment 5A. Meyer took the doorknob in his hand and waited. When the answering click came, he twisted the knob, and silently they headed for the steps to the second floor.

Kicking in a door is an essentially rude practice. Neither Carella nor Meyer were particularly lacking in good manners, but they were looking for a man accused of murder, and a man who had successfully broken jail. It was not unnatural to assume this was a desperate man, and so they didn't even discuss whether or not they would kick in the door. They aligned themselves in the corridor outside apartment 2B. The wall opposite the door was too far away to serve as a springboard. Meyer, the heavier of the two men, backed away from the door, then hit it with his shoulder. He hit it hard and close to the lock. He wasn't attempting to shatter the door itself, an all but impossible feat. All he wanted to do was spring the lock. All the weight of his body concentrated in the padded spot of arm and shoulder which collided with the door just above the lock. The lock itself remained locked, but the screws holding it to the jamb could not resist the force of Meyer's fleshy battering ram. The wood around the screws splintered, the threads lost their friction grip, the door shot inwards and Meyer followed it into the room. Carella, like a quarterback carrying the ball behind powerful interference, followed Meyer.

It's rare that a cop encounters raw sex in his daily routine. The naked bodies he sees are generally cold and covered with caked blood. Even vice-squad cops find the act of love sordid rather than enticing. Eleanor Fay was lying full length on the living-room couch with a man. The television set in front of the couch was going, but nobody was watching either the news or the weather.

142

When the two men with drawn guns piled into the room behind the imploding door, Eleanor Fay sat bolt upright on the couch, her eyes wide in surprise. She was naked to the waist. She was wearing tight-fitting black tapered slacks and black high-heeled pumps. Her hair was disarranged and her lipstick had been kissed from her mouth, and she tried to cover her exposed breasts with her hands the moment the cops entered, realized the task was impossible, and grabbed the nearest article of clothing, which happened to be the man's suit jacket. She held it up in front of her like the classic, surprised heroine in a pirate movie. The man beside her sat up with equal suddenness, turned towards the cops, then turned back to Eleanor, puzzled, as if seeking an explanation from her.

The man was not Arthur Finch.

He was a man in his late twenties. He had a lot of pimples on his face, and a lot of lipstick stains. His white shirt was open to the waist. He wore no undershirt.

'Hello, Miss Fay,' Meyer said.

'I didn't hear you knock,' Eleanor answered. She seemed to recover instantly from her initial surprise and embarrassment. With total disdain for the two detectives, she threw the jacket aside, rose and walked like a burlesque queen to a hard-backed chair over which her missing clothing was draped. She lifted a brassiere, shrugged into it, clasped it, all as if she were alone in the room. Then she pulled a black, long-sleeved sweater over her head, shook out her hair, lighted a cigarette, and said. 'Is breaking and entering only a crime for criminals?'

'We're sorry, Miss,' Carella said. 'We're looking for your boyfriend.'

'Me?' the man on the couch asked. 'What'd I do?'

A glance of puzzlement passed between Meyer and

Carella. Something like understanding, faint and none too clear, touched Carella's face.

'Who are you?' he said.

'You don't have to tell them anything,' Eleanor cautioned. 'They're not allowed to break in like this. Private citizens have rights, too.'

'That's right, Miss Fay,' Meyer said. 'Why'd you lie to us?'

'I didn't lie to anybody.'

'You gave us false information about Finch's whereabouts on—'

'I wasn't aware I was under oath at the time.'

'You weren't. But you were damn well maliciously impeding the progress of an investigation.'

'The hell with you *and* your investigation. You horny bastards bust in here like—'

'We're sorry we spoiled your party,' Carella said. 'Why'd you lie about Finch?'

'I thought I was helping you,' Eleanor said. 'Now get the hell out of here.'

'We're staying a while, Miss Fay,' Meyer said, 'so get off your high horse. How'd you figure you were helping us? By sending us on a wild-goose chase confirming alibis you knew were false?'

'I didn't know anything. I told you just what Arthur told me.'

'That's a lie.'

'Why don't you get out?' Eleanor said. 'Or are you hoping I'll take off my sweater again?'

'What you've got, we've already seen, lady,' Carella said. He turned to the man. 'What's your name?'

'Don't tell him,' Eleanor said.

'Here or uptown, take your choice,' Carella said. 'Arthur Finch has broken jail, and we're trying to find him. If you want to be accessories to—'

144

'Broken jail?' Eleanor went a trifle pale. She glanced at the man on the couch, and their eyes met.

'Wh-when did this happen?' the man asked.

'About ten o'clock tonight.'

The man was silent for several moments. 'That's not so good,' he said at last.

'How about telling us who you are,' Carella suggested.

'Frederick Schultz,' the man said.

'That makes it all very cosy, doesn't it?' Meyer said.

'Get your mind out of the gutter,' Eleanor said. 'I'm not Finch's girl, and I never was.'

'Then why'd you say you were?'

'I didn't want Freddie to get involved in this thing.'

'How could he possibly get involved?'

Eleanor shrugged.

'What is it? Was Finch with Freddie on Saturday night?'

Eleanor nodded reluctantly.

'From what time to what time?'

'From seven to ten,' Freddie said.

'Then he couldn't have killed the rabbi.'

'Who said he did?' Freddie answered.

'Why didn't you tell us this?'

'Because . . .' Eleanor started, and then stopped dead.

'Because they had something to hide,' Carella said. 'Why'd he come to see you, Freddie?'

Freddie did not answer.

'Hold it,' Meyer said. 'This is the other Jew-hater, Steve. The one Finch's sister told me about. Isn't that right, Freddie?'

Freddie did not answer.

'Why'd he come to see you, Freddie? To pick up those pamphlets we found in his closet?'

'You the guy who prints that crap, Freddie?'

'What's the matter, Freddie? Weren't you sure how much of a crime was involved?'

'Did you figure he'd tell us where he got the stuff, Freddie?'

'You're a real good pal, aren't you, Freddie? You'd send your friend to the chair rather than—'

'I don't owe him anything!' Freddie said.

'Maybe you owe him a lot. He was facing a murder rap, but he never once mentioned your name. You went to all that trouble for nothing, Miss Fay.'

'It was no trouble,' Eleanor said thinly.

'No,' Meyer said. 'You marched into the precinct with a tight dress and a cockamamie bunch of alibis that you knew we'd check. You figured once we found those to be phony, we wouldn't believe anything else Finch said. Even if he told us where he *really* was, we wouldn't believe it. That's right, isn't it?'

'You finished?' Eleanor asked.

'No, but I think you are,' Meyer answered.

'You had no right to bust in here. There's no law against making love.'

'Sister,' Carella said, '*you* were making hate.'

11.

ARTHUR FINCH WASN'T making anything when they found him.

They found him at ten minutes past two, on the morning of April fourth. They found him in his apartment because a patrolman had been sent there to pick up the pamphlets in his closet. They found him lying in front of the kitchen table. He was still handcuffed. A file and rasp were on the table top, and there were metal filings covering the enamel and a spot on the linoleum floor, but Finch had made only a small dent in the manacles. The filings on the floor were floating in a red, sticky substance.

Finch's throat was open from ear to ear.

The patrolman, expecting to make a routine pickup, found the body and had the presence of mind to call his patrol-car partner before he panicked. His partner went down to the car and radioed the homicide to Headquarters, who informed Homicide South and the detectives of the 87th Squad.

The patrolmen were busy that night. At three a.m., a citizen called in to report what he thought was a leak in a water main on South Fifth. The radio dispatcher at Headquarters sent a car to investigate, and the patrolman found that nothing was wrong with the water main, but something was interfering with the city's fine sewage system.

The men were not members of the Department of Sanitation, but they nonetheless climbed down a manhole into the stink and garbage, and located a man's black suit caught on an orange crate and blocking a pipe, causing the water to back up into the street. The man's suit was spattered with white and blue paint. The patrolmen were ready to throw it into the nearest garbage can when one of them noticed it was also spattered with something that could have been dried blood. Being conscientious law-enforcement officers, they combed the garbage out of their hair and delivered the garment to their precinct house – which happened to be the 87th.

Meyer and Carella were delighted to receive the suit.

It didn't tell them a goddamned thing about who owned it, but it nonetheless indicated to them that whoever had killed the rabbi was now busily engaged in covering his tracks and this, in turn, indicated a high state of anxiety. Somebody had heard the news broadcast announcing Finch's escape. Somebody had been worried about Finch establishing an alibi for himself that would doubtlessly clear him.

With twisted reasoning somebody figured the best way to cover one homicide was to commit another. And somebody had hastily decided to get rid of the garments he'd worn while disposing of the rabbi.

The detectives weren't psychologists, but two mistakes had been committed in the same early morning, and they figured their prey was getting slightly desperate.

'It has to be another of Finch's crowd,' Carella said. 'Whoever killed Solomon painted a J on the wall. If he'd had time, he probably would have drawn a swastika as well.'

'But why would he do that?' Meyer asked. 'He'd automatically be telling us that an anti-Semite killed the rabbi.'

'So? How many anti-Semites do you suppose there are in this city?'

148

'How many?' Meyer asked.

'I wouldn't want to count them,' Carella said. 'Whoever killed Yaakov Solomon was bold enough to—'

'Jacob,' Meyer corrected.

'Yaakov, Jacob, what's the difference? The killer was bold enough to presume there were plenty of people who felt exactly the way he did. He painted that J on the wall and dared us to find *which* Jew-hater had done the job.' Carella paused. 'Does this bother you very much, Meyer?'

'Sure, it bothers me.'

'I mean, my saying—'

'Don't be a boob, Steve.'

'Okay. I think we ought to look up this woman again. What was her name? Hannah something. Maybe she knows—'

'I don't think that'll help us. Maybe we ought to talk to the rabbi's wife. There's indication in his diary that he knew the killer, that he'd had threats. Maybe she knows who was baiting him.'

'It's four o'clock in the morning,' Carella said. 'I don't think it's a good idea right now.'

'We'll go after breakfast.'

'It won't hurt to talk to Yirmiyahu again, either. If the rabbi was threatened, maybe—'

'Jeremiah,' Meyer corrected.

'What?'

'Jeremiah. Yirmiyahu is Hebrew for Jeremiah.'

'Oh. Well, anyway, him. It's possible the rabbi took him into his confidence, mentioned this—'

'Jeremiah,' Meyer said again.

'What?'

'No.' Meyer shook his head. 'That's impossible. He's a holy man. And if there's anything a really good Jew despises, it's—'

'What are you talking about?' Carella said.

'—it's killing. Judaism teaches that you don't murder, unless in self-defence.' His brow suddenly furrowed into a frown. 'Still, remember when I was about to light that cigarette? He asked me if I was Jewish – remember? He was shocked that I would smoke on the second day of Passover.'

'Meyer, I'm a little sleepy. Who are you talking about?' Carella wanted to know.

'Yirmiyahu. Jeremiah. Steve, you don't think—'

'I'm just not following you, Meyer.'

'You don't think . . . you don't think the rabbi painted that wall *himself*, do you?'

'Why would . . . what do you mean?'

'To tell us who'd stabbed him? To tell us who the killer was?'

'How would—'

'Jeremiah,' Meyer said.

Carella looked at Meyer silently for a full thirty seconds. Then he nodded and said, 'J.'

12.

HE WAS BURYING something in the back yard behind the synagogue when they found him. They had gone to his home first and awakened his wife. She was an old Jewish woman, her head shaved in keeping with the Orthodox tradition. She covered her head with a shawl, and she sat in the kitchen of her ground-floor apartment and tried to remember what had happened on the second night of Passover. Yes, her husband had gone to the synagogue for evening services. Yes, he had come home directly after services.

'Did you see him when he came in?' Meyer asked.

'I was in the kitchen,' Mrs Cohen answered. 'I was preparing the *seder*. I heard the door open, and he went in the bedroom.'

'Did you see what he was wearing?'

'No.'

'What was he wearing during the *seder*?'

'I don't remember.'

'Had he changed his clothes, Mrs Cohen? Would you remember that?'

'I think so, yes. He had on a black suit when he went to temple. I think he wore a different suit after.' The old woman looked bewildered. She didn't know why they were asking these questions. Nonetheless, she answered them.

'Did you smell anything strange in the house, Mrs Cohen?'

'Smell?'

'Yes. Did you smell paint?'

151

'Paint? No. I smelled nothing strange.'

They found him in the yard behind the synagogue.

He was an old man with sorrow in his eyes and in the stoop of his posture. He had a shovel in his hands, and he was patting the earth with the blade. He nodded, as if he knew why they were there. They faced each other across the small mound of freshly turned earth at Yirmiyahu's feet.

Carella did not say a solitary word during the questioning and arrest. He stood next to Meyer Meyer, and he felt only an odd sort of pain.

'What did you bury, Mr Cohen?' Meyer asked. He spoke very softly. It was five o'clock in the morning, and night was fleeing the sky. There was a slight chill on the air. The wind seemed to penetrate to the sexton's marrow. He seemed on the verge of shivering. 'What did you bury, Mr Cohen? Tell me.'

'A ritual object,' the sexton answered.

'*What*, Mr Cohen?'

'I have no further use for it. It is a ritual object. I am sure it had to be buried. I must ask the *rov*. I must ask him what the Talmud says.' Yirmiyahu fell silent. He looked at the mound of earth at his feet. The *rov* is dead, isn't he?' he said, almost to himself. 'He is dead.' He looked sadly into Meyer's eyes.

'Yes,' Meyer answered.

'*Baruch dayyan haernet*,' Yirmiyahu said. 'You are Jewish?'

'Yes,' Meyer answered.

'Blessed be God the true judge,' Yirmiyahu translated, as if he had not heard Meyer.

'What did you bury, Mr Cohen?'

'The knife,' Yirmiyahu said. 'The knife I used to trim the wick. It *is* a ritual object, don't you think? It should be buried, don't you think?' He paused. 'You see . . .'

His shoulders began to shake. He began weeping suddenly. 'I killed,' he said. The sobs started somewhere deep within the man, started wherever his roots were, started in the soul of the man, in the knowledge that he had committed the unspeakable crime – thou shalt not kill, thou shalt not kill. 'I killed,' he said again, but this time there were only tears, no sobs.

'Did you kill Arthur Finch?' Meyer asked.

The sexton nodded.

'Did you kill Rabbi Solomon?'

'He . . . you see . . . he was working. It was the second day of Passover, and he was working. I was inside when I heard the noise. I went to look and . . . he was carrying paints, paint cans in one hand, and . . . a ladder in the other. He was *working*. I . . . took the knife from the ark, the knife I used to trim the wick. I had told him before this. I had told him he was not a real Jew, that his new . . . his new ways would be the end of the Jewish people. And this, *this*! To work on the second day of Passover!'

'What happened, Mr Cohen?' Meyer asked gently.

'I – the knife was in my hand. I went at him with the knife. He – he tried to stop me. He threw paint at me. I – I—' The sexton's right hand came up as if clasped around a knife. The hand trembled as it unconsciously re-enacted the events of that night. 'I cut him. I cut him . . . I killed him.'

Yirmiyahu stood in the alley with the sun intimidating the peaks of the buildings now. He stood with his head bent, staring down at the mound of earth which covered the buried knife. His face was thin and gaunt, a face tormented by the centuries. The tears still spilled from his eyes and coursed down his cheeks. His shoulders shook with the sobs that came from somewhere deep in his guts. Carella turned away because it seemed to him in that moment that he was watching the disintegration of a man, and he did not want to see it.

Meyer put his arm around the sexton's shoulder.

'Come, *tsadik*,' he said. 'Come. You must come with me now.'

The old man said nothing. His hands hung loosely at his sides.

They began walking slowly out of the alley. As they passed the painted J on the synagogue wall, the sexton said. *'Olov ha-shalom.'*

'What did he say?' Carella asked.

'He said, "Peace be upon him."'

'Amen,' Carella said.

They walked silently out of the alley together.

Storm

1.

THE GIRL WITH Cotton Hawes had cold feet.

He didn't know what to do about her feet because he'd already tried everything he could think of, and they were still cold. He had to admit that driving in subzero temperatures with a storm some fifteen minutes behind him wasn't exactly conducive to warm pedal extremities. But he had turned the car heater up full, supplied the girl with a blanket, taken off his overcoat and wrapped that around her – and she still had cold feet.

The girl's name was Blanche Colby, a very nice euphonic name which she had adopted the moment she entered show business. That had been a long time ago. Blanche's real name was Bertha Cooley, but a press agent those many years back told her that Bertha Cooley sounded like a mentholated Pullman, and not a dancer. Blanche Colby had class, he told her, and if there was one thing Bertha Cooley wanted, it was class. She had taken the new name and gone into the chorus of a hit musical twenty-two years ago, when she was only fifteen. She was now thirty-seven, but all those years of prancing the boards had left her with a youthful body, lithe and long-legged. She was still, with a slight assist from Clairol, a soft honey-blonde. Her green eyes were intelligent and alert. Her feet, unfortunately, *ahhhh*, her feet.

'How are they now?' he asked her.

'Freezing,' she said.

'We're almost there,' Hawes told her. 'You'll like this place. One of the guys on the squad – Hal Willis –

comes up here almost every weekend he's off. He says the skiing is great.'

'I know a dancer who broke her leg in Switzerland,' Blanche said.

'Skiing?'

'Sure, skiing.'

'You've never skied before?'

'Never.'

'Well . . .' Hawes shrugged. 'Well, I don't think you'll break any legs.'

'That's reassuring,' Blanche said. She glanced through the window on her side of the car. 'I think that storm is catching up to us.'

'Just a few flurries.'

'I wonder how serious it'll be. I have a rehearsal Monday night.'

'Four to six inches, they said. That's not very much.'

'Will the roads be open?'

'Sure. Don't worry.'

'I know a dancer who got snowed in for six days in Vermont,' Blanche said. 'It wouldn't have been so bad, but she was with a Method actor.'

'Well, I'm a cop,' Hawes said.

'Yeah,' Blanche answered noncommittally.

They were silent for several moments. The light snow flurries drifted across the road, turning it into a dream-like, white, flowing stream. The headlights illuminated the shifting macadam. Sitting behind the wheel, Hawes had the peculiar feeling that the road was melting. He was glad to see the sign for Rawson Mountain Inn. He stopped the car, picking out the sign from the tangle of other signs announcing accommodations in the area. He set the car in motion again, turning left over an old wooden bridge, the timbers creaking as the convertible passed over them. A new sign, blatant red and white, shouted the features of the area — a sixteen-hundred-foot mountain, two chair lifts, a T-Barr, a rope tow, and, definitely not needed with a storm on the way, a snow-making machine.

The inn lay nestled in the foothills at the base of the mountain. The trees around the inn were bare, standing in gaunt silhouette against the snow-threatening sky. Snow-nuzzled lights beckoned warmly. He helped Blanche out of the car, put on his overcoat, and walked with her over old packed snow to the entrance. They stamped their feet in the doorway and entered the huge room. A fire was going at one end of the room. Someone was playing the piano. A handful of tired weekday skiers were sprawled around the fireplace, wearing very fashionable after-ski boots and sweaters, drinking from bottles on to which they'd hand-lettered their names. Blanche went directly to the fire, found a place on one of the couches, and stretched her long legs to the blaze. Hawes found the desk, tapped a bell on it, and waited. No one appeared. He tapped the bell again. A skier passing the desk said, 'He's in the office. Over there on your left.'

Hawes nodded, found the door marked OFFICE, and knocked on it. A voice inside called, 'Yes, come in,' and Hawes twisted the knob and entered.

The office was larger than he'd expected, a good fifteen feet separating the entrance door from the desk at the opposite end of the room. A man in his late twenties sat behind the desk. He had dark hair and dark brows pulled low over deep brown eyes. He was wearing a white shirt open at the throat, a bold reindeer-imprinted sweater over it. He was also wearing a plaster cast on his right leg. The leg was stretched out stiffly in front of him, the foot resting on a low ottoman. A pair of crutches leaned against the desk, within easy reach of his hands. Hawes was suddenly glad he'd left Blanche by the fire.

'You're not a new skier, I hope,' the man said.

'No, I'm not.'

'Good. Some of them get scared by the cast and crutches.'

'Was it a skiing accident?' Hawes asked.

The man nodded. 'Spiral break of the tibia and fibula. Someone forgot to fill in a sitzmark. I was going pretty fast, and when I hit the hole . . .' He shrugged. 'I won't be able to walk without the crutches for at least another month.'

'That's too bad,' Hawes said. He paused, and then figured he might as well get down to business. 'I have a reservation,' he said. 'Adjoining rooms with bath.'

'Yes, sir. What was the name on that?'

'Cotton Hawes and Blanche Colby.'

The man opened a drawer in his desk and consulted a typewritten sheet. 'Yes, sir,' he said. 'Two rooms in the annexe.'

'The annexe?' Hawes said. 'Where's that?'

'Oh, just a hundred yards or so from the main building, sir.'

'Oh. Well, I guess that'll be . . .'

'And that's *one* bath, you understand.'

'What do you mean?'

'They're adjoining rooms, but the bathroom is in 104. 105 doesn't have a bath.'

'Oh. Well, I'd like two rooms that *do* have baths,' Hawes said, smiling.

'I'm sorry, sir. 104 and 105 are the only available rooms in the house.'

'The fellow I spoke to on the phone . . .'

'Yes, sir, that's me. Elmer Wollender.'

'How do you do?' Hawes said. 'You told me both rooms had baths.'

'No, sir. You said you wanted adjoining rooms with

bath, and I said I could give you adjoining rooms with bath. And that's what I've given you. Bath. Singular.'

'Are you a lawyer, Mr Wollender?' Hawes asked, no longer smiling.

'No, sir. Out of season, I'm a locksmith.'

'What are you in season?'

'Why, a hotel-keeper, sir,' Wollender said.

'Don't test the theory,' Hawes answered. 'Let me have my deposit back, Mr Wollender. We'll find another place to stay.'

'Well, sir, to begin with, we can't make any cash refunds, but we'll be happy to keep your deposit here against another time when you may wish . . .'

'Look, Mr Wollender,' Hawes said menacingly, 'I don't know what kind of a . . .'

'And of course, sir, there *are* lots of places to stay here in town, but none of them, sir, *none* of them have any private baths at all. Now if you don't mind walking down the hall . . .'

'All I know is . . .'

'. . . and sharing the john with a hundred other skiers, why then . . .'

'You told me on the phone . . .'

'I'm sure you can find other accommodations. The *lady*, however, might enjoy a little privacy.' Wollender waited while Hawes considered.

'If I give her 104 . . .' Hawes started and then paused. 'Is that the room with the bath?'

'Yes, sir, 104.'

'If I give her that room, where's the bath for 105?'

'Down at the end of the hall, sir. And we *are* right at the base of the mountain, sir, and the skiing *has* been excellent, and we're expecting at least twelve inches of fresh powder.'

'The radio said four to six.'

'That's in the city, sir. We normally get a lot more snow.'

'Like what I got on the phone?' Hawes asked. 'Where do I sign?'

2.

COTTON HAWES WAS a detective, and as a member of the 87th Squad he had flopped down in a great many desirable and undesirable rooms throughout the city and its suburbs. Once, while posing as a dock walloper, he had taken a furnished room overlooking the River Harb, and had been surprised during the night by what sounded like a band of midgets marching at the foot of his bed. The midgets turned out to be giants, or at least giants of the species *Rattus muridae* – or as they say in English, rats. He had turned on the light and picked up a broom, but those brazen rat bastards had reared back on their hind legs like boxers and bared their teeth, and he was certain the pack of them would leap for his throat. He had checked out immediately.

There were no rats in rooms 104 and 105 of the annexe to Rawsou Mountain Inn. Nor was there very much of anything else, either. Whoever had designed the accommodations was undoubtedly steeped in Spartan philosophy. The walls were white and bare, save for a single skiing poster over each bed. There was a single bed in each room, and a wooden dresser painted white. A portable cardboard clothes closet nestled in the corner of each room. The room Hawes hoped to occupy, the one without the bath, was excruciatingly hot, the vents sending in great waves of heated air. The room with the bath, Blanche's room, was unbearably cold. The single window was rimmed with frost, the floor was cold, the bed was cold, the heating ducts and vents were either clogged or blocked, but certainly inoperative.

'And *I'm* the one with the cold feet,' Blanche said.

'I'd let you have the heated room,' Hawes said gallantly, 'but this is the one with the bath.'

'Well, we'll manage,' Blanche said. 'Shall we go down for the bags?'

'I'll get them,' Hawes answered. 'Stay in my room for now, will you? There's no sense freezing in here.'

'I may get to like your room,' Blanche said archly, and then turned and walked past him through the connecting door.

He went down the long flight of steps to the front porch, and then beyond to where the car was parked. The rooms were over the ski shop, which was closed for the night now, silent and dark. He took the two valises out of the trunk, and then pulled his skis from the rack on top of the car. He was not a particularly distrustful man, but a pair of Head skis had been stolen from him the season before, and he'd been a cop long enough to know that lightning sometimes *did* strike twice in the same place. In his right hand, and under his right arm, he carried the two bags. In his left hand, and under his left arm, he carried his skis and his boots. He struggled through the deepening snow and on to the front porch. He was about to put down the bags in order to open the door when he heard the heavy thud of ski boots on the steps inside. Someone was coming down those steps in a hell of a hurry.

The door opened suddenly, and a tall thin man wearing black ski pants and a black-hooded parka came on to the porch, almost colliding with Hawes. His face was narrow, handsome in a fine-honed way, the sharply hooked nose giving it the edged striking appearance of an axe. Even in the pale light filtering from the hallway, Hawes saw that the man was deeply tanned, and automatically assumed he was an instructor. The guess was

164

corroborated by the Rawson Mountain insignia on the man's right sleeve, an interlocking R and M in bright red letters. Incongruously, the man was carrying a pair of white figure skates in his left hand.

'Oh, I'm sorry,' he said. His face broke into a grin. He had spoken with an accent, German or Swedish, Hawes couldn't tell which.

'That's all right,' Hawes said.

'May I help you?'

'No, I think I can manage. If you'd just hold the door open for me . . .'

'It will be my pleasure,' the man said, and he almost clicked his heels together.

'Has the skiing been good?' Hawes asked as he struggled through the narrow doorway.

'Fairly good,' the man answered. 'It will be better tomorrow.'

'Well, thanks,' Hawes said.

'My pleasure.'

'See you on the mountain,' Hawes said cheerfully and continued up the steps. There was something slightly ridiculous about the entire situation, the adjoining rooms with only one bath, the pristine cells the rooms had turned out to be, the heat in one, the cold in the other, the fact that they were over the ski shop, the fact that it had begun snowing very heavily, even the hurried ski instructor with his polite Teutonic manners and his guttural voice and his figure skates, there was something faintly reminiscent of farce about the whole set up. He began chuckling as he climbed the steps. When he came into his room, Blanche was stretched out on his bed. He put down the bags.

'What's so funny?' she asked.

'I've decided this is a comic-opera hotel,' Hawes said. 'I'll bet the mountain out there is only a backdrop. We'll go out there tomorrow morning and discover it's painted on canvas.'

'This room is nice and warm,' Blanche said.

'Yes, it is,' Hawes answered. He slid his skis under the bed, and she watched him silently.

'Are you expecting burglars?'

'You never can tell.' He took off his jacket and pulled his holstered service revolver from his back hip pocket.

'You going to wear that on the slopes tomorrow?' Blanche asked.

'No. You can't get a gun into those zippered pockets.'

'I think I'll stay in *this* room tonight,' Blanche said suddenly.

'Whatever you like,' Hawes said. 'I'll take the icebox next door.'

'Well, actually,' she said, 'that wasn't exactly what I had in mind.'

'Huh?'

'Don't detectives kiss people?'

'Huh?'

'We've been out twice together in the city, and we've just driven three hours alone together in a car, and you've never once tried to kiss me.'

'Well, I . . .'

'I wish you would,' Blanche said thoughtfully. 'Unless, of course, there's a department regulation against it.'

'None that I can think of,' Hawes said.

Blanche, her hands behind her head, her legs stretched luxuriously, suddenly took a deep breath and said, 'I think I'm going to like this place.'

3.

THERE WERE SOUNDS in the night.

Huddled together in the single bed, the first sound of which they were aware was the noise of the oil burner. At regularly spaced intervals, the thermostat would click, and there would be a thirty-second pause, and then a 707 jet aircraft would take off from the basement of the old wooden building. Hawes had never heard a noisier oil burner in his life. The aluminium ducts and vents provided a symphony all their own, too, expanding, contracting, banging, clanking, sighing, exhaling, whooshing. Down the hall, the toilet would be flushed every now and again, the noise sounding with cataract sharpness on the still mountain air.

There was another noise. A rasping sound, the narrow shrill squeak of metal upon metal. He got out of bed and went to the window. A light was burning in the ski shop below, casting a yellow rectangle on to the snow. Sighing, he went back to bed and tried to sleep.

Down the corridor, there was the constant thud of ski boots as guests returned to their rooms, the slamming of doors, the occasional high giggle of a girl skier intoxicated by the mountain air.

Voices.

'. . . will mean a slower track for the slalom . . .'

'Sure, but everyone'll have the same handicap . . .'

Fading.

More voices.

'. . . don't even think they'll open the upper trails.'

'They have to, don't they?'

'Not Dead Man's Fall. They won't even be able to get up there with all this snow. Seventeen inches already, and no end in sight.'

The 707 taking off again from the basement. The vents beginning their orchestral suite, the ducts supplying counterpoint. And more voices, raised in anger.

'. . . because he thinks he's God almighty!'

'I tell you you're imagining things.'

'I'm warning you! Stay away from him!'

A young girl's laughter.

'I'm warning you. If I see him . . .'

Fading.

At two o'clock in the morning, the Cats started up the mountain. They sounded like Rommel's mechanized cavalry. Hawes was certain they would knock down the outside walls and come lumbering into the room. Blanche began giggling.

'This is the noisiest hotel I've ever slept in,' she said.

'How are your feet?'

'Nice and warm. You're a very warm man.'

'You're a very warm girl.'

'Do you mind my sleeping in long johns?'

'I thought they were leotards.'

'Leotard is singular,' Blanche said.

'Singular or plural, those are the sexiest long johns I've ever seen.'

'It's only the girl in them,' Blanche said modestly. 'Why don't you kiss me again?'

'I will. In a minute.'

'What are you listening for?'

'I thought I heard an unscheduled flight a moment ago.'

'What?'

'Didn't you hear it? A funny buzzing sound?'

'There are so many noises . . .'

'Shhhh.'

They were silent for several moments. They could hear the Cats grinding their way up the mountain. Someone down the hall flushed the toilet. More boots in the corridor outside.

'Hey!' Blanche said.

'What?'

'You asleep?'

'No,' Hawes answered.

'That buzzing sound you heard?'

'Yes?'

'It was my blood,' she told him, and she kissed him on the mouth.

4.

IT WAS STILL snowing on Saturday morning. The promised storm had turned into a full-fledged blizzard. They dressed in the warm comfort of the room, Blanche putting on thermal underwear, and then two sweaters and stretch pants, the extra clothing padding out her slender figure. Hawes, standing six feet two inches tall in his double-stockinged feet, black pants and black sweater, presented a one-hundred-and-ninety-pound V-shaped silhouette to the window and the grey day outside.

'Do you think I'll get back in time for Monday night's rehearsal?' Blanche asked.

'I don't know. I'm supposed to be back at the squad by six tomorrow night. I wonder if the roads are open.'

They learned during breakfast that a state of emergency had been declared in the city and in most of the towns lining the upstate route. Blanche seemed blithely indifferent to the concept of being snowbound. 'If there's that much snow,' she said, 'they'll cancel the rehearsal, anyway.'

'They won't cancel the police department,' Hawes said.

'The hell with it,' Blanche said happily. 'We're here now, and there's marvellous snow, and if the skiing is good it'll be a wonderful weekend.'

'Even if the skiing is *lousy*,' Hawes said, 'it'll be a wonderful weekend.'

They rented boots and skis for her in the ski rental shop, and then took to the mountain. Both chair lifts were in operation, but as one of the midnight voices had

170

prophesied, the upper trails were not yet opened. A strong wind had arisen, and it blew the snow in driving white sheets across the slopes. Hawes took Blanche to the rope tow first, had her practise climbing for a while, teaching her to edge and to herringbone, and then illustrated the use of the tow – left hand clamped around the rope, right hand and arm behind the back and gripping the rope. The beginners' slope was a gentle one, but Blanche seemed immediately capable of more difficult skiing. She was a trained dancer, and she automatically thought of the skis as part of a difficult stage costume, encumbering movement, but simply something to overcome. With remarkable coordination, she learned how to snow-plough on the beginners' slope. By midmorning, she had graduated to the T-Bar, and was beginning to learn the rudiments of the stem christie. Hawes patiently stayed with her all morning, restricting his own skiing to the elementary slopes. He was becoming more and more grateful for the snow-clogged roads. With the roads impassable, the number of weekend skiers was limited; he and Blanche were enjoying weekday skiing on a Saturday, and the fresh snow made everything a delight.

After lunch, she suggested that he leave her alone to practise for a while. Hawes, who was itching to get at the chair lift and the real trails, nonetheless protested that he was perfectly content to ski with her on the baby slopes. But Blanche insisted, and he finally left her on the slope serviced by the T-Bar, and went to the longest of the chair lifts, Lift A.

He grinned unconsciously as he approached the lift. Eight or ten skiers were waiting to use the chairs, as compared to the long lines one usually encountered on weekends. As he approached the loading area, he caught a blur of black movement from the corner of his eye, turned and saw his German or Swedish ski instructor from the night before *wedeln* down the mountain, and then turning, parallel in a snow-spraying stop near the lift. He did not seem to recognize Hawes, but Hawes was not at all surprised. Every skier on the line was wearing a hooded parka, the hoods covering their heads and tied securely beneath their chins. In addition, all the skiers were wearing goggles, most with tinted yellow lenses in defence against the greyness of the day, some with darker lenses in spite of the greyness. The result, in any case, was almost total anonymity. Male and female, they all looked very much alike. They could have been a band of Martians waiting to be taken to a leader. Instead, they were waiting for chairs. They did not have to wait very long.

The chairs on their cable kept rounding the bend, came past the grinding machinery. Hawes moved into position, watched the girl ahead of him sit abruptly as the chair came up under her behind. He noticed that the chair gave a decided lurch as it cleared the platform, and he braced himself for the expected force, glanced back over his shoulder as another chair rounded the turn. Ski poles clutched in his left hand, his right hand behind him to grip the edge of the chair as it approached, he waited. The chair was faster and had a stronger lurch than he'd anticipated. For a moment, he thought it would knock him down. He gripped the edge of the seat with his mittened right hand, felt himself sliding off the seat, and automatically grabbed for the upright supporting rod with his left hand, dropping his poles.

'Dropped your poles!' one of the loaders shouted behind him.

'We'll send them up!' the other loader called.

He turned slightly in the chair and looked back. He could see one of the loaders scrambling to pick up his poles. There were two empty chairs behind him, and then a skier got into the third chair, and the loader handed him the poles Hawes had dropped. Behind that chair, two other skiers shared a chair. The wind and the snow made it difficult to see. Hawes turned his head abruptly, but the wind was even stronger coming down the mountain. The chair ahead of him was perhaps thirty feet away, but he could barely make out the shadowy figure of the person sitting in it. All he saw was a dim silhouette obscured by blinding snow and keening wind. He could feel snow seeping under the edges of his hood. He took off his mittens and tightened the string. Quickly, before the biting cold numbed his fingers, he put the mittens on again.

The lift was a new one, and it pulled the chairs silently up the mountain. On his right, Hawes could see the skiers descending, a damn fool snowploughing out of control down a steep embankment pocked with moguls, an excellent skier navigating turns in parallel precision. The wind keened around and under his hood, the only sound on the mountain. The ride was a pleasant one, except for the wind and the cold. In some spots, the chair was suspended some thirty feet above the snow below. In other places, the chair came as close as six feet to the ground. He was beginning to anticipate the descent. He saw the unloading station ahead, saw the sign advising him to keep the tips of his skis up, and prepared to disembark. The skier ahead of him met with difficulty as he tried to get off his chair. The snow had been falling too heavily to clear, and there was no natural downgrade at the top of the lift; the chair followed its occupant, rather than rising overhead at the unloading point. The girl ahead of Hawes was almost knocked off her feet by her own chair. She managed to free herself as the chair gave a sharp lurch around the bend to begin its trip down the mountain again. Hawes concentrated on getting off the chair. Surprisingly, he did so with a minimum of effort and without poles, and then waited while the two empty chairs passed by. The third following chair approached the station. A man clambered off the chair, handed Hawes his poles with a 'These yours?' and skied to the crest of the slope. Hawes stood just outside the station booth, hanging his poles over his wrists. He was certain that the fourth chair behind his had contained *two* skiers at the bottom of the lift, and yet it seemed to be approaching now with only a single person in it. Hawes squinted through the snow, puzzled. Something seemed odd about the person in the fourth chair, something was jutting into the air at a curious angle – a ski? a leg? a . . . ?

The chair approached rapidly.

The skier made no move to disembark.

Hawes opened his eyes wide behind his yellow-tinted goggles as the chair swept past the station.

Through the driving snow, he had seen a skier slumped back into the passing chair, gloved hands dangling limply. And sticking out of the skier's chest at a malicious angle over the heart, buffeted by the wind and snow so that it trembled as if it were alive, thrust deep through the parka and the clothing beneath it like an oversized, slender aluminium sword, was a ski pole.

5.

THE CHAIR GAVE its sharp lurch as it rounded the bend.

The skier slid from the seat as the chair made its abrupt turn. Skis touched snow, the body fell forward, there was a terrible snapping sound over the keening of the wind, and Hawes knew instantly that a leg had been broken as bone yielded to the unresisting laminated wood and the vicelike binding. The skier fell face downwards, the ski pole bending as the body struck the snow, one leg twisted at an impossible angle, the boot still held firmly in its binding.

For a moment, there was only confusion compounded. The wind and the snow filled the air, the body lay motionless, face down in the snow as the chair whipped around the turn and started its descent. An empty chair swept past, another, a third, and then a chair came into view with a man poised to disembark, and Hawes shouted to the boom attendant, 'Stop the lift!'

'What?'

'Stop the goddamn lift!'

'What? What?'

Hawes moved towards the body lying in the snow just as the man on the chair decided to get off. They collided in a tangle of poles and skis, the relentless chair pushing them along like a bulldozer, sending them sprawling on to the body in the snow, before it snapped around for its downward passage. The booth attendant finally got the message. He ran into the small wooden shack and threw the control switch. The lift stopped. There was a deeper silence on the mountain.

'You okay?' he called.

'I'm fine,' Hawes said. He got to his feet and quickly unsnapped his bindings. The man who'd knocked him down was apologizing profusely, but Hawes wasn't listening. There was a bright red stain spreading into the snow where the impaled skier had fallen. He turned the body over and saw the ashen face and sightless eyes, saw the blood-soaked parka where the pole had been pushed through the soft and curving breast into the heart.

The dead skier was a young girl, no more than nineteen years old.

On the right sleeve of her black parka was the insignia of a Rawson Mountain ski instructor, the interlocking R and M in red as bright as the blood, which seeped into the thirsty snow.

'What is it?' the booth attendant shouted. 'Shall I get the ski patrol? Is it an accident?'

'It's no accident,' Hawes said, but his voice was so low that no one heard him.

6.

AS BEFITTED THIS farcical hotel in this comic-opera town, the police were a band of Keystone cops led by an inept sheriff who worked on the premise that a thing worth doing was a thing worth doing badly. Hawes stood by helplessly as he watched these cracker-barrel cops violate each and every rule of investigation, watched as they mishandled evidence, watched as they made it hopelessly impossible to gain any information at all from whatever slender clues were available.

The sheriff was a gangling oaf named Theodore Watt who, instead of putting Lift A out of commission instantly while his men tried to locate the victim's chair, instead rode that very lift to the top of the mountain, followed by at least three dozen skiers, hotel officials, reporters, and local cretins who undoubtedly smeared any latent prints lingering on *any* of the chairs, and made the task of reconstructing the crime almost impossible. One girl, wearing bright lavender stretch-pants and a white parka, climbed off the chair near the booth and was promptly informed there was blood all over the seat of her pants. The girl craned her neck to examine her shapely behind, touched the smear of blood, decided it was sticky and obscene, and almost fainted dead away. The chair, meantime, was happily whisking its way down the mountain again to the loading station where, presumably, another skier would again sit into a puddle of the dead girl's blood.

The dead girl's name, as it turned out, was Helga Nilson. She was nineteen years old and had learned to ski before she'd learned to walk, as the old Swedish saying goes. She had come to America when she was fifteen, had taught in the ski school at Stowe, Vermont, for two years before moving down to Mt Snow in that same fair state, and then abandoning Vermont and moving to Rawson Mountain, further south. She had joined the Rawson ski school at the beginning of the season, and seemed to be well-liked by all the instructors and especially by many beginning skiers who, after one lesson with her, repeatedly asked for 'Helga, the little Swedish girl'.

The little Swedish girl had had a ski pole driven into her heart with such force that it had almost exited through her back. The pole, bent out of shape when Helga fell from the chair, was the first piece of real evidence that the Keystone cops mishandled. Hawes saw one of the deputies kneel down beside the dead girl, grasp the pole with both hands, and attempt to pull it out of her body.

'Hey, what are you doing?' he shouted, and he shoved the man away from the body.

The man glanced up at him with a baleful upstate eye. 'And just who in hell're *you?*' he asked.

'My name's Cotton Hawes,' Hawes said. 'I'm a detective. From the city.' He unzipped the left hip pocket of his ski pants, pulled out his wallet, and flashed the tin. The deputy seemed singularly unimpressed.

'You're a little bit aways from your jurisdiction, ain't you?' he said.

'Who taught you how to handle evidence?' Hawes asked heatedly.

Sheriff Watt sauntered over to where the pair were arguing. He grinned amiably and said, 'What seems to be the trouble here, hmmm?' He sang out the 'hmmm', his voice rising pleasantly and cheerfully. A nineteen-year-old girl lay dead at his feet, but Sheriff Watt thought he was an old alumnus at Dartmouth's Winter Carnival.

'Feller here's a city detective,' the deputy said.

'That's good,' Watt said. 'Pleased to have you with us.'

'Thanks,' Hawes said. 'Your man here was just smearing any latent prints there may be on that weapon.'

'What weapon?'

'The ski pole,' Hawes said. 'What weapon do you think I . . . ?'

'Oh, won't be no fingerprints on that, anyway,' Watt said.

'How do you know?'

'No damn fool's gonna grab a piece of metal with his bare hands, is he? Not when the temperature's ten below zero, now is he?'

'He might have,' Hawes said. 'And while we're at it, don't you think it'd be a good idea to stop that lift? You've already had one person smearing up whatever stuff you could have found in the . . .'

'I got to get my men up here before I order the lift stopped,' Watt said.

'Then restrict it to the use of your men.'

'I've already done that,' Watt said briefly. He turned back to his deputy. 'Want to let me see that pole, Fred?'

'Sheriff, you let him touch that pole again, and—'

'And *what*?'

'—and you may ruin—'

'Mister, you just let me handle this my own whichway, hmmum? We been in this business a long time now, and we know all about skiing accidents.'

'This wasn't an accident,' Hawes said angrily. 'Somebody shoved a ski pole into that girl's chest, and that's not . . .'

'I know it wasn't an accident,' Watt said. 'That was just a manner of speaking. Let me have the pole, Fred.'

'Sheriff . . .'

'Mister, you better just shut up, hmmm? Else I'll have one of my men escort you down the mountain, and you can warm your feet by the fire.'

Hawes shut up. Impotently, he watched while the deputy named Fred seized the ski pole in both hands and yanked it from Helga's chest. A spurt of blood followed the retreating pole, welled up into the open wound, overflowed it, was sopped up by the sodden sweater. Fred handed the bent pole to the sheriff. Watt turned it over and over in his big hands.

'Looks like the basket's been taken off this thing,' he said.

The basket, Hawes saw, had indeed been removed from the bottom of the aluminium pole. The basket on a ski pole is a circular metal ring perhaps five inches in diameter, crossed by a pair of leather thongs. A smaller ring stamped into the thongs fits over the end of the pointed pole and is usually fastened by a cotter pin or a tight rubber washer. When the basket is in place on the end of a pole, it prevents the pole from sinking into the snow, thereby enabling the skier to use it in executing turns or maintaining balance. The basket had been removed from this particular pole and, in addition, someone had sharpened the normally sharp point so that it was as thin as a rapier. Hawes noticed this at once. It took the sheriff a little while longer to see that he was holding a razor-sharp weapon in his hands, and not a normally pointed pole.

'Somebody been working on the end of this thing,' he said, the dawn gradually breaking.

A doctor had come up the lift and was kneeling beside the dead girl. To no one's particular surprise, he pronounced her dead. One of the sheriff's bumbling associates began marking the position of the body, tracing its outline on the snow with a blue powder he poured liberally from a can.

Hawes couldn't imagine what possible use this imitation of investigatory technique would serve. They were marking the position of the body, true, but this didn't happen to be the scene of the crime. The girl had been murdered on a chair somewhere between the base of the mountain and the top of the lift. So far, no one had made any attempt to locate and examine the chair. Instead, they were sprinkling blue powder on to the snow, and passing their big paws all over the murder weapon.

'May I make a suggestion?' he asked.

'Sure,' Watt said.

'That girl got on the lift with someone else. I know because I dropped my poles down there, and when I turned for a look, there were two people in that chair. But when she reached the station here, she was alone.'

'Yeah?' Watt said.

'Yeah. I suggest you talk to the loader down below. The girl was a ski instructor, and they may have recognized her. Maybe they know who got on the chair with her.'

'Provided anyone did.'

'Someone did,' Hawes said.

'How do you know?'

'Because . . .' Hawes took a deep breath. 'I just told you. I *saw* two people in that chair.'

'How far behind you?'

'Four chairs behind.'

'And you could see four chairs behind you in this storm, hmmm?'

'Yes. Not clearly, but I could see.'

'I'll just bet you could,' Watt said.

'Look,' Hawes insisted, 'someone was in that chair

181

with her. And he undoubtedly jumped from the chair right after he killed her. I suggest you start combing the ground under the lift before this snow covers any tracks that might be there.'

'Yes, we'll do that,' Watt said. 'When we get around to it.'

'You'd better get around to it soon,' Hawes said. 'You've got a blizzard here, and a strong wind piling up drifts. If . . .'

'Mister, I hadn't *better* do anything. You're the one who'd just better butt his nose out of what we're trying to do here.'

'What is it you're trying to do?' Hawes asked. 'Compound a felony? Do you think your murderer's going to sit around and wait for you to catch up to him? He's probably halfway out of the state by now.'

'Ain't nobody going noplace, mister,' Watt said. 'Not with the condition of the roads. So don't you worry about that. I hate to see anybody worrying.'

'Tell that to the dead girl,' Hawes said, and he watched as the ski patrol loaded her into a basket and began taking her on her last trip down the mountain.

7.

DEATH IS A cliché, a tired old saw.

He had been a cop for a good long time now, starting as a rookie who saw death only from the sidelines, who kept a timetable while the detectives and the photographers and the assistant ME and the laboratory boys swarmed around the victim like flies around a prime cut of rotten meat. Death to him, at that time, had been motion-picture death. Standing apart from death, being as it were a uniformed secretary who took the names of witnesses and jotted in a black book the arrivals and departures of those actually concerned with the investigation, he had watched the proceedings dispassionately. The person lying lifeless on the sidewalk, the person lying on blood-soaked sheets, the person hanging from a light fixture, the person eviscerated by the onrushing front grille of an automobile, these were all a trifle unreal to Hawes, representations of death, but not death itself, not that grisly son of a bitch.

When he became a detective, they really introduced him to death.

The introduction was informal, almost casual. He was working with the 30th Squad at the time, a very nice respectable squad in a nice respectable precinct where death by violence hardly ever came. The introduction was made in a rooming house. The patrolman who answered the initial squeal was waiting for the detectives when they had arrived. The detective with Hawes asked, 'Where's the stiff?' and the patrolman answered, 'He's in there,' and the other detective turned to Hawes and said, 'Come on, let's take a look.'

That was the introduction.

They had gone into the bedroom where the man was lying at the foot of the dresser. The man was fifty-three years old. He lay in his undershorts on the floor in the sticky coagulation of his own blood. He was a small man with a pinched chest. His hair was black and thinning, and bald patches showed his flaking scalp. He had probably never been handsome, even when he was a youth. Some men do not improve with age, and time and alcohol had squeezed everything out of this man, and drained him dry until all he possessed was sagging flesh and, of course, life. The flesh was still there. The life had been taken from him. He lay at the foot of the dresser in his undershorts, ludicrously piled into a heap of inert flesh, so relaxed, so impossibly relaxed. Someone had worked him over with a hatchet. The hatchet was still in the room, blood-flecked, entangled with thin black hair. The killer had viciously attacked him around the head and the throat and the chest. He had stopped bleeding by the time they arrived, but the wounds were still there to see, open and raw.

Hawes vomited.

He went into the bathroom and vomited. That was his introduction to death.

He had seen a lot of death since, had come close to being dead himself. The closest, perhaps, was the time he'd been stabbed while investigating a burglary. The woman who'd been burglarized was still pretty hysterical when he got there. He asked his questions and tried to comfort her, and then started downstairs to get a patrolman. The woman, terrified, began screaming when he left. He could hear her screams as he went down the stairwell. The superintendent of the building caught him on the second floor landing. He was carrying a bread knife, and he thought that Hawes was the burglar returned, and he stabbed repeatedly at his head, ripping a wound over his left temple before Hawes finally subdued him. They let the super go; the poor guy had actually thought Hawes was the thief. And then they'd shaved Hawes' red hair to get to the wound, which time of course healed as it does all wounds, leaving however a reminder of death, of the closeness of death. The red hair had grown white. He still carried the streak over his temple. Sometimes, particularly when it rained, death sent little signals of pain to accompany the new hair.

He had seen a lot of death, especially since he'd joined the 87th, and a lot of dying. He no longer vomited. The vomiting had happened to a very young Cotton Hawes, a very young and innocent cop who suddenly awoke to the knowledge that he was in a dirty business where the facts of life were the facts of violence, where he dealt daily with the sordid and grotesque. He no longer vomited. But he still got angry.

He had felt anger on the mountain when the young girl fell out of the chair and struck the snow, the ski pole bending as she dropped into that ludicrously ridiculous posture of the dead, that totally relaxed and utterly frightening posture. He had felt anger by juxtaposition, the reconstruction of a vibrant and life-bursting athlete against the very real image of the same girl, no longer a girl, only a worthless heap of flesh and bones, only a body now, a corpse. 'Where's the stiff?'

He felt anger when Theodore Watt and his witless assistants muddied the residue of sudden death, allowing the killer a precious edge, presenting him with the opportunity for escape — escape from the law and from the outrage of humanity. He felt anger now as he walked back to the building which housed the ski shop and the rooms overhead.

The anger seemed out of place on the silent mountain.

The snow still fell, still and gentle. The wind had died, and now the flakes drifted aimlessly from overhead, large and wet and white, and there was a stillness and a peace to Rawson Mountain and the countryside beyond, a lazy white quiet which denied the presence of death.

He kicked the packed snow from his boots and went up the steps.

He was starting down the corridor towards his room when he noticed the door was slightly ajar. He hesitated. Perhaps Blanche had come back to the room, perhaps . . .

But there was silence in the corridor, a silence as large as noise. He stooped and untied the laces on his boots. Gently, he slipped them from his feet. Walking as softly as he could – he was a big man and the floor boards in the old building creaked beneath his weight – he approached the room. He did not like the idea of being in his stockinged feet. He had had to kick men too often, and he knew the value of shoes. He hesitated just outside the door. There was no sound in the room. The door was open no more than three inches. He put his hand against the wood. Somewhere in the basement, the oil burner clicked and then *whoooomed* into action. He shoved open the door.

Elmer Wollender, his crutches under his arms, whirled to face him. His head had been bent in an attitude of . . . prayer, was it? No. Not prayer. He had been listening, that was it, listening *to* something, or *for* something.

'Oh, hello, Mr Hawes,' he said. He was wearing a red ski parka over his white shirt. He leaned on his crutches and grinned a boyish, disarming grin.

'Hello, Mr Wollender,' Hawes said. 'Would you mind telling me, Mr Wollender, just what the hell you're doing in my room?'

Wollender seemed surprised. His eyebrows arched. He

186

tilted his head to one side, almost in admiration, almost as if he too would have behaved in much the same way had he come back to *his* room and found a stranger in it. But the admiration was also tinged with surprise. This was obviously a mistake. Head cocked to one side, eyebrows arched, the boyish smile on his mouth, Wollender leaned on his crutches and prepared to explain. Hawes waited.

'You said the heat wasn't working, didn't you?' Wollender said. 'I was just checking it.'

'The heat's working fine in this room,' Hawes said. 'It's the room next door.'

'Oh.' Wollender nodded. 'Oh, is that it?'

'That's it, yes.'

'No wonder. I stuck my hand up there to check the vent, and it seemed fine to me.'

'Yes, it would be fine,' Hawes said, 'since there was never anything wrong with it. I told you at the desk this morning that the heat wasn't working in 104. This is 105. Are you new here, Mr Wollender?'

'I guess I misunderstood you.'

'Yes, I guess so. Misunderstanding isn't a wise practice, Mr Wollender, especially with your local cops crawling all over the mountain.'

'What are you talking about?'

'I'm talking about the girl. When those imitation cops begin asking questions, I suggest . . .'

'What girl?'

Hawes looked at Wollender for a long time. The question on Wollender's face and in his eyes looked genuine enough, but could there possibly be someone on the mountain who still had not heard of the murder? Was it possible that Wollender, who ran the inn, the centre of all activity and gossip, did not know Helga Nilson was dead?

187

'The girl,' Hawes said. 'Helga Nilson.'

'What about her?'

Hawes knew enough about baseball to realize you didn't throw your fast ball until you'd tried a few curves. 'Do you know her?' he asked.

'Of course I know her. I know all the ski instructors. She rooms right here, down the hall.'

'Who else rooms here?'

'Why?'

'I want to know.'

'Just her and Maria,' Wollender said. 'Maria Fiers. She's an instructor, too. And, oh yes, the new man. Larry Davidson.'

'Is he an instructor?' Hawes asked. 'About this tall?'

'Yes.'

'Hooked nose? German accent.'

'No, no. You're thinking of Helmut Kurtz. And that's an Austrian accent.' Wolleader paused. 'Why? Why do you want to . . . ?'

'Anything between him and Helga?'

'Why, no. Not that I know of. They teach together, but . . .'

'What about Davidson?'

'Larry Davidson?'

'Yes.'

'Do you mean, is he dating Helga, or . . .'

'Yes, that's right.'

'Larry's married,' Wollender said. 'I would hardly think . . .'

'What about you?'

'I don't understand.'

'You and Helga. Anything?'

'Helga's a good friend of mine,' Wollender said.

'Was,' Hawes corrected.

'Huh?'

188

'She's dead. She was killed on the mountain this afternoon.'

There was the fast ball, and it took Wollender smack between the eyes. 'Dea—' he started, and then his jaw fell slack, and his eyes went blank. He staggered back a pace, colliding with the white dresser. The crutches dropped from his hands. He struggled to maintain his balance, the leg with the cast stiff and unwieldy; he seemed about to fall. Hawes grabbed at his elbow and pulled him erect. He stooped down for Wollender's crutches and handed them to him. Wollender was still dazed. He groped for the crutches, fumbled, dropped them again. Hawes picked them up a second time, and forced them under Wollender's arms. Wollender leaned back against the dresser. He kept staring at the wall opposite, where a poster advertising the pleasures of Kitzbühel was hanging.

'She . . . she took too many chances,' he said. 'She always went too fast. I told her . . .'

'This wasn't a skiing accident,' Hawes said. 'She was murdered.'

'No.' Wollender shook his head,' 'No.'

'Yes.'

'No. Everyone liked Helga. No one would . . .' He kept shaking his head. His eyes stayed riveted to the Kitzbühel poster.

'There are going to be cops here, Mr Wollender,' Hawes said. 'You seem like a nice kid. When they start asking questions, you'd better have a more plausible story than the one you invented about being in my room. They're not going to fool around. They're looking for a killer.'

'Why . . . why do you *think* I came here?' Wollender asked.

'I don't know. Maybe you were looking for some pocket money. Skiers often leave their wallets and their valu—'

'I'm not a thief, Mr Hawes,' Wollender said with dignity. 'I only came here to give you some heat.'

'That makes it even,' Hawes answered. 'The cops'll be coming here to give *you* some.'

8.

HE FOUND THE two loaders in the lodge cafeteria. The lifts had been closed at four-thirty, the area management having reached the conclusion that most skiing accidents took place in the waning hours of the afternoon, when poor visibility and physical exhaustion combined to create gentle havoc. They were both burly, grizzled men wearing Mackinaws, their thick hands curled around coffee mugs. They had been loading skiers on to chairs ever since the area was opened, and they worked well together as a team. Even their dialogue seemed concocted in one mind, though it issued from two mouths.

'My name's Jake,' the first loader said. 'This here is Obey, short for Obadiah.'

'Only I ain't so short,' Obadiah said.

'He's short on brains,' Jake said and grinned. Obadiah returned the grin. 'You're a cop, huh?'

'Yes,' Hawes said. He had shown them his buzzer the moment he approached them. He had also told an outright lie, saying he was helping with the investigation of the case, having been sent up from the city because there was the possibility a known and wanted criminal had perpetrated the crime, confusing his own doubletalk as he wove a fantastic monologue which Jake and Obadiah seemed to accept.

'And you want to know who we loaded on them chairs, right? Same as Teddy wanted to know.'

'Teddy?'

'Teddy Watt. The sheriff.'

'Oh. Yes,' Hawes said. 'That's right'

191

'Whyn't you just ask *him*?' Obadiah said.

'Well, I have,' Hawes lied. 'But sometimes a fresh angle will come up if witnesses can be questioned directly, do you see?'

'Well, we ain't exactly witnesses,' Jake said. 'We didn't see her get killed, you know.'

'Yes, but you did load her on the chair, didn't you?'

'That's right. We did, all right.'

'And someone was in the chair with her, is that right?'

'That's right,' Jake said.

'Who?' Hawes asked.

'Seems like everybody wants to know *who*,' Jake said.

'Ain't it the damndest thing?' Obadiah said.

'Do you remember?' Hawes asked.

'We remember it was snowing, that's for sure.'

'Couldn't hardly see the chairs, it was snowing that hard.'

'Pretty tough to reckernize one skier from another with all that wind and snow, wouldn't you say, Obey?'

'Next to impossible,' Obadiah answered.

'But you did recognize Helga,' Hawes suggested.

'Oh, sure. But she said hello to us, you see. She said, "Hello, Jake. Hello, Obey." And also, she took the chair closest to the loading platform, the inside chair. The guy took the other chair.'

'Guy?' Hawes asked. 'It was a man then? The person who took the chair next to her was a man?'

'Well, can't say for sure,' Jake said. 'Was a time when men's ski clothes was different from the ladies', but that don't hold true no more.'

'Not by a long shot,' Obadiah said.

'Nowadays, you find yourself following some pretty girl in purple pants, she turns out to be a man. It ain't so easy to tell them apart no more.'

'Then you don't know whether the person who sat

next to her was a man or a woman, is that right?' Hawes asked.

'That's right.'

'Coulda been either.'

'Did this person say anything?'

'Not a word.'

'What was he wearing?'

'Well, we ain't established it was a *he*,' Jake reminded him.

'Yes, I know. I meant the . . . the person who took the chair. It'll be easier if we give him a gender.'

'Give him a *what*?'

'A gen— if we assume for the moment that the person was a man.'

'Oh.' Jake thought this over. 'Okay, if you say so. Seems like pretty sloppy deduction to me, though.'

'Well, I'm not actually making a deduction. I'm simply trying to facilitate . . .'

'Sure, I understand,' Jake said. 'But it's sure pretty sloppy.'

Hawes sighed, 'Well . . . what *was* he wearing?'

'Black,' Jake said.

'Black ski pants, black parka,' Obadiah said.

'Any hat?' Hawes asked.

'Nope. Hood on the parka was pulled clear up over the head. Sunglasses over the eyes.'

'Gloves or mittens?' Hawes asked.

'Gloves. Black gloves.'

'Did you notice whether or not there was an insignia on the man's parka?'

'What kind of insignia?'

'An R-M interlocked,' Hawes said.

'Like the instructors wear?' Jake asked.

'Exactly.'

'They wear it on their *right* sleeves,' Obadiah said. 'We

told you this person took the outside chair. We couldn'ta seen the right sleeve, even if there *was* anything on it.'

Hawes suddenly had a wild idea. He hesitated before he asked, and then thought, *What the hell, try it*.

'This person,' he said, 'was he . . . was he carrying crutches?'

'Carrying *what*?' Jake asked incredulously.

'Crutches. Was his leg in a cast?'

'Now how in hell . . . of *course* not,' Jake said. 'He was wearing skis and he was carrying ski poles. Crutches and a cast! My God! It's hard enough getting on that damn lift as it is. Can you just picture . . .'

'Never mind,' Hawes said. 'Forget it. Did this person say anything to Helga?'

'Not a word.'

'Did she say anything to him?'

'Nothing we could hear. The wind was blowing pretty fierce.'

'But you heard her when she said hello to you.'

'That's right.'

'Then if she'd said anything to this person, you might have heard that, too.'

'That's right. We didn't hear nothing.'

'You said he was carrying poles. Did you notice anything unusual about the poles?'

'Seemed like ordinary poles to me,' Jake said.

'Did both poles have baskets?'

Jake shrugged. 'I didn't notice. Did you, Obey?'

'Both seemed to have baskets,' Obadiah said. 'Who'd notice a thing like that?'

'Well, you might have,' Hawes said. 'If there'd been anything unusual, you might have noticed.'

'I didn't notice nothing unusual,' Obadiah said. 'Except I thought to myself this feller must be pretty cold.'

'Why?'

'Well, the hood pulled up over his head, and the scarf wrapped almost clear around his face.'

'What scarf? You didn't mention that before.'

'Sure. He was wearing a red scarf. Covered his mouth and his nose, reached right up to the sunglasses.'

'Hmmm,' Hawes said, and the table went still.

'You're the fellow dropped his poles on the way up, ain't you?' Jake asked.

'Yes.'

'Thought I remembered you.'

'If you remember *me*, how come you can't remember the person who took that chair alongside Helga's?'

'You saying I *should*, mister?'

'I'm only asking.'

'Well, like maybe if I seen a guy wearing black pants and a black hood, and sunglasses, and a scarf wrapped clear around his face, why maybe then I would recognize him. But, the way I figure it, he ain't likely to be wearing the same clothes right now, is he?'

'I don't suppose so,' Hawes said, sighing.

'Yeah, neither do I,' Jake answered. 'And I ain't even a cop.'

9.

DUSK WAS SETTLING upon the mountain.

It spread into the sky and stained the snow a purple-red. The storm was beginning to taper off, the clouds vanishing before the final triumphant breakthrough of the setting sun. There was an unimaginable hush to the mountain, and the town, and the valley beyond, a hush broken only by the sound of gently jingling skid-chains on hard-packed snow.

He had found Blanche and taken her to the fireplace in the inn, settling her there with a brace of double Scotches and a half-dozen copies of a skiing magazine. Now, with the mountain and the town still, the lifts inoperative, the distant snow brushed with dying colour, he started climbing the mountain. He worked through the deep snow directly under the lift, the chairs hanging motionless over his head. He was wearing ski pants and after-ski boots designed for lounging beside a fire. He had forsaken his light parka for two sweaters. Before he'd left the room, he had unholstered the .38 and slipped it into the elastic-reinforced waistband of his trousers. He could feel it digging into his abdomen now as he climbed.

The climb was not an easy one.

The snow under the lift had not been packed, and he struggled against it as he climbed, encountering drifts which were impassable, working his way in a zigzagging manner across the lift line, sometimes being forced to leave the high snow for the Cat-packed trail to the right of the lift. The light was waning. He did not know how much longer it would last. He had taken a flashlight from the glove compartment of his car, but he began to wonder whether its glow would illuminate very much once the sun had set. He began to wonder, too, exactly what he hoped to find. He was almost certain that any tracks the killer had left would already have been covered by the drifting snow. Again he cursed Theodore Watt and his inefficient slobs. Someone should have made this climb immediately after they discovered the dead girl, while there was still a possibility of finding a trail.

He continued climbing. After a day of skiing, he was physically and mentally exhausted, his muscles protesting, his eyes burning. He thumbed on the flashlight as darkness claimed the mountain, and pushed his way through knee-deep snow. He stumbled and got to his feet again. The snow had tapered almost completely, but the wind had returned with early evening, a high keening wind that rushed through the trees on either side of the lift line, pushing the clouds from the sky. There was a thin sliver of moon and a scattering of stars. The clouds raced past them like silent dark horsemen, and everywhere on the mountain was the piercing shriek of the wind, a thin scream that penetrated to the marrow.

He fell again.

Loose snow caught under the neck of his sweater, slid down his back. He shivered and tried to brush it away, got to his feet, and doggedly began climbing again. His after-ski boots had not been designed for deep snow. The tops ended just above his ankles, offering no protection whatever. He realized abruptly that the boots were already packed with snow, that his feet were literally encased in snow. He was beginning to regret this whole foolhardy mission, when he saw it.

He had come perhaps a third of the way up the lift line, the mountain in absolute darkness now, still except for the maiden scream of the wind. The flashlight played a small circle of light on the snow ahead of him as he stumbled upwards, the climb more difficult now, the clouds rushing by overhead, skirting the thin moon. The light touched something which glinted momentarily, passed on as he continued climbing, stopped. He swung the flashlight back. Whatever had glinted was no longer there. Swearing, he swung the flashlight in a slow steady arc. The glint again. He swung the light back.

The basket was half-covered by the snow. Only one edge of its metallic ring showed in the beam of his light. It had probably been covered completely earlier in the day, but the strong fresh wind had exposed it to view again, and he stooped quickly to pick it up, almost as if he were afraid it would vanish. He was still bending, studying the basket in the light of the flash, when the man jumped on to his back.

The attack came suddenly and swiftly. He had heard nothing but the wind. He had been so occupied with his find, so intent on studying the basket which, he was certain, had come from the end of the ski pole weapon, and when he felt the sudden weight on his back he did not connect it immediately with an attack. He was simply surprised, and his first thought was that one of the pines had dropped a heavy load of snow from its laden branches, and then he realized this was no heavy load of snow, but by that time he was flat on his belly.

He rolled over instantly. He held the ski pole basket in his left hand, refusing to let go of it. In his right hand, he held the flashlight, and he swung that instantly at the man's head, felt it hitting the man's forearm instead. Something solid struck Hawes' shoulder; a wrench? a hammer? and he realized at once that the man was armed, and suddenly the situation became serious. He threw away the flashlight and groped for the .38 in his waistband.

The clouds cleared the moon. The figure kneeling over him, straddling him, was wearing a black parka, the hood pulled up over his head. A red scarf was wrapped over his chin and his mouth and his nose. He was holding a hammer in his right hand, and he raised the hammer over his head just as the moon disappeared again. Hawes' fingers closed on the butt of the .38. The hammer descended.

It descended in darkness, striking Hawes on his cheek, ripping the flesh, glancing downwards and catching his shoulder. Hawes swore violently, drew the .38 in a ridiculously clumsy draw, brought it into firing position, and felt again the driving blow of the other man's weapon, the hammer lashing out of the darkness, slamming with brute force against his wrist, almost cracking the bone. His fingers opened involuntarily. The gun dropped into the snow. He bellowed in pain and tried to kick out at his attacker, but the man moved away quickly, gained his feet, and braced himself in the deep snow for the final assault. The moon appeared again. A thin silvery light put the man in silhouette against the sky, the black hooded head, the face masked by a scarf. The hammer went up over his head.

Hawes kicked out at his groin.

The blow did nothing to stop the man's attack. It glanced off his thigh, missing target as the hammer came down, but throwing him off balance slightly so that the hammer struck without real force. Hawes threw a fist at him, and the man grunted and again the hammer came out of the new darkness. The man fought desperately and silently, frightening Hawes with the fury of his animal strength. They rolled over in the snow, and Hawes grasped at the hood, tried to pull it from the man's head, found it was securely tied in place, and reached for the scarf. The scarf began to unravel. The man lashed out with the hammer, felt the scarf coming free, pulled back to avoid exposing his face, and suddenly staggered as Hawes' fist struck home. He fell into the snow, and all at once, he panicked. Instead of attacking again, he pulled the scarf around his face and began to half run, half stumble through the deep snow. Hawes leaped at him, missing, his hands grabbing air. The man scrambled over the snow, heading for the pines lining the lift. By the times Hawes was on his feet again, the man had gone into the trees. Hawes went after him. It was dark under the trees. The world went black and silent under the pines.

He hesitated for a moment. He could see nothing, could hear nothing. He fully expected the hammer to come lashing out of the darkness.

Instead, there came the voice.

'Hold it right there.'

The voice startled him, but he reacted intuitively, whirling, his fist pulling back reflexively, and then firing into the darkness. He felt it connecting with solid flesh, heard someone swearing in the dark, and then – surprisingly, shockingly – Hawes heard the sound of a pistol shot. It rang on the mountain air, reverberated under the pines. Hawes opened his eyes wide. A pistol? But the man had only a hammer. Why hadn't . . . ?

'Next time, I go for your heart,' the voice said.

Hawes stared into the darkness. He could no longer locate the voice. He did not know where to jump, and the man was holding a pistol.

'You finished?' the man asked.

The beam of a flashlight suddenly stabbed through the darkness. Hawes blinked his eyes against it, tried to shield his face.

'Well, well,' the man said. 'You never can tell, can you? Stick out your hands.'

'What?' Hawes said.

'Stick out your goddamn hands.'

Hesitantly he held out his hands. He was the most surprised human being in the world when he felt the handcuffs being snapped on to his wrists.

10.

THE OFFICE FROM which Theodore Watt, sheriff of the town of Rawson, operated was on the main street alongside an Italian restaurant whose neon sign advertised LASAGNA * SPAGHETTI * RAVIOLI. Now that the snow had stopped, the ploughs had come through and banked snow on either side of the road so that the door of the office was partially hidden by a natural fortress of white. Inside the office, Theodore Watt was partially hidden by the fortress of his desk, the top of which was covered with Wanted circulars, FBI flyers, carbon copies of police reports, a pair of manacles, a cardboard container of coffee, a half-dozen chewed pencil stubs, and a framed picture of his wife and three children. Theodore Watt was not in a very friendly mood. He sat behind his desk-fortress, a frown on his face. Cotton Hawes stood before the desk, still wearing the handcuffs which had been clamped on to his wrists on the mountain. The deputy who'd made the collar, the self-same Fred who had earlier pulled the ski pole from Helga Nilson's chest, stood alongside Hawes, wearing the sheriff's frown, and also wearing a mouse under his left eye, where Hawes had hit him.

'I could lock you up, you know,' Watt said, frowning. 'You hit one of my deputies.'

'You ought to lock *him* up,' Hawes said angrily. 'If he hadn't come along, I might have had our man.'

'You might have, huh?'

'Yes.'

'You had no right being on that damn mountain,' Watt said. 'What were you doing up there?'

'Looking.'

'For what?'

'Anything. He gave you the basket I found. Apparently it was important enough for the killer to have wanted it, too. He fought hard enough for it. Look at my cheek.'

'Well now, that's a shame,' Watt said drily.

'There may be fingerprints on that basket,' Hawes said. 'I suggest . . .'

'I doubt it. Weren't none on the ski pole, and none on the chair, neither. We talked to the two loaders, and they told us the one riding up with Helga Nilson was wearing gloves. I doubt if there's any fingerprints on that basket at all.'

'Well . . .' Hawes said, and he shrugged.

'What it amounts to, hmmmm,' Watt said, 'is that you figured we wasn't handling this case to your satisfaction, ain't that it? So you figured you'd give us local hicks a little big-time help, hmmmm? Ain't that about it?'

'I thought I could possibly assist in some . . .'

'Then you shoulda come to me,' Watt said, 'and *asked* if you could help. This way, you only fouled up what we was trying to do.'

'I don't understand.'

'I've got six men on that mountain,' Watt said, 'waiting for whoever killed that girl to come back and cover his mistakes. This basket here was one of the mistakes. But did our killer find it? No. Our helpful big-city detective found it. You're a lot of help, mister, you sure are. With all that ruckus on the mountain, that damn killer won't go anywhere near it for a month!'

'I almost had him,' Hawes said. 'I was going after him when your man stopped me.'

'Stopped him, hell! *You're* the one who was stopping

203

him from doing his job. Maybe I *ought* to lock you up. There's a thing known as impeding the progress of an investigation. But, of course, you know all about that, don't you? Being a big-city detective. Hmmm?'

'I'm sorry if I . . .'

'And of course we're just a bunch of local hicks who don't know nothing at all about police work. Why, we wouldn't even know enough to have a autopsy performed on that little girl, now would we? Or to have tests made of the blood on that chair, now would we? We wouldn't have no crime lab in the next biggest town to Rawson, would we?'

'The way you were handling the investigation . . .' Hawes started.

'. . . was none of your damn business,' Watt concluded. 'Maybe we like to make our own mistakes, Hawes! But naturally, you city cops never make mistakes. That's why there ain't no crime at all where you come from.'

'Look,' Hawes said, 'you were mishandling evidence. I don't give a damn what you . . .'

'As it turns out, it don't matter because there wasn't no fingerprints on that pole, anyway. And we had to get our men up the mountain, so we had to use the lift. There was a hell of a lot of confusion there today, mister. But I don't suppose big-city cops ever get confused, hmmmm?' Watt looked at him sourly. 'Take the cuffs off him, Fred,' he said.

Fred looked surprised, but he unlocked the handcuffs. 'He hit me right in the eye,' he said to Watt.

'Well, you still got the other eye,' Watt said drily. 'Go to bed, Hawes. We had enough of you for one night.'

'What did the autopsy report say?' Hawes asked.

Watt looked at him in something close to astonishment. 'You still sticking your nose in this?'

'I'd still like to help, yes.'

'Maybe we don't need your help.'

'Maybe you can use it. No one here knows . . .'

'There we go with the damn big-city attitu—'

'I was going to say,' Hawes said, overriding Watt's voice, 'that no one in the area knows I'm a cop. That could be helpful to you.'

Watt was silent. 'Maybe,' he said at last.

'*May* I hear the autopsy report?'

Watt was silent again. Then he nodded. He picked up a sheet of paper from his desk and said, 'Death caused by fatal stab wound of the heart, penetration of the auricles and pulmonary artery. That's where all the blood came from, Hawes. Wounds of the ventricles don't usually bleed that much. Coroner figures the girl died in maybe two or three minutes, there was that much loss of blood.'

'Anything else?'

'Broke her ankle when she fell out of that chair. Oblique fracture of the lateral malleolus. Examiner also found traces of human skin under the girl's fingernails. Seems like she clawed out at whoever stabbed her, and took a goodly part of him away with her.'

'What did the skin tell you?'

'Not a hell of a lot. Our killer is white and adult.'

'That's all?'

'That's all. At least, that's all from the skin, except the possibility of using it later for comparison tests – if we ever get anybody to compare it with. We found traces of blood on her fingers and nails, too, not her own.'

'How do you know?'

'Blood on the chair, the girl's blood, was in the AB grouping. Blood we found on her hands was in the O grouping, most likely the killer's.'

'Then she scratched him enough to cause bleeding.'

'She took a big chunk of skin from him, Hawes.'

'From the face?'

'Now how in hell would I know?'

'I thought maybe . . .'

'Couldn't tell from the skin sample whether it came from the neck or the face or wherever. She coulda scratched him anyplace.'

'Anything else?'

'We found a trail of the girl's blood in the snow under the lift. Plenty of it, believe me, she bled like a stuck pig. The trail started about four minutes from the top. Took her two or three minutes to die. So, assuming the killer jumped from the chair right soon's he stabbed her, then the girl . . .'

'. . . was still alive when he jumped.'

'That's right.'

'Find any tracks in the snow?'

'Nothing. Too many drifts. We don't know whether he jumped with his skis on or not. Have to have been a pretty good skier to attempt that, we figure.'

'Well, anyway, he's got a scratch,' Hawes said. 'That's *something* to look for.'

'You gonna start looking tonight?' Watt asked sarcastically.

11.

BLANCHE COLBY WAS waiting for him when he got back to the room. She was sitting up in his bed propped against the pillows, wearing a shapeless flannel nightgown which covered her from her throat to her ankles. She was holding an apple in her hand, and she bit into it angrily as he entered the room, and then went back to reading the open book in her lap.

'Hi,' he said.

She did not answer him, nor did she even look up at him. She continued destroying the apple, continued her pretence of reading.

'Good book?'

'*Excellent* book,' she answered.

'Miss me?'

'Drop dead,' Blanche said.

'I'm sorry. I. . .'

'Don't be. I enjoyed myself immensely in your absence.'

'I got arrested, you see.'

'You got *what*?'

'Arrested. Pinched. Pulled in. Collared. Apprehen—'

'I understood you the first time. Who arrested you?'

'The cops,' Hawes said, and he shrugged.

'Serves you right.' She put down the book. 'Wasn't it you who told me a girl was killed on this mountain today? Murdered? And you run off and leave me when a killer . . .'

'I told you where I was going. I told you . . .'

'You said you'd be back in an hour!'

'Yes, but I didn't know I was going to be arrested.'

'What happened to your cheek?'

'I got hit with a hammer.'

'Good,' Blanche said, and she nodded emphatically.

'Aren't you going to kiss my wound?' Hawes asked.

'*You* can kiss my . . .'

'Ah-ah,' he cautioned.

'I sat by that damn fireplace until eleven o'clock. Then I came up here and . . . what time is it, anyway?'

'After midnight.'

Blanche nodded again. 'I would have packed up and gone home, believe me, if the roads were open.'

'Yes, but they're closed.'

'Yes, damn it!'

'Aren't you glad I'm back?'

Blanche shrugged. 'I couldn't care less. I was just about to go to sleep.'

'In here?'

'In the other room, naturally.'

'Honey, honey . . .'

'Yes, honey-honey?' she mimicked. '*What*, honey-honey baby?'

Hawes grinned. 'That's a very lovely nightgown. My grandmother used to wear a nightgown like that.'

'I thought you'd like it,' Blanche said sourly. 'I put it on especially for you.'

'I always liked the touch of flannel,' he said.

'Get your big hands . . .' she started, and moved away from him swiftly. Folding her arms across the front of her gown, she sat in the centre of the bed and stared at the opposite wall. Hawes studied her for a moment, took off his sweaters, and then began unbuttoning his shirt.

'If you're going to undress,' Blanche said evenly, 'you could at least have the modesty to go into the . . .'

'Shhh!' Hawes said sharply. His hands had stopped on

the buttons of his shirt. He cocked his head to one side now and listened. Blanche, watching him, frowned.

'What . . . ?'

'Shhh!' he said again, and again he listened attentively. The room was silent. Into the silence came the sound.

'Do you hear it?' he asked.

'Do I hear what?'

'Listen.'

They listened together. The sound was unmistakable, faint and faraway, but unmistakable.

'It's the same buzzing I heard last night,' Hawes said. 'I'll be right back.'

'Where are you going?'

'Downstairs. To the ski shop,' he answered, and swiftly left the room. As he went down the corridor towards the steps, a door at the opposite end of the hall opened. A young girl wearing a quilted robe over her pyjamas, her hair done in curlers, came into the hallway carrying a towel and a tooth brush. She smiled at Hawes and then walked past him. He heard the bathroom door locking behind her as he went down the steps.

The lights were on in the ski shop. The buzzing sound came from somewhere in the shop, intermittent, hanging on the silent night air, ceasing abruptly, beginning again. He walked silently over the snow, stopping just outside the door to the shop. He put his ear to the wood and listened, but the only sound he heard was the buzzing. He debated kicking in the door. Instead, he knocked gently.

'Yes?' a voice from inside called.

'Could you open up, please?' Hawes said.

He waited. He could hear the heavy sound of ski boots approaching the locked door. The door opened a crack. A sun-tanned face appeared in the opening. He recognized the face at once – Helmut Kurtz, the ski instructor who had helped him the night before, the man he'd seen today on the mountain just before he'd got on the chair lift.

'Oh, hello there,' Hawes said.

'Yes? What is it?' Kurtz asked.

'Mind if I come in?'

'I'm sorry, no one is allowed in the shop. The shop is closed.'

'Yes, but *you're* in it, aren't you?'

'I'm an instructor,' Kurtz said. 'We are permitted . . .'

'I just saw a light,' Hawes said, 'and I felt like talking to someone.'

'Well . . .'

'What are you doing, anyway?' Hawes asked casually, and casually he wedged one shoulder against the door and gently eased it open, casually pushing it into the room, casually squeezing his way into the opening, casually shouldering his way past Kurtz and then squinting past the naked hanging light bulb to the work bench at the far end of the room, trying to locate the source of the buzzing sound which filled the shop.

'You are really not allowed . . .' Kurtz started, but Hawes was already halfway across the room, moving towards the other small area of light where a green-shaded bulb hung over the work bench. The buzzing sound was louder, the sound of an old machine, the sound of . . .

He located it almost at once. A grinding wheel was set up on one end of the bench. The wheel was still spinning. He looked at it, nodded and then flicked the switch to turn it off. Turning to Kurtz, he smiled and said, 'Were you sharpening something?'

'Yes, those skates,' Kurtz said. He pointed to a pair of white figure skates on the bench.

'Yours?' Hawes asked.

Kurtz smiled. 'No. Those are women's skates.'

'Whose?'

'Well, I don't think that is any of your business, do you?' Kurtz asked politely.

'I suppose not,' Hawes answered gently, still smiling. 'Were you in here sharpening something last night, too, Mr Kurtz?'

'I beg your pardon?'

'I said, were you . . .'

'No, I was not.' Kurtz walked up to the bench and studied Hawes slowly and deliberately. 'Who *are* you?' he asked.

'My name's Cotton Hawes.'

'How do you do? Mr Hawes, I'm sorry to have to be so abrupt, but you are really not allowed . . .'

'Yes, I know. Only instructors are allowed in here, isn't that right, Mr Kurtz?'

'After closing, yes. We sometimes come in to make minor repairs on our skis or . . .'

'Or sharpen up some things, huh, Mr Kurtz?'

'Yes. Like the skates.'

'Yes,' Hawes repeated. 'Like the skates. But you weren't in here last night, were you, Mr Kurtz?'

'No, I was not'

'Because, you see, I heard what could have been the sound of a file or a rasp or something, and then the sound of this grinding wheel. So you're sure you weren't in here sharpening something? Like skates? Or . . .' Hawes shrugged, 'A ski pole?'

'A ski pole? Why would anyone . . . ?' Kurtz fell suddenly silent. He studied Hawes again. 'What are you?' he asked. 'A policeman?'

'Why? Don't you like policemen?'

'I had nothing to do with Helga's death,' Kurtz said immediately.

'No one said you did.'

'You implied it.'

'I implied nothing, Mr Kurtz.'

'You asked if I were sharpening a ski pole last night. The implication is . . .'

'But you weren't.'

'No, I was *not*!' Kurtz said angrily.

'What *were* you sharpening last night?'

'Nothing. I was nowhere near this shop last night.'

'Ahh, but you were, Mr Kurtz. I met you outside, remember? You were coming down the steps. Very fast Don't you remember?'

'That was earlier in the evening.'

'But I didn't say anything about time, Mr Kurtz. I didn't ask you *when* you were in this shop.'

'I was *not* in this shop! Not at any time!'

'But you just said, 'That was earlier in the evening.' Earlier than what, Mr Kurtz?'

Kurtz was silent for a moment. Then he said, 'Earlier than . . . than whoever was here.'

'You saw someone here?'

'I . . . I saw a light burning.'

'When? What time?'

'I don't remember. I went to the bar after I met you . . . and I had a few drinks, and then I went for a walk. That was when I saw the light.'

'Where do you room, Mr Kurtz?'

'In the main building.'

'Did you see Helga at any time last night?'

'No.'

'Not at any time?'

'No.'

'Then what were you doing upstairs?'

'I came to get Maria's skates. Those.' He pointed to the figure skates on the bench.

'Maria who?'

'Maria Fiers.'

'Is she a small girl with dark hair?'

'Yes. Do you know her?'

'I think I just saw her in the hallway,' Hawes said. 'So you came to get her skates, and then you went for a drink, and then you went for a walk. What time was that?'

'It must have been after midnight.'

'And a light was burning in the ski shop?'

'Yes.'

'But you didn't see who was in here?'

'No, I did not.'

'How well did you know Helga?'

'Very well. We taught together.'

'How well is very well?'

'We were good friends.'

'How good, Mr Kurtz?'

'I *told* you!'

'Were you sleeping with her?'

'How dare you . . .'

'Okay, okay.' Hawes pointed to the skates. 'These are Maria's, you said?'

'Yes. She's an instructor here, too. But she skates well, almost as well as she skis.'

'Are you good friends with her, too, Mr Kurtz?'

'I am good friends with *everyone*!' Kurtz said angrily. 'I am normally a friendly person.' He paused. '*Are* you a policeman?'

'Yes. I am.'

'I don't like policemen,' Kurtz said, his voice low. 'I didn't like them in Vienna, where they wore swastikas on their arms, and I don't like them here, either. I had nothing to do with Helga's death.'

'Do you have a key to this shop, Mr Kurtz?'

'Yes. We *all* do. We make our own minor repairs. During the day, there are too many people here. At night, we can . . .'

'What do you mean by *all*? The instructors?'

'Yes.'

'I see. Then any of the instructors could have . . .'

The scream was a sentient thing which invaded the room suddenly and startlingly. It came from somewhere upstairs, ripping down through the ancient floor boards and the ancient ceiling timbers. It struck the room with its blunt force, and both men looked up towards the ceiling, speechless, waiting. The scream came again. Hawes got to his feet and ran for the door. '*Blanche*,' he whispered, and slammed the door behind him.

She was standing in the corridor outside the hall bathroom, not really standing, but leaning limply against the wall, her supporting dancer's legs robbed of stance, robbed of control. She wore the long flannel nightgown with a robe over it, and she leaned against the wall with her eyes shut tight, her blonde hair disarrayed, the scream unvoiced now, but frozen in the set of her face and the trembling openness of her mouth. Hawes came stamping up the steps and turned abruptly right, and stopped stock still when he saw her, an interruption of movement for only a fraction of a second, the turn, the stop, and then a forward motion again which carried him to her in four headlong strides.

'What is it?' he said.

She could not answer. She clung to the wall with the flat palms of her hands, her eyes still squeezed shut tightly, the scream frozen in her throat and blocking articulation. She shook her head.

'*Blanche, what is it?*'

She shook her head again, and then pulled one hand from the wall, as if afraid that by doing so she would lose

214

her grip and tumble to the floor. The hand rose limply. It did not point, it only indicated, and that in the vaguest manner, as if it too were dazed.

'The bathroom?' he asked.

She nodded. He turned from her. The bathroom door was partly open. He opened it the rest of the way, rushing into the room, and then stopping instantly, as if he had run into a stone wall.

Maria Fiers was inside her clothing and outside of it. The killer had caught her either dressing or undressing, had caught her in what she supposed was privacy, so that one leg was in the trousers of her pyjamas and the other lay twisted beneath her body, naked. Her pyjama top had ridden up over one delicately curved breast, perhaps as she fell, perhaps as she struggled. Even her hair seemed in a state of uncertain transition, some of it held firmly in place by curlers, the rest hanging in haphazard abandon, the loose curlers scattered on the bathroom floor. The hook latch on the inside of the door had been ripped from the jamb when the door was forced. The water in the sink was still running. The girl lay still and dead in her invaded privacy, partially clothed, partially disrobed, surprise and terror wedded in the death mask of her face. A towel was twisted about her throat. It had been twisted there with tremendous force, biting into the skin with such power that it remained twisted there now, the flesh torn and overlapping it in places, the coarse cloth almost embedded into her neck and throat. Her tongue protruded from her mouth. She was bleeding from her nose where her face had struck the bathroom tile in falling.

He backed out of the room.

He found a pay telephone in the main building, and from there he called Theodore Watt.

12.

BLANCHE SAT ON the edge of the bed in room 105, shivering inside her gown, her robe, and a blanket which had been thrown over her shoulders. Theodore Watt leaned disjointedly against the dresser, puffed on his cigar, and said, 'Now you want to tell me exactly what happened, Miss Colby?'

Blanche sat shivering and hunched, her face pale. She searched for her voice, seemed unable to find it, shook her head, nodded, cleared her throat, and seemed surprised that she could speak. 'I . . . I was alone. Cotton had gone down to see what . . . what the noise was.'

'What noise, Hawes?' Watt asked.

'A grinding wheel,' he answered. 'Downstairs in the ski shop. I heard it last night, too.'

'Did you find who was running the wheel?'

'Tonight, it was a guy named Helmut Kurtz. He's an instructor here, too. Claims he was nowhere near the shop last night. But he did see a light burning after midnight.'

'Where's he now?'

'I don't know. Sheriff, he was with me when the girl was killed. He couldn't possibly have . . .'

Watt ignored him and walked to the door. He opened it, and leaned into the corridor. 'Fred,' he said, 'find me Helmut Kurtz, an instructor here.'

'I got that other guy from down the hall,' Fred answered.

'I'll be right with him. Tell him to wait.'

'What other guy?' Hawes asked.

'Instructor in 102. Larry Davidson.' Watt shook his head. 'Place is crawling with goddamn instructors, excuse me, miss. Wonder there's any room for guests.' He shook his head again. 'You said you were alone, Miss Colby.'

'Yes. And I . . . I thought I heard something down the hall . . . like . . . I didn't know what. A loud sudden noise.'

'Probably the bathroom door being kicked in,' Watt said. 'Go on.'

'And then I . . . I heard a girl's voice saying, "Get out of here! Do you hear me? Get out of here!" And . . . and it was quiet, and I heard someone running down the hall and down the steps, so I . . . I thought I ought to . . . to look.'

'Yes, go on.'

'I went down the . . . the hallway and looked down the steps, but I didn't see anyone. And then, when I . . . when I was starting back for the room, I . . . I heard the water running in the bathroom. The . . . the door was open, so I . . . Oh Jesus, do I *have* to?'

'You found the girl, is that right?'

'Yes,' Blanche said, her voice very low.

'And then you screamed.'

'Yes.'

'And then Hawes came upstairs, is that right?'

'Yes,' Hawes said. 'And I called you from the main building.'

'Um-huh,' Watt said. He went to the door and opened it. 'Want to come in here, Mr Davidson?' he asked.

Larry Davidson came into the room hesitantly. He was a tall man, and he stooped as he came through the doorway, giving an impression of even greater height, as if he had to stoop to avoid the top of the door frame. He was wearing dark trousers and a plaid woollen sports shirt.

His hair was clipped close to his scalp. His blue eyes were alert, if not wary.

'Guess you know what this is all about, huh, Mr Davidson?' Watt asked.

'Yes, I think so,' Davidson answered.

'You don't mind answering a few questions, do you?'

'No. I'll . . . I'll answer anything you . . .'

'Fine. Were you in your room all night, Mr Davidson?'

'Not all night, no. I was up at the main building part of the time.'

'Doing what?'

'Well, I . . .'

'Yes, Mr Davidson, what were you doing?'

'I . . . I was fencing. Look, I didn't have anything to do with this.'

'You were *what*, Mr Davidson?'

'Fencing. We've got some foils and masks up there, and I . . . I was just fooling around. Look, I *know* Helga was stabbed, but . . .'

'What time did you get back here, Mr Davidson?'

'About . . . about ten-thirty, eleven.'

'And you've been in your room since then?'

'Yes.'

'What did you do when you got back here?'

'I wrote a letter to my wife, and then I went to sleep.'

'What time did you go to sleep?'

'About midnight.'

'Did you hear any loud noise in the hall?'

'No.'

'Did you hear any voices?'

'No.'

'Did you hear Miss Colby when she screamed?'

'No.'

'Why not?'

'I guess I was asleep.'

'You sleep in your clothes, Mr Davidson?'

'What? Oh. Oh, no. Your fellow . . . your deputy said I could put on some clothes.'

'What *were* you sleeping in?'

'My pyjamas. Listen, I barely knew those girls. I only joined the school here two weeks ago. I mean, I knew them to talk to, but that's all. And the fencing is just a coincidence. I mean, we always fool around with the foils. I mean, ever since I came here, somebody's been up there fooling around with . . .'

'How many times did you scream, Miss Colby?' Watt asked.

'I don't remember,' Blanche said.

'She screamed twice,' Hawes said.

'Where were you when you heard the screams, Hawes?'

'Downstairs. In the ski shop.'

'But you were in your room, right down the hall, Mr Davidson, and you didn't hear anything, hmmm? Maybe you were too busy . . .'

And suddenly Davidson began crying. His face twisted into a grimace, and the tears began flowing, and he said, 'I didn't have anything to do with this, I swear. Please, I didn't have anything to do with it. Please, I'm married, my wife's in the city expecting a baby, I *need* this job, I didn't even *look* at those girls, I swear to God, what do you want me to do? Please, please.'

The room was silent except for his sobbing.

'I swear to God,' he said softly. 'I swear to God. I'm a heavy sleeper. I'm very tired at night. I swear. Please. I didn't do it. I only knew them to say hello. I didn't hear anything. Please. Believe me. Please. I *have* to keep this job. It's the only thing I know, skiing. I can't get involved in this. Please.'

He lowered his head, trying to hide the tears that streamed down his face, his shoulders heaving, the deep sobs starting deep inside him and reverberating through his entire body.

'Please,' he said.

For the first time since the whole thing had started, Watt turned to Hawes and asked his advice.

'What do you think?' he said.

'I'm a heavy sleeper, too,' Hawes said. 'You could blow up the building, and I wouldn't hear it.'

13.

ON SUNDAY MORNING, the church bells rang out over the valley.

They started in the town of Rawson, and they rang sharp and clear on the mountain air, drifting over the snow and down the valley. He went to the window and pulled up the shade, and listened to the sound of the bells, and remembered his own youth and the Reverend Jeremiah Hawes who had been his father, and the sound of Sunday church bells, and the rolling, sonorous voice of his father delivering the sermon. There had always been logic in his father's sermons. Hawes had not come away from his childhood background with any abiding religious fervour – but he had come away with a great respect for logic. 'To be believed,' his father had told him, 'it must be reasonable. And to be reasonable, it must be logical. You could do worse than remembering that, Cotton.'

There did not seem to be much logic in the killing of Helga Nilson and Maria Fiers, unless there was logic in wanton brutality. He tried to piece together the facts as he looked out over the peaceful valley and listened to the steady tolling of the bells. Behind him, Blanche was curled in sleep, gently breathing, her arms wrapped around the pillow. He did not want to wake her yet, not after what she'd been through last night. So far as he was concerned, the weekend was over; he could not ski with pleasure any more, not this weekend. He wanted nothing more than to get away from Rawson Mountain, no, that wasn't quite true. He wanted to find the killer. That was what he wanted more than anything else. Not because he was being paid for the job, not because he wanted to prove to Theodore Watt that maybe big-city detectives *did* have a little something on the ball – but only because the double murders filled him with a sense of outrage. He could still remember the animal strength of the man who'd attacked him on the mountain, and the thought of that power directed against two helpless young girls angered Hawes beyond all reason.

Why? he asked himself.

Where is the logic?

There was none. No logic in the choice of the victims, and no logic in the choice of the scene. Why would anyone have chosen to kill Helga in broad daylight, on a chair suspended anywhere from six to thirty feet above the ground, using a ski pole as a weapon? A ski pole sharpened to a deadly point, Hawes reminded himself, don't forget that. This thing didn't just happen, this was no spur-of-the-moment impulse, this was planned and premeditated, a pure and simple Murder One. Somebody had been in that ski shop the night before the first murder, using a file and then a grinding wheel, sharpening that damn pole, making certain its end could penetrate a heavy ski parka, *and* a ski sweater, *and* a heart.

Then there must have been logic to the choice of locale, Hawes thought. Whoever killed Helga had at least planned far enough ahead to have prepared a weapon the night before. And admitting the existence of a plan, then logic could be presupposed, and it could further be assumed that killing her on the chair lift was a *part* of the plan – perhaps a very necessary part of it.

Yes, that's logic, he thought – *except that it's illogical*.

Behind him, Blanche stirred. He turned to look at her briefly, remembering the horror on her face last night, contrasting it now with her features relaxed in sleep. She had told the story to Watt three times, had told him again and again how she'd found the dead girl.

Maria Fiers, twenty-one years old, brunette, a native of Montpelier, Vermont. She had begun skiing when she was six years old, had won the women's slalom four times running, had been an instructor since she was seventeen. She skated, too, and had been on her high school swimming team, an all-round athlete, a nice girl with a gentle manner and a pleasant smile – dead.

Why?

She lived in the room next door to Helga's, had known Helga for close to a year. She had been nowhere near the chair lift on the day Helga was killed. In fact, she had been teaching a beginners' class near the T-Bar, a good distance from the chair lift. She could not have seen Helga's murder, nor Helga's murderer.

But someone had killed her nonetheless.

And if there were a plan, and if there were supposed logic to the plan, and if killing Helga on a chair halfway up the mountain was part of that logic, then the death of Maria Fiers was also a part of it.

But how?

The hell with it, Hawes thought. I can't think straight any more. I want to crack this so badly that I can't think straight, and that makes me worse than useless. So the thing to do is to get out of here, wake Blanche and tell her to dress and pack, and then pay my bill and get out, back to the city, back to the 87th where death comes more frequently perhaps, and just as brutally – but not as a surprise. I'll leave this to Theodore Watt, the sheriff who wants to make his own mistakes. I'll leave it to him and his nimble-fingered deputies, and maybe they'll bust it wide open, or maybe they won't, but it's too much for me, I can't think straight any more.

He went to the bed and woke Blanche, and then he

walked over to the main building, anxious to pay his bill and get on his way. Someone was at the piano, practising scales. Hawes walked past the piano and the fireplace and around the corner to Wollender's office. He knocked on the door, and waited. There was a slight hesitation on the other side of the door, and then Wollender said, 'Yes, come in,' and Hawes turned the knob.

Everything looked exactly the way it had looked, when Hawes checked in on Friday night, an eternity ago. Wollender was sitting behind his desk, a man in his late twenties with dark hair and dark brows pulled low over deep brown eyes. He was wearing a white shirt open at the throat, a bold reindeer-imprinted sweater over it. The plaster cast was still on his right leg, the leg stretched out stiffly in front of him, the foot resting on a low ottoman. Everything looked exactly the same.

'I want to pay my bill,' Hawes said. 'We're checking out.'

He stood just inside the door, some fifteen feet from the desk. Wollender's crutches leaned against the wall near the door. There was a smile on Wollender's face as he said, 'Certainly,' and then opened the bottom drawer of the desk and took out his register and carefully made out a bill. Hawes walked to the desk, added the bill, and then wrote a cheque. As he waved it in the air to dry the ink, he said, 'What *were* you doing in my room yesterday, Mr Wollender?'

'Checking the heat,' Wollender said.

Hawes nodded. 'Here's your cheque. Will you mark this bill "Paid", please?'

'Be happy to,' Wollender said. He stamped the bill and handed it back to Hawes. For a moment, Hawes had the oddest feeling that something was wrong. The knowledge pushed itself into his mind in the form of an absurd caption: WHAT'S WRONG WITH THIS PICTURE? He looked at Wollender, at his hair, and his eyes, and his white shirt, and his reindeer sweater, and his extended leg, and the cast on it, and the ottoman. Something was different. This was not the room, not the picture as it had been on Friday night. WHAT'S WRONG WITH THIS PICTURE? he thought, and he did not know.

He took the bill. 'Thanks,' he said. 'Have you heard any news about the roads?'

'They're open all the way to the Thruway. You shouldn't have any trouble.'

'Thanks,' Hawes said. He hesitated, staring at Wollender. 'My room's right over the ski shop, you know,' he said.

'Yes, I know that.'

'Do you have a key to the shop, Mr Wollender?'

Wollender shook his head. 'No. The shop is privately owned. It doesn't belong to the hotel. I believe the proprietor allows the ski instructors to . . .'

'But then, you're a locksmith, aren't you?'

'What?'

'Isn't that what you told me when I checked in? You said you were a locksmith out of season, didn't you?'

'Oh. Oh, yes. Yes, I did.' Wollender shifted uneasily in the chair, trying to make his leg comfortable. Hawes looked at the leg again, and then he thought, Damn it, what's wrong?

'Maybe you went to my room to listen, Mr Wollender. Is that possible?'

'Listen to what?'

'To the sounds coming from the ski shop below,' Hawes said.

'Are the sounds that interesting?'

'In the middle of the night, they are. You can hear all sorts of things in the middle of the night. I'm just beginning to remember all the things I heard.'

'Oh? What did you hear?'

'I heard the oil burner clicking, and the toilet flushing, and the Cats going up the mountain, and someone arguing down the hall, and somebody filing and grinding in the ski shop.' He was speaking to Wollender, but not really speaking to him. He was, instead, remembering those midnight voices raised in anger, and remembering that it was only later he had heard the noises in the shop, and gone to the window, and seen the light burning below. And then a curious thing happened. Instead of calling him 'Mr Wollender', he suddenly called him 'Elmer'.

'Elmer,' he said, 'something's just occurred to me.'

Elmer. And with the word, something new came into the room. With the word, he was suddenly transported back to the interrogation room at the 87th, where common thieves and criminals were called by their first names, Charlie, and Harry, and Martin, and Joe, and where this familiarity somehow put them on the defensive, somehow rattled them and made them know their questioners weren't playing games.

'Elmer,' he said, leaning over the desk, 'it's just occurred to me that since Maria couldn't have *seen* anything on the mountain, maybe she was killed because she *heard* something. And maybe what she heard was the same arguing I heard. Only *her* room is right next door to Helga's. And maybe she knew *who* was arguing.' He hesitated. 'That's pretty logical, don't you think, Elmer?'

'I suppose so,' Wollender said pleasantly. 'But if you know who killed Maria, why don't you go to . . .'

'I don't know, Elmer. Do *you* know?'

'I'm sorry. I don't.'

'Yeah, neither do I, Elmer, All I have is a feeling.'

'And what's the feeling?' Wollender asked.

'That you came to my room to listen, Elmer. To find out how much *I* had heard the night before Helga was murdered. And maybe you decided I heard too damn much, and maybe that's why I was attacked on the mountain yesterday.'

'Please, Mr Hawes,' Wollender said, and a faint superior smile touched his mouth, and his hand opened limply to indicate the leg in the cast.

'Sure, sure,' Hawes said. 'How could I have been attacked by a man with his leg in a cast, a man who can't get around without crutches? Sure, Elmer. Don't think that hasn't been bugg—' He stopped dead. 'Your crutches,' he said.

'What?'

'Your crutches! Where the hell are they?'

For just an instant, the colour went out of Wollender's face. Then, quite calmly, he said, 'Right over there. Behind you.'

Hawes turned and looked at the crutches, leaning against the wall near the door.

'Fifteen feet from your desk,' he said. 'I thought you couldn't walk without them.'

'I . . . I used the furniture to . . . to get to the desk. I . . .'

'You're lying, Elmer,' Hawes said, and he reached across the desk and pulled Wollender out of the chair.

'My leg!' Wollender shouted.

'Your leg, my ass! How long have you been walking on it, Elmer? Was that why you killed her on the mountain? So that . . .'

'I didn't kill anybody!'

'. . . so that you'd have a perfect alibi? A man with his leg in a cast couldn't possibly ride a lift or jump from it, could he? Unless he'd been in and out of that cast for God knows how long!'

'My leg is broken! I can't walk!'

'Can you *kill*, Elmer?'

'I didn't kill her!'

'Did Maria hear you arguing, Elmer?'

'No. No . . .'

'Then why'd you go after her?'

'I didn't!' He tried to pull away from Hawes. 'You're crazy. You're hurting my leg! Let go of . . .'

'*I'm* crazy? You son of a bitch, *I'm* crazy? You stuck a ski pole in one girl and twisted a towel around . . .'

'I didn't, I didn't!'

'We found the basket from your pole!' Hawes shouted.

'What basket? I don't know what . . .'

'Your fingerprints are all over it!' he lied.

'You're crazy,' Wollender said. 'How could I get on the lift? I can't walk. I broke the leg in two places. One of the bones came right through the skin. I couldn't get on a lift if I wanted . . .'

'The skin,' Hawes said.

'What?'

'The skin!' There was a wild look in his eyes now. He pulled Wollender closer to him and yelled. 'Where'd she scratch you?'

'What?'

He seized the front of Wollender's shirt with both hands, and then ripped it open. 'Where's the cut, Elmer? On your chest? On your neck?'

Wollender struggled to get away from him, but Hawes had his head captured in both huge hands now. He twisted Wollender's face viciously, forced his head forward, pulled back the shirt collar.

'Let go of me!' Wollender screamed.

'What's this, Elmer?' His fingers grasped the adhesive bandage on the back of Wollender's neck. Angrily, he tore it loose. A healing cut, two inches long and smeared with iodine, ran diagonally from a spot just below Wollender's hairline.

'I did that myself,' Wollender said. 'I bumped into . . .'

'Helga did it,' Hawes said. 'When you stabbed her! The sheriff's got the skin, Elmer. It was under her fingernails.'

'No,' Wollender said. He shook his head.

The room was suddenly very still. Both men were exhausted. Hawes kept clinging to the front of Wollender's shirt, breathing hard, waiting. Wollender kept shaking his head.

'You want to tell me?'

Wollender shook his head.

'How long have you been walking?'

Wollender shook his head again.

'Why'd you keep your leg in the cast?'

Again, Wollender shook his head.

'*You killed two young girls!*' Hawes bellowed. He was surprised to find himself trembling. His hand tightened on the shirt front, the knuckles showing white through his skin. Perhaps Wollender felt the sudden tension, perhaps Wollender knew that in the next instant Hawes would throttle him.

'All right,' he said. His voice was very low. 'All right.'

'Why'd you keep wearing the cast?'

'So . . . so . . . so she wouldn't know. So she would think I . . . I was . . . was unable to walk. And that way, I could . . . could watch her. Without her knowing.'

'Watch who?'

'Helga. She . . . She was my girl, you see. I . . . I loved her, you see.'

'Yeah, you loved her enough to kill her,' Hawes said.

'That's *not* why I . . .' He shook his head. 'It was because of Kurtz. She kept denying it, but I knew about them. And I warned her. You have to believe that I warned her. And I . . . I kept the cast on my leg to . . . to fool her.'

'When did it come off?' Hawes asked.

'Last week. The . . . the doctor took it off right in this room. He did a bivalve, with an electric saw, cut it right down the side. And . . . and when he was gone, I . . . I figured I could put the two halves together again, and . . . and . . . hold it in place with . . . with tape. That way, I could watch her. Without her knowing I could get around.'

'And what did you see?'

'You *know* what I saw!'

'Tell me.'

'Friday night, she . . . I . . . I saw Kurtz leaving the annexe. I knew he'd been with her.'

'He was there to pick up Maria's skates,' Hawes said. 'To sharpen them.'

'No!' Wollender shouted, and for a moment there was force in his voice, a vocal explosion, fury and power, and Hawes remembered again the brute strength of Wollender's attack on the mountain. Wollender's voice died again. 'No,' he said softly, 'you're mistaken. He was with Helga. I know. Do you think I'd have killed her if . . .' His voice caught. His eyes suddenly misted. He turned his head, not looking at Hawes, staring across the room, the tears solidifying his eyes. 'When I went up to her room, I warned her,' he said, his voice low. 'I told her I had seen him, seen him with my own eyes, and she . . . she said I was imagining things. And she laughed.' His face went suddenly tight. 'She laughed, you see. She . . . she shouldn't have laughed.' His eyes filled with tears, had a curiously opaque look. 'She shouldn't have laughed,' he said. 'It wasn't funny. I loved her. It wasn't funny.'

'No,' Hawes said wearily. 'It wasn't funny at all.'

14.

THE STORM WAS over.

The storm which had started suddenly and filled the air with fury was gone. The wind had died after scattering the clouds from the sky. They drove in the warm comfort of the convertible, the sky a clear blue ahead of them, the snow banked on either side of the road.

The storm was over.

There were only the remains of its fury now, the hard-packed snow beneath the automobile, and the snow lining the roads, and the snow hanging in the branches of the trees. But now it was over and done, and now there was only the damage to count, and the repairs to be made.

He sat silently behind the wheel of the car, a big redheaded man who drove effortlessly. His anger was gone, too, like the anger of the storm. There was only a vast sadness inside him.

'Cotton?' Blanche said.

'Mmmm?' He did not take his eyes from the road. He watched the winding white ribbon and listened to the crunch of snow beneath his heavy-duty tyres, and over that the sound of her voice.

'Cotton,' she said, 'I'm very glad to be with you.'

'I am, too.'

'In spite of everything,' she said, 'I'm very, very glad.'

He did a curious thing then. He suddenly took his right hand from the wheel and put it on her thigh, and squeezed her gently. He thought he did it because Blanche was a very attractive girl with whom he had just shared a moment of communication.

But perhaps he touched her because death had suddenly shouldered its way into that automobile, and he had remembered again the two young girls who had been Wollender's victims.

Perhaps he touched her thigh, soft and warm, only as a reaffirmation of life.

The Pusher

Two a.m. in the bitter cold of winter: the young Hispanic man's body is found in a tenement basement. The rope around his neck suggests a clear case of suicide – until the autopsy reveals he'd overdosed on heroin.

He was a pusher, and now a thousand questions press down on the detectives of the 87th Precinct.

Who set up the phony hanging? Whose fingerprints were on the syringe found at the scene? Who was making threatening phone calls, attempting to implicate Lieutenant Byrnes' teenage son? Somebody is pushing the 87th Precinct hard, and Detective Steve Carella and Lieutenant Pete Byrnes have to push back harder – before a frightening and deadly chain tightens its grip.

See Them Die

Kill me if you can – that was Pepe Miranda's challenge.
Murderer, two-bit hero of the street gangs, he was holed up
somewhere in the 87th Precinct, making the cops look like fools
and cheered on by every neighbourhood punk.

It was not a challenge Lieutenant Pete Byrnes and the detectives
in the squad room could leave alone. Not in the sticky, July
heat of the city with the gangs just waiting to explode into
violence . . .

The Heckler

All over town, phones were ringing. Shopkeepers and merchants were being threatened by anonymous cranks. And the threats were getting more and more serious.

When the angry victims started yelling to the local cops for help, Steve Carella and the boys of the 87th Precinct didn't know what to make of the whole thing. Were they facing a plague of harmless pranksters – or the danger of a city-wide wave of violence?

All they had to go on were the constant attention of 'the deaf man' and the knowledge that if they didn't catch their cold-blooded callers before the end of the month, the prophecies of murder and mayhem might prove all too true.

Give The Boys
a Great Big Hand

The mystery man wore black, and he was a real cut-up king. Why else was he leaving blood-red severed hands all over the city? Was he an everyday maniac with a meat cleaver, or did he have a special grudge against the 87th Precinct?

Steve Carella and Cotton Hawes went along with the grudge theory, because the black-cloaked killer didn't leave any clues to go on – the grisly hands even had the fingertips sliced off. And how do you nail a murderer when you can't identity or unearth most of his victims?

That's what the boys of the 87th Precinct have to do: find a killer before he carves up any more corpseless hands.

'Til Death

The groom in question is Tommy Giordano – and he's about to marry Steve Carella's sister, Angela. So the wedding party suddenly becomes a deadly game of hide-and-seek for Steve and the boys of the 87th Precinct.

Tommy is 'it' and Steve has only a few hours to find a killer and prevent Tommy from being tagged out for good.

But how do you find a murderer with hundreds of wedding guests to choose from? Is it Tommy's best man, who would collect everything the groom owns if the killer finds his mark? Or Ben Darcy, who is still madly in love with the bride and would do anything to get her back? Or what about the crazy ex-GI who swore he'd get revenge against Tommy?

Carella has to work fast, or someone is going to make Angela a widow on her wedding day . . .

The Con Man

A trickster taking money from an old woman for his own private charity. A cheater fleecing the businessmen of their thousands with the oldest gimmick in town. A lady-killer after the ladies' dollars with just a little bit of love ...

The guys of the 87th Precinct thought they knew every trick in the book – so why are there bodies still washing up on the shore?

The Con Man: handsome, charming – and deadly.

Alice in Jeopardy

Alice thought she had lost everything when her husband's yacht was found empty and adrift. He had slipped out to sail under the stars and is never going to come back. A year on, Alice and her two children are still struggling to come to terms with their new life – but troubles are only just beginning . . .

One sunny day, Alice's children don't come home. The police are caught up in interdepartmental battles and Alice, now very much alone in the world, believes that the only way to save her children is to find them herself. But as the questions multiply, the answers seem more elusive than ever.

☐ Alice in Jeopardy £6.99
9780752865034

☐ The Pusher £6.99
9780752857930

☐ The Con Man £6.99
9780752857947

☐ 'Til Death £6.99
9780752857954

☐ King's Ransom £6.99
9780752857961

☐ Give the Boys a Great Big Hand £6.99
9780752859798

☐ The Heckler £6.99
9780752863788

☐ See Them Die £6.99
9780752863795

☐ Lady, Lady I Did It! £6.99
9780752864105

☐ The Empty Hours £6.99
9780752864112

☐ Like Love £6.99
9780752865461

☐ Money, Money, Money £6.99
9780752848396

☐ Fat Ollie's Book £6.99
9780752842769

☐ The Frumious Bandersnatch £6.99
9780752859163

☐ Hark £6.99
9780752865645

☐ Fiddlers £6.99
9780752878027

All Orion/Phoenix titles are available at your local bookshop or from the following address:

Mail Order Department
Littlehampton Book Services
FREEPOST BR535
Worthing, West Sussex, BN13 3BR
telephone 01903 828503, *facsimile* 01903 828802
e-mail MailOrders@lbsltd.co.uk
(Please ensure that you include full postal address details)

Payment can be made either by credit/debit card (Visa, Mastercard, Access and Switch accepted) or by sending a £ Sterling cheque or postal order made payable to *Littlehampton Book Services*.
DO NOT SEND CASH OR CURRENCY

Please add the following to cover postage and packing

UK and BFPO:
£1.50 for the first book, and 50p for each additional book to a maximum of £3.50

Overseas and Eire:
£2.50 for the first book plus £1.00 for the second book and 50p for each additional book ordered

---

BLOCK CAPITALS PLEASE

name of cardholder ....

address of cardholder ....

postcode ....

delivery address
(if different from cardholder)

....

postcode ....

☐ I enclose my remittance for £ ....

☐ please debit my Mastercard/Visa/Access/Switch (delete as appropriate)

card number ☐☐☐☐☐☐☐☐☐☐☐☐☐☐☐☐

expiry date ☐☐☐☐   Switch issue no. ☐☐

signature ....

prices and availability are subject to change without notice